*Lady of the Imperial City*

by

Laura Kitchell

Lady of the Imperial City
A novel

Copyright© 2015 Laura Kitchell
Print Edition
ISBN 13: 978-1512022421
ISBN 10: 151202242X

Cover Art Photographer: Allegra Christopher
Editor: Katherine Alexander

www.laurakitchell.com

# DEDICATION

Thank you, Kathy, for your tireless efforts and endless support. To Sara, for always believing in me and for your precious time and input. To my mother, for your gentle and sometimes not-so-gentle insistence that I continue to write and evolve. To Kristen, for your wisdom, creativity, and honesty. And to the ladies of Chesapeake Romance Writers, for your shared knowledge and encouragement.

# A NOTE FROM THE AUTHOR

For those of you who enjoy historicals, you may find this one a bit different in terms of style. An historical novel set in western culture prior to the late 1800's typically should not contain speech with contractions. We must understand, however, that eastern peoples have spoken in an abbreviated fashion far longer, and especially so within the Japanese language. As such, I have endeavored to capture this through the use of contractions.

Also, you will find words in this novel that were not in use yet within the western world. Both the Japanese and the Chinese languages were vast even during this time in history and, therefore, had words equivalent to those I have used. As this story is not written in Japanese and Chinese, I found it necessary to employ words in use today that were not in use when this story takes place.

Chapter One

Kyō, Japan
March 31, 1001

"I don't want a house full of women." Yūkan drained his cup of *sake*, smoothing an appreciative finger along his friend's porcelain. He'd traded some of the finest dishes throughout the eastern world and recognized that Lord Yoki had acquired the best. "As it is, I'm not used to this aristocratic life you *good people* live. What makes you think I want to infect my home with the arguing and cackling of women?"

"You only think that because you've never experienced the pleasure of having lovely ladies at your beck and call," said Lord Yoki from across a low, beautifully wrought black pine table. His effeminate features thoughtful and still smooth despite his thirty-one years, he gestured toward his servant who stood at the far side of the vast common area of his mansion's main building. "Ladies ready and willing. Eager to please. Working hard to gain your favor above the others."

It only showed how little this dandy of a gentleman knew. Yūkan naïve? Ha! Annoyance nudging him, he returned, "You're naïve. You've been doing business with me for years. Both of you. Can you imagine me with a bevy of women? I can barely manage one at a time." He shuddered, not having to fake his horror.

Shizuka, the too-thin minister of trade in his staid robe of office and his face bearing his thirty years far less gracefully than Yoki's, snuffled his mirth. He took the *sake* bottle and refilled Yūkan's cup. "Don't blame the ideal for the fact that you've never wished to add to your household. All those women you've bedded, and you're trying to tell me you never wanted to make a single one a permanent part of your life?"

"Not one." Yūkan made a derisory snort then thrust his hands from inside his sleeves and pressed warm palms to his stiff, ice-cold cheeks. A servant stoked a brazier, but the heat it emitted didn't begin to warm the room's massive area. "You've both done well. Minister, you've taken a wife who represents what a wife should be. I've no interest whatsoever in meeting any of your consorts. And you, Yoki, don't have a single permanent lover in your house, so you can't criticize. Believe me, though. I wouldn't want to trade places with either of you. You're suited to this life. Even though we share an age, I'm not interested in making any woman a part of my household."

"So you've not found a wife because of your own skittishness then?" Yoki sipped his rice wine and ran a hand down the glittering peacock blue damask of his rich array.

"Skittishness? You compare me with a lamb or doe?" Yūkan sniffed with disdain then laughed at the idea. "I haven't married partly in dread and partly in kindness. Dread of marrying the wrong woman and having to live with a harridan, or worse, a mindless, uneducated dolt. Kindness in sparing a woman, or women as you'd have me take, the unfortunate fate of having to live with my unrefined, manly ways."

"As an import shipper, you've traveled the world. You can't claim ignorance of women. I suspect your knowledge is in pleasuring, however. A lady of this fine city can enhance your life. Bring beauty and culture into your home."

Shizuka plunked his empty cup upon the table. "I imagine we wouldn't even be having this conversation if you'd gotten your meeting with the emperor, but I'm glad we're talking. Will you spend the rest of your days wasting away with drink and common one-night rendezvous, never begetting an heir or achieving enlightenment through love? I won't have it.

You're a son of the finest of our families. A Minamoto."

"You say this to me but not Lord Yoki? You describe his life better than mine." The *sake* began to cloud his thinking, and Yūkan gave his head a vigorous shake. "I didn't come to Kyō to find a wife or consort, and I certainly didn't come to argue. I need to meet with Emperor Ichijō. Despite our family name, now that my brother, Fudōno, has taken over our family shipping business, I have to ensure he has rights to the trade agreement my father set in place with the former emperor."

Shizuka shook his head. "Even so, I'm determined to help you see the error of your ways. Now that you've retired from trade, you're free to stay. You may not have our friend's ideal roundness of face, and you'd do well to grow a bit of hair on that bare, brown chin of yours, but I think there are ladies in our fair city who would find you attractive."

Yoki nodded then slapped the table and barked a drunken laugh. "You're ugly. It's true, but I've seen worse. Listen, the emperor's schedule is relentless. It could be three months before I can arrange a time for you to meet. There's time to make you appealing."

"Three months?" asked Yūkan in dismay. "What am I to do for three months in this city?"

"Ichijō knows you're in Kyō. I told him this morning while I went over his day's agenda. He invites you to stay at the palace. I'll sponsor you in society. He's found you a tutor to teach you the way of this city's *good people*, and we'll see if you don't come to embrace our lifestyle."

"Three months of you and some tutor preaching to me the benefits of aristocratic morality and ideals of domesticity?" Yūkan rolled his eyes. "My aunt has already tried. You waste your time."

His friends shared a glance. He'd known them for ten years, before any of them had achieved anywhere the greatness they now enjoyed. Yūkan's father had brought him to Kyō right before he took over the family trading business and introduced him to Ichijō's father, the previous emperor. Shizuka had just been appointed as an apprentice to the ministry of trade and complained often about the humiliation of his Seventh Rank robes of office. Now he ran the ministry and had no shame in his apparel. In the trade district those many years ago, he'd met Lord Yoki who had recently accepted a promotion that earned him a mansion, and he shopped for items to fill this home where they sat tonight. Now Yoki served the emperor directly as Supreme Minister of Personal Affairs.

Every time he had brought wares to the city through the years, they had met to dine and drink. He knew them well, and he understood that look. They were about to counsel him. If he weren't so set on paving the way for his brother to trade with ease in Kyō, as their father had done for him, he'd return to his home province.

"Let's get serious," said Yoki, filling the minister's cup. "What do you think you're doing?"

Shizuka leaned against a wide, elaborately carved ceiling support column and arched anemic eyebrows. "Yes. Tell us, what do you think you're doing?"

"What do you mean?" Yūkan blinked. Had he consumed too much *sake*? He could usually read these two like a scroll.

"You're set on retiring, and I understand. I really do. But this is an uncertain world we live in. Fudōno is sailing the seas."

"So? He's been doing that for years with me."

Shizuka leaned forward, causing his tall, skinny black hat to tip forward and pull at his shiny, ebony topknot. "And the gods have granted you safety and good fortune. Don't be so complacent that you think it may not change. What happens if you lose your brother? If you have no heirs, who will continue? Fudōno is eight years younger, only twenty-three and in no mind or position to start a family. It's on you."

Interesting. He hadn't expected them to come at him from the perspective of family. It showed how well they knew him, too. Family meant everything to him.

Yoki nodded. "You're acting careless. Heedless. Rash."

"Rash!" Yūkan threw back his head and laughed. "And I

thought *I'd* had too much wine. My not taking a wife is acting rash? That's ridiculous."

The minister's lips formed a moue then slowly widened into a sly smile. "You're ready."

"For what?"

Shizuka leaned nearer still, his stiff robe puffing above the edge of the table. "Oh, yes. I see it now. When you see her, you'll know."

"What are you talking about?" Yūkan didn't even try to hide his irritation.

"You protest the same way I did right before I was introduced to Izumi. The moment I met her, I knew she'd be my wife."

"Then how come I haven't met my wife yet?" asked Yoki, his voice a bit whiny. "I protest all the time."

The minister sat back and grinned.

"Look," said Yūkan, crossing his arms. "My prospects are different from yours. You're both happy, and that works for you."

"I'm not happy," cut in Yoki, a slight pout pulling the edges of his small mouth downward.

Yūkan sent him a dismissive glance. "As for me, I don't want a proper and fine life in Kyō." He signaled to the servant to bring another bottle. "And I think I've been very generous in my willingness to listen to the two of you prattle on about the supposed virtues of surrounding oneself with women galore—"

"Three months," cut in Shizuka. "Honestly, what have you got to lose?"

That gave him pause. He had nothing waiting for him on his country estate but servants and workers who functioned quite well under the guidance of his manager. Without acquisition trips and sales contracts, what did he have to do? Time was the one thing of which he had plenty.

He studied his friends. They'd always been good for a diversion. Their attempts to win him to their way of thinking could only prove entertaining in the extreme.

"Fine. Three months. But don't hope too hard. I'm me, after all."

Shizuka beamed, making his too-wide mouth appear garish, and brought his hands together in a single clap of delight. "Excellent. We'll start tonight."

*   *   *   *

"It'll be fun. Come with me tonight," Amai said, a hopeful smile upon her delicate face while she stepped as light as a cherry blossom petal floating on a garden pond. She emerged from the hallway that led to individual bedchambers and came into the common area of the wing her father had built onto his mansion especially for her. "Everyone will be disappointed if you don't."

Kirei adored her sweet cousin's youthful enthusiasm. Excitement colored the young woman's round face a becoming pink. She almost envied her. Almost.

Amai had beauty and taste ladies would envy if they didn't like her so well. Her thick, glossy hair fell heavy and straight to pool upon the outermost layer of her many silk robes in shades of maroon, pink, and white. The color combination, a tribute to winter with a nod toward the coming change in season, complimented her cousin's delicate youth and ideal face. Her narrow eyes gleamed with anticipation.

Kirei had also enjoyed this kind of excitement her first year in high society. Now, she had spent too much time with Kyō's jaded and fickle aristocrats to eagerly seek their company. Well, with the exception of a few. Fingering the soft silk of her innermost layer of robes, a pale green chemise that spilled at sleeves and hem, she allowed a brief smile. "I can't. It takes weeks to prepare for an incense contest. I haven't blended anything new or chosen an elaborate bowl or burner."

"You don't need to and you know it." Amai's soft brown eyes widened a fraction. "You always create new scents."

Sometimes having a person know her so well was *not* a

good thing.

"You're the best smelling lady in the city. Besides, you use the very best containers and burners. Nothing but the finest for you."

Kirei plucked at the heavy flower-patterned burgundy silk of her outermost layer, her dress garment, and changed tactics. "But I have to wash my hair tonight. My usual washing night won't be auspicious. I might get sick."

"Nonsense. We both wash our hair the day after tomorrow. It's a most auspicious day for it. Nobody follows the celestial calendar as closely as I." Amai laughed and rolled her eyes. "As if I have a choice. With my brother promoted at the Yin-Yang Bureau, is it any wonder? It's all he talks about these days."

Too true, unfortunately. "Can I give you any reason not to go to this party that you'll accept?"

"No." The young woman stood in a single, fluid motion. Her maroon and pink silk layers swayed in glimmering loveliness as her floor-length hair spooled off of her cushion. Like a dancer, she threw her arms wide and spun. The polished dark wood floor offered no resistance to her white socks. She hugged her arms across the front of her multi-layered *uchigi* robes. "Yours will be the most beguiling fragrance, and you'll surely win the contest. I must go choose what to wear."

"Indeed," Kirei said under her breath as Amai shuffled away. The gods forbid she should appear with any less than twelve colors showing at her neckline. In frustration, she gently kicked her six-foot portable *kichō*, its two opaque curtains fluttering.

She hated the screen of state and the restrictive life it represented. In the country, she'd been free to come and go as she pleased. She could wear far fewer layers of silk and didn't have to hide from every man around. Here in the imperial city, if she didn't demure behind a fan, she was tied to the *kichō*.

She fell onto her back, her head landing on a yellow silk pillow, and gazed out at delicate pink cherry blossoms shining in a rare beam of afternoon sunlight cheating its way through a gray sky. Morning rain had left the ground wet, and a cool breeze blowing in had a rich, loamy quality.

The recent rain caused aches where broken bones had healed. The more time that passed since her injuries, the more she ached when rain and snow fell. It offered an inescapable reminder of her suffering. An inescapable reminder of her guilt. Of the pain in her heart. Warui. She would never forget his name and what he had done to her and her brother.

She had been glad when her father sent her to Kyō because she wanted to leave the horrors of Shinano Province behind. In recent weeks, however, her uncle's behavior had indicated he moved to make a match for her.

She had never intended to find a gentleman. Perhaps her father had. Certainly her uncle did. She only wanted peace, though.

Perhaps if she had a chance to marry, to meet a gentleman she could respect and love, she might not resist. Were she to love, she wouldn't easily share him with a wife and multiple concubines.

She gave her head a vigorous shake and covered her eyes with a hand. This line of thinking could only lead to deeper unhappiness. A true lady of Kyō wasn't to harbor such selfish ideas. Not that she'd ever be considered a true lady of the imperial city. Her country upbringing made her unsuitable for marriage. She could only hope to become a consort. Shivering with distaste, she removed her hand and stared up into the pale blossoms of the cherry tree.

City life had its benefits. Art. Religious choice. Stimulating conversation. She had even managed to make associations with people she genuinely called friends. Country life would always be her preference, however. Unfortunately, her home province held too many painful memories to return. She'd nearly lost her sanity to grief before her father sent her to his brother's house. If only she had a relative in another province. Lately, her lack of freedom in this city suffocated her.

She was trapped. With her uncle's intentions growing clearer, she now stood to become a pawn, as well.

"Have you no correspondence to write?" came a deep, guttural voice from the main house.

"Ojisan." Kirei sat up like a shot. She smoothed a hand over her ruffled hair and peeked through her screen of state's loose strips of curtain. "Um, no. I wrote my notes and responses this morning. No correspondence has come this afternoon."

"That's disappointing. You need to get out more." Her uncle stepped into the doorframe separating her and Amai's wing of rooms from the main part of his Fourth Ward mansion. "I might've suggested you spend your idle time in writing poetry or perfecting your drawing, but I understand you've been invited to Prince Hansamu's perfume party tonight."

His balding pate gleamed in white light filtering through rice paper. His hard eyes showed no kindness as he assessed what he could see of her past her *kichō*. To appease his curiosity, she extended her arm so he could admire the arrangement of colors showing at the end of her sleeve. His gaze fell upon her silks and he appeared to relax a fraction, so she rested her hand on her knee to keep her layers in his view. At his waist, he fingered a jeweled sword that he wore for show.

She fought a smirk at the thought of him trying to wield such a weapon in earnest. With his narrow shoulders and thin arms, she doubted he could lift the blade over his head. He was more likely to send robbers into peals of laughter rather than running for their lives.

Her voice tight from restrained humor, she said, "Yes, Ojisan. Amai has the party's particulars."

He grunted. "Then you should go speak with her. Prince Hansamu, it's rumored, has expressed an interest in you. I won't deny him if he seeks to take you as a consort, so you'd do well to encourage him. I want you looking your best tonight."

"Of course." Her fun evaporated, and when he left, she released a disgusted huff.

Prince Hansamu was entirely too aware of his good

looks. She couldn't think of a more unfaithful gentleman in the capital city. Half the ladies she knew had shared a bed with him at one time or another. Encourage him, indeed. If anything, she'd spend her night protecting her naive cousin from his considerable charms.

A consort. She didn't want a man who would take her as less than a wife. Regardless of the fact that she came from the best family and shared the blood of the city's most powerful aristocrats, her childhood spent away from the imperial city's refinements automatically reduced her status to second class citizen. She fisted an angry hand in the heavy garments draping her trousers.

She stood with nowhere near the grace of Amai and moved toward their hallway as fast as her seven layers would allow. Despite the minutes of bright light reflecting off of polished wooden floors and round column supports, a chill cooled her nose and cheeks. Though she appreciated the warmth her thicker robes offered, she looked forward to Change of Dress Day when she could trade her heavy *uchigi* in winter colors for lightweight silk in spring hues.

If only she could've stayed in Shinano. Too many demons haunted her there, however. Kirei preferred a happy, peaceful life in the country, perhaps married to a governor like her father. Just not in her home province.

In her sparse chamber, her two maids met her in a flurry of activity. It took every bit of her self-control not to issue an irritated groan. In a corner, her caged birds twittered their agitation. She went and opened their door so they could fly about the room.

"My lady," said Uma, her plain features pinching into a frown. "They will poop."

"Then raise a blind. Let them gaze at the sunset and soil the sill."

The maid moved to do her bidding. "I don't understand why they don't simply fly away. I think they must love you very much."

Kirei scoffed. "Hardly. They were born and raised in captivity. It's more a matter of being too frightened to fly into that big, unknown world than to stay here where they feel safe."

In so many ways, the aristocracy were human versions of her tiny birds. Born and raised in the imperial city, they only ventured from the walls of their elaborate cage to visit the nearby Mount Hiei and its temples and breathtaking views. Their window ledge of sorts. To the *good people* of this city, the world was savage - large, coarse, and not meant for refined sensibilities. Even the rural vastness of their own country beyond the city walls was ventured into only by those cast from their society.

Uma stood a moment, her gaze blank as if Kirei's request that she consider a bird's perspective tasked her faculties too greatly. Smoothing a weathered hand down her simple but quality gray *kosode*, she cast the feathered creatures a fleeting glance. Then she gave herself a little shake and scurried past, indicating a rack draped with rich worked silk. "I've prepared three color combinations, my lady. You must choose quickly. We have so much to do."

Her other maid, Zo, lifted her sizable girth to reveal she held Kirei's hair accessories box on her limited lap. "I can't set out your decorations and dress your hair until you tell us what you'll wear."

Kirei moved to the rack and fingered a pale purple damask. Only her connection to her uncle allowed her to wear such fine fabrics, and still there would be some who'd dis- approve of a governor's daughter in finery reserved for the city's elite. As she traced a delicate crane sewn into the silk's texture, she wished she had a reason to care. "Ojisan says I have to look my best tonight."

Uma exchanged a wide-eyed glance with Zo. "You must wear the sky blue then." She slid a hand under a *mo* apron-skirt artfully weaved into a random floating of diaphanous white clouds amidst a sky that started in pale blue at the waist and gradually darkened to deepest indigo where the hem formed a train. "You'll appear as if a piece of the heavens settled to earth to move among the cherry blossoms."

"Will I?" She found it hard to believe. In her mood, she couldn't compare herself to heaven in any way.

"You will. You will." Zo set aside the box and grunted low while struggling to get her rotund body off the floor. When she heaved to her feet, she had a red face and breathed hard. It didn't stop her, though. She hurried over and began smoothing Kirei's hair. "Today's the last day you can wear it. Tomorrow is the first day of the fourth month. It's Change of Dress."

Uma lit incense near the open window where the two small birds hopped, fluffing their feathers against the chill, and happily sang. A cold breeze pushed the smoke throughout her room, infusing it with the sweet scent of white and pink cherry blossoms that grew just outside. Wisps of pale gray snaked through the air, and Kirei inhaled deeply while fingering a loosened length of hair. The flower's perfume mingled with her unique preparation of rich wood tones and exotic Chinese spices to soothe her nerves.

She relaxed her shoulders. "What will Amai wear?"

Uma shrugged then squatted, helping Kirei out of her socks. "Do you want me to ask?"

"Yes. She needs to shine brightly tonight. My uncle wants me matched well and quickly, but I'll put my effort into seeing my cousin wed for happiness."

Kirei swallowed a lump of jealousy. Amai's city upbringing and Fujiwara family connections made it possible for her to actually wed. Preferably as a primary wife. One day, she would be an official wife to a very important man.

Zo finished freeing Kirei's hair then went to work removing the many layers of her robes. "You'll wear your hair down and loose tonight? It's so thick and lovely."

And risk attracting attention away from Amai? Not tonight. "I think it would be better to fashion it gathered with a ribbon halfway down my back." Kirei drew the ebony length over one shoulder to clear the way for her maid to work. The ends tickled her bare toes, and she fed it like a thick rope through a fist to help dispel her nervous energy. "I wish I could think of some excuse to get out of going to this party."

"Why?" Zo removed the final robe, leaving Kirei in the faded jade chemise and her white *kosode* tucked into dark purple-red raw silk *hakama* skirt-trousers.

"I have a bad feeling."

Her maid went still then came around to face her, the multiple swaths of material draped over an arm. Pink drained from her cheeks, and her unfashionably round eyes widened. "Have you had a dream? Was there an omen?"

"No." She had a bad feeling Prince Hansamu would try to insinuate his way into her *hakama*. She was nobody's one-night of pleasure. Kirei put a hand on the good-natured young woman's arm, contrite for causing alarm. "Not at all. I don't like these gatherings. Simple as that."

She shivered, her single raw silk *kosode* offering no protection against the evening's chill. Stepping to the window, she shooed the adorable birds back to their cage and rolled the bamboo blind down to close the window.

Zo relaxed, her cheeks finding color once again and her lips puckering. She carefully folded each robe in plain paper and placed them into separate thin shelves built into a long black lacquered drawer. "You'll enjoy yourself. You'll see. When you get there and meet friends, you'll have stimulating conversation and discover your happiness. Why be bored in your uncle's house when you can enjoy society and entertainments?"

"Entertainment is subjective, I think. What amuses one may bore another." Not everyone could stay home and entertain themselves as she did. Though to be completely fair, she'd been hard pressed to amuse herself these last days of winter. Poor Amai had cried once in sheer boredom. Perhaps she shouldn't fight this outing so much. It might do them both good.

"Except for me." Zo laughed, her double chin jiggling in

her mirth. "I'm amused by most anything."

"I envy you. I wish I could find joy like that." Did her father ruin her disposition by educating her on equal level with her brother? Kirei wouldn't trade her knowledge and thirst of learning for all the possibilities of joy, however. It was her secret delight.

"Why do you say you find no joy, my lady? Is there something you would rather do?"

"I would rather accomplish something worthwhile and meaningful. The people I'm expected to spend time with move through this life as if asleep. Their eyes only touch on each other and the beauty of nature and our surroundings. Their thoughts never seem to move past seeking the next pleasure or criticizing their peers."

"I think your dark mood is clouding your view," said Zo, sliding the drawer into a tall bureau against the far wall. "I see a lot of goodness in the *good people* of Kyō. Charity. Artwork. A constant striving for perfection. You are among the best, Lady Kirei, for your excellent taste and very high opinions, and for your skill with a brush and your rare ability to turn a phrase. I hear what the *good people* say about you."

It reassured Kirei to hear of her acceptance and admiration by the aristocracy, but that had never been her goal. She was herself, true to her upbringing and beliefs. "You sound like Ojisan."

"You pay me a compliment." Zo laughed. "Fujiwara no Rikō is a wise and caring lord. I'm the luckiest of maids to have work in his house."

Her maid was right. If her uncle didn't care, he would've immediately matched her to whomever he deemed could best advance his career without a thought to her wants and desires. Since coming to live in the imperial city, Kirei had seen it happen again and again to ladies of her acquaintance. Ojisan insisted she seek a gentleman of high rank, but he'd already given her a year and the freedom to do so in her own way and time.

He wouldn't be so kind and generous if he learned of her and Uma's late-night forays into less pristine areas of the city. She refused to confine her charitable works to simple handouts when people in genuine crisis needed help.

"Why do you easily accept the place society says you must hold? The only obstacle between you and a birthright like mine is one marriage." Kirei pulled her chemise closed over her *kosode*, as if the flimsy material could offer any added warmth.

Zo's smile widened as she stoked a brazier under the birdcage then moved to a hairbrush waiting next to the accessories box. "Yes, my mother came from an aristocratic family, but I wouldn't be a lady for anything if it meant she had to marry a man other than my father. My parents *love*. Really love each other. And I rejoice in my position because I'm free to love where I will. A governor's son. A soldier. Even a gentleman could have me as a consort if I loved him."

"You would do that?"

"For love, yes. My mother was ostracized for her choice. Her mother disowned her. She lost all of her friends. She was no longer welcome among Kyō's *good people*, but she lives a life filled with joy and told me how glad she is that her children have a chance at the same. Were I a lady like you, I might not. In fact, with my looks, I'd practically be guaranteed not to." She patted her generous hip and chuckled.

Love. In her circles, love was only talked of in terms of clandestine meetings and extra-marital affairs. Rarely was love associated with a spouse. Her own father had loved her mother, his primary and only wife, and had refused to take other women into his bed. His 'unnatural' love had cost him his brilliant career as a Fifth Rank official in the emperor's court. When it became clear he wouldn't add women to his household, the emperor took *some* pity on him by assigning him a wealthy and prestigious governorship. It was banishment nonetheless.

"You feel sorry for me?" asked Kirei with a teasing grin. "A moment ago, you expounded on the entertainments I should pursue."

Zo shrugged and set down the hairbrush unused. Settling to the floor, she released a heavy breath. "We have to make the best of our situations. I'm trying to help you see the good in yours."

"Am I wrong to want more?"

Her maid didn't respond, her eyes on the box of accessories she moved to her knees.

She did want more. Was she being selfish?

Uma hurried in and quickly bowed then scurried to the displayed *uwagi* over-robes and *mo*. "Amai wears plum layers – plum and red robes with a blue-green chemise. They're all lined, so she'll have twelve colors showing under her *uwagi*."

Kirei shook her head. "She'll be stunning in the forbidden colors, but she's a tiny woman. After she dons an *uwagi*, *mo*, and *karaginu* jacket over her lined robes and *kosode*, how will she walk?"

Uma laughed. "Why does she need to walk? She will only be sitting, anyway."

"Embarrassing," Kirei said under her breath. "Well, the colors will make her skin glow. She's chosen wisely."

Uma placed fingertips on the purple damask. "This over-robe, I think, is the best choice."

"Maybe so, but the colors will be too striking next to Amai's. I don't want to draw attention." She moved, her feet cold on the bare wood floor. She stepped lightly to the third *uwagi* – a pale yellow confection with red lanterns applied in watered dye that made them blur at their edges and gave an abstract impression. "This one, with only five *uchigi* layers – all dark golden yellow – and this green chemise I already wear. No *mo*. No *karaginu*."

"But—"

"No. I don't go to court tonight, so I have no need or desire to dress formally. It's just a party in the Sixth Ward."

Uma's countenance drooped with disappointment. "You'll pale in comparison."

Kirei shook her head. "I'll compliment her. This is what I want."

Zo frowned but drew a plain yellow ribbon from the box and waved Kirei to turn around. "Very well. I'll dress your hair."

## Chapter Two

As Yūkan smoothed a hand down the front of his silk jacket and made his way through his aunt's First Ward mansion, he grimaced. How had he let Yoki talk him into attending a society party where he would know nobody and likely appear a fool?

From an outer ring of chambers, a woman's voice floated through flimsy partitions of bamboo and rice paper. "Lady Minikui's ensemble lacked taste this morning."

He smiled, halting. His carriage awaited, but it didn't matter. The gossip shared between the court ladies who attended his aunt might aid him, so he sidled a bit closer to the partition. At this point, any amount of information had to help.

"She does herself a disservice to snub Lady Kirei. She could only benefit from time spent with such a lady of refined taste."

"So true. Lady Kirei's sense of style is only surpassed by the empress. She showed me how to layer this green between the white and yellow to imply a happy bush rising from snow and reaching for the sun."

"I was admiring that, actually. It's no surprise Fujiwara no Kirei inspired it. Her fashion sense is a perfect reflection of her poetry. I love when she reads her poems for our empress. They're so fine. So profound and fitting."

"It's a shame. She's a stunning woman. The loveliest of us all. I'm not shy or too proud to say so. She'd make a perfect wife."

"Yes. A true shame."

Yūkan frowned. The women spoke of a paragon. How

could such fineness be a shame? They now discussed which jackets to wear, so he continued on his way. Better to face the evening with courage than put it off until it grated upon his nerves. Whatever Prince Hansamu's party held for him, he would hold his head high.

*   *   *   *

Lamplight created punctuated bright points against the orange glow of dusk along the wall surrounding the Fujiwara estate. At a line in the sky where brush-stroked clouds floated in stark contrast to gray nothingness beyond, a flock of birds silently crossed. Behind the distant peaks of Mount Hiei, cloud cover in coral hues bled finally into crimson against a purple dome.

On the veranda outside the mansion's main entrance, her uncle assessed Kirei's hair and attire. "I approve."

She guessed he might not be so pleased were he to see her next to her resplendent cousin. Adjusting her fan a bit higher, she took in his beige silk decorated with a five-sided blue medallion print. He rarely dressed in such finery. In fact, she tried to recall when she had last seen him in anything but his robes of office.

"You'll surely win Prince Hansamu's heart." He gestured to a servant who ran to the mansion's wall gate and threw it open. On the busy Fourth Ward street beyond, an ox-pulled carriage appeared in the gateway.

"Ojisan, Prince Hansamu's heart is fickle. I could only attract his favor for a short time. He has a wife and two consorts, none of whom he beds any longer. Is that what you want for me? A master who'll ignore me? Leave me to rot while he spends his nights in other women's beds?" She flicked her fan in agitation.

His eyes shifted to his waiting carriage, and he cleared his throat. "That's not something you should concern yourself about."

She glanced at his lighted conveyance, and it dawned on her where he headed. *He* was on his way to another woman's bed. "Is this my future? Is this what I have to look forward to?"

He turned his back and accepted a wrapped gift from a servant who joined them on the mansion's north veranda. Was that present bound for the hands of his lover? "Your only concern, Niece, should be in making the very best political and financial match. Do your family proud and bring us honor in choosing wisely. Once you're bound, worry about being the very best companion. The very best mother. What your master does is his business."

The temperature had steadily dropped over the past hour, and into the cold evening, he strode down a set of steps. He offered a wave over his shoulder without turning then passed out of the north gate.

She didn't miss how he hadn't given her a chance to reply. Frustration burned at the bottom of her stomach. She couldn't hate him, however. He simply expressed what everyone seemed to believe. Everyone but her.

She didn't move as he climbed in, causing the carriage to sway upon its large wheels. He cast her a final stern look out his window then gave the driver a curt wave. In seconds, he had disappeared amidst the flow of other carriages.

Before she turned to go collect Amai from her room, Kirei felt a draw. Tiny prickles dotted her nape, and hairs on her arms tried to stand on end under the weight of her eight layers of fabric. Lowering her fan, she searched the street for its source. Would she spy a ghost, or worse?

A carriage more elegant than her uncle's approached in the sea of conveyances. It stood out because it was drawn by a horse and its driver sat on a seat near the roof rather than walking ahead. It slowed. Its black lacquered finish gleamed in the glow of torches lining the thoroughfare. Yellow light spilled from the carriage's lush interior.

She held her breath. Who rode inside? The horse blatantly proclaimed him a foreigner. The *good people* of town would never have anything but proper oxen pull their carriages. Why did she care? And why couldn't she take her eyes from it?

A man leaned forward and captured her gaze. The carriage's window framed his square, masculine face. In her year in Kyō, she had never seen him, yet he was obviously a man of great riches. Was he a visitor from China? From Korea?

He wore his hair long, the black length smoothed into a high ponytail and reflecting lantern light rather than in a topknot hidden under a hat. His lips held no rouge yet had nice color and a fine, bow shape. He wore no cream or powder to lighten his skin tone, yet his brown hue didn't offend her. On the contrary, it lent added strength to the power he exuded.

His spell held her enthralled until his carriage continued along the avenue and his black stare broke. She blinked. Too late, she realized she'd lowered her fan. He'd seen her face.

What had just happened?

*    *    *    *

Yūkan sat dazed, the woman's lovely face imbedded in his mind until the cart hit a rut and jarred him. *Focus.* Emperor Ichijō wanted him in Kyō for the next three months, so much he'd provided him quarters in the imperial palace and arranged a tutor. Was Ichijō testing him? In order to continue the family's business in the imperial city and with the royal house, he had to make a good social impression.

His father had done it for him, and now he had to do it to pave the way for Fudōno. In the capital city, social failure made success in business and politics impossible.

He ran a thumb along the neckline of his jacket for the fifth time, making sure it rested at the correct angle with no gaping. When he'd taken over his father's business, importing luxuries from China had brought him often to Kyō and the court. This was the first time he'd been asked to stay, however.

He wished he knew why. Did the Fujiwaras seek to end his family's trade by disgracing him with his clients now that they had gained their own wealth through the purchase of rice manor rights? It seemed unlikely. The Fujiwara Family enjoyed power and their ability to rule Japan in the emperor's shadow. They didn't *work* for a living, so they definitely didn't intend to assume the trade in his place.

Besides, Fujiwara no Michinaga, his uncle and the father of the empress, was married to his father's sister. Rinshi was Michinaga's primary wife, and Yūkan's money had built the mansion in which they lived after their prior one burned. Michinaga wouldn't amputate the hand of the family that had built his home. He was no fool.

Perhaps Japan wanted to resume diplomatic relations with China. It made sense to keep him here to help them work through the details, since his ships would be their source of transportation.

Before he could explore that idea further, the woman's face came unbidden to his mind. She had beguiled him. In four seconds, without a word spoken, he had discerned her to be a well-born lady of superior taste based upon her attire, a woman of excellent family based upon her residence in the Fourth Ward, and an available beauty based upon the color of her *hakama* trousers. All compelling reasons to avoid her. But when she lowered her fan, he caught something intriguing in her expression that haunted him. Something sad yet hopeful. Something exciting swirling beneath the calm stillness of her exterior.

His cart arrived in the Sixth Ward and stopped at the second wall gate along Red Bird Avenue, the three-hundred-foot-wide main roadway his carriage had traveled after dropping Yoki at home in the Fourth Ward. After the party, this avenue would take him directly to the imperial compound.

Red Bird Avenue glittered like a jewel in the waning light. On either side, water channels reflected lantern light from passing carriages. Weeping willows bent low, their frothy white flowering boughs a reminder of snows past yet promising the warmth of spring in their delicate beauty.

The great willow trees dipped and swayed, their branches caressing the avenue's edges. From carriage windows, ladies displayed their colorful, layered silk sleeves. Everything appeared clean and perfect, as though a painting had sprung to life. The beautiful sight was an obscene contradiction to the riotous turmoil threatening to upset the contents of Yūkan's stomach.

He had no time to ruminate, however. His driver drew the horse under a fine gateway portico painted green and gold. A servant opened the door of his carriage, and another beckoned him through the gate. This was it. He had to do well for the family business. For his brother's future.

Inside, the sounds of Prince Hansamu's party filled the night. Music, fine and light, drifted along air made damp by a morning rain left moist in the ground by a sunless day. A servant escorted him along a wing of the prince's mansion and around a pavilion. From the pavilion's eaves, long lengths of red and yellow silk hung. The wide swaths billowed and undulated in a sweet-smelling breeze, as if they wished to detach from their moorings and join the party.

Behind the dancing silk, Yūkan glimpsed an occasional curve of cheek and colorful sleeve to accompany a symphony of women's voices within. He followed the servant around to a vast garden lit by pole lanterns casting golden glow upon gentlemen sitting along an anemic pond. Only a few screens of state rose from the grass behind the noblemen.

Prince Hansamu waved him over. "Lord Yūkan. Sit next to me. I'm happy you could come."

Yūkan cleared his throat to avoid saying something offensive. After all, Yoki had said Emperor Ichijō *suggested* he attend, at Fujiwara no Michinaga's urging. In essence, he'd had no choice. He settled to the mat and accepted a cup of *sake*.

"This damp air is perfect for a perfume contest. The fragrant smoke will hang on the moisture much longer, letting us appreciate each scent to its fullest." The prince inclined his head, his almost feminine features catching moonlight and appearing ghost-like in their pallor. Hansamu had no facial hair, and Yūkan couldn't help thinking that if the man traded his damask jacket for the layered robes of a lady, he might pass as a woman.

He took a sip of wine and forced his shoulders to relax. "Will you judge?"

"Oh, no," Hansamu said on a chortle. "I'm entering two mixtures of my own. I bury them next to my river like His Majesty. Emperor Ichijō matures his incense in the ground near the moat of the Inner Palace Guard's headquarters."

"Interesting." *Not really.* Yūkan glanced at a trickle of water trailing from the pond toward the main building and considered it a pitiful *river.* "Then who will judge? Don't say me. I won't have an unbiased opinion. I prefer *jijū* blends and have no appreciation for the sweeter *kurōbo* and *baika* scents."

Half the gentlemen looked more like women, with their small lips, round cheeks, and painted white faces appearing pasty and artificial. What did they think of his undecorated visage?

Hansamu nodded sagely, not seeming to mind Yūkan's lack of cosmetics. "Indeed. We didn't get a chance to talk at the palace this afternoon. Do you enjoy mixing your own scents?"

He didn't know if he was about to make a social blunder, but he had always lived by the belief that speaking truth carried the best karma. "I haven't been fortunate enough to explore the art of perfume. I travel a great deal, so I haven't had the time necessary to cultivate such a skill. I'm forced to purchase my incense."

Hansamu sent a critical gaze over him but simply nodded. "I respect that. A man should only pursue those things to which he can devote himself. Lord Yoki told me you regularly travel to China. Will you come inside and see my collection of Chinese artwork?"

Yūkan couldn't imagine this man's collection compared to what he had seen during his visits to the Chinese imperial palace, but he stood. The prince led the way inside the mansion's east wing where a surprisingly diverse exhibit formed three galleries of rare and particularly vibrant pieces displaying representations from China's rich history. A vase in bold colors, pristine in its condition and lovely in its finely wrought design of curls, reminded him of the lady in yellow and her striking beauty enhanced by her understated manner and sheer elegance.

Prince Hansamu clearly had an eye for quality, though Yūkan would've enjoyed the tour better had the man not incessantly boasted about how his tastes and collection fed jealousies around Kyō.

When they returned to the garden veranda, the prince stopped a moment to survey his party. His eyes, no more than bare slits, wandered to the pavilion, and his small lips parted on a genuine grin. He waved servants toward two approaching ladies. "Ah, Ladies Kirei and Amai have chosen to grace us."

The Lady Kirei spoken of by the ladies in his aunt's household. The paragon. Intrigued, he descended to a gravel courtyard. He kept his gaze on the advancing ladies while making his way to softer grass then his seat near the pond's shore.

The first lady wore a burdensome amount of fabric, extensive layering of exquisite pink and purple in a pattern showing at neckline, cuff and hem. The material clearly weighed upon her, causing her to stoop and shuffle. Youth clung to the smooth skin of her ivory brow and shone like a beacon of sheltered innocence from her eyes. She cast him a single glance above the edge of her green fan, obvious distaste flashing across her delicate forehead before she averted her gaze.

The second made him catch his breath. His heart beat a bit faster and he blinked, unsure if he imagined her. The yellow fan before her face did nothing to disguise her. The moment her eyes met his and gleamed with recognition, he realized the stakes against his reputation had just climbed.

Her eyes, a warm brown in the garden's light, held an

edge in their set that spoke of knowledge and understanding. This woman's intelligence wafted from her as if it were a scent emanating from her pores. In her erect spine and searching gaze, she exuded a confidence that almost dared anyone to challenge her. He smiled, recognizing a kindred spirit.

As servants swarmed about the newly arrived ladies then came behind him to erect their two *kichō*, Yūkan inhaled slowly to regain his control. Here came the lady in yellow from the Fourth Ward. Her bold gaze didn't leave his, and he liked how her fewer layers allowed her to walk gracefully at her full height.

Conversations continued, but all eyes were on them. Their pleasure and excitement over her attendance said a great deal about the lady and her place in the adoration of these people. Would he have a chance to share words with a woman who obviously enjoyed an elevated status as favorite among Kyō's elite? That she moved toward her screen behind *him* gave him hope.

On the other hand, two words from his mouth said in the wrong context could reveal his lack of city culture, and he'd lose his chance to win her approval. Somehow, he suspected her approval, more than anyone's, would determine his acceptance into the noblemen's world.

She passed behind the lords, and Yūkan reluctantly released her gaze. He stared at golden lamp-lit ripples on the pond, but hardly noticed.

"You brought an entry," declared Hansamu. "We're truly blessed by you."

"I see you have many entries," came her rich, warm voice. "We are blessed by everyone, it seems."

Yūkan stifled a chuckle. A woman of wit was rare, and he appreciated how she didn't succumb to the prince's flattery. Though her words sounded correct in tone, he sensed a crisp defiance in their delivery. It intrigued him.

"Who will judge?" asked a sweet, winded voice he assumed belonged to her companion.

"Yes!" cried Hansamu a bit too enthusiastically. How much *sake* had the prince consumed already? "The noble adventurer, Lord Yūkan, and I were discussing that very subject when you arrived. Any suggestions? Anyone?"

Noble adventurer? Hardly. Then again, these *good people* barely wandered beyond the walls of their great city. A man who traveled the seas and visited foreign lands surely appeared a grand adventurer in their limited view.

The party went quiet.

"I believe the choice is obvious," said the lady in yellow. "Only Lord Hana has the superior discernment necessary to do this contest justice."

Third from the end of lords lined along the pond, an older, thin man all in black, with a nose like a hawk, stood and bowed. "Lady Kirei, I'm grateful you hold me in such high esteem but I can't accept. There are others here who know more than I."

Lady Kirei. Everything about her appealed to him. He fought a laugh at his own ridiculousness. Of course he would want the paragon. Of course he would want the woman who wore so many eyes upon her when he sought as little attention as he could manage. He hid his smile in a sip of *sake*.

Hansamu sent her a look that left no one in doubt of his desire for her. Yūkan began to dislike the *kichō* because hers blocked her reactions from him. Though the two brocade curtains attached to the top moved back and forth in the breeze, they didn't shift enough to let him see anything but the yellow silk that draped her dark *hakama*.

The prince checked the placement of his tall, thin black hat and said, "I believe the lady's correct. Lord Hana is the best judge among us, and since he hasn't entered the contest, he's the ideal man for the job. Shall we put him to the test?"

All around, voices lifted in assent. Curious, Yūkan stood to join gentlemen who made their way to a room adjacent to the crowded pavilion. A servant who had worked to display the contestants' entries bowed and exited. Guests crowded in, and it became quickly clear the room had insufficient space. Yūkan laughed when a young man in the robes of a Seventh Rank official trod on Hansamu's toes, earning a swift and unmanly reprimand.

"I'll fix this," Yūkan said, waving over the only man who appeared to have any strength. Together, they removed a heavy wooden partition separating the bottom half of this room from the next. He flipped up a screen that partitioned the top half, securing it to a roof support and effectively doubling the space. Murmurs of approval accompanied a comfortable shift while two servants hauled away the partitions.

"Let the judging begin," announced the prince.

A manservant hurried in and lit the incense on display. The few women who had submitted entries came out from behind their screens and curtains. They appeared unsure and vulnerable behind their hand-held fans as they joined the men inside. Women of the court stood out in their extravagant displays of worked silks in vibrant, forbidden colors, but Kirei's simpler color combination and plain silk lent her an elegance that appealed to him.

They filed in, their eyes downcast and their countenances demure. Except Lady Kirei's. She boldly entered, her eyes meeting any that glanced her way. He offered her a bow, but she turned her back and faced Lord Hana at the display board.

A line of candles behind the entries lent a golden tinge to thin smoke emanating from each ball. Soon, the cold room grew rich with scent. It surprised Yūkan that the culmination of fragrances somehow created a pleasant aroma rather than the pungent one he'd expected.

He insinuated a position behind her but didn't dare attempt to make conversation until they had an official introduction. Especially since her smaller companion in purple had come to stand next to her. Still, his nearness to Lady Kirei held an almost mystical thrill.

The skinny judge stepped to the first ball, its reddish-brown top peeking from a plain pinewood box sporting random dragonflies painted in browns and reds. A very young gentleman went forward to claim credit.

"A fresh, untamed quality with warm undertones," said Lord Hana, his hawkish nose nearly in the smoke. "Perhaps it could've used a bit more time to age?"

The young man's face slid from hopeful to stoic, as if he didn't want to show his disappointment.

The judge addressed his nostrils to each successive stream of smoke and gave his opinion. The man had an understanding and discernment of fragrance that surpassed anything Yūkan had witnessed. Most of his comments were positive and encouraging, and even his criticisms held a constructive note. Always, Yūkan had the lady in yellow in his vision, a mere hand's breadth away. He imagined he could feel her warmth in that brief space between them.

At a bowl painted red with intricate snowflakes detailing its rim, Hana examined a lacy twist of smoke rising from incense as black as a clouded night sky. "Unusual. Plum. Gentle but deep in a spiced wood foundation. This one has an exotic quality, a Chinese spice perhaps, that I can't quite place."

Lady Kirei moved forward and bowed, accepting the praise. Yūkan experienced a moment of unexpected deprivation, but she almost immediately returned to her place before him. She cast him a furtive glance that contained enough curiosity to give him hope.

The final fragrance, a dark brown mixture in a box of black lacquer inlaid with mother-of-pearl, was judged and found exceptional, as well. It belonged to a court lady they called Lady Winter Garden. She stepped forward, her stiff demeanor and averted gaze proclaiming her uncomfortable to be seen by everyone, though she looked resplendent in a spectacularly flamboyant layering of colors called Mixed Maples – an intricate combination of blue green, scarlet pink, and yellow silks that dazzled the eye.

While in China, he had personally selected for import

the damask she wore. His knowledge of silk layering and color ensembles enabled him to make wise purchasing choices and had thrust their family's trading company to top standing in Kyō.

"What's your decision?" asked Prince Hansamu. "Who won?"

Lord Hana retreated from the display board. "It's very smoky in here. Let's go outside and clear our noses. Then I can think better."

Yūkan agreed that the smoke had become a bit oppressive, weighing the air and making it a job to breathe. Yet he hesitated to leave and lose his close proximity to the lovely lady in yellow, plus the space had gained some warmth from so many people. The garden, though charming in its way, meant returning to cold air *and* the chill of being a stranger among a closed society.

Sighing, he put up his guard and followed Lady Kirei out.

Everyone resumed their places in the pavilions or along the pond's grassy bank. Yūkan refilled Hansamu's *sake* cup, and the prince returned the favor. Behind him, Kirei settled to the security of her *kichō*. He was acutely aware of each movement, each breath, each rustle of her silk.

Near the end of noblemen, Lord Hana stood and bowed to their host. "We have an abundance of superior mixtures in tonight's contest. True artists of incense are in attendance here. In all fairness and good conscience, however, I have to say there are only two from which I must choose a winner."

"Lady Winter Garden's and Lady Kirei's," said the young man who had entered a scent found wanting.

"Too true. Too true." The judge flicked his beak then sniffed. "It's not an easy decision, but I've made it. Lady Winter Garden's fragrance contained a slightly more earthy quality, a beautiful tribute, I believe, to this final day of winter. Therefore, I declare Lady Winter Garden's incense the winner of tonight's contest."

"It was a risk," said Lady Kirei. "An incense that suits her own season rarely competes with more fragrant months, but I agree that her gentle aroma contains a touching tenderness lacking from the rest of ours. Lord Hana chooses most wisely."

Sounds of agreement radiated about the garden. Yūkan admired Kirei's gracious loss.

Clapping, Prince Hansamu stood and waved a servant to the pavilion. "For your delightful win, Lady Winter Garden, I present you with two rolls of plain white silk so you may have them dyed to your liking."

The court lady's slim hands emerged from between the pavilion's swaying red and yellow curtains. She accepted the silk, then the top of her head appeared ever so briefly in a bow of thanks before she disappeared entirely behind the curtains.

"You should've won," said the dainty lady next to Kirei.

Yūkan turned a bit to hear better.

"Lord Hana made his decision, which was a difficult one. There were many outstanding scents presented in competition. I don't envy his position as judge tonight."

"But yours was the best."

"I disagree. The winner can't be picked solely on fragrance and presentation. The season and weather have to be considered, too. Under tonight's circumstance, Lady Winter Garden earned her win. She deserves it."

A gentleman between Yūkan and Lord Hana turned at the waist, his bright blue robe of rank rustling pleasantly. "Well said, Lady Kirei. Will you write us a poem to commemorate the win?"

The partygoers buzzed. Someone yelled, "A poem!"

"Yes, a poem," shouted another.

Yūkan held his breath. If she wrote one, would she be asked to stand and read it? Would he get a chance to gaze upon her face?

\*   \*   \*   \*

A groan of nerves threatened, and Kirei swallowed it.

"I'm not the most qualified. Perhaps Lady Winter Garden will grace us with her words. I'm sure we'd like to hear a poem sprung from her elation of winning."

"Nonsense." Hansamu waved over a servant. "Bring my writing box to Lady Kirei."

The servant bowed and ran to do the prince's bidding.

Wholly unprepared to compose a *tanka,* and irritated that he insisted, she slightly separated the curtains of her screen of state and looked Hansamu in the face. "I don't think so much of myself as to write poetry on a spontaneous whim. Verses like that tend to be weak, barely hanging together. Or worse, sound pretentious. Any poem I write without careful consideration could only be odious and pathetic in the extreme."

The prince stood, his narrow eyes gone wider and wider during her lament until they bugged far larger than she thought possible. His shoulders sagged, and his mouth opened only to snap shut again. His distress left her contrite for giving their host a hard time.

The newcomer laughed. The handsome man's broad shoulders shook, and his quiet chortling grew to great guffaws. He threw back his head and put a hand to his stomach.

Prince Hansamu shifted his attention from her to the man, his caterpillar-like eyebrows inching upward. In moments, his features tightened until he laughed, too. Others joined in until the garden resounded in mirth.

Kirei slowly let the stiff curtains close, unsure whether to be offended by the man's laughter or relieved she no longer attracted so much notice. To Amai, she said, "You see? I *should've* stayed home. Nobody wants a peevish shrew at a party."

"Your poetry is never faulty, but they were wrong to ask. Besides, it's cold." Her cousin exhaled a misty breath as if to demonstrate. Her cousin flicked a trailing cuff. "You'll freeze your fingers if they leave your sleeves."

True, though the cold evening air barely seeped through

her many layers. Still, nobody deserved the unkind berating she had given to the prince.

"Do you have any idea who that man is?" she asked, indicating by a nod of her head toward the laughing visitor in front of her *kichō*.

"No, though I heard from the Governor of Tanba's wife that he stays in the Nine-Fold Enclosure and spent the entire day with His Excellency, Fujiwara no Michinaga."

"So he's important." Maybe she wasn't wrong in guessing he visited as a diplomat from China. As the laughing quieted, she peeked through her screen at him. Somehow, Chinese diplomat didn't fit. Besides, when was the last time Michinaga had accepted an audience with a diplomat of any kind? Plus, the rare ones she'd seen had always worn judgmental and disapproving scowls. He didn't. No diplomats had ever been invited into the imperial compound, much less resided there for their stay.

He wore his hair pulled high but hanging loose from its stay rather than caught in an uptight topknot. It lent him a casual air that somehow fit well with this outdoor gathering. His garments gleamed in the lamplight, their fine silk and stiff movement proof of superior craftsmanship. Despite his impeccable apparel, however, he wore no cosmetics to lighten the natural brown tone of his skin. He was a contradiction in every way. His bearing and grooming declared him an aristocrat of the best breeding, yet he lacked any pretention. She couldn't comprehend his position, and it confounded her.

He started to turn, and she quickly retreated to the privacy her screen offered. Who was he, and why did he fascinate her to the point of distraction?

# Chapter Three

Kirei wilted as Hansamu's servant came out of a rear door of the sprawling, one-story mansion's east wing and knelt. He placed the prince's writing box on the veranda in front of his knees and slid the door closed. With care and reverence, he collected the box and hurried down a set of steps into the garden. If she accepted the box from him, she couldn't continue to protest. She'd have to write a poem.

At the east gate behind the pavilion, a ruckus disturbed the night. Servants darted. Male voices rose above the roofline.

Prince Hansamu strode toward the pavilion's corner but stopped short and dropped out of sight.

"I can't see," Kirei said to Amai. She swayed, trying to catch a glimpse between the shoulders of seated gentlemen.

"His Majesty!" whispered Shinsetsu, the young nobleman who'd received Lord Hana's gentle criticism in the contest. His crisp, green robes of rank practically crackled as he shifted off of his mat and stood.

Amai's eyes widened, but Kirei suspected it had more to do with Shinsetsu's appeal and less to do with the emperor's arrival. Especially since her cousin's gaze never left the young man.

Gasps sounded, lingering a moment over the pond. Everyone stood. Kirei reached to help Amai get up amidst the burden of her many layers. By the time they reached their feet and had fans protecting their faces, the partygoers had already dropped into bows.

"Quick," hissed Kirei, gesturing for Amai to bend.

"There you are," said Emperor Ichijō, spotting her as he

rounded the pavilion's corner.

"I told you she'd be here," said Lord Yoki at his shoulder.

The emperor looked for her and had Yoki, of all men, with him? This couldn't be good. Before bowing deeply, she greeted, "Your Majesty."

"Please. Everyone sit. Let's have some wine."

The emperor dazzled in his brilliance. He wore red and gold court dress, his wide red pants gathered at the ankles, as if he had left the palace compound in a hurry without a thought to changing.

Kirei settled behind her *kichō*. It unnerved her how he headed straight for her. Would *he* insist on a poem? Embarrass her? Humiliate her? At least the servant bearing Hansamu's box had halted halfway from the veranda and still huddled on the cold ground. If he didn't carry the means to her final failure at this party, she might actually feel sorry for him.

Ichijō stopped next to the newcomer. "Lord Yūkan, you've passed my test."

"Test, Your Majesty?" the man asked, his voice deep and smooth.

"Yes. Test. You took my advice and came to Hansamu's party."

The prince bowed then waved madly at servants to bring mats and cups for the emperor and Yoki.

Ichijō ignored him. "Her Majesty and I agree that you should make time to spend with Lady Kirei."

Her heart skipped a beat, and Yoki handed her a folded parchment through her screen. In the empress' impeccable hand were written two words. *Teach him.* Teach him what?

"Nothing would give me more pleasure, Your Majesty," said Lord Yūkan, his head disappearing from view as he bowed.

"Good, good. Let me introduce you."

Introduce them? Was this an association she wanted? Who was this man with a horse-drawn carriage and who warranted an introduction by the emperor himself? He had a Japanese name, which meant he didn't merely visit as a foreign diplomat. His title of *lord* told her he hailed from a family of Kyō. So why hadn't she seen him before tonight? Kirei fisted her trembling hands inside the warmth of her sleeves.

"Lady Kirei, I bid you accept Yūkan into your acquaintance. His father was a friend to my father, and I believe you will get on well."

She tipped forward where she sat. "Lord Yūkan, *dozo yoroshiku. Hajimemashite.*"

"Lady Kirei, *dozo yoroshiku. Hajimemashite.*"

She swallowed a sigh. There was no avoiding the association now.

"Let's celebrate this new acquaintance," said Ichijō, sitting next to Yūkan and holding his cup for Hansamu to fill.

Biting her lip, Kirei fought the urge to crumple the empress' note. She didn't like how the newcomer made her feel vulnerable and more unfulfilled than ever. Now she had to spend time with him. Ojisan wouldn't like it one bit.

"Prince Hansamu looks ready to spit," whispered Yoki, leaning near her screen from his place next to Ichijō.

She leaned to see. The prince, usually talkative and eager to draw attention, sat quietly sipping his *sake*. His features in profile drooped, something she'd never witnessed in him.

"What's the reason, do you think?" she asked. He should've been overjoyed to have the emperor honor his party.

"You," said Yoki on a chuckle. His perky black hat quivered atop his head. He offered to pour her wine, but she declined with a flip of her thick sleeve.

Ojisan had said Prince Hansamu expressed an interest in her.

"He'll get over it soon enough," she said, glancing over her shoulder. The servant had gone, and she released a relieved breath. "He doesn't need another consort – certainly not me with my bold opinions and unconventional education."

"Indeed," said Yoki, staring toward the pavilion as if he hoped to glimpse the ladies within. "Any man in his right mind would be intimidated by a woman as learned in Chinese history and classics as you."

"Sh!" she hissed.

He leaned nearer and whispered, "So apparently, he's not in his right mind."

"Maybe he doesn't know. I go to great lengths to hide my learning."

"You can't hide it. It shows in your poetry. Only the truly ignorant wouldn't see it...which would be most people. Okay. Hint taken."

She laughed softly, but grew serious. "Maybe I don't want to get lost and forgotten in a household full of consorts."

She peeped around at Yūkan and found him gazing in her direction. Did he listen to her conversation while Ichijō talked? Surely not. Shrugging, she set a plate of cubed fruit next to her mat and tried to decide which piece to try first.

"Maybe think of it this way," said Yoki. "When a man fills his home with women, but obviously singles one out above the others, people admire her."

"And here's the problem with your argument. Who's to say he'll single me out? Who's to say he wants me for anything other than to say he has taken one of the empress' favorites as one of his own? I hate the thought of being reduced to a prize."

"Maybe you should ask him."

"Ha! I'll avoid this subject with him at any cost."

"The Minister of the Center—"

"Leave my uncle out of it."

"Fine." He drained his *sake*. While she reached through her screen and refilled it, he launched into the latest gossip. Amai joined in, always eager for diverting tidbits, and the hours slipped past.

As a hint of gray took the edge off the sky's darkness, the party began to degenerate. Gentlemen gathered near the pavilion's swinging curtains and exchanged suggestive comments with the court ladies inside.

"Everyone's drunk," Kirei said to Yoki. She cut a gaze toward Yūkan, but he didn't meet her assessment.

Wide-awake and sober, he glanced her way.

"Let's leave," she suggested.

Yoki straightened his listing hat, stood and stretched. "I want to see the sunrise."

"That sounds wonderful," said Amai, defying her natural grace by getting on all fours the heaving to her feet. She scraped white frost from her jacket and gazed at a dozing Shinsetsu. "The dew is freezing. Lord Yoki, do you think you would mind company in your carriage?"

He followed her line of vision. "You fancy young Shinsetsu? A wise choice if you can turn his head. He won't be in those lowly green robes for long." He went over and nudged the boy. "Come on, little man. We're going for a ride."

Shinsetsu rubbed his eyes and staggered to his feet. "We are?"

"Places to go. Things to see. Gather yourself."

Emperor Ichijō stirred then stood. He cast Kirei a hopeful smile that made her want to groan. "You're going? Lord Yūkan will join you. He has a very fine carriage. Take his."

Yūkan stood and bowed. He sent her a lazy look that caused a flutter in her stomach. "It would be my honor."

Servants hurried over and collected the two *kichō* and mats. Flipping open her fan, she put her head down, hoping she came across as gentle and demure, and ushered her cousin past the drunken noblemen, around the pavilion, and to the main east gate. A number of carriages loomed, large square shadows waiting along Red Bird Avenue. She recognized her driver, who waved, and she moved from the gate to stand under the covered entrance. Her carriage came forward.

"Meet you there?" asked Yoki from the wall opening, Yūkan and Shinsetsu at his shoulders. "The usual place."

She nodded and stepped to her conveyance. Amai took her hand.

Through the predawn dark, Yūkan's quiet voice caught up with her. "I've never met anyone like Lady Kirei."

"And you never will," replied Yoki.

                    *    *    *    *

"Wake up," Yūkan said, giving the young pup, Shinsetsu, a gentle nudge. "We're here."

The ladies' ox-drawn cart sat unmoving on a grassy patch under a stand of black pines, the sunrise casting fiery hues upon its shiny finish. Its finely-split palm-leaf roof thatching proclaimed the ladies' family as fourth rank or above. Their driver snoozed upon a mat on the ground, his back resting against one of the large wheels.

Yūkan stifled a groan as his stiff muscles protested. He opened his carriage door and unfolded his long legs to climb out.

"Aa! I'm sore. Whose idea was this, anyway?" Yoki fairly fell from the carriage, barely catching himself before he went to the ground. He clutched a hand to the small of his back like an old woman.

"Yours," said Shinsetsu, rubbing his eyes and exiting the carriage with the lithe ease of youth. He stood tall and stretched as if he'd just rolled from bed, his green robes practically glowing in the promise of sunrise.

Shaking his head, Yūkan turned his back to them and admired the view. They had traveled up Mount Hiei, but only far enough to gaze down at hills that ran north and east of the city. While he stared, trying to ignore Yoki's moans behind him, the sun crested the east hills to create a sparkling brilliance on the Kamo River below. The sun brought warmth. Frost began to melt, and a delicate mist rose from the ground.

The ladies' driver stirred and pointed.

"This way," said Yūkan, leading the way past the black pines to a gentle slope lit by the rising sun. "I wish I had addressed the issue of our trade agreement last night. I spent six hours in the emperor's presence. It seems a wasted opportunity."

Yoki shook his head. "Your instincts were good. A party

at Prince Hansamu's mansion isn't the place to discuss business. No, your conversation last night went farther to ensure the continuation of your family's agreement than you realize. Damn, my knees hurt."

The ladies sat upon silk-draped mats, their many voluminous robes situated about them in glimmering opulence. Her yellow fan hiding her face, Lady Kirei glanced over her shoulder and offered a wave.

He wanted her greeting to be for him, but when Yoki hurried past, he realized the wave was meant for the gentleman.

His friend tossed a cushion next to her mat and settled to the ground, his attire puffing. He thrust a hand toward hyalescent clouds burnished coral and gold. "I always feel abused by that ride, but then I forget the discomfort when I see this. Look at that. It takes my breath away."

Lady Amai nodded in admiring agreement, but Kirei rolled her eyes. Yūkan smiled. He'd forgotten to grab something from his carriage to sit on, so he stood. Distant honking drove their eyes to the purple sky where a tiny line of geese flew north.

Yoki put a hand to his chest and gasped. "So beautiful."

The geese were nice, certainly, but Yūkan didn't see how they were gasp-worthy.

"Their song is so mournful," said Amai.

"Yes. It reminds us of how fragile our lives are," said Yoki, his voice thick. He sobbed, covering his face with his hands.

Yūkan stared at the man, suddenly uncomfortable and confused. He went around and bent to Lady Kirei's ear. "Is he being real?"

"Yes," she whispered.

"He's crying over geese." He couldn't keep disbelief from his tone. Did his friend suffer the effects of too much *sake* in combination with too little sleep?

"Lord Yoki's an *ideal* gentleman," she said low, using a

patient tone like that of a mother to a child. "He recognizes that our world is impermanent, and the sadness in the geese' cry mirrors the sadness in his heart."

Yūkan fought a laugh. "The sadness in his heart?"

She nodded. "His mother and father died in an earthquake when he was very young. His aunt took him in but died of a fever a few years later. He has watched nearly every member of his closest family die young, so we must understand his keen awareness of how precarious our lives are. Of how he can expect to die young, too."

"I didn't realize." He glanced at his friend with new eyes. How had he not known any of this?

"It seems you have a lot to learn," she said, the patience gone.

"Why do you say that?" Though he agreed.

She released a heavy breath. "A true gentleman wouldn't stand when ladies are seated behind their *kichō*."

"Why?"

"It puts us at risk."

"Of what?" He blinked and gave his head a small shake. When had they stopped talking of Yoki?

"Being seen," she snapped, raising her fan a fraction. She glanced past him to Amai, but the younger woman was engrossed in quiet conversation with Shinsetsu.

He clenched his jaw and lowered his gaze before retreating a few steps. He swished a foot over the grass to test its moisture. His slippers were soaked.

Yoki composed his demeanor and glanced over a shoulder. His tears had coursed tracks through his white face powder. "It's not seemly that you stand. Come share my mat." He scooted and pulled the voluminous silk of his outfit close to reveal ample room.

It didn't escape Yūkan's notice that the gentleman had moved *away* from Kirei. Before his friend could change his mind, he accepted. He sank to the mat, enjoying his immediate proximity to the lovely lady. She kept her eyes on the sunrise and didn't adjust her screen or fan to block his unrestricted view of her elegant profile.

Why didn't she shut him out? She obviously disdained him.

In part, he couldn't help disdaining himself. As an importer, he was an expert. Other traders sought him with questions regarding trade winds and currents, corrupt merchants, foreign dealings, and evading pirates. He knew the rules and tricks. Here, however, he knew none of the rules. His lack of social diplomacy made him appear oafish. Perhaps the emperor had been wise to arrange lessons for him. Unfortunately, the chosen tutor already despised him.

Yoki cleared his throat, and she looked his way.

"Honestly," she said on a faint smile. "You've made a mess of your face."

Amai leaned forward to see then laughed. "You look like a patch of dark ground where snow has melted in spots."

"Do I?" He averted his countenance and gently wiped his face. When he turned back, he had smoothed the white evenly over his features. He wasn't as white, since he'd thinned his makeup, but the women made approving sounds and returned to admiring the sky. He glanced at Yūkan and said, "The emperor has a real liking for you. Are your fathers close friends?"

"Yes. Like brothers in some ways. When I was a young boy, they exchanged letters often. They retired as monks together." He withheld the fact that his father had died. He didn't want the gentleman bursting into tears.

"But you're not an aristocrat from Kyō," said Lady Kirei. "I haven't seen you before."

Yūkan shook his head. "I've been traveling. There's little leisure time in my family's import business."

"Travel?" Kirei cut her dark gaze in his direction. "Do you mean in the savage countryside?"

Yūkan detected sarcasm, but both Yoki and Amai shuddered. "All over Japan, yes. The countryside may be rustic and lacking the finery Kyō has to offer, but I'd hardly call it savage. I travel to other countries, too. China. Korea. And farther south, to the Dong Son and Sa Huynh Fu Nan kingdoms."

Yoki and Amai gave him blank looks as if he talked of traveling to the stars. Shinsetsu emitted a soft snore where he slumped.

Kirei, however, sent him a curious glance. "Dong Son? Isn't that very far?"

He nodded, surprised both by her interest and knowledge. "It's south of China. It can be a treacherous journey, so I take our sturdiest ships, and only when ocean conditions are right. Sometimes we set out but have to return without making it that far. There are entire years when I can't trade there."

"Where do you live?"

"Echigo Province."

"Maybe we can talk about something that's actually interesting," suggested Amai.

"I find it interesting," said Kirei, lowering her fan to her chest and giving Yūkan her full attention.

His heart beat faster with her lovely dark eyes on him. In a society where screens of state and curtains meant a man could go a lifetime without glimpsing the countenance of his own daughter, much less a new female acquaintance, Kirei's revealing of her face showed an honor of favor he found humbling...and arousing. Had he misread her disdain?

Amai harrumphed. "Did you hear about Lady Hendesu?"

"I heard she was acting strange," said Kirei, gazing at the color-washed sky. "Didn't they call the Masters of Yin-Yang to perform an exorcism?"

"Yes. My brother attended. It turns out she was a *virgin*." She said the last word as though it were an expletive. "No wonder she got possessed. What lady in her right mind goes so long with her maidenhead intact? She was asking for it."

Lady Kirei straightened her spine with a jerk, her gaze

going to the swaying fabric of her *kichō*.

Lord Yoki cast her a worried glance.

Yūkan opened his mouth to ask what had her upset, but the sun broke free of the hills' tentative hold, bringing full morning and robbing him of any further chance to explore the topic.

"Lady Amai, give Lord Shinsetsu a shove." Yoki stood and stretched. "It's time to go. I don't know why he came. He slept through it."

Amai giggled and shook the young gentleman. "Wake up."

Kirei lost her tension and rolled her eyes, which made Yūkan want to laugh. He enjoyed her expressive features. She was refreshing in a city of people who went around with stoic, painted faces. Her lack of white powder made her appear more delicate in her pale countenance. He also liked that the top of her head exceeded his shoulder where most women would have to stand on tip-toe to come level.

She waved a dismissive hand at Yoki and warned, "Don't let anyone see you returning home."

The gentleman's eyebrows arched. "Why? I haven't been misbehaving."

She sent Yūkan a playful glance then said, "Today is Change of Dress. You're out of season."

Wide eyes and a gaping mouth transformed Yoki's face into a look of horror.

Kirei snorted a laugh, placing a dainty hand in front of her pert mouth. She waved, and her driver came running from the carriage. While he gathered the mats and *kichō*, the lady shifted her shoulders in Yūkan's direction. She kept her eyes low. "I found your conversation interesting."

He leaned closer but avoided touching her, fighting a desire to take her hand.

"It's likely we won't see each other again, so I'll wish you a pleasant stay in Kyō and a safe journey home."

Her words sounded courteous, but they cut into his gut

as sharply as a blade. He stood straighter. "You may not wish to dismiss me so easily. Emperor Ichijō isn't eager to see me leave the city, and I'd be embarrassed for you if we meet again after you've prematurely issued your farewell."

Her fine eyebrows approached one another above the sloping bridge of her nose. "I'm growing less fond of you by the second, Lord Yūkan."

"So you're fond of me." He couldn't prevent a smile.

She snuck a peek at him then huffed and turned her back. "Come on, Amai. Let's go home." When the diminutive lady couldn't get off of her mat for the weight of her many layers, Kirei let loose a dainty giggle. She gestured toward her driver. "Oh, for humanity's sake. Makoto, help my cousin to her feet."

"I've got her," announced Shinsetsu, his voice cracking. He stumbled, teetering in his attempt to rise, then tangling his feet beneath him.

"Silly boy," Kirei whispered, shaking her head.

Shinsetsu righted himself, squared his shoulders, and offered Lady Amai a hand with formal ceremony.

Yūkan shook his head. Kirei had him right. How had such an awkward youth earned an invitation to attend such a private gathering with two of the city's most acclaimed and sought after women? For that matter, he didn't deserve such an honor, either.

Amai appeared impressed, however. Her face pinked, despite her white makeup. She placed a tiny hand in his. Then the antics began anew as his face turned red in his effort to get the lady and her heavy robes off the ground.

Yūkan leaned near Kirei. "This is so much more entertaining than the sunrise."

Behind her fan, she showed him her profile, her focus on the glistening grass. Her lips formed an amused smile. "I have to agree."

Finally, the small party headed up the rise toward the waiting carriages. Yūkan hung close to Kirei. "Tell me I may visit you."

"No."

"Why?"

She sighed. "We are no good for one another. We cannot further each other's social standing."

"Isn't it enough that we enjoy each other's company?"

"Not to my uncle. It's his house in which I live, and it's him you have to impress. I promise you, as unrefined as you are, any attempt at acceptance from him would fail." Her words made sense, but something in her demeanor told him she held back. That she didn't tell a whole truth.

He had to learn the rules of this city's peculiar high society. He moved easily among the gentility of China and Korea, but the aristocracy of his own Japan had such an exclusive way that he began to wonder if he'd ever gain acceptance. Yoki was right. Discussing business at the party last night had been out of the question, so he had to show Ichijō he was worthy of an official audience. "His Majesty has asked that you teach me. Does that mean nothing to your uncle?"

"An imperial request versus the distaste of having a provincial upstart in his home? I think his choice is apparent."

Irritation prickled at his nape. "Aren't you judging me too harshly?"

She halted at the edge of shadow leading to the sheltered carriages. "I'm not your judge, Lord Yūkan. In the eyes of Kyō's *good people,* my country upbringing makes me as low and unacceptable as you. I'm not your better. I'm your equal. As such, my statement regarding my uncle's disapproval is one of fact. Not censure. He only accepts me because my father is his brother and because Their Majesties took an instant liking to me. I really do wish you well and safe, but I must return home." A small smile touched the outer edges of her eyes over the trim of her fan. "I'm so tired I might drop at any second. Now *that* would be embarrassing."

He couldn't help liking her more than ever for her frank humility, but he suspected she underestimated her standing among the *good people*. They revered her poetry and sense of style. Her beauty fueled more than one conversation he'd overheard. She was admired and adored.

He'd only benefit from more time spent in her company.

## Chapter Four

Chaos. When Kirei arrived home, servants scurried here and there, arms loaded with piles of fabric. Change of Dress Day meant a flurry of work. Curtains, robes, even pillows in winter colors and textiles headed for storage. Dust hung in the air, creating a musty odor and making Kirei sneeze.

With the screens and curtains removed and leaving the main room of her west wing open, she realized how large the space was. Elaborate carved trusses supporting the expansive roof stood exposed, and the blinds were rolled up and secured. Servants worked along the veranda outside to lift and anchor the upper portions of removable screens that formed the outer walls of the mansion. The cypress floorboards gleamed from a fresh washing, and amidst the dust hung a scent of pine and cherry.

Uma and one of Amai's maids hurried from the sleeping chambers near the rear of their residential wing. They bowed then followed as Kirei led Amai and the two servants toward their private rooms at the back. Her feet dragged, and she blinked dry, gritty eyes.

She found her bedroom blessedly calm. Winter hangings remained, and she was glad. The heavier panels covering her blinds would do a better job blocking daylight, though she could do nothing about the glow seeping through rice panels lining the wall common to the hallway. She gave Amai a small wave, and Uma slid her chamber door closed.

"I hope you weren't up all night waiting for us," she said to her maid.

Uma removed Kirei's outer jacket. "No, my lady. We

received word that the emperor made an appearance at the party. I knew it would go through the night, so I went to bed. Gossip this morning let us know Lady Amai and you went to Mount Hiei for a sunrise gathering with Lords Yoki and Shinsetsu."

Kirei chuckled. "Your sources are extremely reliable."

"Yes, my lady." She unfastened the thin belt around Kirei's waist and removed it along with the golden yellow mantle. "We servants can't prepare unless we know what to expect."

"Any word from the lower wards?"

Her maid paused. In a near whisper, she said, "I am hearing disturbing reports."

Zo slid open the door enough to insert her round face, making further discussion impossible. "We heard about the excitement. Did you have fun, my lady?"

"It was all right. I don't know that I'd classify it as fun." Though Yūkan had certainly added an interesting element. "What excitement are you talking about? The contest?"

"No, no. The emperor coming and bringing that wild country savage with him."

Kirei laughed and shrugged out of her many layers of thin *uchigi*. "Lord Yūkan arrived and left apart from the emperor. And he's hardly a savage. His carriage and clothing are finer than anything Ojisan owns."

Zo's features lapsed to a pout, and she left, closing the door.

"I think she hoped for tales of a barbarian madman wreaking havoc on Prince Hansamu's estate."

Uma smiled, helping her adjust her *hakama* for sleeping. "No doubt. Surely his manners are atrocious, though. Was he offensive? What was Emperor Ichijō thinking to invite such a man into gentle company?"

Kirei cleared her throat, provoked on his behalf by prejudice from people who hadn't even met him. He had a genuine interest in others, and he had a way about him that spoke of a generosity of spirit. "I'm sure some found him offensive. Personally, I didn't mind his lack of refinement. The emperor calls him friend. I think that says a lot for his character."

Uma nodded thoughtfully, her eyebrows arching a bit. "And is he handsome?"

In only her white *kosode* and dark *hakama*, she went to a luxurious futon her maid had unrolled. She settled with relief under her cotton counterpane. "Not handsome in terms of what we normally consider good-looking. He wears no white on his face. His eyebrows are not fine, and his mouth is wide and thin instead of small and well-shaped. Though a round face is considered ideal, his square features are surprisingly easy on the eyes." She smiled. "This might sound strange, but looking at his manly visage makes me feel more like a woman."

Uma had stopped working and stood at the center of the chamber, staring at her. "Tell me more."

Kirei chuckled. "This isn't some story I made up. You stand enthralled as if I'm reading one of my tales to you."

"He sounds so interesting."

"I think he is. Amai considers him a bore. I imagine most would. It doesn't matter. With his untamed ways, he won't last in town very long. I doubt I'll see him again."

"What a shame." Her maid came to the bedside and draped a heavy brocade mantle atop the counterpane to chase away the chill. "Let's get your hair bound or we'll never get a brush through it later."

"I'm so tired." She turned her back so Uma could work her hair.

"I'm sure you are, but about that disturbing report I mentioned... Would you be up for helping an unfortunate tonight?"

Kirei sat straighter. "Of course. Where?"

"The eighth ward. She's a fourteen-year-old farmer's daughter come to town to learn how to dye silk and find a husband. She's been taken in by Hen Na."

"No." Kirei gasped. "She's only fourteen. He'll use her as slave labor. She'll be lucky to survive a year under him."

"Exactly."

"We'll get her out tonight."

"The eighth ward is very far, my lady. How will we do this?"

Kirei immediately thought of Yūkan and his carriage outfitted for a horse. His conveyance would be so much faster than an ox-drawn rig. "I might have an idea. Let me sleep only a few hours. I have a visit to make this afternoon." She settled her weary head for a much needed rest.

When sleep took her, she dreamt of strong hands, angular features, and broad shoulders. She stood on the deck of a merchant ship, wind whipping her hair and robes as China's shore came into view. She woke with her heart pounding. Leave Japan? The very idea should appall her, but it didn't.

"My lady. My lady."

She stirred, groaning when her sore shoulders protested. A nudge made her open her eyes. Zo, red-faced and ringing her chubby hands, whimpered at the bedside.

"Is the mansion on fire?" Kirei asked. She sat and rubbed stiff eyelids.

"Your uncle's demanding you attend him."

"Why?"

Zo's face practically went purple. "I don't know, but an imperial messenger left a little while ago."

She flipped aside her covers and sat. "Where's Uma?"

The maid's voice rose an octave. "I don't know. She went to the textile district to see about new summer silks for you, and she's been gone for hours."

The girl in the eighth ward. Uma had gone to get information. Of course.

Kirei patted Zo's dimpled fingers. "It'll be fine. I didn't get home until dawn, so Ojisan knows I've been sleeping and need to dress."

"But I'm still pulling your summer robes and mantles

from the storage room. The boxes are stacked next to the kitchen."

"Does Ojisan have a guest with him?"

"No," the maid whined.

"Then it doesn't matter if I wear my winter silks. Let's do a very simple version of *Iro*." She went to her wardrobe and pulled a clean *hakama* from the bottom drawer. "I can get into this pant-skirt myself. See if you can find my light maroon *uchigi*. The one with a dark lining." She stepped into the *hakama*, tucking in her white *kosode*, and tying the waist tight. She donned a glossy white chemise rather than the flashy scarlet the color combination called for.

"Found it."

She took the robe and put it on while saying, "Now a pale golden yellow."

Zo brought it, unfolding it and holding it out by the neckline.

Kirei accepted it. "Lavender."

Her maid hesitated. "But what about the plum-pink and sprout-green?"

"The pink is a forbidden color, and I'm not going before the court. There's no one to impress. I'm just trying to dress enough to pass for decent."

Zo huffed then rummaged through long box-drawers. "Found it." She brought the final *uchigi*. "Only five layers. Thank goodness you aren't going out in public."

Kirei grinned. "These are winter *uchigi*. They're lined, so really I'm actually wearing eight layers. Besides, do you want to keep Ojisan waiting?"

Her maid squeaked.

"Exactly." She headed for the door.

"Wait!" Zo flapped her arms like a fat duck trying to take flight. "You can't go to your uncle like that. You need at least a *ko-uchigi*."

Kirei sighed and tapped her bare foot. "Fine. Pick out whichever dressing gown you like."

Her maid selected a white, plain silk gown boasting a maroon wavy line along its edge.

She made small adjustments to her *uchigi* to make sure each layer showed in equal measure then let Zo help her into the *ko-uchigi*, which topped the ensemble to perfection. "A very nice effect," Kirei said.

"Thank you, my lady. Let me do your hair." She stripped off the binding Uma had applied that morning then brushed the length until it smoothly rode down the back of her dressing gown nearly to the hem of the protruding chemise's slight train. Bowing, Zo declared, "You're ready."

"Thank you." Kirei left, heading down the hall separating her chamber from Amai's. Her maid followed. The main common area of their wing had undergone a transformation from heavy winter textiles to lighter fabrics in paler colors. She much preferred the cheerful summer décor and apparel.

She settled behind her screen of state and waved Zo past to notify her uncle that she was ready for his visit. While she waited for him to be summoned, she arranged her layered robes past the screen's edge so he could enjoy the *irome no kasane* of her modified *Iro Iro* combination.

A board creaked, announcing his approach.

"Ojisan," she said when his rustling clothes came within earshot. "*Konnichiwa.*"

"Niece. *Konnichiwa,*" he said, his voice deep and rough. He must've been out all night, too, since he sounded as if he'd just woken. His tone tightened when he said, "I have a message from Emperor Ichijō."

Her insides sank. Ichijō would apparently push this association with Yūkan to its limits. "A message having to do with me?"

"A special assignment for you as a court favorite." Another board creaked as he stepped from the main mansion into her private wing. He grunted, settling to a cushion near her screen.

She stared at gray silk dotted with black circles that

covered his knee. Feigning ignorance, she asked, "An assignment for me? Does it involve poetry?"

A knock prevented him from answering. A manservant announced, "Another messenger."

Kirei peeked through her *kichō*. A beautiful boy in very fine green and black patterned damask bowed to her uncle.

"Give it to me," said Ojisan with an impatient thrust of his hand.

The boy bowed. "I'm sorry, Minister, but my master instructed me only to give it into the hands of his lady love."

Oh, by the gods. Kirei swallowed a laugh. She put out her hand, and the boy placed a neatly folded piece of lavender parchment adorned with a sprig from a budding plum tree.

The boy bowed again then left.

"I knew you were out all night, but I didn't suspect you'd spent it in a gentleman's bed," said Ojisan on a hopeful pitch.

She held her tongue, preferring he believe the lie of her promiscuity than learn the awful truth of her virginity. At her age, she could never give him an excuse he would accept. Her very reputation wouldn't survive such a brutal truth.

"Who's it from?" he asked.

"I cannot say. I'll read it in a minute. What's this assignment the emperor makes?"

"Yes. A waste of time, if you ask me." He huffed and handed her the missive. "It's an honor, to be sure, for the emperor to ask such a personal favor..."

Kirei opened the cream parchment and read the artistic script inside.

> The Emperor Ichijō hereby commissions the Department of Personal Affairs with the honorable distinction of appointing the most trusted Lady Kirei of the Fujiwara Family as tutor to His Majesty's social charge, Minamoto no Yūkan.

Minamoto? "Ojisan, I hadn't realized Lord Yūkan is

related to Empress Akiko."

He grunted. "A country cousin. Certainly a less civilized branch of her family. I'm not happy about this. Your time is better spent finding a worthy gentleman to take you as his consort. You're smart. Provide me a reason I can give to the Department of Personal Affairs that would excuse you from this onerous and distasteful task. The emperor wouldn't blame me if I don't want a savage in my house."

"A savage, you say? You must be secure in your position to contemplate denying the emperor his request. Though it's true, I don't look forward to teaching Lord Minamoto the ways of refinement." What the emperor planned to gain by it, she had no idea. Personally, she considered Yūkan a hopeless case. He'd only disappoint. Then again, she'd be open to spending more time talking to him of his travels...if she hadn't so rudely bid him a permanent farewell this morning. She could use the emperor's edict as the rationale for having to see him.

"What excuse will we give?" her uncle asked, his voice gruff.

"Maybe I should interview him," she said.

"Interview him?" His clothing shifted, then his footsteps told her he paced. "For what, Niece?"

"He might not be as bad as you suspect."

"I don't need to meet him to know the rumors are true. He keeps an estate in Echigo, of all places. Do you know where Echigo Province is? It would take a month of treacherous travel through merciless countryside to reach it, if the trip is survived."

"Then perhaps it's good that he owns a fleet of ships. I imagine travel by sea is much faster and more comfortable than through mountain trails. Echigo is a sizeable province. I'd guess his income from rice shares is huge."

Her uncle huffed. "You're too learned. It's unseemly for a woman to know so much about geography and economics."

"Why? So men can take advantage of my ignorance? Of course my education is better than most. What inducement does any man, even the Fujiwaras, have to seek higher learning when all the best posts are saved for our Fujiwara kin and doled out by Michinaga with no mind whatsoever to individual talent or ability?"

His feet ceased. "Fine. You vex me to no end, Kirei. If you want to torture yourself teaching that country bumpkin, who am I to stop you? As far as I'm concerned, you deserve it for being such a pain."

She was a pain because she had knowledge? Well, from his point of view, she imagined perhaps she was. "Consider when you were a boy. I think of my brother, Mezurashii, who struggled to memorize events in China's ancient history in Chinese, a written language he'd never heard spoken and never would, and who received practically no other instruction except from my father. He was bound to an unnatural literature. A captive of too narrow a classic system of teaching that left him understandably mind-numbed and uninspired. Is it any wonder—?"

"Cease, Niece. Just stop."

She sighed. "The emperor will be pleased if I at least consider tutoring this man, Ojisan. It'll earn you favor."

He sighed. "Very well. Keep him in your own wing during your *interview*. I don't want his barbaric spirit poisoning the rest of my home."

The gods grant her patience! "Of course. Shall I respond, or do you want to?"

He headed for the doorway to the main building. "I don't want anything to do with this. You take care of it." His stomping footsteps faded.

\*     \*     \*     \*

"Lord Yūkan!"

He recognized Yoki's shout and set aside a scroll of sutras he'd been reciting. He wiped a section of sweat off of his forehead. Better to seek spiritual merit than venture into the bustle of Change of Dress Day that had servants turning the palace grounds upside down.

Smoothing a hand around the neckline of his *agekubi* round-necked robe, he stood and slid open his chamber door. Yoki stood at the end of the hall near the building's entrance. He waved at the gentleman over the heads of shuffling workers.

"Ah, there you are." Yoki laughed and weaved through the sea of servants. "This is crazy. I left my house to avoid this, and here I am, in the worst of it."

Yūkan chuckled. "Quick. Come inside where it's quieter."

The gentleman sidestepped with a jump, his sock-clad toes sliding on the chamber's shiny wood floor. "Ai! They're on a mission out there."

"That's why I'm hiding in here."

Yoki fingered the pine green brocade of Yūkan's *agekubi* sleeve and wrinkled his nose. "I thought you were hiding because of *this*."

"What's wrong with it?" He took in the gentleman's glossy pale blue silk designed with a light gray mosquito pattern. It appeared lightweight and cool.

"It's fine if we were still in winter garb, but today's Change of Dress. Where are your summer clothes?"

"I didn't bring any." A cool breeze came in his open window, and he breathed it its fragrant freshness. "I only expected to stay a few days."

"Not if Emperor Ichijō has a say. He wants you here permanently." His friend ran a palm over his glossy hair, flattening it and making his fine, round face appear more feminine than usual.

"I don't know why. Other than the perfume party last night, I haven't seen him."

Yoki offered a sage nod. "As emperor, he can be a slave to protocol. It doesn't leave him much personal time. That's why having friends near and available means a lot to him." He chuckled. "We're his sanity."

"*We're* his sanity? Then what are the empress and his consorts?"

"Drama." Yoki threw back his head and laughed. "Come on. Let's go to the textile district. We'll get you a whole new wardrobe for the warm season."

"I'm not planning to stay much longer."

"You will." The gentleman waggled his eyebrows and slid open the chamber door.

Yūkan collected his sandals from a corner. "Why? What do you know?"

"As Supreme Minister of Personal Affairs, I can tell you you're about to spend a great deal of time with a certain gorgeous lady of learning and wit."

Yūkan paused. "Lady Kirei?"

"The very same."

He slowly smiled. Now *there* was a reason to stay.

*   *   *   *

"Ugh. Insufferable man." Kirei threw the lavender parchment which caught Amai's topmost *uchigi* as she came around Kirei's screen of state.

"What's this? A poem?" Her cousin bent and retrieved the note. She read it then sent Kirei an incredulous look. "Why'd Lord Hansamu send you a lover's *tanka*?"

"Because he's a cad. It's five measures of meaningless, coarse verse intended to imply an intimacy we don't share. He's hoping to force me into his bed through public perception." She swallowed against a wave of nausea.

"Maybe you're reading too much into it." Amai pulled over a wide seat, its dark wooden framework showcasing intricate carvings under round, upholstered armrests. She sank onto it. Her many colored, thin *uchigi* splayed upon the floor behind her in an elegant display.

"Read it again."

Her cousin spread it on her lap and bent her slender

neck. The lavender paper made a pretty contrast to Amai's dark purple-red raw silk *hakama*. "Okay. I see your point."

How to respond? Certainly not in kind. She didn't want to be rude, either. It was beneath her. "I have it."

Her cousin stood. "I'll get your writing box."

Kirei pulled a second pillow close and fell forward onto it with a giggle. *Geese cry in lament.* Perfect. *A prince's love brings a return of winter.* If he didn't get the message, he was more ignorant than she thought. Ojisan would be so mad. She grinned.

Amai knelt with youthful dexterity onto her fancy cushion and presented Kirei's writing box of aloes-wood inlaid with mother-of-pearl. Kirei made a slight bow, accepting it in both hands. Uma hurried in and set an ink stone on the floor next to her knee. She appeared harried and smelled of dust.

Amai wrinkled her nose.

She shook a finger at her cousin as her maid rushed away. Kirei chastised, "The sign of good taste and charm in a woman is to be gentle, calm, *pleasant*, and self-possessed."

"Servants don't enter into it," Amai argued.

"They should. It embarrasses me when you're pretentious because I know you're genuinely sweet-natured. Don't put yourself into a position where others find fault in what you say or do. Your kindness should earn you high regard. As long as you're careful to avoid criticism, people won't want to hear gossip about you from those few who'll talk badly about anyone, and you'll receive sympathy when it happens."

"*When* it happens?" Her cousin's countenance pulled tight as her eyes widened a fraction.

Kirei opened her box and nodded. She selected an excellent thin paper in exactly the same shade of lavender. "Only the ugly or invisible avoid the attention of Lady Minikui and Lord Kowai. Sometimes not. But you're beautiful and young. You have impeccable manners and sensitivity in choosing your *uchigi* color combinations. Now you've attracted the handsome and promising Lord Shinsetsu. Yes, it's only a matter of time."

"They haven't attacked you. They wouldn't dare."

She laughed and chose a fine brush given to her by Empress Akiko. "They have. Many times."

Her cousin's lovely slanted eyes studied her. "What did you do?"

She put a bit of ink on the stone then inserted the brush's tip in her mouth to wet it before touching it to the ink. "At first, I was terrified they'd ruin me. But like I said, when we behave in a way which others can't find fault, the people who truly matter can only sympathize. Sometimes merely in politeness. Sympathy in the face of malicious gossip has a nullifying effect."

"And now?"

Kirei shrugged. "Now I ignore them. They're petty. It would be useless to argue or refute. Since I won't be baited by their hateful words, they call me a bore."

Amai barked an unladylike laugh. "You? A bore? You're one of the most interesting people I know."

"I hardly believe that." Kirei went silent, putting total concentration into forming her characters with artistic perfection. When she'd finished 'Geese cry in lament,' she gathered more ink into her brush and glanced at her lovely cousin. "Please don't use me as your role model. Be the ideal, Amai. I'm not. I'll never reach the social heights you will. Plus, I annoy your father at every turn. This *tanka* alone, if he ever has occasion to learn of it, will make him want to return me to my parents more than ever."

"Is that what you want?"

Kirei hesitated. Yesterday morning, she'd have gone to the country in an instant. Not Shinano, of course. Yet Yūkan's strong features came to mind. His straightforward smile and frank wit. Then there was the emperor's unusual assignment. A slow smile came unbidden, and she forced it away as soon as she noticed. "No. I don't want to return to the country...yet."

## Chapter Five

When Yūkan returned to the Nine Fold Enclosure from the market, a servant met him at Yoki's carriage before he could climb out.

"My Lord Minamoto," said the man. "Lady Fujiwara no Kirei awaits you in the dragonfly garden."

Yūkan shared a surprised glance with his friend. "Has she been waiting long?"

"Not long, my lord."

"Thank you." When the servant left, he met Yoki at the rear of the conveyance. "What do you think?"

"I sent the emperor's edict to her uncle today. The one where she's officially assigned as your tutor."

Yūkan swallowed an urge to groan. "Right. So she's basically here to tell me to go piss myself. Okay then. This ought to be fun."

His friend laughed. "She's not one you want to keep waiting. Go on. I'll take care of these bolts of fabric. Please be at my house first thing tomorrow. I'll have a tailor ready. You can't walk the streets of Kyō in last season's fashions."

He shook his head. In this town, he broke rules without even trying. It was getting old. He offered the gentleman a wave and strode for the dragonfly garden behind the emperor's offices.

Lady Kirei stood in bright sunlight on a walkway hidden by chest-high brown reeds that lined one side of a tranquil pond. He halted, admiring her profile. She was heart-stopping gorgeous. It looked as though she watched something on the ground, but he suspected she had gotten lost in thought. A slight pucker between her eyebrows gave her away.

"Lady Kirei," he said, moving toward her along a gravel path.

Her head jerked upright, and she turned while bringing a blue fan decorated in tiny white blossoms before her face. "Lord Minamoto."

"I'm told you came to see me. I'm delighted."

"Are you?" Her eyes held a troubled glint.

Immediately serious, he went as close as he dared before stopping. "Do you need help?"

Her eyes narrowed above the edge of the pleats. "You're remarkably perceptive."

"It comes with being in charge of people in dangerous circumstances."

"Dangerous circumstances. Yes. Speaking of that..." She cut her glance sideways then back at him.

"I'm at your service." He fought a smile. This gorgeous creature was in need, and she'd thought to come to him. He'd jump at the chance to be her hero, but what could a fine lady in the high society of this imperial city need that qualified as a dangerous circumstance?

Her lack of response spoke to the enormity of her situation. Worry shone in her gaze.

His stomach tensed, and he fought an urge to touch her. "My lady, I am the last person to judge you. If you need something, simply ask."

Her fan trembled a moment, and she lowered it.

He held his breath. He wanted to kiss her so badly he had to physically resist his desire to lean near.

"Lord Minamoto," she whispered. Her breath caught in a slight hiccough. "Someone needs our help. I need to go to her in the dark of night, but she's far. She's being held at the other end of the city. I require the speed of your horse-drawn carriage."

Her words caught him short. She spoke of some kind of rescue mission. "Lady Kirei, what have you gotten into?"

She opened her mouth, and he waited for her to say something, but she didn't. She clamped closed her lips, turned her back, and walked three steps toward the water. Before he could follow, she spun in the gravel and returned.

"What are your views on the lower classes?"

Huh? "Are you changing the subject?"

"No. This is important. I need to know."

"I'm a Buddhist. All people have a soul and a purpose. In my personal experience, I've had to put my life in the hands of men some would disregard. If you want to know the horrifying truth, my lady, some of the best men I've ever worked with are members of the lower classes. Men on my ships. Laborers in port. People working my lands."

She sighed and appeared to relax. "Many of the *good people* think them odd, dirty, and abstruse. You've already discovered how they scorn us provincials. They consider military men and their families worse. So you can only imagine how they consider peasants to have no human existence at all. Some go so far as to say they're not really people."

"That's reprehensible. I can assure you I don't share that view. I'm sorry if you do. Is that what this is about?"

She shook her head, and her tone dropped to an almost whisper. "No. I share your view. When someone poor finds himself in a desperate situation, my maid and I call him unfortunate. I help where I can."

"You imply a rescue. That goes beyond charity."

She came a step closer. "Charity is good, of course. Sometimes more is needed than a handout of food and clothing."

His opinion of this lady increased tenfold in an instant. "I agree."

"So you'll let me borrow your horse and carriage?"

"No." A thrill ran through him. Finally, he had something worthwhile to do in this city of walls and quiet arrogance. "I'm coming with you."

*   *   *   *

"He's here," whispered Uma, scurrying in and sliding closed the chamber door.

Kirei secured the tie of her deep purple *uchiginu*. "Let's go."

Her maid, dressed in black slippers and a dark cotton *kosode* the color of soot, led the way to the northern gate. They slipped out unnoticed as the sky bled lavender into pale gray. Yūkan's carriage and driver waited at the curb.

Kirei quickly climbed in, followed by Uma. Yūkan wore all black, which made him appear stronger and more capable than usual.

"Your driver won't tell anyone of our activities tonight?" she asked. "I don't need my uncle to find out about this."

"My driver is loyal to a fault. I promise he won't say anything."

Her maid offered a single nod then climbed out. She gave directions to the man then returned. "The horse is drawing attention. People are looking."

Yūkan shook his head. "I've been through here enough times on my way to and from Yoki's house that these people aren't alarmed. My concern will be when we get to the eighth ward. We'll be remembered."

The carriage started forward, and Kirei situated her posture to a more comfortable position for the trip. "We'll be careful."

Uma pulled a ribbon from her sleeve and motioned for Kirei to turn. "Let me put your hair up. It's likely to attract as much attention, if not more, than the horse. Besides, I told the driver to use the side streets and park two blocks from Hen Na's warehouse."

Yūkan eyed the maid's hands in her hair. "Going on foot is the best course. The eighth ward isn't teeming with carriages and finely dressed noblemen, so we'll gain less notice if we stay in shadow and move along the walkways. This warehouse owner, is he a nasty sort?"

"Extremely," said Kirei, wincing a bit when Uma yanked a section of hair while forming the length into a knot. This isn't the first time he's done something that required our intervention."

His countenance hardened. "This man could be dangerous. Why put yourself at risk?"

"What if I were the one in a bad situation? Wouldn't you hope someone would put themselves at risk to help me?"

He studied her a long moment. "Why are you so passionate about this?"

She glanced at Uma who gave her jaw a nudge to make her turn back around. She considered Yūkan's masculine features and wondered how much she should reveal. Since she wanted to know about him, the best way to encourage him to talk was to speak honestly about her past.

"I am. I can't deny it. These are hardworking, honest people. I lived most of my life in Shinano where the people work the land and labor in the mountains. I played with their children and attended festivals with them. I knew so many by name. They may be illiterate and lack fine manners, but most have good hearts. We all want the same things. To have food in our bellies. To love and be loved. To have purpose and meaning for our existence."

"You've thought a lot about this."

She wanted to grab him and make him feel her conviction. "They have nobody to advocate when harm or ill will is aimed their way."

"I see." He gazed at his knees.

"Do you?" Frustration jerked at the vertebrae in her neck, sending a vibration through her shoulders. She really wanted him to understand.

His gaze met hers. "Yes, I honestly do. As long as I'm in town, let me come with you. Let me take the risk. Let me advocate with you."

An unexpected joy suffused her. Behind her, Uma's

hands went still. Kirei asked, "Really?"

He nodded. "Really."

"Thank you."

"Don't thank me. I want to help. Life is good for the people in my province, and if I can make life better for some here in this city, I want to put forth that effort."

She grinned. "Okay. Now tell me something about yourself."

"What do you want to know?"

Uma finished with her hair and scooted aside. Kirei moved backward next to her maid. "Why do you want to learn the ways of the *good people* of Kyō?"

He stroked his chin while glancing at the covered window. "Well, I actually didn't think I wanted to. Emperor Ichijō wanted it so I'll move more easily among society. He has asked me to stay for an extended time. After last night, I realize I have a great many rules to learn. Breaking rules is something I don't do; yet here, it seems to be the only area where I excel."

She chuckled. "Following rules has always been important to you?"

He faced her, and his eyes seemed to bore into hers. An intensity emanated from him. "No. Not always. Maybe we shouldn't talk about this. We recently met, and this is a less-than-pleasant subject."

"Less-than-pleasant like the exploitation and neglect of common workers?" She tilted her head and arched her brows.

He released a breathy laugh. "Right. So I guess uncomfortable subjects will be our common ground."

She shook her head. "It's not about being uncomfortable. It's about being honest. Who are you, Minamoto no Yūkan?"

He opened his hands and stared at his palms for a long second as if reading a book. "Who am I? Until a couple of months ago, I was a businessman. A trader. An explorer of culture and, in a way, a diplomat. I speak Korean and three dialects of Chinese. I searched for beautiful goods to bring back to Japan, and I took satisfaction in providing for my family.

Now, I guess I'm starting over. I'll redefine what's important to me."

She released a breath she didn't realize she held. She adored how he opened and showed her his doubt. "Tell me about following rules."

"Ah, yes." His eyebrows lowered, and a tightness formed about his mouth. "I told you that my father was close friends with Emperor Ichijō's father and that they retired as monks together."

"Yes."

"I was a boy. To me, the most important part of living was exploring. I didn't worry about getting hurt or lost. I was curious. I didn't want to follow rules that made me stand back and watch the world go by. I wanted to be *in* the world, experiencing it firsthand." He closed his hands and planted his fists on his thighs.

"What made you change your view of rules?"

Beside her, Uma nodded with an eager expression.

His neck muscles went taut then relaxed. "An accident."

"I'm sorry." Maybe he was right. Maybe she shouldn't have asked him to tell this part of his past. "You don't need to talk about this if you don't want."

"This is good for me. I haven't talked about what happened since that day. My mother, brother and I went to the temple to visit my father. I was told to stay close and be on my best behavior. What could be more boring for a boy?"

Dread crept up her nape and sent the hairs on her arms on end.

"At my first opportunity, I snuck away. I explored the temple, and after I'd disturbed one monk too many, I ran out the back. The mountaintop was unlike anything I had ever encountered. I could see the entire world. I went to the edge to learn how far I could see down. My father shouted my name, and I lost my footing."

"No." She bit her lip. Her heart contracted. His guilt mirrored her own, and she wished she could ask him to stop.

"I caught the ledge with my fingertips. My father ran to me and pulled me up. He wore hard sandals, and his feet went out from under him as I came over the edge to safety. He scrambled for a handhold but he went over."

Tears smarted, and she blinked. How awful for him that his father died while saving his life. Her own brother had died in defense of her. She would've prevented him if she could have. If she had known. Here, unfortunately, was something she shared with Lord Yūkan.

"I decided right then that I'd try never to break another rule."

She wrapped her fingers over one of his fists. "I'll teach you what I can."

"Thank you."

The carriage came to a halt, and Uma led the way through dark night toward the warehouse. People walked the narrow streets, their weathered faces and threadbare clothing declaring their class without a word spoken. Despite the lack of nobility in this ward, they kept their eyes on the ground, a habit Kirei suspected they never broke. Hard work and life outdoors had formed deep lines on many faces, yet the late hour allowed for casual stances and an occasional laugh that belied a sense of hardship. Even those in conversation rarely glanced up, so Kirei and her maid moved easily through the Eighth Ward while residents paid them no notice.

Hen Na wasn't in the warehouse when they arrived, and Yūkan went right to work untying six girls bound by ropes to a wall behind a line of soaking tubs. Six. She'd had no clue Hen Na had enslaved so many.

She marveled at his calm strength. He merely touched a finger to his lips, and the weeping girls went silent. She held the door, and he and her maid ushered the ragged and weeping girls to freedom. Kirei took them to a family she knew would give them a safe place to stay until good jobs could be found. Then she hurried after Uma to the carriage.

The ride home didn't hold the satisfaction she'd

expected. Nobody spoke, and a tension set in. She had promised to teach him the rules of Kyō high society, but would he do well? He had spoken of interest in culture, but did he have the skills and knowledge necessary to learn even the basics? She had doubts.

## Chapter Six

The Minister of the Center wasn't home when Yūkan arrived the next day. He understood that Kirei's uncle meant it as a slight, but he didn't care. He came to see her, not her self-important, bigoted uncle.

He stifled his surprise when a servant led him along an outer veranda directly to a residential wing. Had the lady changed her mind? Was she now open to a romantic liaison with him? She hadn't seemed the changeable type, but maybe he'd misread her. Perhaps he'd misjudged her silence after their rescue last night.

The servant slid open a door leading into the wing, ushered him in, bowed and closed the door. He went to protest that the servant showed him to private quarters without proper announcement, but found he faced a closed door and so left the words unsaid. What difference would it make, anyway?

He realized he stood in a lavishly wide sitting room where brightly colored cushions and skillfully painted screens created a rich but happy atmosphere. Beautiful instruments hung on a solid wall that appeared to separate the sitting room from a sleeping area. White natural light from a removed section of the opposite wall reflected off of polished black floorboards. Beyond, a garden brought the fragrance of pine and grass inside.

Other than a group of playful ducks on a garden pond, all was still and quiet. Yūkan contemplated returning to the main mansion. He put a hand on the door.

"Do you like my home?"

He startled, snatching his hand to his side. "Lady Kirei?"

A movement next to a screen caught his attention. A many-layered sleeve showing two different shades of blue green and two shades of purplish pink decorated innermost and outermost layers around a plain white one. It appeared clean and cool, though how so many layers could be cool he had no idea. Still, she wore far fewer layers than he had seen on Kyō's other ladies.

"I'm sorry. I didn't see you there," he said. "I like it very much. It's spacious and reminds me of my home in the province."

"Come and sit. I'm surprised Yoki didn't join you. He visits here often."

"He sends his regards. The emperor had personal business today and needed his supreme minister nearby." Yūkan chose an orange cushion and slid it in front of her screen. He settled cross-legged to the thick, comfortable pillow.

"Poor Yoki. He's not used to having to work so much."

"Yes, I gathered that." He laughed.

The open view to the garden fed light in behind her, and he could make out a hint of her silhouette through white raw silk hangings on her kichō. Her sleeve shifted, and he wondered if her fingers would make an appearance.

"Speaking of the emperor, my uncle received an interesting communication from him yesterday," she said, her tone matter-of-fact with no hint of emotion to clue him in to her mood.

"I'm aware."

"I told you he wouldn't be happy about my tutoring you." Her head tilted slightly.

He wished he could see her lovely face. "You gave me much to compel me. I might've been bold enough to come visit, even if the emperor hadn't issued a formal request."

"It would've been extremely bold. I'd have been within protocol to turn you away." She peeked around the edge with a playful glint in her eye.

"Then I would've found another opportunity to see you."

He paused. "Would you have turned me away if I'd come to visit without orders from Emperor Ichijō?"

She disappeared behind the screen, and humor laced her tone. "Probably. Maybe not. I *do* enjoy harassing Ojisan."

Interesting. "Yoki only told me I'd be seeing a lot of you and to come today at this time."

"That's all he said?"

"Yes."

Her head straightened and she laughed. "Leave it to him to be cryptic for his own amusement. No doubt he planned to be here to witness your expression when I tell you."

"Tell me what?"

Her dark eyes peeked between the curtains of the screen. A light of fun glinted in her gaze. "That I'm to teach you good manners."

"Is that so?"

The gap widened, allowing her face from the nose up to show. "Without a doubt. The perfect example is when you criticized Yoki for weeping when he heard the geese's cries."

"Are you trying to tell me that crying is a rule? I have to cry? Because I don't know if I can weep at the sound of a bird's chirp." A laugh tried to emerge, and he stifled it by clearing his throat.

"The *good people* don't simply express emotion. We experience it. Emotional sensitivity is an identifier of a true gentleman. There are limits to showing emotion, however. He doesn't flail with wild passion or abandon. A nobleman is restrained. There's something we call *aware*. It's the emotional quality and beauty we recognize in the world around us, and the recognition of its innate worth. It's the understanding that this beauty is fated to disappear. Death. Natural disasters. Everything is connected."

He studied her flawless white forehead and arching ebony eyebrows. He appreciated how her hairline formed a gently rounded shape. "Except when they're drunk. Believe me, I've seen it. As far as I'm concerned, I think it's safe to say you shouldn't expect tears. So do you still want to teach me?"

"Are you staying in Kyō?"

Did she want him to? "You answer a question with a question."

"Why not?" Her cheeks bunched below her eyes, proof of a smile hidden behind the edge of her curtain.

"You're toying with me." He liked it.

"A bit."

"Should I go? Am I wasting your time?"

"No." She disappeared behind her *kichō*. "This is the most amusing diversion I've had in a long time."

"I'm glad to be of use."

"Are you?"

He sighed. "Not back to that."

She chuckled. "Fine. Answer me this, then. Are you staying in Kyō?"

"The emperor has asked me to stay. I wasn't planning to, but I'm willing. Nothing at my estate needs my attention anytime soon."

"What about your trade?"

She remembered. He was flattered. None of the nobility seemed interested in work. Their interest focused primarily on who did what with whom, and whether anything artistic could be construed from any particular moment or event. "My younger brother, Fudōno, has taken over as head of the business. I've given him a portion of my lands, and he builds his own estate. I have a manager who sees to the rice farming and estate maintenance."

"You're free."

For what? Boredom? "As I said last night, I haven't decided what to do now. I'm not of a mind to join a monastery like my father."

"If you have no reason to leave, why haven't you decided to stay?" Her fingers emerged from her sleeve and gripped the wooden frame.

"I have friends here, but I feel out of place in Kyō. So

many unwritten rules. So many ideas and sensibilities I find strange."

"Are you at all artistic?"

Where did she go with that question? "I play music well."

Her sigh rustled a panel of her screen of state. "That's something, at least. I feared you'd say no."

"Why?"

"Because I'd like to see you have a chance at succeeding."

"Do you have a choice about teaching me? Could you have said no?" He leaned nearer her *kichō*.

"Always."

"The emperor—"

"*Asked* it of me. He did it in an official manner to overcome my uncle's objections."

"Then why do you agree if you don't have to? Am I to serve as no more than an entertainment? A social experiment?" If it meant time spend with the most magnificent woman he'd ever met, did he care?

"In part, certainly. I have a lot of affection for Empress Akiko, and she asked me first. Don't you think this'll be interesting?"

Undoubtedly. Her pointing out his flaws and inadequacies wasn't what he considered *interesting*. Though this presented a rare chance to spend hours with her, and he definitely considered *her* interesting. "Should I come back tomorrow, or would you prefer to start right away?"

She didn't move or speak. Yūkan resisted the urge to flick aside one of her *kichō's* curtains. Did she smile or frown?

Kirei handed a rough-cut piece of white parchment through the unfastened bottom of the opaque curtain. She sent a box through next, and said, "Write for me."

He hated the sense that she tested him. He put the paper on the floor then selected a brush. "What do you want me to write?"

"Anything."

"How about an inventory of cargo?" He stroked his chin.

"No. You're missing the point. I want to see your characters. I need to watch you form your ideas. *What* you write can only be enjoyed if you've taken proper care in *how* you write. A fine hand can earn you acceptance. It's the most important identifier of a good person, and without it, you'll be viewed as lacking moral virtue."

"Because of sloppy brushwork?"

"Absolutely."

"This is what I mean about unwritten rules and strange sensibilities. You can't tell me there aren't aristocrats in Kyō who have imperfect writing."

"There are, of course. But they're also open to criticism for it. They, however, have a Kyō upbringing to recommend them among the *good people*. You don't."

He had no argument to her sound logic. He ought to get up now, walk away from Kyō and refuse to look back. He'd never shied from a challenge, however. Not for as long as he could remember. In that way, he was like his father. His family called them brave. Proud. Strong.

Also, whether he liked it or not, he wanted Kirei. She'd told him they couldn't form any kind of friendship, much less a romantic connection, but there again was an unspoken challenge. It made him want her that much more.

Determined to learn the ways of the imperial city's nobility, Yūkan inked her stone and set brush to paper. Total focus, total concentration went into the movement of the bristles to the point where he had to pause from time to time to remember what it was he wrote.

"Writing is the window to your soul," she said.

He felt her gaze upon his hand holding the brush.

"If you take a lover, she'll be anxious for your first letter. If it's poorly written, either in message or penmanship, she may refuse to see you again. Most ladies will refuse you their bed until they have a letter or poem from you...to make sure you're worthy of their favor."

He finished his brief note and passed it to her. "Am I worthy?"

"Your style is wanting."

Well, damn. "I've been writing since I was a boy. My own father taught me, and I've never had complaint from those who've had to read it."

"Those who've had to read your writing apparently don't share our sensibility. Our appreciation of beauty."

They didn't share the aristocracy's over-sensitivity. "Am I beyond redemption?"

"Maybe. Maybe not. Refrain from writing. We don't want anyone judging you by it until you've had a chance to perfect it...if you can."

If he could? She didn't sound like she held out much hope. He'd have to show her he could be the finest calligrapher in all of Kyō. Then she'd see his heart. Then she'd want him as he wanted her.

\*     \*     \*     \*

When the door closed behind Yūkan, Kirei breathed a sigh. How could a man be so opposite of beauty's ideal yet attract her as none other? Her friends would call his dark skin and wide, thin lips coarse. They'd find his lack of perception toward natural esthetics lowly. The fact that he shared her country rearing only added to his lack of appeal. And once they learned he'd *earned* his fortune through work, not just rice yields, well...

"He's doomed."

"My lady?" Zo presented a tray with two cups and a small pitcher of water. A square white saucer contained two slices of dried octopus and four slices of dried apple. She set it on the floor next to Kirei's cushion. "Did you say he's doomed?"

"I did. Thanks for the snack, but he's gone. You didn't need to bring this much." She shouldn't have sent him on his way so soon. Examining his eating habits might've provided her a better chance to observe his personal grace, or lack thereof.

"That must've been an ordeal for you, my lady. At least it's over and you never have to see that odious, back-country buffoon again." Her maid offered a bright smile.

"I know you mean well, Zo, but I take umbrage to insulting someone you've never met. How can you, who've been reduced to servitude due to the circumstances of your birth and rearing, harshly judge someone for theirs?"

"You think I'm being unfair."

"Wholly. Consider holding off on forming an opinion until you get to know him. You'll have the opportunity. Many, in fact. I've decided to accept the emperor's request. Maybe he's not the hopeless cause everyone thinks." Kirei genuinely hoped she didn't merely indulge in wishful thinking.

She didn't get a chance to find out the next day, however. The Yin-Yang Department declared that the divinity had stopped in the south, and they closed that sector for the entire day. Nobody but commoners and servants could travel in the unlucky southerly direction. Since Yūkan resided in the imperial compound at the northernmost point of the city, he was stuck.

Kirei spent the morning letting Zo wash her hair. It had barely dried when Yoki came to call. She shrugged into a lightweight green mantle over top of the five layers of spring-colored *uchigi* robes she'd donned at sunrise.

"It's a good thing you live to the west of here," she said as she settled behind her *kichō*. She grinned, managing to stave off a laugh and glad he couldn't see her amusement. "I couldn't live with myself if I knew you'd have to travel in an unlucky direction to visit me."

He completely missed the fact that she teased. "You're such a kind person, Lady Kirei. I'm blessed to call you a friend. Because you're such a dear friend, and because I knew you, of all my acquaintances, would appreciate this as much as I, I've brought you an entertaining treat."

Yoki had a way of producing the most interesting

diversions, and she smiled in anticipation. "What do you have?"

"A record I dug up while visiting Shinsetsu at the Bureau of Divination."

She laughed. "Anything from the Yin-Yang Bureau ought to be amusing in the extreme."

He opened the book and said, "This one, especially. Listen to this. 'On the fourth day of the eighth month, *ki* appeared in the sky above the Datchi Gate. It appeared to be smoke, but it wasn't smoke. It resembled a rainbow, but it wasn't a rainbow. It looked like a cloud, but it wasn't a cloud. People gathered near and decided that nothing like it had appeared before. The master of Yin-Yang proclaimed the strange colorful wisps an omen. He predicted a typhoon, floods, and fire.'"

"No." Kirei giggled.

"Wait. It gets better. 'Scared people ran into the streets for safety. Shortly thereafter, the city was rocked by an earthquake.'"

"Ah!" She laughed. "The one cataclysm they didn't predict." She laughed harder.

Yoki joined in. "I knew you'd love that."

"The Yin-Yang Bureau can be ridiculous. I have to give them credit, though. They try hard, and they're passionate about what they do."

"They're the hardest working bureau in the Ministry of Central Affairs. I'm so glad I avoided a position there."

"Right. Because we know how little you actually like to work."

"Precisely," he agreed with no pretense. "Which brings me to the subject of our new friend, Yūkan."

"He's no friend of mine."

"Don't lie. You like him, even if you don't want to. I know because I'm the same way. What drives me crazy is Emperor Ichijō wants a report on his *happiness* every afternoon."

"Are you serious? How does someone gauge another

person's happiness?"

"Exactly," he drawled. "How am I supposed to know? And every afternoon? Do you have any idea what this is going to do to my social life?"

"Heaven forbid work should get in the way of pleasure," she said, making no attempt to camouflage her sarcasm.

"I knew you'd understand."

Kirei smiled. He was being intentionally obtuse, but she enjoyed his flamboyant disregard for any value not adherently noble by Kyō standards. He didn't share her ideals, completely embracing the principles of the *good people* in everything he did and said. It was why they'd never be more than friends. They appreciated each other's differences and admired their many mutual qualities.

"Why does the emperor want a daily report of our *friend's* happiness, do you think?"

"I have no idea." His tone lifted on a bit of a whine.

Kirei sighed. "You spend more time with Ichijō than his own wife. Guess."

"Pushy," he accused.

"Whiny," she tossed right back.

He laughed. "All right. My guess, and I could be wrong, is that he wants to keep our friend in Kyō."

"Why is that?"

"More guessing?"

"Of course." She chortled.

Yoki huffed a dramatic breath. "My *guess* is that Emperor Ichijō is bored. All day every day he's devoted to ceremonies and observances. When he's not being told what he must do by ministers and advisors, he tries to make time for his music and painting and to encourage the traditional arts. When does he get to meet truly interesting people like you and me?"

"Speak for yourself."

"Stop it. You like to think you're a dullard, but you're not. You're the most artistic person at court."

It didn't matter that he couldn't see her through the

*kichō*. Heat still crept into her face, and she smoothed the intricate mantle covering her many inner robes. "So what will you report today?"

"Nothing. I'm not going to the Nine Fold Enclosure. If I go north, I can't come back south until tomorrow, and I refuse to give up my bed tonight. Not when I expect to have such diverting company in it." He chuckled.

"Anyone I know?" She peeked between the hangings of her screen.

"I love you, Lady Kirei, but you know I never tell." He picked at the hem of his jacket, a small smile playing about his tiny, doll-like lips.

As the picture of male beauty in the eyes of Kyō's ladies, and with no wife yet to compete for his attention, he made the ideal lover. Kirei wondered why she'd never had a single hint of attraction to him when women around her sighed for him almost as much as they did for Prince Hansamu. She shook her head. No matter.

"Can't you tell me anything?" she asked.

He hesitated, his sweeping, slightly bushy eyebrows meeting at a scrunched center as his features grew thoughtful. Then his face melded into a wolfish grin. "I'll say this. If you hear rumors tomorrow, they're probably true."

"Intriguing. You're limited in choice of lady, so I may be able to determine who she is based on her proximity to your estate." Kirei paused for effect. "I must do some clever deducing. If she lives along the fourth avenue, both of you are saved from having to travel south. Therefore, she may be any lady here in the fourth ward. You said she'd be in *your* bed. If she comes to you on her own, she could live in any of the lower wards, especially if she plans to stay until morning when the southerly direction is reopened as a lucky one."

He didn't reveal anything in his expression as she spoke, giving her no clue as to whether the lady in question fell into the fourth ward category or the lower ward category. Disgusted, she closed the screen hanging and reclined on her cushion.

"I suppose," she said, "I'll have to wait for the gossip...if there is any. You're entirely too discreet. You rarely give us anything to talk about."

"I almost feel sorry for you," he said, a smile in his voice.

"I won't have time for gossip tomorrow, anyway," she declared, staring at lacquered beam supports under the shallow roof. "Yūkan comes tomorrow for tutoring."

"Is it bad?"

She grinned. "Not as bad as I made him think he is. His writing's passable. To be accepted, considering his upbringing, it's going to have to be impeccable."

"Do you dread it?"

"I thought I would, but I'm actually looking forward to this."

"But he's so..."

"Coarse?"

"Yes." Yoki sniffed. "I'd be a hypocrite if I declared him unlikable, however. I find myself seeking his company. I like his candor. It's so refreshing. But he isn't from Kyō, which stands to reason that he can't be anything but the most uncivilized brute."

## Chapter Seven

The mansion in the fourth ward greeted Yūkan in silence, the same as before. Another slight by the Minister of the Center. For Kirei's sake, he'd let it pass and hope the emperor didn't learn of it.

He entered the common room of her wing where writing materials waited in massive quantities. Stacks of paper in every color and thickness imaginable sat lined along the middle of the large room. Three writing boxes designed in elegant style stood open and displayed handsome brushes of the best quality. Ink stones waited next to a black cushion he assumed had been positioned for his use. It made him glad he had spent a large portion of yesterday practicing his calligraphy.

"Lady Kirei?"

"Welcome, Lord Yūkan," she said quietly from behind her *kichō*.

The servant who'd accompanied him to her wing closed her door with a firm clack. Kirei peeked through the screen's loose hangings then slid it out from between them. She didn't hide behind a fan.

Yūkan held his breath at her loveliness. She wore a serene smile, though it didn't reach her eyes. A pale blue gown with a pink cherry blossom print covered a white *uchigi* lined in pale blue-green. The semi-translucence of the white gave the blue-green a frail, frosty quality. Under it, she'd layered a pure white *uchigi* followed by a white one lined in pink. The long layer of her white chemise showed at throat and sleeve, and extended a full eight inches past the hems of her *uchigi* robes where they fanned across the floor behind her.

She wore her hair loose, its shiny, smooth length riding her gown and its neat ends reaching the edge of her protruding chemise. Its ebony strands contrasted starkly against the naturally pale hue of her face and slender neck as well as the pure white of her chemise.

Where she sat, the dark purple of her *hakama* bunched in stiff raw silk folds over her legs and provided an almost shocking foil to her pristine chemise where it peeled backward from the trouser skirt in its turn toward the fanning spread of material behind her.

"You're a man of integrity and discretion, I believe." Her expression remained placid.

A compliment? With these odd nobles, he couldn't tell. "I value these traits, yes."

"Good. Then I trust you not to speak of the removal of my *kichō*."

"You may. It was never necessary with me. I'd never force my attention on you." If she invited it, however...

She gestured toward the black cushion. "Please sit."

He settled before her and accepted a lightweight pinewood writing table, which he set in front of his knees. "You're teaching me about correspondence today."

Her serene smile disappeared. "Writing letters is an art. Your skill in this will determine your initial reputation. Excel, and you'll be given a chance. Fail, and you won't."

"Isn't that harsh?"

"No. We've already discussed this. Now, the thickness, color, size, and design of the paper you choose has to match the emotion in your message, the weather of the day you send it, and the season. This is extremely important."

"Sounds complicated."

"Give it a chance."

She broke down each paper's representation. It took an hour, but it made sense. He didn't know how, but he could provide a sheet of paper to match each of the scenarios she presented by the end.

"I'm impressed," she said.

Her praise meant more than he liked. He sat straighter and fought a smile.

Uma, dressed in a white cotton apron and a solid gray *kosode* of high-quality glossed silk, shuffled in with a tray. Her dull hair formed a bun at her nape and quivered a bit when she bowed to Lady Kirei. "Refreshment, my lady. And I brought a *tasuki* so you can write."

"Thank you." Kirei took the looped cord from the tray.

Yūkan nodded approval of her kind treatment of the maid. She not only provided her quality clothing, but she interacted with her in a respectful manner. She'd told him she was unlike her Kyō contemporaries. Apparently, she differed from them in more than location of upbringing.

Uma bowed and offered him a gentle smile. "I've had word from the girls we helped. They're doing well and send you both their kindest regards."

He offered the servant a slight bow of gratitude for the good news.

Kirei grinned and wrapped the cord across her upper back then sent her arms through the loops. The thin rope bunched her sleeves, baring her arms to the elbows. She gestured to the woman to set down the tray.

He accepted a cup of water and saucer of biscuits from the maid before she bowed to her lady and left.

Not wanting to embarrass his gorgeous tutor, he didn't comment on the fascinating exchange. It made him want to learn more about her. She was clearly more than a lovely face and an expert on Kyō aristocracy. He suspected he'd only begun to glimpse this woman's complexities.

After swallowing some water, she said, "Your calligraphy is equally important to the message you write. You may need to write your correspondence a few times, using different brushes until you achieve the effect you want. Most of your correspondence will be in the form of a poem."

Yūkan groaned inwardly.

"I see your discomfort."

Great. He was not only a pathetic poet, he was also as transparent as the water in his cup.

"Don't worry about the poetry right now. Today, we're focusing on presentation. In addition to paper choice and word choice, you'll need to select a small piece of nature that helps symbolize your gesture. Perhaps a willow twig or white iris root." She gave examples of how to match nature to paper color and mood then quizzed him.

He didn't do as well, not sure really why adding a leaf or chunk of bark meant anything.

She demonstrated how to use care in folding paper into various accepted shapes then how to attach a spray of blossoms or branch. It took him a few tries, but he eventually received her nod of approval.

Finally, she explained the necessity of summoning an intelligent, attractive messenger to deliver his package. He tried not to laugh, but a chortle escaped.

"Forgive me," he said.

"I can't know, but I can imagine how foreign this is in comparison to your matter-of-fact business lifestyle."

He studied her a long moment, taking in her sharp eyes. "That's both generous and insightful of you. It's also unlike anything an aristocrat would think, much less say. They don't seem to see beyond themselves. It's as if the world doesn't exist beyond the city gates. Anyone not born into the correct bloodline and raised in Kyō isn't worth the silk on his back. Servants and common workers are sub-human. Animal, even."

"Your criticism is severe, but you won't hear an argument from me. I've spent enough time among them to agree with your assessment. Before you completely dismiss them as a waste of your time, however, consider this. They keep art alive and thriving. Music, writing, dance, painting. Even the creation of incense and the dying of silk are arts in themselves."

"But there are other things that matter. Learning. Work to improve lands and lives. Planning toward a future men like

Yoki claim don't exist." He took a bite of biscuit and followed it with a swallow of water.

"I approve of your gentlemanly eating. I feared you'd stuff the entire biscuit in your mouth like the workers hired by Ojisan to make improvements and repairs to the mansion and outer property wall." She smiled then had a small bite of her own. "In all fairness, there are great scholars among the *good people*, though they're few. Work and living conditions are up to each individual landowner, and some are better at directing and monitoring their estates' managers than others. As for planning and politics, there's only one man in charge."

Yūkan narrowed his eyes, wishing he didn't already know the truth. "My aunt's husband, Fujiwara no Michinaga."

"Exactly. Are you aware of the history?" She tilted her head in a charming way that had him resisting a smile.

"Not really. Are you?"

"Very well. The Fujiwara clans warred with each other right up until about thirty years ago. It's what kept any one faction from claiming total political power, since they each provided daughters as wives and consorts to the emperors. The Fujiwara who won an emperor's hand for his daughter became the father of the empress, and eventually the regent and chancellor to the next emperor."

"You know this because you're a Fujiwara?" He took another bite of his sweet rice biscuit. He found the unusual marriage politics in Kyō intriguing. It provided insight into the thinking of the city's noblemen.

"Partly, but not really. Fujiwara women have an understanding of this system and their role within it, if chosen as a pawn to participate. But most know nothing of what brought His Excellency, Michinaga, to his current reign of power. Do you realize he has more power than the emperor?"

"Yes. I'm in the Nine Fold Enclosure, and I see firsthand how Emperor Ichijō is essentially a figurehead. I'm also welcome at my aunt's home. I've observed her husband making the real decisions concerning military actions, distribution of food and wealth, and work assignments around the city. His Excellency even decides who gets promoted and hired in the ministries. Emperor Ichijō's signatures on the appointment papers are a mere formality to the decisions Michinaga already made."

"Right. Thirty years ago, the post of chancellor became empty, and it came down to two Fujiwaras who could succeed. Kaneie, an educated politician with experience and position, and Kanemichi, his older brother. Their sister was dowager empress, and she influenced the emperor to name Kanemichi because he was the elder."

Yūkan studied the lady. "You *read* this, didn't you? This is an official record of some kind."

"Of course. As I was saying, Kaneie wasn't deterred. He had a daughter married to the retired emperor, and he arranged another into position as imperial lady to the current emperor. This is where he won. Both of his daughters bore sons who became emperors. Now it gets really interesting." She paused to take a sip of water.

"Official records are written in Chinese," he said.

"True." She cut him a mysterious look, but before he could say more, she continued her family's tale. "Kanemichi was mad over Kaneie's marriage maneuvers, but he became sick before he had a chance to counter with his own. When he learned Kaneie headed for his mansion, he assumed his brother was coming to ask forgiveness and pay final respects. Imagine how upset he felt when Kaneie's carriage went right past on its way to the imperial palace."

"Was he so heartless?"

She smiled. "No. Kaneie had a false report that his brother already died. He headed immediately to the Nine Fold Enclosure to claim the chancellor post before anyone else could. It made Kanemichi so irate that he gathered enough strength to go to the palace and announce he'd make the last appointments of his life. He named Yoritada, his cousin, as his post successor then demoted Kaneie to Minister of Civil

Administration." Kirei made a sour face then let loose a quiet laugh.

"Before we go any further, tell me how you learned to read Chinese. Ladies don't, as a rule, I understand." Especially ladies under the protection of the Minister of the Center, a man known as a stickler when it came to rules and observances of proper behavior.

"Don't you want to hear about Michinaga's rise to power?"

"I do—"

"Let me finish, and if it's not too late, I'll tell you some about my education." She closed her eyes, but when she raised her lids, she gazed at the tray.

He suspected she had no intention of talking about herself. But he would have it from her. If not now, soon. "Okay. Please continue."

"So Michinaga is Kaneie's son."

"Then his rival was Kanemichi's son?" Yūkan leaned nearer, enthralled as her features grew open and dramatic in her oration.

"Close. His nephew. Korechika was Kanemichi's handsome, young nephew. The rivalry wasn't hidden, and nearly everyone had chosen a side. Korechika was popular, was the son of a Fujiwara who'd served as both Regent and Chancellor, and had support from Sadako, his sister and the emperor's favorite consort."

"I know Michinaga, though," said Yūkan. "I believe your description of Kaneie, because His Excellency inherited his father's cleverness, ambition, and motivation."

"You're right. Michinaga also had a more influential ally. His sister was Dowager Empress, and with her help, he received the appointment as Imperial Examiner six years ago."

"And he rose from there. Fascinating." He sent his gaze over her stunning face. "Let's talk about you."

"I haven't gotten to the most interesting part." Her countenance melted into a knowing smile but quickly grew serious. "This all happened in the last six years, yet everyone seems to have conveniently forgotten. Let this next part of the history be a lesson to you about the *good people*'s fickle nature and selective memory.

"Michinaga never liked having Korechika in Kyō. It made him nervous. The Fujiwaras haven't committed violence to gain position in a very long time, so Michinaga had to get creative."

A niggling of conversation a number of years back came to mind. Yūkan asked, "Did it have something to do with his sister?"

Kirei nodded. "The dowager empress came down with an illness, and he used it to fuel a rumor that Korechika cursed her. Then he accused him of officiating at *Daigen no Hō*."

"That's a religious service, isn't it?"

"Yes. Only the emperor is allowed to perform that service."

"So it would be a grave offense."

"A grossly inappropriate undertaking, to be sure...if Korechika had actually done it." Kirei frowned. "The accusation placed Korechika into a precarious place both socially and legally, but provided his own rope for his social execution."

"How?" He finished his biscuit and drained the last of his water.

"Korechika loved one of his distant cousins and was seeing her in secret. It turns out that Kazan, an important priest, also paid visits to her home. When Korechika learned of Kazan's visits, he placed some of his servants in her garden. They shot at the priest with arrows when he came out."

"They killed him?" Yūkan definitely would've remembered news of that.

She shook her head. "Korechika only meant to frighten his rival. Two facts came to light. First, the priest was a retired emperor, and second, he wasn't a rival at all. He was seeing the distant cousin's younger sister."

Yūkan barked a laugh. "Is this a joke?"

"No, though it sounds like one, I know. Anyway, one of

those arrows brushed Kazan's robe. The retired emperor was incensed and had Korechika removed from the premises. As punishment, palace officials appointed Korechika as Provisional Governor-General of Kyūshū's government headquarters."

Yūkan shrugged. "So?"

Kirei's mouth fell open. "An appointment in the provinces is banishment. If the appointment is for too long a time, a nobleman may never be able to reestablish his social standing in Kyō."

"That makes no sense." He stared at her, hoping he'd find in her gaze some reasonable explanation for such silliness.

"Maybe not, but that's the reality here. The rumors and banishment all added up to discredit Korechika. Michinaga stood unopposed, and two years ago, he had Akiko appointed as Imperial Lady. He helped her win Emperor Ichijō's favor. When Empress Sadako died last year, Akiko became empress. She's shy and kind and everything good in a woman, though she's only thirteen years old. But her rise secured Michinaga as the most powerful man in the land, especially if she eventually has a son."

"The lesson to be learned," he said, settling back on his cushion, "is not to cross Michinaga."

She nodded. "He can ruin you with a snap of his fingers. I hope you also learned that intrigue can destroy a man in Kyō as surely as an arrow or censure from the emperor. Are you certain you still want to stay?"

\*   \*   \*   \*

"He's so ugly," said Amai, coming in through their private entrance. "I passed him on his way to his carriage. He has the finest clothes and conveyance, but he's so brown. Why doesn't he at least use powder to lighten his face?"

Kirei hid a smile. She liked that he was different. In his looks, he was the opposite of what ladies found attractive. He had dark skin, not pale. He had an angular face, not round. He had wide, thin lips, and she could actually see his eyes when he looked at her. Yoki's lids had such a dramatic slant that he appeared to go around with his eyes closed. She chuckled.

"Are you laughing at me?" Amai scowled.

"I think you don't like his looks because they're not like yours. He makes you uncomfortable."

Her cousin plopped onto his abandoned cushion and fiddled with the pale *uchigi* layers at her sleeves. "He does make me uncomfortable. He makes me feel strange in my own skin. Does that sound odd?"

Kirei closed her eyes and savored a tingling awareness. "No, because he makes me feel the same way. I like it, though."

"I thought you despised him for his uncouth manners." Amai picked up a discarded sheet of tan parchment with one of his attempts at *tanka*.

"Maybe I do." Maybe she didn't. "Or maybe I'm indifferent. At least he switched his horse for a proper ox. Be glad for any improvement."

"Harrumph." Her cousin eyed the poem. "His handwriting's okay. Better than Shinsetsu's, that's for sure. This poem is terrible, though. I can't make out the emotion or the message. It's random."

"I know. That's his *best* one today, too. I haven't decided if he's uninspired or if he's out of touch with his emotions." Both, probably.

"Why are you using your time trying to teach this savage to be a gentleman? You'd have better luck teaching a monkey to be emperor."

Kirei released a disbelieving laugh and threw a small pillow at her cousin. "You're a mean one today. I'm beginning to wonder if your sweet face is a mask for a darker disposition. I always thought your temperament matched your appearance." She shot her a suspicious glance.

Amai blinked rapidly, her mouth opening and closing in a perfect imitation of a fish removed from water. "I'm not mean-spirited. It's just that I appreciate things and people that have some element of beauty or art. He's got neither."

"Most people don't. I recognize potential in him." He was already a favorite of the emperor, though Kirei didn't really understand why. With more refinement, he could fit into Kyō society. Maybe.

"How can he have potential? He's from the country." Amai screwed up her face into a distasteful squint, her tiny nose wrinkling and the corner of her mouth curling.

Kirei schooled her features to hide the pain of her cousin's unintended dig. "*I'm* from the country."

"It's not the same. Your parents are both of noble families, and they made sure you had an excellent education. Too excellent, some say. You're a paragon, and sometimes I even forget you weren't raised in Kyō. But him...? One look at his stoic expression and stiff shoulders says he's not easy or sensitive. Not a true gentleman. He's *countrified*," she spat with a sour expression.

Kirei leaned forward, and in a conspiratorial whisper, said, "He's of noble blood."

"No." Amai smacked her knee. "You're trying to fool me."

She shook her head. "He's nephew to Her Excellency."

"Minamoto no Rinshi? He's a Minamoto? But how...? Why...?"

Kirei chuckled. "The same way I'm a Fujiwara. My family wasn't sent to the provinces. My father chose it. We're richer than most here in the city, and my brother, Mezurashii, and I had a far better education than anything we could've received here, where I'd have been refused access to Chinese texts and Mezurashii would've had to go to that asthenic university."

"Yūkan's family is that way, too?" Her cousin's features softened a bit.

"Maybe. I don't know. I haven't asked. But I do know they're very wealthy. Probably more wealthy than my father. He owns tremendous rice shares, and they're legitimate, which means he contributes to the emperor's coffers. He also reads Chinese, though I don't know the extent of his education. So maybe, if I'm not a savage country bumpkin, he might not be either."

Amai slowly grinned. "Indifferent, huh?"

Kirei took the poem from her cousin and studied his carefully formed and much improved characters. "Indifferent enough."

Chapter Eight

Carriages arrived in a steady stream, bumping and teetering across the metal base bar of the Nine Fold Enclosure's main gate when Yūkan accompanied Yoki over a gravel walkway to the Divine Spring Garden. Enough lamps lit the grounds and garden to transform the night to day and dim the stars in their cloudless, inky sky. Noblemen sat along the shoreline of a large pond that reflected a white moon weakly competing with the golden lamps. Forming a second row, ladies hid behind *kichō*.

Yūkan recognized Lady Kirei's screen. She didn't sit behind it, however. He accepted a cushioned mat from a servant, and managed to earn a couple scowls as he claimed a space in front of her gently billowing hangings. Yoki was less discreet. He simply waved a lesser ranking gentleman away and claimed the abandoned mat.

"You're shameless," Yūkan accused.

Yoki grinned. "What's the use of being a Supreme Minister if I can't use my position in situations like these?"

He laughed, but it quickly faded when the gathering quieted. The assemblage tipped forward, their foreheads aiming for soft grass as the emperor made his way from the palace offices. Yūkan bowed, too, but peeked.

The emperor's black hat towered and barely bobbed as the man's smooth gait brought him to a luxuriantly appointed sitting area that overlooked the assemblage. Ichijō wore black. Each layer of his attire formed impeccable folds and tucks. His outermost layer, a glossed black silk jacket that reached nearly to the ground, boasted gold swirling dragons that flashed in the glow of moonlight.

The small empress, dressed entirely in white except for a trail of elegant red dragons trimming the edges of her damask jacket and *mo*, followed close behind. Three ladies-in-waiting trailed her. Fans held before their faces made it impossible to discern their features, but he identified Kirei immediately. He knew the curve of her brow. The slant of her eyes above the edge of her fan. The way one lock of hair always separated from the mass to fall forward and hug her cheek.

She wore red, a forbidden color, which told him Her Majesty had singled her out for special acknowledgment of something she'd done that pleased the girl-empress. Kirei cast him a furtive glance, her fan lending her a coquettish air he enjoyed. Though he doubted she smiled at the sight of him, he liked to imagine she did. He liked to imagine she was as attracted to him as he was to her. The bowing ended, and Yūkan straightened.

The empress sat beside Emperor Ichijō. After Kirei helped arrange the girl's many layers of sumptuous fabric, she skirted the gathering and took her seat behind her screen.

The emperor faced a gentleman to his right and began a quiet conversation. Everyone relaxed and commenced socializing.

Leaning backward, Yūkan greeted, "My lady."

"Good evening," she said.

"Where is the pretty lady who seems to accompany you everywhere?"

"Why? Do you miss her?" She sounded peevish.

He smiled. "Are you jealous?"

She didn't answer. Finally, she huffed. "Again with questions. Why do you play this game?"

He laughed at her unwarranted accusation. "You started it."

"True," she conceded. "Amai, my cousin, isn't here tonight. I wouldn't have come either, except Empress Akiko specifically requested I attend her tonight."

"Why don't you want to be here?" He held his breath, half expecting her to say it was because he'd been invited.

"This is a drinking party." Her quiet voice dripped with disapproval.

"I was told it's a poem party." He shifted on his cushion. "I only hope they don't ask me to compose one. You know how bad I am at it."

That earned him a soft laugh. "You'll be fine. Simply recite one you've memorized."

"If there's to be poetry, why do you call it a drinking party?" He took a chance and rested his fingertips on her silk layers so fine they felt like butterfly's wings.

She didn't pull away. "Do you see that cup in front of the emperor?"

Yūkan glanced past the six noblemen between him and the emperor and spotted an elaborately painted wooden dish on the grass in front of him. "That bowl?"

"It's a large wine cup. When he gives the signal, a servant will fill it halfway with *sake* and float it on the water. A stream feeds this lake and creates a current that'll carry the cup along the shoreline. Each gentleman will be expected to take the cup, have a swallow, recite a poem or compose an appropriate verse on the spot, and return the cup to the water for the next to take a turn."

He stroked his thumb over the silk at her sleeves' ends. "How long does this go on?"

"All night. It'll only take a few hours until most are drunk. Especially considering *sake* will flow into each of our own cups throughout the party. I feel sorry for the empress."

"Why?" He eyed the demure royal who kept her gaze downcast and her hands hidden in the seemingly endless yards of fabric encasing her lap.

"People forget how to behave properly when they've had too much to drink. Even the ladies. She's so young and unsure. I think I'll try to find a way to remove her when manners and language begin to slip."

Yūkan wanted to see her face so badly. Despite her elite social celebrity and apparent charms, she had no false pride. She showed a generosity of spirit and care of others that he found tremendously endearing. "Will you drink and recite poetry?"

"I'm in attendance to Empress Akiko tonight. I'm in service to the court, and that dictates that I must participate. I'd rather have stayed home with Amai." Her voice held no complaint, yet her matter-of-fact tone had him wishing he could spare her the scene she believed would take place.

"Don't mind Lady Kirei," said Yoki. He grinned and waved a servant over to serve them food and rice wine. "We'll put her on display because her poetry's so poignant, and she can't stand being the center of attention." The dandy shook his head. "You'd think she'd be used to it by now."

"My poetry isn't the best. Lady Rikō and Lady Minikui are both extremely beautiful, and both are able to trip a lovely, perfectly fitting verse off their tongues at a moment's notice."

Yūkan detected a hint of envy in her voice.

Yoki coughed a laugh. "You can't compare yourself to that evil-spirited Lady Minikui. She may be quick-minded, but her poetry lacks depth. I agree with you about Lady Rikō, however. She's clever, that one."

The emperor raised a hand, and the cup was placed in the water. Behind her *kichō*, Kirei released a heavy sigh. Yūkan still learned about this strange society, but he understood her discomfort.

When the cup reached him, he scooped it from the water and leaned forward to prevent drips from staining his silk brocade while taking a small sip. He recited a Chinese poem he'd learned as a boy, and received approving nods as his reward. Yoki cast him a sly grin and tilted his head toward Kirei's screen of state, but he set the cup back into the pond.

"Thank you," she whispered.

He returned his hand to her soft *uchigi* layers, and this time, her fingers emerged to settle upon his. He smiled.

Progress.

"You're no fun," accused Yoki.

Yūkan shrugged.

"It's just like my dream last night, which makes me nervous because there was an earthquake in that dream, too. I went to an interpreter this morning, and he assured me it has no particular significance." Yoki sighed with a dramatic arch of his brows and lift of his shoulders. "It's one of my favorite things – to be told that a troubling dream isn't some kind of premonition."

Kirei chuckled. "What else was in this dream of yours?"

"A sorcerer," he whispered when a nobleman shot them a scowl. A few mats down, a man not much more than a boy recited a lengthy poem, but that didn't stop Yoki. "The sorcerer made himself invisible when he put on a straw cloak, and I thought he'd strangle me. I woke up, instead. I couldn't stand it. I was so afraid I'd have another scary dream that I got up, took all my clothes off then put them on inside out and went back to bed."

"Did it work?" asked Yūkan, trying not to burst out laughing at the silly aristocrat.

"I think so. I don't remember any more dreams, so they must've been pleasant. I woke up sneezing, which scared me witless. I've been waiting all day for some disaster to strike because of those ominous sneezes."

"Ominous sneezes?" Yūkan clamped his lips closed as a chortle made its way into his throat.

"Yes. And thank the gods I was alone. If I'd been talking to someone, those sneezes would've made me a liar."

"Nonsense," said Lady Kirei, sounding composed in a way Yūkan couldn't have attempted. "A sneeze, especially someone else's sneeze, doesn't lend any falseness to your words. It's not your lips that lie, but the sneezer's nose."

"If only everyone believed that, but even I don't," said Yoki with a mournful pout that made his lower lip jut. "Just look how many sneezes occur around that hateful Lady

Minikui. She constantly spouts lies."

"Maybe it's her fragrance," offered Kirei, a slight quaver in her voice finally revealing her amusement.

Yūkan smiled. No wonder he had earned a position as the emperor's Supreme Minister of Personal Affairs. Who wouldn't want such an entertaining gentleman around?

They quieted in deference to the poetry recitations, especially since the cup had come full circle and would reach Yoki soon.

This time, Kirei didn't escape the rotation. Emperor Ichijō clapped his hands, earning everyone's attention and demanding a poem from the reluctant lady. At first, Yūkan wanted to step between her and the curious eyes. Then it occurred to him that he wasn't her protector. She hadn't asked him to be her hero. In addition, she knew these people and their ways much better than he. He had to trust she could handle the situation. She'd been doing it far longer than he and without any interference.

She stood, her silks rustling softly, and gazed at him over the edge of her red and silver fan. All conversation ceased, making Yūkan glance around to see if the royals were on the move. They weren't. The party had quieted to hear her verse. Amazed, he returned his attention to her.

She continued to stare at him as she began her poem. She didn't pause once as she slowly told a rhythmic story of the night. Her words ideally captured the moon's reflection on the water and the cup's lazy spin upon the current. She spoke of season's change, bringing natural elements into the verse. In her gentle delivery, she paid homage to the night. When she finished, she offered a shallow bow of tribute to the emperor.

Nobody made a sound. Even Yūkan sat in awe of her poem's perfect reflection of this very moment. This very event. This very experience.

Then the emperor shared a smile with his young wife and threw his arms wide. He declared, "Delightful!"

Kirei handed Yūkan the cup then disappeared behind

her *kichō*. Placing the cup gently on the water, he determined in that moment that he'd earn her respect. He'd earn her affection and win her for his bed. Staying in Kyō hadn't been a waste.

He enjoyed the foods served with an eye to artistic arrangement, and wished before long that he sipped water instead of *sake*. He struggled to follow along with Kirei's and Yoki's talk of Hiei Mountain temples.

A mere hour into the party, gentlemen began speaking with slurred words and laughing openly at slips in each other's verses. Some noblemen made lewd comments to the ladies behind them, and were so bold as to reach through screens to tug on women's clothing. The ladies didn't mind, if their giggles and quips indicated correctly. The emperor's eyelids drooped, and the empress appeared ready to cry.

"Lady Kirei," Yūkan whispered, nudging her hand.

"I know. I see. I'm not sure..." She peeked through her screen at him.

"Follow my lead." He stood and stretched with a loud yawn. Then he stumbled sideways, catching Yoki's knee with his foot.

"Watch it," cried her friend, shaking his fist and frowning. "You're too drunk to be up and about."

A number of gentlemen laughed, their comments centered on both his and their own drunkenness.

He stumbled further past two more gentlemen and headed straight for Empress Akiko. Kirei stood, fan in place and eyes wide. She reached a hand out to him.

He pretended to reach for it but careened backward, closer to the royals.

Emperor Ichijō came alert. He laughed as Yūkan kneed a minister in the shoulder then shuffled away. Kirei hurried toward him, but seated aristocrats and her heavy court apparel slowed her ability to get to him. He made a show of regaining his balance to give her a chance to get near. When she touched her fingertips to his, he flailed for a second then leaned. He sent his feet scuffling rapidly toward the seated empress.

Shrieks of alarm filled the night and echoed slightly off the water. He carefully maneuvered so as not to make contact with the young woman who appeared ready to scream. He scuffed his shoe along the edge of her *karaginu* jacket of white damask.

Gasps sounded, and her other ladies-in-waiting rose on unsteady legs from behind their screens. Kirei had already reached her, however. Yūkan slurred a murmur about finding a place to relieve himself, and stumbled out of sight past a wing of the greater imperial palace.

He hung in the shadows until Lady Kirei arrived with the struggling empress. He went to the girl's side and offered his arm. When she shied on a whimper, he said, "I'm sorry I scared you. I only pretended so we could make an excuse for you to leave. Please let me help you, Your Majesty? I can tell your heavy fabrics are making it difficult to walk."

She offered a small nod and placed a tiny hand on his arm.

*    *    *    *

Delivering the empress into the waiting and capable hands of her maids at the First Ward Ichijō mansion outside the palace walls, Kirei sighed and smiled. Yūkan had been brilliant. He would receive criticism of his bumbling antics, but not censure. In another hour, someone else would follow suit, but in earnest drunkenness.

She shook her head and left the empress' curtained sleeping area to find a palace carriage driver awake enough to drive her home. She stepped out onto the veranda and bumped into Yūkan.

"My lady," he said, his voice deep, surprisingly sober, and containing a lacing of humor. He took her shoulders and steadied her.

"I'm sorry," she said, managing a step backward without

toppling. "I thought you were still in the Nine Fold Enclosure."

Despite the eleven layers of material between his hands and her shoulders, she was acutely aware of his touch. She was also aware that he didn't let go. Moonlight spilled past the overhead eave to scatter his sharp, masculine features in abstract illumination. His dark eyes remained in shadow, though she felt them on her face. Her heart beat faster.

"I came to make sure you got her home alright. Are you returning to the party?" he asked.

"With the empress retired, my duties are finished." Was that *her* breathless-sounding voice?

"Allow me to take you home." He glanced at an imperial guard who passed with a nod and shallow bow.

She needed some distance. He had her wanting things she shouldn't. *Sake* had reduced her natural defensiveness, so she needed to proceed carefully.

"That won't be necessary." An image of him next to her in his carriage flashed through her mind. His hand holding hers. His lips curved in a generous smile. She found it difficult to catch her breath. "I came by imperial transport. A palace carriage can take me home."

His voice went quieter and deeper. "It seems like a lot of trouble to find someone to drive you."

"It is," she whispered, lulled by his soothing tone.

"My conveyance is waiting, my driver prepared to take us wherever we wish to go." He released her shoulder and put two fingers on her wrist, effectively lowering her fan.

Kirei fought against the *sake's* numbing of her brain. "But you live near, at the palace. Why not just return?"

He smiled. "Your uncle's mansion in the Fourth Ward isn't that far from here. I have my driver up and ready. Let's take advantage, shall we? I thought you might need him."

She tried to raise her fan, but he kept her hand weighted. "You're very thoughtful. I'm tempted, but you should stay. You could return to the party."

"I've heard enough poetry and drank enough wine for

one night."

"You should find your rest. You're staying here. Why leave just to have to return?"

He put his hand to her back and urged her down steps leading from the wing's veranda to a pale graveled walkway. "You talk too much."

She grinned. "You mean I *think* too much."

"Maybe." He encouraged her toward a gate in the Ichijō mansion's wall surround. "Maybe I'm not interested in sleep when I have fascinating conversation to pursue with you."

"Is my conversation fascinating?" she teased, enjoying how he didn't back down or hesitate to command the situation. She hadn't realized how tired she'd grown of demurring and indecisive men until he arrived.

"Enthralling. I can't get enough."

She chuckled. "Are you being sarcastic?"

He stepped through the gate first and signaled to his driver. While the carriage pulled forward, he faced her. Moonlight fully bathed his features, revealing a slight pull of amusement at his lips. "Not in the least. You are, by far, the most intriguing person I've met." He opened the carriage door and gave her an assisting hand in. "There are other things I'd like to do with you besides conversing."

She quickly settled to keep from thumping her head in the limited space. Before he could climb in, she said, "You really don't have to come with me. I'll send your driver after he delivers me to my uncle's home."

"I know I don't have to. I want to, Lady Kirei." He climbed in and closed the door then rapped a single knock to the side of the cabin. He called, "You know where to go."

"Yes, my lord," said the driver. The carriage lurched, and soon, the wheels crunched along wide streets east of the Nine Fold Enclosure.

"Normally, I'd worry my uncle will see me with you, but he's at the party." Because of the late hour and remoteness of their entry, she didn't have any concern about wagging tongues, either.

"He doesn't like me."

"He doesn't know you." A lantern mounted on the carriage wall let her see his face, but she wished they sat in the dark so he couldn't see hers...and so she wouldn't be so aware of how the damask of her jacket rested against the brocade of his sleeve.

His gaze met hers. "He doesn't want to. Your uncle decided his opinion of me already."

Her fan slid from her fingers, but she couldn't look away from his stare. He had a gentle, intelligent strength in his gaze. An affection and genuine interest that held her spellbound. Why'd the emperor have to pick her to be his tutor? "I liked your recitation of Po Chü-i's poem."

He leaned closer an inch. "You're familiar with Chinese poetry?"

Whoops. She blinked but still couldn't avert her gaze. He was entirely too handsome. "A little."

"You're lying," he said softly, his eyes lowering to her mouth. "You're very familiar, aren't you? I didn't think they let women study Chinese works."

A clump of discomfort settled in her esophagus, and she cleared her throat. "Women are discouraged from learning to read Chinese, it's true."

"But you do." His gaze, curious and lacking any condemnation, lifted to her eyes.

"I had an unusual education." She wondered why she cared if he approved or not. Yoki adored her learned mind. Would Yūkan?

"I suspected as much, since you know geography better than anyone I've met yet in Kyō, including Emperor Ichijō. And because I believe you read the history of my uncle, Michinaga, from official records written in Chinese. So since you've read Po Chü-i, tell me you've also read Li Po and Tu Fu."

Kirei shook her head. "Are they poets, too?"

He looked away and groaned, breaking the spell.

She breathed a sigh, partly in relief and partly in disappointment of...what?

"Li Po and Tu Fu were great masters of poetry during Po Chü-i's time. In China, they're even more respected than Po Chü-i. I don't get it. What perversity takes place in Kyō that decides one Chinese poet takes precedence to the exclusion of all others?" He slapped her folded fan against his other palm.

"I thought you hated poetry." She studied his profile, captivated by his unexpected passion for something she enjoyed so much.

He faced her. "I don't hate poetry. I just accept that I'm no good at writing it."

"That makes sense." Too much sense. Had she underestimated him like everyone else seemed to want to do? Had she become a Kyō aristocrat, regardless of her protests and resistance? She laughed. "Yes. You make perfect sense."

His gaze went to her lips. Her stomach jumped, and for the first time in her life, she actually wanted a man to kiss her.

## Chapter Nine

Yūkan closed in, his lids going heavy.

Kirei stiffened. "Don't."

She put a palm to the front of his *uenoginu*, astonished to discover he wore no padding underneath to make his chest appear larger. He had hard, thick muscle, and he filled out his clothing without aid.

"Lady Kirei," he murmured, still approaching.

"Please don't." What was she saying? She wanted this. She pressed her palm more firmly against his chest.

The carriage came to a halt, but he didn't move.

His gaze searched hers. "Since that first time I saw you standing on the veranda of your uncle's mansion, I've been drawn to you. Say you don't feel it and I'll leave you in peace."

She couldn't lie so blatantly. Besides, she didn't want him to leave. "The emperor asked me to teach you. If you... If we... It would become awkward."

He leaned away, his features going intense. "I see your point."

"Do you agree?"

"No." He handed her the fan.

She released a slow breath between tense lips. "I meant it when I said we're no good for each other. My father would want me matched with a true gentleman. A man born and raised here, who lives as an aristocrat should."

His eyes narrowed. "As an aristocrat *should*? According to whom? It seems to me this tiny society in this one city is too bold in its attempt to dictate propriety."

Hairs stood on end at the nape of her neck, and a chill

shivered down her spine. "This 'tiny society' makes up the bulk of our country's nobility. They own the land, make the laws, and control most of the money. This 'one city' is the only *true* city in a land full of villages, farms, and castle estates. So yes, they're bold. And yes, they dictate propriety. They do because they can."

His lips curved into a gradual smile. "I've put you on the defensive. You like to act as if they get on your nerves, but you sit here defending them. You're one of them, even if you can't enjoy the full benefits of true membership."

His words rankled because of the truth in them. They stung. She met his gaze straight on. "I'm not here by choice, Lord Yūkan. I'm not content to hide the extent of my knowledge and to play the part of an imperial pet. I can't, however, change the fact that in order to be an obedient and loyal daughter and niece, I have to somehow make the best of it. Somehow fit in. Somehow bide my time until an acceptable alternative to a life of sexual servitude comes along."

She wilted, fisting her hands. She'd said too much.

His smile melted. He sat staring at her a long minute, his expression unreadable. Then he opened the carriage door. "I'll let you go."

"Thank you for bringing me home." Kirei opened her fan and accepted his hand as he helped her climb out.

"Get some good sleep," he said while she arranged her robes' layers. "I'll be here for a lesson this afternoon."

She couldn't discern his thoughts, and her stomach roiled at the idea that he might think less of her now. She didn't want to care, but she couldn't seem to help it. She offered a slight bow. "I'll see you later."

The carriage didn't leave as she headed inside. She opened the west gate leading to her wing of the mansion then stepped through. Before closing the gate, she glanced over her shoulder.

He sat in the carriage, unmoving, the door still open. His eyes remained on her until she closed the gate.

\*    \*    \*    \*

Yūkan loved that Kirei had revealed her reality to him. It bothered him that she'd appeared to immediately regret it. She had practically confessed to not wanting the life this society offered her. He stood and stretched. Sleeping on a mat made him stiff. At home, and even when he traveled by ship, he slept on a padded futon. Maybe he was spoiled. He'd been spoiled in many ways.

While he chose his day's clothing, Yoki came in and settled onto a square cushion, his posture relaxed as if he planned to stay for hours. He poured a cup of water then took a long drink. "Going to see Lady Kirei today?"

"Of course. Isn't that what the emperor wants?" Yūkan selected off-white trousers and a tan raw silk *tarikubi* kimono-style robe dyed in a way to make it appear as if it had been painted by a brush.

Yoki snorted. "You can't fool me. I see the way you look at her. I look at women that way all the time, but you look only at her that way."

"You're talking nonsense. I don't look at her any special way." He folded a clean *fundoshi* around his hips then exchanged the gray *kosode* he'd slept in for a fresh white one before shrugging off a niggling irritation.

"Lie to me if you want, but don't lie to yourself."

Yūkan drew on his trousers and tucked in the *kosode*. He settled to a cushion next to his odd friend and said, "You know her fairly well, don't you?"

"Better than anyone." He made a show of leaning near in a conspiratorial manner. "She's one of those rare people who'll be honest and forthright with you if you are with her." He leaned backward, jutting his finely haired chin in a preening pose. "And she knows I'll never betray her. She trusts me because I'm discreet. I keep her secrets."

"What secrets?" he asked, glad his tone sounded casual,

almost bored. His interest peaked, Yūkan poured a second cup of water.

"Ha! You won't get them out of me. You'll have to learn them for yourself."

"Secrets like the fact that she reads Chinese and is probably better educated than half the gentlemen in Kyō?"

Yoki went still. "You know that, do you? She told you?"

He hid a smile in his cup while he took a swallow. "She did. Last night when I took her home."

For the first time, the nobleman's too-slanted lids widened enough to show the color of his eyes. "She let you go home with her? And did she...? Did you...?"

How was that any of his business? "Why do you ask?"

The man's eyes disappeared behind his slits. "You know what? It doesn't matter."

"Apparently it does." Was this related to another of her supposed secrets?

"She's special," said Yoki in a reverent voice. "A truly good person – not in sensibility and birth but in her heart and in her actions."

"You love her then." Why did that bother him so much? Yūkan had witnessed the affection between Yoki and Kirei, so it shouldn't have surprised him. Still, a wave of jealousy upped his temperature. "You're not married. Why haven't you offered for her hand?"

Yoki barked a laugh. "Me? Married to Lady Kirei? There are *so* many reasons why not."

"Is it because she's country-raised?" Anger replaced his jealousy. He couldn't understand this stupidity of prejudice.

The nobleman sighed. "She's beautiful, but don't take it the wrong way when I say I have no interest in sharing her bed. She's entirely *too* good for the likes of me. I enjoy my nightly rendezvous with various women – whoever strikes my fancy. If I gave Lady Kirei my heart, she'd have all of me. Does that make sense?"

Yūkan relaxed. "Perfect."

"She deserves better than me. Not that I'm interested in her that way. I love her, but she's too smart for me. Thank the gods I don't have romantic notions about her. I'd be doomed to a life of feeling inferior next to her." He laughed. "No, I'm satisfied to call her a friend and be the keeper of her secrets. Which brings us to you."

Yūkan stood and shrugged into his robe. "What about me?"

"You admire her. I can see that. And you're attracted to her. Who wouldn't be? Then last night you took her home. Despite that drunken scene you made at the party, I knew you weren't inebriated to that degree. Emperor Ichijō knew it, too."

"So?"

"You shared her bed." Nervous energy radiated from the aristocrat.

"Are you saying I'm not capable of being a gentleman? Of escorting a lady home without seducing her?" He took extra seconds to ensure the lines of his robes were straight before he secured a thin cord around his waist to keep the front closed.

"Did you?"

He faced the nobleman. "Why's it your concern? If you're not interested in her for yourself, why do you want to know?"

A slow smile curved Yoki's lips. "You didn't."

Yūkan unfastened his long hair and combed fingers through it to smooth it and remove tangles. "How do you know?"

"I told you. She's special. If you'd gotten into her *hakama*, you wouldn't be so casual."

That was alarming. "Why? Does she have a penis or something?"

Yoki's eyes became visible, and his small mouth formed an O.

Yūkan chuckled while tying a ribbon around his hair's length. "There are some. You talk about bedding women and enjoying a variety. You should try it while traveling the world.

The things I've seen..."

"I'm fascinated. Tell me more."

"I'm sure you are, but I won't keep the lovely Lady Kirei waiting. The sun's already past its zenith, and I told her I'd be over for a lesson this afternoon. I didn't expect to sleep this long, so no. I have to go." He picked up a set of chopsticks from atop his chest of drawers and slid them into the pocket portion of his left sleeve.

"Let me come." Yoki stood and went to the door.

"So we can talk about my sexual exploits? No. I don't think she'd find that conversation interesting." Yūkan tied his coin bag to his belt then slid open the door.

Yoki walked at his side down the hallway toward the exit. "She might surprise us."

"I don't agree. She's highly educated, that's for sure, but this isn't an appropriate topic for a lady's ears. I say with certainty that her education didn't include sexual deviations."

"Neither did mine, but I'm a willing and eager student. Tell me everything."

Yūkan laughed. "I won't play the role of corruptor. You'll have to go to China to experience it for yourself."

Yoki halted, sliding a bit on the wooden floor. "Leave Kyō? Have you lost your mind?"

He didn't stop. Over his shoulder, he said, "This city is but a tiny speck, Lord Yoki. There's an entire world out there worth exploring. Go to it."

"Not going to happen," called the nobleman.

Yūkan slipped his feet into his wooden sandals at the edge of the veranda. He offered a dismissive wave and descended to a gravel walkway. His carriage waited, thanks to the efficiency of Ichijō's servants. Yoki would stay, and he was glad. He wanted Kirei to himself today.

*    *    *    *

Kirei's heart thudded at the sight of Yūkan entering her

common room. Amai had gone to a garden party with Lord Shinsetsu, and both Uma and Zo had the afternoon off. With her uncle and his women at the Kamo shrine for the day, she'd have the handsome world traveler alone.

"Please come and sit," she said, indicating cushions scattered before her.

His dark eyes didn't leave her face as he sank cross-legged to a large red pillow directly in front of her. "How are you?"

"I'm well, thank you. Let's get right to business, shall we?" Before she dissembled under this strange and unwanted desire he sparked in her.

"Whatever you wish, my lady." His gaze devoured her.

Hiding trembling hands in the folds of her pale green and yellow mantle, she swallowed hard. "Have you been studying your brush technique?"

"I have." He offered a lazy, sexy smile.

"Good. I'll have you show me your progress tomorrow." She indicated the far wall where her instruments hung on display. "Today, we'll concentrate on the seven-string zither. You'll need to play it better than anyone else."

He gazed at her zither, saying, "I'd rather learn more about Kyō's *good people*."

"But—"

He turned his full attention on her. "Please."

She really needed to assess his skill, but they had time. "Fine. If you're going to live in Kyō and become one of the *good people*, as Emperor Ichijō wants, there are things you should know."

He relaxed, his shoulders relaxing a bit as he settled. He teased, "Teach me, wise lady."

She liked his attempt at badinage but prevented a smile by biting the inside of her cheek. "A nobleman's rank in the government dictates in which ward he may live. My uncle is of the fourth rank, which places us in the Fourth Ward. Family connection is everything. As a Fujiwara, he's related to nearly every emperor and empress four generations back."

"I see. I've noticed most gentlemen don't work, not even in their government posts. How do they earn their wealth?"

His question put focus on the lesson and eased her nerves. She took a deep breath and relaxed. "They don't earn it. The first five ranks obtain income from special rice land grants. It also helps that their expenses are reduced."

He frowned. "What do you mean by 'reduced'?"

"Any official of the Fifth Rank or higher receives silk and cloth allowances, so they don't have to buy them. Guards and messengers are assigned by the ministry, which means they don't have to bear the burden of payroll for such services. My uncle also employs his house retainers at government expense. The greatest expense relief, however, comes from the fact that they aren't required to pay taxes or tributes."

He sat a moment, his eyes dropping to the front of her mantle where it hung loose and open along the crossed front of her dress. "I had no idea. All the income they receive is theirs to do with as they choose."

"Mainly. It's important to know that the higher the rank, the greater regulation is enforced. With that comes vast expense."

"What kind of regulation?" He shifted, and the toes of one foot poked past the fabric of his trousers.

"What men and women can wear is dictated by rank. For example, fans have to be of a certain kind. Fans held by people below the Fifth Rank may only have twelve folds. Fourth and Fifth Ward residents hold fans with twenty-three folds. Anyone above the Fourth Rank owns fans with twenty-five. Rank also determines what type of carriage a person must own and how many outriders to have in attendance. Regulation even controls how high a gatepost can stand."

"That's interesting. Only Fujiwaras can hold ranks higher than Sixth?" His lips pursed.

"Not at all. We have members in the Fourth and Fifth Ranks from clans who came from the Yamato region, and there are a few from important foreign families that immigrated a couple hundred years ago."

"So people born within a rank are relegated to that rank for life?"

She laughed. "No. Many officials are absolutely obsessed with gaining promotion. Pay attention to officials in the green robes of the Sixth Rank, and see if you can catch them talking of anything other than escaping the rank for something higher."

His gaze went to her mouth. "I like your laugh."

"Thank you," she said, uncomfortable with how much she wanted his kiss.

"I notice you don't stain your teeth. Yoki tells me white teeth are garish. He's been trying to talk me into darkening mine, but I don't think he minds yours."

"He accepts my idiosyncrasies. Probably because he knows I won't let him influence me. I am who I am." As difficult as that was when she'd first moved to Kyō.

"It's fortunate you fit so well into what the *good people* expect from a lady of their city." He tilted his head.

"I suppose. Some qualities they like and value to excess. Others, they tolerate." A small smile tugged at the corners of her lips. Her glaring teeth and prudish attitude were a minimal price to pay for her poetry, music, and sense of style. Silly aristocrats.

"Am I wasting my time?" he asked, growing serious.

She considered him closely. What exactly did he want? "Actually, no, you're not. You may be countrified, which is the worst thing any *good person* could say to or about you."

"Right. Thanks for that." He bowed slightly, sending her a crooked grin.

She returned his smile. "If you truly wanted a position as a nobleman in Kyō, it could happen. Your bloodline makes you eligible for a Fourth or Fifth Rank position. The emperor's approval of you will earn you acceptance into certain elevated circles. As for a post in the government, it'd just be a matter of Michinaga appointing you."

## Chapter Ten

Simple as that? Yūkan hadn't imagined he'd ever want to live in Kyō as one of these *good people*. Had anyone told him last week that he would, he'd have laughed outright. Now, however, he only had one desire, and she sat in front of him. If becoming one of the social elite in the imperial city was what it took to win Kirei, he'd do it.

"Would you like it if I made Kyō my permanent home?" he asked.

One moment, she studied her sleeves in her lap, her lips relaxed and her brow smooth, and the next, her forehead wrinkled slightly while her mouth tightened. Finally, she settled into a serene smile.

"My opinion doesn't matter," she said, brushing a drape of hair off of her shoulder. "That's between you and Emperor Ichijō."

"Your opinion matters to me."

"But I'm nobody, really." She plucked at a fold in her outermost layer of silk.

"That's not true. Their Majesties think very highly of you, and so does Yoki. Imagine if Lord Yoki didn't have you as a friend. He can be honest with you and speak frankly. Without you, I think the poor man would go mad. He'd probably cry himself to death."

She laughed. "We really don't have many people we can talk with. Too much honesty in the wrong ear could cause a tremendous amount of discontent. Before I came to Kyō, Lord Yoki spent time with Lady Minikui because she does speak openly. But she's vindictive and abusive and often wrong in her opinions. You have to be mindful around her."

"I will." To test her interest, he leaned forward and plucked boldly at her salmon-colored chemise, the longest layer of her ensemble. What he wouldn't give to have her out of these clothes and in his arms. "I won't even think about such a move without your approval."

"Why?" She eyed where his fingers caressed her inner layer.

"As I said before, your opinion means more to me than anyone's." He tugged a bit harder. Did she have any idea how much he hungered for her kiss? Her touch?

She adjusted her legs but didn't discourage him.

"Tell me you want me to stay," he said, deepening his voice to a more intimate level. "Tell me you wanted my kiss in the carriage last night."

Her visage went blank. Then a slight smile allowed a peek at her teeth. Placing her warm hand on his fingers at her hem, she said, "I'll tell you this. I'll be glad for your company and conversation if you stay. I'll consider you part of my inner-most circle."

He frowned. "You won't encourage me?"

Her eyes met his, but she said nothing.

"I must know." Clenching his jaw, he crossed the space between their cushions. Letting go of her chemise, he touched his lips to hers at the same time he combed his fingers into her luxurious hair.

She inhaled a sharp breath through her nostrils, but she didn't push him away. Desire ignited in his belly, and he growled quietly in his throat as he slanted across her lips. Kirei made a contented-sounding hum. Her lips moved against his.

She closed her eyes, her hands going to his shoulders. He closed his eyes, too. Sending his hands inside her mantle, he could barely gauge her true size and shape under the many layers. Still, he could tell she was slender.

The heat of need grew, spreading to his groin. He wanted to carry her to her chamber and peel away each layer.

To reveal her secrets and explore what she hid so well. To make her gasp. Sigh. Cry out his name in pleasure.

Not today. Not yet. She would love him first. She would invite him.

He settled a knee onto her mantle where her dress, five *uchigi* and her chemise formed a thin padding. He gathered her close. Deepened his kiss. Breathed in the heavenly scent of her unique perfume.

She issued a quiet groan, her mouth opening under his sensual onslaught. When he swept his tongue inside, hers met his in a dance of the senses. She tasted of roasted sesame and sweet rice. Her soft breaths, deep and quickening, filled his ears with proof of her growing arousal. His own excitement pressed against the restraint of his *fundoshi*.

Withdrawing his tongue, he placed several more slanting kisses on her willing lips then settled onto his heels. "I took without asking, but I had to know."

She only offered a nod, but her gaze went to his mouth.

"If you don't stop looking at me like that, I may not be responsible for what ensues," he warned.

She didn't love him, he was certain. Her unexpected responsiveness had been more than he'd expected, however. As hard as she'd made him, he didn't know if he could refuse if she asked him to lie with her.

\*   \*   \*   \*

Kirei trembled. She hadn't realized how badly she'd wanted Yūkan to kiss her until his lips touched hers. Her entire body had combusted. Now, she fought for air. Her lungs couldn't seem to get enough.

She averted her gaze because he spoke the truth. She could only think how she wanted him to do that again. How she wanted his hands on her. In her hair. Under her robes. How she wanted to taste his masculine flavor.

She wanted Yūkan in a way she'd never wanted anyone.

She wished she knew why. He was like her - a royal favorite but still only a noble-born, provincial nobody. In her uncle's view, he could never be more than an acquaintance, and even then, reluctantly. If she took him as a lover, she'd have to do so in secret. They'd have to sneak and whisper and steal moments of affection.

She despised that. When she'd realized men snuck into the beds of women they 'loved,' she'd vowed not to sink so low. That if she couldn't love openly, she wouldn't love at all. Yūkan changed everything.

He made her want something she couldn't have. He tempted her to defy her own values. To step outside the bounds she'd set. Would he understand? She had to try and make him.

Kirei cleared her throat, testing her voice around an emotional clog. "I'm a woman of means. My father is ambitious, and as a successful official, he has acquired a great deal of wealth in the provinces. For you and me, our homes are beautiful and natural and peopled with the strong and generous of spirit. To the *good people* of Kyō, the provinces are harsh, sad, backward places; and the less they hear about them, the better."

"Lady Kirei—"

"Please let me continue." Before she lost her courage. "My brother died a year ago, which leaves me as sole heir to my father's wealth. I'll be entitled by law to keep most of it. My uncle will help with the administration, and after him, I have a number of cousins. My uncle is growing anxious to see me matched and settled, but you can see why I'm in no hurry or have no great interest."

He nodded, his countenance serious. "I'm in no hurry, either."

"Yes, but your circumstance is far different than mine." She fell back, resting her head on her thin padding of sleeves. "You have no one in authority over you, dictating with whom you may or may not form a connection. You can actually *marry*, whereas I'm only good enough to enter a gentleman's house as a consort. Though I'm given some choice, ultimately my uncle and father must approve."

Yūkan stretched alongside her, resting his cheek on his propped-up palm. He gazed down on her, spiking her awareness of his nearness. When he reached over and fingered the innermost neckline of her white *kosode*, she held her breath. An insistent pulsing infused the tender folds between her thighs.

"What if you don't choose?" he asked.

"They'll choose for me. My uncle has already made his choice and warns me that I'm running out of time." She closed her eyes, savoring the wanton sensations he aroused.

Yūkan's voice dropped to a quiet, lazy quality. "Who has he chosen?"

"I believe he has chosen Prince Hansamu."

"Why him? Even I can see he values nobody as much as himself."

She rolled to her side and buried her face in his silken *tarikubi*. He smelled of cedar and plum incense burned in many of the greater palace buildings. "Because he's rich beyond most, even though he resides in the Sixth Ward, and he's directly related to Emperor Ichijō. Any children I bear him will be legitimized if his wife adopts them. And she will. She can't have any of her own."

"You sound miserable." He stroked her hair and kissed her cheek.

She loved the security of his affection. It offered her a sense of safe acceptance she hadn't experienced since childhood. He seemed to genuinely cherish and adore her. She'd made it a rule to stay on guard with men, but Yūkan wouldn't betray her. She didn't know how he had won her confidence or why she trusted him. She just did. She had since that second night when he'd helped her rescue those girls from the dye warehouse. He was different from the gentlemen of her acquaintance and similar to her in many ways.

"I'm not like other ladies," she whispered. "They call me

a prude. I won't enter into a casual love affair. Not with you. Not with anyone."

*   *   *   *

Yūkan managed to maintain his dignity as he bid Lady Kirei farewell and climbed into his carriage. He wanted to shout his victory to the sky. Finally, he had gotten past that stiff formality she'd always shown him. She'd spoken openly, letting him see the real her, and he liked her more than he'd anticipated.

He wanted her with a greater urgency than ever.

His stomach rumbled, and he had his driver head south and stop at an inn restaurant Yoki had mentioned. Inside, it took a second for his vision to adjust to the darker interior. When he could see, he realized someone waved to him from the back.

Lord Shinsetsu sat at a low table with Kirei's cousin and Prince Hansamu. Grinning, the young man waved harder. Lady Amai glanced down, doing a fairly poor job of hiding her displeasure at the prospect of sharing a table with Yūkan. The prince arched his eyebrows.

Why not? Yūkan always liked entertainment with his meals. He chuckled.

"Eat with us," said Shinsetsu when he reached their table. "We haven't ordered yet."

Bowing his gratitude for the invitation, Yūkan snuck a peek at the young lady. She kept her eyes downcast, and her fan hid the rest of her face. He imagined her mouth must be as tight as a clam. Smiling, he settled to an elaborately patterned red and gold cushion boasting embroidered free-floating koi.

"I understand the emperor considers you a close personal friend," said Prince Hansamu. He smoothed his already perfect hair and gave Yūkan a raking look. "It's an honor to be called a favorite."

"If it's so, it's news to me. I've never heard myself called a favorite. I can only say that I've enjoyed what little time I've spent with him. We have a few interests in common."

Kirei's cousin snorted behind her fan but didn't raise her eyes.

"Like what?" asked Shinsetsu.

A waiter arrived, set four metal cups upon the table and poured water from a pitcher. After the young gentleman told him what food to bring, he left the pitcher. Overhead, footsteps sounded a few seconds before a staircase creaked in the next room. Yūkan imagined this inn stayed at full capacity with traders bringing wares to market, and deputies to provincial governors visiting on estate business. He'd never stayed here, however. He'd either sent an agent to deliver goods, or stayed at his aunt's mansion in the First Ward.

"Well," he said, "we have a very similar education. Though I didn't attend the university like he did, we share interests in our studies."

"So you studied the Confucian classics," said the prince with an approving nod.

"Yes, though like Emperor Ichijō, my beliefs and practices are grounded in the Lotus Sutra of Buddhist teaching."

Shinsetsu eagerly leaned forward. "Really? Tendai or Shingon?"

"I believe in salvation by Amida Buddha." Yūkan held his breath. Would they dismiss him from the table and attempt to humiliate him for not supporting the impressive pomp and colorful ceremonies of the Shingon sect?

"My cousin, Lady Kirei, owns a copy of The Essentials of Salvation," said Amai, meeting his gaze for once. "She'll lend it to you if you ask, though it's practically falling apart, she's read it so many times."

He smiled, careful to hide his white teeth behind his lips. "You're kind to think of me, Lady Amai. I already have a copy of my own."

"Come early tomorrow and pray with her. She'd like

that. She's always complaining that she has to intone alone."

His mind did a little dance at the idea. He offered her a shallow bow of acknowledgement. The more he learned about Kirei, the more he discovered how right she was for him. She had it in her head that she couldn't consider an association with him beyond the platonic. He'd have to prove otherwise.

Prince Hansamu frowned. "You would pray with her? Maybe I should come and pray with her, too."

Yūkan raked the man this time. "You know the *Namu Amida Butsu* formula?"

"Not exactly." The prince fidgeted. "I tend toward Shingon observances, but..."

"But what?" asked Shinsetsu, a glimmer of humor in his dark eyes.

Yūkan decided he liked the young man. So far, Shinsetsu had only been a sleepy, quiet sort of puppy. Here, awake and involved, he showed intelligence and energy. He also showed spine in standing up to Hansamu. Perhaps he deserved the beautiful Amai, after all.

"I could learn," said the prince, a hint of defensiveness in his tone.

"What for?" asked the young man. "So you can make a show of believing something you don't?"

Okay, he liked him a lot. Yūkan stifled a laugh.

"You'll only make yourself despicable in her eyes." Amai cut Hansamu a dismissive glance. She patted the prince's hand. "She admires honesty. Try that."

A chortle gurgled into Yūkan's throat, and he faked a cough to disguise it. Somehow he seriously doubted Hansamu had much practice with honesty - even to himself.

The waiter returned and served them each a small bowl of soup and a large bowl of cooked rice. He placed a platter containing various vegetables and meats at the table's center and bid them a pleasant meal.

Yūkan removed his personal chopsticks from his sleeve and went to work assuaging his hunger.

Shinsetsu leaned near and said quietly, "I need to thank you."

He arched a single eyebrow at the youth. "Why?"

"You've been the reason Lady Amai doesn't like to be home in the afternoons, so I've been spending a lot of time with her." The young man grinned.

"She seems very sweet. I suppose, for your sake, I should be glad she doesn't care for my company."

Shinsetsu nodded. "She's the sweetest. She's the prettiest woman I know, so her trusting, uncalculating nature came as a delightful surprise. I plan to take her as my wife."

"A wise move," he said, giving him a firm nod.

"And she may not like you, but I do. Come to my mansion tonight. I'm having a drinking party. It'll be fun."

He hesitated. He hadn't yet had a chance to learn if Kirei would venture out. He preferred to cross her path whenever possible, and she had told him for a fact that she hated drinking parties.

Shinsentsu's lips parted on a knowing grin, and he cut a watchful glance at Hansamu. "Lady Amai's cousin will attend, and I suspect you've decided to pursue her."

"You're too observant," said Yūkan, relaxing some when the prince entered into conversation with Amai, oblivious. "I can't think you'll be wearing that green robe too much longer."

The young man's grin widened. "I know I won't. Amai's father will make sure I'm promoted when I marry her. Come to my party tonight."

"Kirei won't go. She told me she despises drunkenness."

Shinsetsu laughed. He looked at Prince Hansamu. "You're coming to my party, aren't you?"

"Wouldn't miss it."

"And you're coming to my party, Lady Amai?"

Deep affection shone from her gaze as she faced the young man. "Of course. I always want to be where you are."

Shinsetsu beamed at Yūkan, threw his arms wide, and laughed. "You see? The Minister of the Center will insist a certain niece attend my party."

Then Yūkan would be there, too. He smiled and gave Shinsetsu a nod.

## Chapter Eleven

"Oh!" Kirei fumed as she stared at her uncle's retreating back.

Beside her, Uma shrugged.

"That man is impossible. A drinking party, of all things. I adore Shinsetsu. He's a kind, gentle person. But a drinking party?"

"Let's get you changed, my lady."

Kirei took a second to close her eyes and inhale a deep, calming breath. It didn't work. Following Uma to the bedroom end of the mansion's wing, she said, "He says Prince Hansamu's going to be there."

Zo waited in her chamber and closed the door after Kirei entered. Amai's voice carried through the walls, talking incessantly of how she wanted to look good for Lord Shinsetsu.

Kirei eyed the three choices Uma had set out. "Those are exceptionally tasteful, but I have nobody to impress."

Her thoughts went to Yūkan. Not that she wanted to impress him, though the idea of him finding her attractive did thrill her...a little.

"Your uncle will want you to impress Prince Hansamu."

"All I have to do is *look* perfect and he'll be impressed." The shallow man. Pompous social climber. He only wanted her because of her position as a court favorite. "Why can't he switch his attention to Lady Rikō?"

Uma giggled. "He doesn't stand any more chance of winning her attention than yours. She's cleverer than you."

"She is." Kirei wilted, defeated for now. "And her father's already of the Second Rank, so he's not ambitious for his family.

*She'll* marry."

Zo cast her a sketchy smile. "How would you like your hair?"

"I don't even care. You two chose everything. I'm just going to consider the night a waste. Be sure I'll return home before the party's over, though. What's Amai thinking to go to such an event?"

"She's in love," said Uma, pulling airy-light *uchigi* from various drawers.

Zo came behind Kirei and removed her mantle. "Have you considered accepting Prince Hansamu's advances? He's one of the finest looking men in Kyō. He may not be the most interesting person, but you've got your friends and ladies at court. When he loses interest in your bed—"

"And he will, because he always does," said Kirei.

Uma nodded sagely.

"You can find a man to really love. You'd have some freedom as the princes' consort," said Zo, helping her out of her dress.

"Freedom if I want to spend my life going to clandestine rendezvous and hiding my affairs. What kind of *love* survives having to sneak out of bed in the morning? It's seedy and crude."

"It's not," said Uma, her hands snapping toward the ceiling as she let a crimson chemise fall from its fold and billow on a graceful half-flight. "All the ladies do it."

"Not all," Kirei said under her breath. She really wanted to return to the country. Her father's home held too many painful memories, however. Besides, leaving the city in haste would cause him dishonor in the eyes of their Fujiwara relatives. There had to be another way, but she hadn't found one yet.

\*   \*   \*   \*

Drinking had already begun when Yūkan arrived at

Shinsetsu's simple but majestic mansion in the Sixth Ward. Servants moved through the young official's surprisingly lush garden, making sure everyone had *sake* in his cup. Yūkan barely passed through the main building's garden access when a cup was thrust into his hand.

As he descended a set of wooden steps to the lawn, he studied the partygoers. The ladies looked the same, their stiff, fancy jackets and long, loose hair gleaming in light from torches lit at various points around the garden. Most sat along the rear veranda or upon the pavilion at the end of the west walkway. Shinsetsu hadn't hung panels of fabric to hide them, so they used fans to cover their faces.

When his gaze landed on Kirei, however, he recognized her. He wasn't sure if it was the shape of her hair, the way she turned her head, or the manner in which she sat, but he knew her. She occupied a section of material spread upon a portion of grass near the pavilion, and a wild glint lit her darting gaze.

Prince Hansamu sat diagonally, facing her. His lips moved as he repeatedly offered to fill her cup.

As though she could sense his eyes on her, Kirei showed her profile then offered a smile. Was that relief that caused her eyebrows to relax and her back to straighten? And did she wear powder? She appeared paler than usual.

He waved and bowed at various gentlemen who greeted him while he headed for the seated gathering. This party held a more casual air than Prince Hansamu's perfume party had. A noblewoman sang a pretty song from behind a *kichō*, and when he approached, Shinsetsu stood.

"Thank you for inviting me," Yūkan said on a bow, careful not to spill his drink.

"I'm glad you came. I think it'll rain."

He glanced at a sky too dark to tell. No stars shone, suggesting thick cloud cover. "You might be right."

The young man took a step closer and whispered, "When it does, we'll move to the garden veranda. Some will go to my pavilion." He pointed to the covered walkway that ran from the pavilion to a narrow building west of the main building. "Take Lady Kirei to the west wing. Lady Amai and I will join you there after I get my guests settled and drinking again. I'll try to convince Prince Hansamu to leave. Otherwise he'll come searching for her."

"That should be easy. Tell him the rain has affected his looks."

Shinsetsu laughed. "Good advice. That'll work."

"Why are you helping me?" He liked the young man, but he couldn't discern his motive.

Shinsetsu's smile faded. He stepped to the side, further from people who might overhear. Worry deepened the shadows of his eyes. "Can I trust you?"

"You can. I'm discreet." Yūkan bent his head close, intrigued.

"Last year, I saw Lady Kirei for the first time." He glanced past Yūkan's shoulder at her. "She's gorgeous. I don't need to tell you. She's smart and talented and...well, I decided I loved her. I went to her bed to begin my declaration for her."

Yūkan gave his head a vigorous shake. Had he heard correctly? How old was he, anyway? Seventeen? "Kirei took you to her bed?"

Shinsetsu gazed at the ground. "I'm ashamed to admit she denied me."

He exhaled. "How is this important?"

"This is hardly the place, but you need to understand what she means to me. You see, I wanted her for my wife. She told me I couldn't marry her because it would ruin my career. She said she'd only agree to be a consort to a man she loved, and even though she liked me, she didn't love me. She advised me to take a wife, and if she was still available, I was welcome to try for her heart." He smiled.

"And?" This sounded so different from the impatient, frustrated teacher. So different from the sensual, reluctant woman.

"She helped me escape without notice. She disguised me

in servant's garb and sent me home on foot. That was the longest walk of my life, but it saved me from gossip and ridicule. She saved me from myself that night, and I think the world of her. I'll never deserve her, but I have what I really wanted – actual love with a lovely, sweet woman who'll make the perfect wife for me. Am I wrong to want Lady Kirei to be happy, too?"

"What makes you think I'll make her happy? I vex her. I'm no better for her than she was for you." Yūkan narrowed his eyes and shot her a quick glance over his shoulder. Her eyes met his, and he averted his gaze.

"She can love you. That's all she wants. At least, that's what she told me she needs to be happy. Don't you see the way she looks at you?"

He hadn't. He snuck a glance at her from the corner of his eye. She still watched him, an expression of intense interest and slight worry lifting her brow and pursing her lips. Though her fan concealed her features from the prince, she didn't attempt to hide her face from Yūkan.

A raindrop hit his forehead. Turning his full attention to Shinsetsu, he said, "Thank you for sharing your story. It helps. I'll take your advice and see you later in the west wing."

The young man smiled then signaled to a servant.

Another raindrop landed on Yūkan's cheek as murmuring began among the guests. Some glanced at the black sky. He took his time heading for Kirei.

A rumble of thunder had men on their feet. A second later, shrieks accompanied the beginning of a downpour. Smiling, he ran to her and she offered her hand. A wave of possessiveness washed over him as he helped her to her feet and pointed at the covered walkway. Nodding, she gripped his hold.

"Wait a—" cried Prince Hansamu, trying to shield his face from the rain with ineffective fingers.

Kirei laughed. She ran at Yūkan's side then slowed when they reached the walkway.

He didn't let her stop. Giving her a gentle tug, he said, "This way."

"Where are we going?"

"I'm not sure," he confessed. "In here."

He slid open the door to the west wing. Only a flicker of light beckoned from the wall to his left. He let it show the way and discovered a partitioned room halfway along. Beyond an open doorway, lantern light filled a long, inner room. He released her hand and gestured for her to enter.

A corner brazier radiated heat, making him aware how wet the rain had made his robe. He removed it and spread it on the floor next to the brazier. Going to Kirei where she stood at the center of a bright green rug, he offered to remove her wet jacket.

She gave him a wary look.

"Trust me, my lady. I don't intend to take advantage." Okay, maybe he did a little.

She turned her back. He reached around and took the stiff brocade by its trimmed opening. She shrugged while he lifted it off then down her arms. As he removed the heavy garment, she sighed, making him smile. He spread it next to his *uenoginu*.

"This is wet, too," she said, coming out of her mantle. She handed him the thin, damp silk.

He didn't have much room left on the floor, but he laid it out as best he could. He relaxed, liking how she now wore a dress, *uchigi* layers, and chemise as she did when she taught him at her home.

"It's a garden," she said with a smile, indicating colorful cushions atop the green rug. She sank to a red cushion and brought her long hair over one shoulder. "I think someone planned this."

"It wasn't me," he said in answer to her questioning glance. With his foot, he nudged a brown cushion close to hers then settled upon it. "You're beautiful."

She demurred. "I'm wet. My face must be a mess."

Tentatively, he reached for her hairline. She didn't shy, so he wiped dotted powder from her forehead. Her revealed skin was pale and translucent – far lovelier than the powder that whitened her. Their eyes met, and he held her gaze as he continued to strip away her cosmetic.

"I know you told me you're not one to enter into frivolous love affairs," he said low. There was nothing frivolous about what he felt for her. "You also said I'm no good for you."

She touched a hand to his knee. "I'm no good for you, either."

She was entirely too good for him. "Lady Kirei, sometimes none of that matters. Sometimes what's meant to be defies what men and society say should be."

"You don't want me," she said, shaking her head as a sadness crept into her gaze.

"I want you. I want you so much I can't think straight." He wiped powder from her chin with his thumb then let his gaze go to her mouth as he traced the curve of her bottom lip. "Tell me you want me, too." He looked to her eyes. "Tell me I'm not alone in this."

"You're not alone, but we can't. I'll break your heart. Don't you see? I'll be promised to a gentleman's bed and have to move into his house. I'll belong to him."

His stomach twisted painfully. "I'm a Minamoto, and I'm told I enjoy the emperor's favor. Surely that means something to your uncle."

"It doesn't." She lowered her eyes. "I'm a Fujiwara, and I enjoy both the emperor's and the empress' favor. It's not enough. To him, you're a countrified nobody. He thinks Emperor Ichijō will lose interest in your crude ways, and you'll return to your distant province never to be seen again."

"Is that what you think?" he asked quietly.

"I think..."

He cupped her cheek and braced internally. "Don't be afraid to tell me the truth. Be honest."

"I think Ojisan doesn't know the emperor well at all.

Emperor Ichijō doesn't choose his friends lightly, and he never turns his back on them." She met his gaze, her voice going soft. "I think he doesn't know you, either. You're unrefined in some ways, but never crude. Certainly not insensitive or uneducated. I see a depth in you that's clear evidence of your birth. You're *good people*, Lord Yūkan, and anyone who despises you for being countrified has to equally despise me."

She approved of him. He took a moment to bask in it. How had he come so far in her estimation in only a week?

"Tell me you want me as much as I want you."

The sadness in her gaze multiplied. "It wouldn't make a difference."

"It would to me. Don't say it if you don't feel it. If you do, though, I need to know. Please."

Her eyes went to his mouth. "I want you, too."

Desire consumed him. He moved forward and pressed his lips to hers. He slid his hand into her hair and around her nape. He didn't need to urge her, however. She leaned into him, deepening the kiss. She splayed her hands on his chest. Warmth from her palms penetrated his thin *kosode*.

Overhead, the rain pounded the roof, filling the building with a powerful rumble. Nature's fury reflected the roiling hunger he had for Kirei. He wrapped his arms around her and hugged her close. She sent her arms around his neck. Catching at his shoulders, her sleeves bunched as her bare forearms caressed the sides of his neck.

He groaned his pleasure, and she opened. He sent his tongue along hers, completely absorbed in her taste. Her feel. Completely lost in her scent and softness. In his arms, he held an incredible, intelligent lady of learning and talent. No woman he'd ever encountered came close in comparison.

Yet she was real. She wasn't a goddess or imperial consort. He could kiss her. Touch her. He adored her, and the more he got to know her, the more he was convinced she was meant for him. Him alone.

His task now was to endeavor to deserve her.

\*    \*    \*    \*

The brazier's heat paled next to the inferno bursting within Kirei. Yūkan's kisses set her on fire. This man, whom she'd decided to disdain from their first meeting, had somehow gotten inside her. Whenever he came in sight, she could only think how much she wanted him to kiss her.

This was wrong, and they'd both suffer in the end. At the moment, however, only his kisses mattered. Only being next to him held any importance.

She currently grew closer to taking a man to her bed than she ever had, and it scared her. She couldn't stop, though. He had become irresistible.

"Yūkan," she whispered against his lips when he withdrew his sensual tongue.

"Hm?" The pressure of his hand rode her spine to her hip.

"We should stop." He had to because she couldn't. She moved her lips against his, loving the feel of his kiss and the pulse of pleasure sparking in her womb.

"Why?" He slanted his face over her, one way then the other, commanding the contact of their mouths.

"Before we're discovered." Before she no longer cared if they were discovered. Before she submitted fully and did something she'd regret. She whimpered as the pulse moved lower into her crease.

Pressing harder against him, she opened. He invaded, his moan resonating in her throat. She met his tongue in a questing duel.

The only thing between him and her exploring fingers was his white raw silk *kosode*. He was hard to her soft. Angles and planes to her round curves. Dense to her slender. His rugged man's body made her that much more feminine next to him. He brought out her sensuality and gentleness.

Most of the ladies she knew would wrinkle their noses

and call him ugly. She suspected they wouldn't if they had such a man kissing them like this. They'd only ever had the soft, feminine gentlemen of Kyō to use in forming their ideal of masculine beauty.

Yūkan had a build more like a common laborer, but his intellect and sensibility, not to mention his family of birth, behind it made him sexy rather than coarse. Kirei couldn't stop touching him.

She caressed the hot skin of his neck then reached high and unfastened the ribbon binding his hair. The black length fell past his shoulders. It came forward to mingle with hers while brushing her forehead and cheek with a feather-light grazing.

Everything about him appealed to her.

She withdrew from his kiss. Staring at her lap, she let her fingers slowly descend his firm chest while she attempted to catch her breath.

"Kirei," he said, his voice quiet, reverent, full of tenderness. He sent the backs of his fingers along her cheek to her ear then eased the weight of her hair over her shoulder and down her back. His large hands held her by the waist. "You are...remarkable."

So was he. He made her feel—

Song leeched through the rain.

"Sounds like the party's resumed," he said. He didn't retreat, however. As if still poised to kiss her, he stared at her lips. The corners of his eyes crinkled slightly.

"Should we join the others?" *Say no.*

"Our robes are still wet." He inched closer.

"Are they?" she whispered, acutely aware of his desire. *Kiss me.*

"Probably better to stay here," he murmured. His nose nearly touched hers.

"In that case..." She tipped her chin, pressing her lips to his.

"You're wonderful," he said against her mouth. He

embraced her. Falling backward, he took her with him.

She giggled. Lying atop him, she stared into his eyes while her voluminous robes settled around him and her hair tumbled to his side. She admitted, "You're not who I thought you were."

"Come here." He put his hand to the back of her head and brought her down so their lips could touch.

Even through her many layers, her body reacted to his strong length stretched beneath her. Her legs sank between his. Despite the amount of clothing between them, she didn't miss that she was pelvis to pelvis with him.

The clothing was too much. She wanted his hands on her. On her skin. In her hair.

Her heart pounded. Her swelling crease throbbed. She wanted relief, and only Yūkan could provide it.

She broke the kiss and parted her lips to suggest they take his carriage to her uncle's mansion when a voice clearing at the door caught her words in her throat.

## Chapter Twelve

Yūkan helped Kirei into a more dignified position on a bright orange cushion. Shinsetsu shot him a conspiratorial smile while Amai followed him in.

The young lady sent Kirei a frown, and whispered to their host, "I thought we were going to be alone."

*Hypocrite.* Lady Amai could be alone with Shinsetsu, but her cousin wasn't allowed to sneak away with Yūkan? It should've bothered him more, but Kirei had prepared him for this kind of prejudice.

"Join us," he said, waving their host to sit. Glad for the billow of his trousers that hid proof of his arousal, he asked, "Are your robes wet? We're drying ours near the brazier."

The young gentleman shrugged and plopped onto the red cushion Kirei had occupied earlier. Amai, however, removed her tan and orange damask jacket. She spread it on the floor in a far corner then adjusted her yellow and orange checked mantle.

"Come sit by me," said Kirei, patting a dark green cushion next to hers. She cut Yūkan a disappointed smile, which gave him hope.

Amai settled and touched fingertips to her cousin's cheek. "What happened? All your powder's gone and your face is red. Are you sick? He helped you?" She sent a contrite glance his way. "Thank you for bringing my cousin in out of the cold rain. I'm sorry for judging you. I put too much faith in what my father says, and sometimes he's wrong."

"Lady Kirei's well-being is my first priority." Yūkan hid silent laughter in a long bow. He didn't straighten until he had his features securely schooled. It wasn't exactly a lie.

Amai's eyes widened with a genuine smile. "You really are a good person. You do honor to the Minamoto name. Kirei tried to tell me, and now I see it."

He looked to Kirei. She'd spoken well of him to others? Against the opinions already established about him? He whispered close to her ear, "Thank you."

She offered the faintest of nods.

Oblivious, Amai worked to artfully arrange her robes around her. "Shall we play a game?"

"What game?" asked Shinsetsu, yawning and stretching his arms over his head.

The young woman pouted. "You're not going to take a nap, are you? You've got guests...and me."

Yūkan tapped Kirei's arm and raised his eyebrows in question. Her young cousin's conclusion provided the perfect excuse, and he'd take full advantage if she wanted. She nodded again then dramatically placed the back of her hand to her forehead.

He cleared his throat. "I can see Lady Kirei's still not feeling better. I should take her home."

"Oh." Amai sent her a worried look. "Do you want to take my father's carriage? Shinsetsu can escort me home in his when the party's over."

"Or you can stay," offered the young gentleman. "I have to get back to my party soon, anyway. I wouldn't want anyone to accuse me of being rude."

Yūkan went to the end of the room and collected his mostly-dry *uenoginu*. He put it on then gave his host a courteous bow. "Lord Shinsetsu, I'm grateful for your kind generosity. I suspect Lady Amai would appreciate a private conversation with you, however. It's best I get Lady Kirei home where she can rest."

Amai's sweet features brightened.

Standing, Kirei said, "I'll go home in Yūkan's carriage. Something tells me you'll be wanting Ojisan's carriage for the sake of propriety."

Her pretty cousin giggled.

"Okay," he said, retrieving her mantle from the floor and holding it open so she could put it on. "Everything's decided. Let's get going."

The rain quieted some. From the main building's veranda, a cheer arose. Shinsetsu grinned. "They're playing a game. Somebody's had to drink from the *cup of defeat*. It's early. They're going to be drunk sooner than usual." He laughed.

"All the more reason for us to leave now," said Kirei. She fetched her jacket from beside the brazier and draped it over her head. "Goodnight."

Amai and Shinsetsu only had eyes for each other, though.

Chuckling, Yūkan ushered Kirei out. They put on their shoes at the back exit, but he turned her around. "Let's go out the north side. We don't want half the gentlemen in the Sixth Ward to see you leaving with me."

When they passed by the warm room, he glanced inside. Shinsetsu and Amai were engaged in a long kiss, and three layers of her robes already hung off of her shoulders. Grinning, he hurried his own beautiful lady outside.

He led her along the front veranda, making sure at each corner that they'd go unobserved. The wide porch followed the entire west wing and main building. A small bridge formed a crossing over a wide creek feeding Shinsetsu's garden pond, and linked the main building to the east wing.

He sent her across ahead of him, making sure not to look back in case anyone from the party glimpsed them. Shadows obscured their clothing, so from the back, they could be any couple.

He followed the veranda around to the east wing's wall side, then descended a set of steps to wet grass and escorted her to the east gate where the guests' carriages lined the street outside. Her soft hand briefly brushed his as they passed through. He couldn't get her alone fast enough.

Stepping out onto the street, he hailed his driver. Kirei kept to the gateway's added darkness until his conveyance pulled under the cover. Once he had her safely in, he waved to his driver.

"Take the long way, and go slowly," he said.

His servant nodded, and he climbed in. The carriage rocked gently as he settled onto his cushion. Light from the cabin's lantern cast a romantic glow on her bare face, and he marveled that such an accomplished beauty as she could have affection for a 'countrified' provincial like him.

He had enjoyed success in the world, and he'd earned his grandfather's pride when it mattered most. Fudōno admired him, and his servants respected him. So, in his way, he was accomplished, too. Just not in the eyes of Kyō society. Not in *her* eyes.

"Have you considered living somewhere other than the imperial city?" he asked then immediately regretted it. Of the characteristics of the *good people* he'd learned, Kyō was the only place worth living.

A small smile curled the corners of her mouth. "I miss the country, of course. It was my home and all I knew most of my life. Think of yourself, though. This is the only place a person can enjoy the pleasure of polite society. Nowhere else offers the kind of artistic sharing and displays this city does. Where else would we hear poetry as fine as Lady Rikō's, or singing as perfect as Lord Kowai's?"

"So you're saying you wouldn't want to leave?" He'd live in the city if it meant being near her. If she could love him, though, and agree to marry him, he'd prefer knowing whether or not she'd be open to living at his estate in Echigo.

*    *    *    *

Kirei fisted a hand in her jacket's brocade and dragged it off of her head. Since moving to Kyō, she had only wanted to return to the country. In this strange and unexpected twist, however, she had begun to develop an esteem, no, a passion for this man. She didn't want it, but she also couldn't deny it. He needed to know she wouldn't leave him, especially since he'd expressed an interest in joining the community.

"Living away from the imperial city can make it nearly impossible for an official to earn promotion," she warned.

"You're not an official." His eyes narrowed as he studied her.

"No, but you might become one."

"That's what you want? For me to become an official?" He leaned closer, despite the sway of the carriage. "For me to become a true gentleman of Kyō?"

He'd implied it's what *he* wanted, and leaving the imperial city would cripple such a career. He'd have to stay here. At the moment, she couldn't stand the thought of being where he wasn't. She didn't know how it'd happened or why, but she also couldn't ignore what formed between them.

She wanted his good opinion. She wanted his kisses and caresses. And she wanted him to know she'd support his wishes. For the first time since coming here, she actually wanted to live in Kyō.

"Yes," she said. "I'll do everything I can to teach you what's expected. What you need to know. But nobody can know about..."

He closed the distance between them and captured her lips in a brief but sensual kiss. "This?" he asked. "They can't know about this?" He kissed her again, longer and deeper.

When his lips left hers, she sighed. "Yes. They can't know." Her voice sounded rough and breathy, even to her own ears.

"Because of my *career*."

"Yes." She sought his lips once more, but he backed out of reach.

"You think our being together will harm my chances."

Not harm. Destroy. "Yes. It might not matter if you also

showed interest in a lady of legitimate standing—"

"Another lady?" His brows slammed together over the bridge of his nose.

"If ministers saw that you pursued a lady of Kyō for your wife, and only spent time with me for fun—"

"For fun?" His scowl darkened.

She laughed. She wanted to kiss the ferocity from his countenance. "Would you please stop interrupting?"

"This is ridiculous," he said.

"This is the way of the aristocracy. I know you don't understand. Bear with me."

He huffed.

Fighting a smile, she said, "Let me tell you about my father. He and my mother are both of good birth and fine sensibility. They met and married here. My mother's family was overjoyed by such an auspicious match. You see, my father was a Minister of the Fifth Rank with potential for promotion."

"I thought you were from the country," he said, his scowl melting.

She nodded and continued. "Theirs was a love-match. They lived in their own mansion in the up-to-date fashion, instead of with her family. She gave him a son, Mezurashii. My father says he was never happier. When I was two years old, my parents had been married ten years, and my father hadn't added a single concubine to his household."

"Where's the problem?" He took her hand as though he couldn't stand to be near without touching her.

She stared at their clasped hands and ran her thumb along his. "My father was exceptional. He wanted only my mother. By that time, he occupied a high position in the Fourth Rank, however. He was encouraged to take consorts to set a good example and to improve his chances of promotion into the Third Rank, but he ignored the advice."

Yūkan squeezed his eyes tightly and gave his head a shake. "Explain to me how the number of women a man has can have anything to do with his work."

She thought for a moment. "It has to do with ability, really. A man of common birth is expected to find it a challenge to divide his attentions after he marries. A man of position, especially if he's serious-minded, is expected to take a wife and at least one consort and a number of concubines. It's normal, respectable behavior for a gentleman."

"It still don't see—"

"Let me put it this way. A large family is invaluable. The reality is that women die young. It's a sad truth. So a gentleman who has several women bearing him children gives him added status. It's an indication of his wealth and position, and it attests to his health and charm." She gave his fingers a squeeze, willing him to understand. "The argument for a man taking many women into his household is eminently reasonable."

"I don't know about that, but I can see now how a man who refuses to take more than one might be considered anti-social." He didn't appear pleased with the prospect, though.

"Or abnormal, in the least. I understand your travels might've skewed—"

"Lovely Kirei, I'm more than familiar with our attitude of marriage as a function of family welfare and separate from love and sex, which are needs of an individual. Your readings in Chinese literature show you that China shares our values. I've been there and seen it firsthand. It's the same in Korea. But have you considered for a second that I, as an educated and thinking man, might have developed my own set of values? That I might've decided for myself, without any outside influence, that one wife is all I want or need? And maybe for me, love and sex aren't separate from marriage."

She inhaled slowly as her stomach somersaulted. Here sat a man she found attractive above any other, and he had come to the same conclusions about what he wanted in his marriage as she had. Her head swam with the idea for a second.

"Tell me I'm wrong," he challenged.

"I can't," she whispered.

The carriage came to a halt, and her heart sank. The

night would stretch for hours yet, and she wasn't ready to end her activities. End her time with him. She stared at him, trying to gain enough courage to invite him to her chamber.

"Damn it," he said to the ceiling. "I told him to take the long way."

"I think he did. I don't live far from Shinsetsu." Her eyes went to his lips. There were so many reasons for her to go inside alone. So many reasons to discourage his pursuit of her. The idea of never kissing that mouth again was more than she could cogitate.

As if reading her thoughts, he cupped her chin and pressed his lips to hers. She sighed, pulling him close and kissing him harder. When he touched the tip of his tongue to her mouth's crease, she opened. Her heart beat faster. She closed her eyes.

Their tongues entered into a leisurely, sensual dance, and Kirei pressed against his muscular, unyielding body. She detested the layers that kept her from truly feeling him. The pace of his kiss didn't match the rhythm of her heartbeat. Every inch of her, every piece of her, yearned for him in a way that was both alarming and exciting.

For once, she would let emotion outweigh reason. She pulled away and met his hooded gaze. For once, she'd decide on an action that wasn't in her best interest. She whispered, "Come inside with me. Come to my bed."

## Chapter Thirteen

Yūkan reeled. He'd longed to hear her say those words since he had set eyes on her the first time. If his hardened member had any say, he'd scramble from his carriage in an instant. Sometime in the past two days, however, he'd realized she could be it. She could be the one woman for him.

He'd waited his entire life for her. He could wait a while longer. He wanted more than lust or passion from her. He wanted her love. Her loyalty. Her undying commitment.

"As much as I want to," he said and placed a chaste kiss to the tip of her nose, "I'm going to return to the Nine Fold Enclosure and claim my own bed tonight."

Hurt and disappointment flashed in her eyes.

"There's time," he said quietly. "We will. Just not yet."

It was too soon. He wanted her forever, not just one night. Still, his desire begged to differ. Hadn't they discussed the benefits of promiscuity? Hadn't she issued an invitation and told him minutes ago that their affair would be commonly accepted if he made a show of pursuing other ladies?

Then again, perhaps she'd said that in way of convincing herself. In all honesty, what legitimate lady would tolerate, much less welcome, his attentions? Kirei had spent the past week telling him how backward and unappealing his countrified manners were. She'd had to defend him to her own cousin.

No, the time wasn't right.

"Don't come for a lesson tomorrow," she said, her face a mask as she moved to pass him.

"Why?" He quickly opened the door and exited then helped her out. Was she angry he wouldn't sleep with her? That couldn't be correct. She had flaws, but a shallow character wasn't one.

"I need time to think." She climbed out then hesitated, glancing at him from the corner of her eye before heading for the wall gate of her uncle's mansion.

After she passed through, he went and leaned on the open gate to watch and make sure she made it inside without mishap. She didn't glance back, and her withdrawal felt like a sharp blade in his gut. He secured the gate closed. At his carriage, he told his driver to take him for a drive through the city.

Before long, they headed south on the main thoroughfare. The early hour made for heavy traffic on Red Bird Avenue and, therefore, slow going. He didn't mind, however. It gave him a chance to admire the view of blooming willows reflected in still waters and the colorful silks spilling from carriage windows.

Kirei had told him not to see her tomorrow, but he suspected she didn't need time to think. He'd thrown her off balance. Had her confused. She wanted time to convince herself to push him away. She'd spend tomorrow thinking of a way to escape her tutoring obligation.

He wouldn't let her. She wanted him, but he doubted she realized it went deeper than physical desire. He needed time with her, and the tutoring gave him the necessary excuse. Besides, if he planned to win a position in the government and in high society to suit her, he needed her expertise to guide him.

Lost in thought, he didn't comprehend that his carriage had come to a halt until a loud knock on the door made him jerk. He glanced out the window to find Yoki grinning at him from his own carriage. The drivers had pulled near the center of the three-hundred-foot-wide roadway, and traffic moved uninterrupted around them.

"I thought you went to Lord Shinsetsu's drinking party," said his friend.

"I did." Yūkan sighed heavily.

"Can you come to my house, or are you on your way somewhere else?"

Did he have the patience for the gentleman's dramatics? Maybe his friend could shed some light on the mystery of Lady Kirei. "I can come. I was headed back to my room to read. Nothing important."

Yoki shuddered. "I've saved you from yourself."

His carriage rolled forward and Yūkan's made a sluggish U-turn to fall in behind. The ride gave him plenty of time to contemplate how he would counter Kirei's attempt to cease their lessons. Yoki lived further down the same lane but on the opposite, more elevated side. As each property was three and a half square acres, however, it was a goodly distance. Soon they stopped in front of a well-lit gate more elaborate than Kirei's.

His friend led the way in with a welcome wave. Inside the mansion's main building, opulence ruled. Mats trimmed in blue damask formed a sitting area in full view of the main entrance. Curtains of matching damask hung from rafters and formed sidewalls for the sitting room. A bank of gaily painted folding screens created the room's backdrop.

Yoki bypassed the room, skirting blue curtains as he beckoned Yūkan to follow him farther into the building. He passed through a gallery where scrolls of gorgeously wrought poetry hung on display from tall wooden partitions, and then into a room created by painted rice paper screens erected between the wooden partitions and the outer section wall. A few lush gray and black arm-cushions dotted a brown rug. Stained green bamboo blinds hung closed from an elegant green and black patterned brocade valance that ran the length of the entire main building.

A low desk sat in one corner, strewn with a plethora of color stationary and clean writing brushes. Yoki, however, sank to a cushion behind a table at the center of the room. He indicated Yūkan should have a seat on a cushion at the table's other side.

"I'm surprised you're home tonight," said Yūkan, accepting the invitation to sit. "I thought you went out every night."

Yoki smiled. "I try, anyway. Sitting home alone with my dreary thoughts is depressing. And I'm not home." He held a finger to his lips. "This is a quick stop before I head to my final destination." He opened a handsome writing box made of nettle tree wood with silver fittings.

"Then why ask me here?" Yūkan didn't attempt to keep irritation from his voice.

"Because I haven't seen you in a while, and I enjoy spending time with you. You may be a favorite of the emperor's, but you're a favorite of mine, too." He studied him a second. "Oh, no."

"What?"

"You're thwarted in love."

He laughed outright. "You're good at reading people, but not perfect. I'm afraid I did the thwarting."

Yoki chuckled and opened his box. "An unattractive lady propositioned you at Shinsetsu's party?"

"Hardly."

"Then wh—" His friend froze, a hand in the box. "Lady Kirei?"

Yūkan held his silence. He refused to gossip about his own life.

"You fool," Yoki whispered. He blinked, his narrow lids barely moving. "Do you have any idea what a rare honor it is to be invited to Kirei's bed?"

Huffing, Yūkan fingered the edge of the table. "I'm beginning to learn being invited to a lady's bed in this city has nothing to do with honor. Married, unmarried, everyone sleeps with whomever they please." Not that Kirei fell in that category, but still... "Isn't that where you're headed?"

"And I thought Kirei was a prig. I think you're actually worse." He pointed toward the gallery. "Go get in that carriage of yours, ride to her uncle's house, and claim that stunning woman like the man you are."

"Maybe she's all I want. Maybe she's all I need. And maybe I don't want to turn something that could be meaningful into something tawdry and carnal by moving too soon and making it solely about pleasure-seeking."

"Speaking of carnal," murmured the nobleman, once again getting busy at his table. He pulled from the box everything he required to draw, including a clean sheet of white vellum. He inked his brush and swept it across the page. "Yūkan, you're making this into a bigger deal than it is, though like I said, it was an enormous privilege to be asked into Kirei's *hakama*."

"I'm not making it into a big deal. It is, in itself, a big deal." He followed the brush's seemingly effortless strokes.

Yoki paused to add more ink to his bristles then resumed his drawing. "Lady Kirei understands better than most the reality of relationships. It's the way of the world. Sleep with her now and offer her reassurance that she'll occupy first place in your heart. She'll never be more than a consort, so it's the most she can expect."

"She deserves better." Anger pushed his temperature hotter.

"She runs in court circles. Casual affairs are commonplace. I often visit women behind their *kichō* then leave at dawn before we can be discovered." His friend's lips parted on a knowing smile.

Yūkan leaned forward. "If it's such an accepted practice, how come I hear Empress Akiko and the higher-ranked ladies-in-waiting criticizing court ladies for their promiscuity?"

"They're not criticized for having sex. They're criticized for not being more discriminating." He laughed. "A lady should be devoted to only one gentleman...at a time."

He sighed. This was getting him nowhere. "I should go."

"To Kirei?"

"I closed *that* blind for tonight."

"There's always tomorrow." Yoki finished his drawing

with a flourish.

Yūkan stood, getting a good look at the erotic picture. "That's disgusting."

"It is not. It'd be disgusting if I'd made her naked," Yoki argued on a shudder.

"You think a naked woman is disgusting?" He fought the urge to gawk at this gentleman who dared call himself a man.

"Anyone naked is disgusting. Like a plucked chicken – all pale and goose bumped and their bone and muscle shapes showing under their skin. Who wants to look at that?" The aristocrat picked up the drawing and fanned it back and forth. He turned it to face Yūkan. "No, this is beautiful. See how her pleasure opening shows only among the many layers of her silk? It's like the center of an opened flower – the petals soft and colorful, and the hidden sex smelling sweet. Promising ultimate pleasure. Irresistible in its soft wetness that I just have to enter."

"Is this lady anyone special?"

Yoki stood. "Tonight she is. Tomorrow? Well, that'll be determined by how we get along tonight."

\*　\*　\*　\*

Her eyes burning, Kirei pulled her lantern closer and read the same Chinese verse for the third time. It did no good. She couldn't concentrate.

He'd turned her down. It made no sense because he'd been eager and excited. She didn't doubt it for a second. So why'd he leave?

Closing her eyes, she relived his kisses. His caresses. The heat coming off of him. His breaths close to her ear. She'd never been so aroused. Thinking about him had her nipples hardening.

"If I don't stop, I'm going to go insane," she whispered.

Maybe he would change his mind and come back. She wouldn't send him away, though she didn't hold out hope. He'd promised they'd make love one day, but not tonight. Had he considered there might not be a someday? That tonight might be all they had?

Giving up on the Chinese poetry altogether, she pushed to her feet and went to her window. She rolled up the bamboo blind, relaxing as cool air hit her face. She inhaled the refreshing night, soaking in the scent of pine and cherry blossom.

Her birds chirped insistently, so she opened their cage. They joined her at the sill. As they hopped and sang, she envied their simple joy. There had been a time not so long ago when a fragrant breeze had held a measure of happiness for her. Life had grown too complicated.

Now, she couldn't get past her unsatisfied longing and the suspicion that this time next year would likely find her trapped and miserable in an unwanted arrangement with a gentleman not of her choosing. Her uncle had given her a year. It was more than most others would've offered. Perhaps he was right. Perhaps she had wiled away too much time already.

Life hadn't always been so cruelly unfair. Maybe it should've been. Maybe her father did her no favor in letting her experience independence and an unladylike higher education in the country. Then maybe she'd be more prepared for this forced limitation. Then maybe she'd be more accepting of her fate. Maybe.

Instead, she wasn't used to this. A year in Kyō had made her acutely aware of her position. People talked of her upbringing in 'undesirable surroundings' and how it was a shame. She didn't regret living her childhood in the country, however. And though a more restricted rearing might've readied her for the life of a consort, she couldn't disallow its value in making her who she was. However, none of her logic helped her accept her uncle's wishes.

Still, her only alternative was to return to her father's estate in Shinano. Which presented the worst circumstance – to go home and suffer the pain and incessant guilt from those hated events that led to her brother's death, or to stay and endure the prince's undesirable attentions but have friends nearby? She had thought the latter might be bearable, but Yūkan changed everything. Now she wanted another choice altogether. A choice her uncle would fight to prevent.

Sighing, she closed the blind. She shooed the birds to their cage but left it open. At least she'd have time to think tomorrow, since she'd told Yūkan not to come. The knowledge didn't get her to sleep any faster, but she could breathe. Under the circumstances, that was something.

Uma's humming woke her, and she blinked at her maid. "Are you early today?"

"You're late abed this morning." Her maid handed her a folded note, lit incense, and worked to set out a simple ensemble in spring colors. "I'd have left you to sleep, but you mentioned saying prayers during the sun's rising. You don't have much longer if you still want to."

If she'd known Yūkan would haunt her night, she'd have withheld her request. It made no sense to try to fall asleep again. She'd be wasting her time. Thoughts of him would only find their way in and sabotage her attempt.

"I'll dress myself," Kirei said, rising. She unfolded the note, a warning from the Yin-Yang Ministry that she should remain home today. She chuckled. "Please open the sitting area to the garden. Removing two wall sections should be enough. It's not raining, is it?"

"No, my lady. Shall I bring you something to eat?"

"Bring a tray to the sitting area. I'll eat after I pray." If she had an appetite. Last night's embarrassing turn down still had her stomach in bunching knots.

Uma bowed and exited, closing the door without a sound.

If Kirei had ever needed blessings from her god, she needed them now. She quickly stripped from her *kosode* and *hakama*. After bathing with a damp, sweet-smelling cloth her maid had left, she donned a clean white *kosode* and newly

laundered *hakama*. In minutes, she'd dressed in five layers of
varying white and green *uchigi* over an extra-long peach
chemise.

She gave her hair a few flicks over her arm to smooth the
strands then hurried to the sitting area. Two manservants
finished rolling a blind. They secured it above its opening at
each end and in the center. With the space now open to a lush
garden view and their work done, the men smoothed their
coarse gray *kosode*, bowed, and rushed from her wing to the
main building.

The sun shone brightly at the horizon. It burnished the
garden in golden light as though artists had spent the night
brushing gold leaf on the eastern side of every tall plant. Two
ducks alighted onto Ojisan's small lake, their wide, orange feet
splashing the water's surface before their fat, brown bodies
settled. One quacked quietly, seeming to admonish the other
for splashing too much.

Kirei chuckled as she fetched her prayer book from a low
table against the wall displaying her instruments. Her mind
sharpened amidst the infusion of cool, fresh air into the room,
and she took a deep breath. No surprises today. No unexpected
summons to court, no irritating conversations with Ojisan, and
no unnerving visits from Yūkan. Though she'd like to admonish
Yūkan for denying her.

She went to her knees, facing the garden, then scooted
so she sat half inside and half on the outer veranda. Setting her
shoulders, she flipped to a well-used page in her book. She
cleared her throat and began intoning. A minute in, a male
voice joined hers.

*   *   *   *

Yūkan closed the door to Kirei's wing and moved across
her public room, his feet keeping time with the rhythm of her
words. He joined her in the *Namu Amida Butsu* formula, its
words a part of him because he'd said them so often.

She looked gorgeous. Clean and young and inviting. Her pale robes mirrored the dew-glistening vegetation serving as her background, and the pinkish-orange of her chemise acted as a dash of sunlight at hem and sleeves.

He sat and scooted into the opening beside her. He'd expected her to demand he leave, or to lacerate his ego with her sharp tongue at the least. She didn't stop, however.

She cut her gaze his way for a second then returned her attention to the garden. He adjusted his pitch a tad deeper. She held steady. Together, they meditated on Amida's name in enchanting harmony. They finished on a long note as sunlight went from molten gold to liquid yellow, signaling dawn's end.

"I'm mad at you," she said quietly, not sparing him a glance.

He followed her gaze to a couple of ducks swimming circles on placid water. "For leaving when you asked me to stay?"

"And for coming today when I said not to."

A breeze ruffled her sleeve, mussing the layers. Restoring their neatness, he smoothed a hand across the incredibly soft fabric. He studied her lovely, pale profile. She didn't wear cosmetics this morning, and he caressed the back of his fingers along her cheek.

"I had to see you. I need you to understand that I refused your bed because..." He swallowed hard.

"Because why?" Her eyebrows arched slightly.

He took a deep breath. "Because there's more to life than beauty and pleasure. I've been watching gentlemen at court, and I doubt any of them have the education necessary to fully understand the Lotus texts. They don't really read them, either. They quote a few memorable lines from the beginning, middle, and end. Or worse, they pay priests to intone the sutras for them. It's shallow and meaningless. They don't care."

"And you do? You fully understand the Lotus? You care?" She looked him in the eyes and arched her eyebrows higher.

He leaned nearer. "Yes, I care. Yes, I read the texts in their entirety again and again. Each time, I discover a new truth. A better understanding. I'm a deeper person than any I've met here, save you and Emperor Ichijō. I need a deeper experience than one night of pleasure with you. You deserve a real commitment."

Her brow furrowed, but she didn't move. "Don't you believe that all is vanity?"

"No."

"Buddha teaches that all existence involves suffering."

He reached into the folds of her sleeve and found her fingers. Taking her hand in his, he said, "He doesn't teach that we have to suffer alone. Amida's merciful. He promised to deny himself nirvana until everyone in the world is saved. Do you believe this?"

She slowly nodded. "I adhere to the Tendai and the belief in salvation by Amida. Whatever anyone else does, I'll always recite my prayers to Amida Buddha."

"Then let's look beyond the present. Beyond this nonsense of day-to-day pleasure with no meaning past the moment. These gentlemen seem either incapable or unwilling to look to the future. They put their energy into seeking enjoyment and securing promotions."

"Are you saying you've changed your mind?" Her bottom lip protruded a bit. "Are you giving up your pursuit of a government position and a place in Kyō society?"

He brought her hand to his lips and placed a lingering kiss upon her smooth fingers. "I plan to stay. I plan to make a place for you in my life."

Chapter Fourteen

A place for her. Kirei pulled her cool hand from his
warm one. Yūkan couldn't have stated more clearly that he'd
begun to think like everyone else. That his position in a
ministry would make it impossible for him to take her as his
proper wife.

Everything he'd said this morning had been right, except
those final hated words.

The more she grew to like and respect him, the more it
bothered her that he wanted a life here. Rank would demand he
obtain multiple women for his household, a proper wife, and
children with each of them. She'd never considered herself a
jealous woman, but with this man, she was in terrible danger of
becoming one of those despised harridans.

Yūkan was so handsome she had to fight the urge to
stare. He wore no hat atop his thick hair, and he let the length
fall to his broad back from its tie rather than securing it in a
topknot. His brown skin radiated health in the warm morning
light, and the square lines of his face spoke of strength and
determination. His blue and gray brocade glimmered when he
moved, representative of his very fine taste and vast wealth.
With him, she would never want for anything. Not even love.

His education rivaled her own, and this morning's visit
revealed he shared her religious beliefs, too. No other man
compared.

"Perhaps," she said in as bored a tone as she could
muster, "it would be best if you go."

"Best for whom?"

For her. She didn't want him to see her confused and

unsure. "Aren't you tired of my lessons?"

"Never."

He lied, but a smile tugged at the corners of her mouth.

He studied her. "I can see you're uncomfortable. I'm not leaving, though. Maybe this would be a good time for music?"

The idea of music after prayers sounded wonderful, if he could actually play. He'd surprised her often enough, however. She didn't know whether to prepare her ears for a performance as poor as his poetry or to expect a melody fit for court. She only had one way to find out.

They scooted inside, and he helped her to her feet. She pointed to a black *biwa* superbly embellished with mother-of-pearl swans, gold leaf flowers, and clusters of red and green painted flower buds made from tiny shells. It belonged to Amai – a gift from Ojisan when she'd been declared a master player.

Kirei settled behind a seven-string zither. Its rich reddish-brown wood gleamed from a recent cleaning. A glance at Yūkan, however, made her frown. He'd set the *biwa* on his lap, strings up.

"That's how you learned to play?" she asked.

He glanced quickly at the instrument and chuckled. His lips quirked into a confident, entirely masculine half-smile she found incredibly sexy. "Funny story. Do you want to hear it?"

"Is it a long story?"

"No."

"Okay, then tell me." She fought a smile as his lips parted on a white tooth-filled grin.

"My grandfather began teaching me the *biwa* when I was seven. An ambitious undertaking, I have to admit, since it was difficult to keep me seated very long at that age. He would meet me the moment I got up in the morning, before I had a chance to run out the door on my all-day adventures." He laughed.

"You ran wild?" Kirei sniffed. No wonder he hadn't perfected his writing. He'd lacked discipline.

"Only during that time. My father traveled for long stretches, and that spring, my mother had stayed to her bed with a difficult pregnancy. Anyway, a month into my *biwa* lessons, I fell from a tree and hurt my wrist." He held up his right arm.

"I'm not surprised." She imagined him as a good-looking boy who climbed mountains and swam rivers. He'd gone from exploring the countryside to exploring the world.

"My grandfather didn't want to stop my lessons. He knew I'd forget everything I'd learned if we took a break. So he had me rest the instrument on my lap." He set the butt of his right hand onto the *biwa* and strummed its strings with his fingers. "See? I can engage the strings without using my wrist much."

She arched her brows. "And you've been playing that way ever since?"

"My wrist didn't stop hurting until the season turned cold. By then, my habits were established. I think my grandfather got so used to seeing me play this way that he never thought about changing it." He strummed a B major chord.

"It's nice that you have a sense of humor about it. You're at a social disadvantage, though, Lord Yūkan. Emperor Ichijō wants you to succeed, so we want to avoid habits that would subject you to public ridicule."

"You're too uptight," he teased.

"You're not taking this seriously enough." She adjusted the collar of her dress with an agitated jerk. He was such a contradiction.

"You're right," he said, plucking a quiet, random melody with the tips of his fingers. "I'm sorry."

She studied his handsome, contrite visage. "Why are you doing this? Why do you want to live in Kyō and be accepted by its *good people*?"

His gaze went to her mouth, and he licked his lips.

A familiar tingling began low in her belly. "Are you doing this because the emperor wants it?"

He slowly shook his head. His lids drooped a bit over obsidian eyes.

"For your aunt? For Fudōno and the business?"

He continued to shake his head.

Her stomach wrenched. She whispered, "For me?"

He went still, his stare intense.

"Lord Yūkan," she said, but her voice broke. She cleared her throat. "Please don't go to this trouble for me. I'll only disappoint you."

His gaze softened then dropped to the *biwa*. "Perhaps I should play you a song."

Kirei held her breath.

"This was my mother's favorite. I composed it myself." He kept his gaze on the lute as he positioned his fingers for the opening chord. Then he closed his eyes and began.

His countenance contained immense tranquility as his fingers wrought a stirring melody. A slight smile touched his shapely lips when notes fairly tripped over themselves in a complex run. The section made her think of clumsy, laughing children playing tag, or little brown birds flitting in overhead branches. Then the song transitioned into a pretty mirror of the beginning before slowing and finishing on three harmonious thrums.

Her heart beat faster. "That was beautiful."

"So now I need to reposition this and try playing it again." He inclined his head and angled the *biwa* to an awkward tilt. "Like this?"

\*   \*   \*   \*

"At least you make striking music. You're not completely hopeless." Kirei shrugged one shoulder.

"You liked my song." Yūkan laughed. "I guess that means I'm not pathetic."

"You're never pathetic. Frighteningly unrefined in some areas, but never pathetic." She stood and came behind him. "Hold it like this."

Her smooth fingers supported the back of his left hand

while she reached around and twisted the lute onto its side with her right. Her chest pressed against him, and her cheek caressed his. Awareness roused in his loins.

"Many men prefer to hold it like this." She adjusted his fingers at the frets. "Does it feel strange?"

"Very." Tendons pulled uncomfortably through his wrist and hand.

"I thought it might. Try this." She angled his hand high, pointing the *biwa's* neck at the ceiling and placing its base on his knee. She let go and backed away. "Your wrists are nearly at the same aspect, and it's a more formal presentation. Go ahead. Please play."

He missed the coolness of her cheek and fingers. It amazed him how she wore so many layers without growing overheated.

"The same song," she said with an encouraging nod.

He positioned his fingers then tested the chord. The rich resonance sounded good.

He took a deep breath and began. The slower melody flowed sweetly from his fingertips, but he struggled with the pluck work of the runs. He'd have to borrow a *biwa* at court so he could practice. He loved music and truly wanted to impress her with his proficiency. He needed to do it properly, though, as she'd said.

"Not bad," she said.

He cringed. It was horrible.

"Let's try something simpler. Maybe a Saibara song?"

"Which one? I only know a few." He'd hoped she'd send him on his way after his atrocious performance a minute ago. He wanted to nurse his wounded pride then stumble over fingerings without the watchful eyes of this beauty.

Her silks rustled, and he glanced over his shoulder. She stood and came around. "That's no good. You need to know them all. How long can you stay?"

The realization that she wanted him with her gave him a bold hope. He schooled his features into what he prayed passed for a thoughtful expression. "I suppose I can stay as long as you think it'll take. Do you have plans this evening?"

"I'm resting today. The Yin-Yang Ministry has declared today inauspicious for anyone with my birth day. Amai's brother sent a note especially to warn me. Are you expected anywhere?" She settled behind her zither.

"My time's free."

"Good." She moved a cascade of hair past her shoulder as a tiny smile touched her lips.

She appeared glad for his company, and he liked how she negotiated for more time. "I can't imagine tutoring me is very restful, though."

"Maybe not." She placed fingertip plectrums on her thumb and each finger of her right hand. "You're an excellent student, usually."

He winced. "Please don't bring up my poetry."

She showed her teeth in a too-brief smile. "You make teaching more of a pleasure than I expected. You clearly have a talent with music. I think you'll quickly learn these songs."

He hoped so. He despised disappointing her. On the other hand, he did enjoy her high color and blazing eyes when he irritated her.

"How about *Koromogo-e*?" he suggested.

"That's a fun song," came Yoki's voice from outside. The door slid open, and he grinned at her. He lifted a lovely, pale stone end-blown flute.

While Kirei opened a fan before her face, Yūkan stifled a groan.

"Come in," said Kirei, waving her friend inside.

"It's a coincidence, I suppose," said Yūkan, "that you just happened by with your flute."

Yoki laughed. "Of course not. I was driving past on my way home, and I heard the most beguiling song played on a *biwa*." He bowed, deepening his compliment. "I had to come and join in."

"You're alone?" Kirei asked.

He nodded. "Why would I bring someone here and take the risk of boring conversation?"

"Have a seat," invited Kirei, closing her fan and slipping it into her sleeve. "We're getting ready to play *Koromogo-e.*"

"One of my favorites." He plunked onto a blue-green cushion.

Opening the song on a few introductory notes, Yūkan tried not to scowl. Kirei and Yoki entered simultaneously.

Then she began to sing. Yūkan couldn't take his eyes off of her. Her notes pure, her voice added to the music as if it were another instrument. On the zither, her fingers worked the strings with grace and accuracy.

What held him enthralled, however, was her stunning face. A light seemed to shine from her, and he wouldn't have been surprised if a divine entity had descended into their midst to get closer to her singing. He didn't know how he managed to keep his hands playing on the lute.

The song came to an end, and he whispered, "I'm amazed you're not asked to sing at every party and function."

"She usually is." Yoki licked his lips then wiped them with the back of his hand. He inclined his head toward the *biwa.* "You're good on that."

He rocked it on his knee. "I'm better, actually, but I'm learning to hold it a different way."

Yoki glanced at Kirei. "You should see Lord Yūkan dance. I took him to try to gain an audience with Emperor Ichijō, but our ruler asked him to dance for the empress, instead."

Yūkan groaned inwardly at the reminder of another failed attempt to speak with the emperor. How would he smooth his brother's way?

"Why hadn't I heard?" she asked. "Was it memorable?"

Yoki grinned. "Ichijō wept at his beauty and grace of movement."

He rolled his eyes. It was true, but he struggled with the sensitivity of the aristocratic men.

"How about we hear you sing?" asked Kirei, flinging aside the excess silk of her sleeves.

He arched his brows and failed to fight a smile. "I like singing. I'd like it more if you sang with me."

Her gaze holding a glint of humor, she plucked a well-known tune and took a breath.

He hit the first note a fraction of a second after she did, but his pitch struck correctly, bringing him into harmony with her. Five words in, Yoki provided a third part to the harmony.

A slow smile stole over her pretty mouth. She held his gaze.

Keen awareness brought her into pinpoint focus, and the world fell away. Electricity charged the air between them. Though their lips worked in unison to form the words of the song, he imagined they worked, instead, in a sensual kiss.

The melody surrounded them, forming a musical curtain they could hide behind. Too soon, however, the curtain collapsed on the final note.

"That was great!" Yoki guffawed.

Frowning at the nobleman for breaking the spell, Yūkan blinked. If their friend didn't visit, he'd have moved to her for a kiss.

"What?" Yoki shrugged. "That was worthy of a court banquet. You have a smooth, deep voice. It perfectly complements Lady Kirei's."

"I agree," she said. "How about we take a break and have something to eat?" She gave the nobleman a pointed look. "Then you have to go. I still have a lot to teach today."

Yoki pouted. "But this is so diverting. Maybe I could help."

She shook her head. "You want to play. You can be just as entertained in the bedroom or sitting room of one of your many lovers."

"True. It's daylight though. I won't have it said of me that I'm indiscreet." He set aside his flute and rubbed his hands together. "I'm so hungry."

Yūkan wondered if Kirei would take offense if he told Yoki to take his snack for the carriage ride home.

As if on cue, Kirei's maid shuffled in bearing a tray laden with saucers of fruit, a plate of rice cakes, cups, and a water pitcher. She bowed before setting her burden on the floor next to the zither. She bowed again, collected the breakfast tray, and left without a word.

"You have your staff well-trained," complimented Yoki.

Yūkan reverently placed the lute on a cushion beside his.

Chuckling, Kirei stood. As she moved to a cushion at Yūkan's other side, she said, "It's more a matter of my maid knowing my stomach's schedule. She's smart. She pays attention."

Leaning sideways, she hooked a finger over the tray's lip and dragged it in front of her. Her exotic, spiced scent reminded him of the Chinese emperor's private chambers after a lavish meal on his last trade visit to China. He closed his eyes and inhaled on a long breath, drinking in her heady fragrance. Her gesture meant something. She had never come to him. He'd always had to find her and make a place near her.

She could've sat anywhere. Facing him. Next to Yoki. Even apart and on her own. But she sat next to him, so close that her robes brushed his trousers and sleeve.

Removing chopsticks from his sleeve, he smiled at her choice, and her choice was him.

Yoki took a set of chopsticks from the tray, arranged them in his hand, and clicked the tips together. "So guess whose carriage I saw parked along Red Bird Avenue outside Prince Hansamu's mansion this morning."

"Gossip," said Kirei with a grin. She handed Yūkan a saucer of fruit. "How delightful. Is it a lady I know?"

Yoki shook his head and picked up a rice cake in his sticks. "Not a lady. It was your uncle."

Chapter Fifteen


Yoki's statement slapped Kirei so hard the world tilted for a second. She could only think of one reason Ojisan visited Prince Hansamu.

Her.

How long did she have? Weeks at the most, surely. Though the fact that her uncle went there rather than meeting the prince someplace neutral made it more likely she had reached her final days of freedom. Her heart pounded.

At this point, she had one remaining recourse. She'd write her father. She should've written weeks ago when Ojisan first appeared interested in consigning her to Prince Hansamu's bed, although she hadn't known he'd truly made his choice until right now. Should she return to Shinano? Surely she could face the memory of her brother's death and avoid the likes of Warui's family. Pain pierced her heart at the thought. How would she return when her grief had nearly destroyed her? Somehow she suspected she wouldn't last a year in Shinano.

She refused to believe it was too late, however. She cut a glance at Yūkan. His eyebrows slanted inward, and his knuckles had gone stark white where he gripped his saucer. She received small consolation in his unhappiness. He was powerless to intercede.

Her father, however, respected her. Throughout her life, he'd praised her on her wit and sense. He'd regularly told her how he was glad she hadn't become a silly, vacuous girl, his opinion of the majority of Kyō's female population. Before she'd left him a year ago, he'd advised her to find a man and to choose wisely. That he couldn't imagine her attached to a gentleman beneath her in intellect and charm. That he'd lose his respect for her if she chose an unworthy man.

Shame on her. Ojisan gave her more than ample room to choose for herself. She'd taken too long. Been too discriminating. Why hadn't an acceptable gentleman made her feel the way Yūkan did? Better yet, why hadn't she found the strength to return to Shinano and deal with her demons?

She hoped she had enough time to get a letter to her father. She'd have to dip into her personal money to pay a messenger to race by horse to her home province. It didn't bother her in the least that she'd have to do it behind Ojisan's back. He'd gone behind hers when he met with the prince this morning.

Yoki prattled nonstop, oblivious to her distress. She had no idea what he went on about, though knowing him, it probably had something to do with which lady slept with which lord that created a scandal at court.

Swallowing the last of his rice cake, her friend raised his eyebrows at her untouched food. "Aren't you going to eat?"

"I've lost my appetite."

Yūkan set his fruit and chopsticks on the tray.

"You, too? Has a foul spirit come inside?" Yoki picked up his flute. His nostrils flared. He stood and glanced at the rafters, his eyes darting as if he expected to glimpse an apparition. "I love you dearly, Lady Kirei, but I can't get sick, or worse, risk being possessed. I'm expected to spend the evening with Emperor Ichijō." He hurried to the door, and while he slid his feet into his shoes, he said, "You are, too, Yūkan. We're expected at the Ichijō mansion an hour after sunset. Don't be late."

When the door closed behind the nobleman, Yūkan took her hand. "Are you okay?"

"No." She averted her face and squeezed her eyes closed.

"I know he's your friend. I like him, too, but Lord Yoki has a tendency to be ridiculous. The only foul invasion here was his news." He gave her fingers a tug.

"Prince Hansamu's very nearly the last man I'd have chosen." She inhaled deeply and slowly then blew the air through tight lips.

"He's a proud man."

"In the worst way. I can't..."

"He has a certain appeal." Yūkan stroked his thumb along her fingers.

She faced him but didn't pull away from his reassuring hold. She gestured toward the wall openings with a flick of her free hand. "It's superficial. The man's no deeper than my uncle's garden lake. I wanted a man as deep as the ocean."

"Mm-hm. That explains why you haven't found a man acceptable. Kyō's the last place you'd find that kind of depth. As far as the choices you've got in the imperial city, however, he's not a bad way to go."

"He is," she whispered, her gaze dropping to her lap.

She felt his stare for long seconds before he asked, "What aren't you saying?"

She yanked her hand from his. Her stomach roiling, she swallowed. "Why are you trying to convince me this is okay? It's not. In fact, I think I'm about to prove Lord Yoki right and be genuinely sick."

That light of humor she adored so much returned to lessen the intensity of his dark eyes. "I'm testing you."

"Well, stop it. I'm the tutor. I do the testing." She didn't sound as angry as she'd meant.

He recaptured her hand and rubbed her palm in a soothing rhythm. "Would you rather I go?"

She shook her head. He kept her grounded. If he left, she'd fly into a panic. "My uncle is forcing me into a corner. I despise this."

"This is the way things are done, but that doesn't make it right." He grew serious. "I wish I could promise to fix this."

"It's out of both our control. I can appeal to my father, though. Would you please arrange for a messenger who can travel to the provinces?"

"Of course." He stood and assisted her to her feet. "I know just the man. He's carried messages for me many times during my business dealings. Will you be okay by yourself for a little while?"

"Yes. I have a letter to write. I feel better taking some kind of action." Kirei released a shaky breath. She reluctantly withdrew her hand from his. "Thank you for helping me."

He cupped her cheek. "You know how I feel. I'll do everything I can to help you."

He kissed her lightly then bent and lifted the lute from its cushion. She didn't doubt his attraction and interest. But could she accept him as anything other than a husband? He was the opposite of Prince Hansamu in every way that mattered.

As he returned the *biwa* to its place on the wall, she considered Yūkan's intent to stay in Kyō. If she couldn't avoid her uncle's maneuvering, would it matter? Prince Hansamu might declare her crazy when he discovered her virginity, especially when she openly denied him her body. He would lose interest in her, but she would be free to pursue a love with Yūkan, assuming her reputation survived.

The door closed behind him, and she realized that it mattered more than anything. If Prince Hansamu took her as his concubine, she'd enter his household. Yūkan might not wait for her. He might even leave town.

The alternative could prove worse. If her letter succeeded, and she returned to Shinano, would Yūkan travel so far to claim her? If he had truly committed to becoming a Kyō official, such a trip would ruin his chances.

A knife twisted in her gut. Pivoting on her heel, she sank teeth into her bottom lip. She had to write a flawless letter. She marched to her room and located her writing box.

Perhaps she should write to her father about what she really wanted. About that third choice which would be distasteful for all but Yūkan and her. Did she dare?

When he returned an hour later, she was signing her

name to the third and final draft. This letter would appeal to her father's love and respect for her, but would it reach him in time to act?

Yūkan placed her folded letter into a leather pouch while she wrote delivery directions on a separate paper. He took both to a messenger who waited with a brown horse at her uncle's west gate.

"You paid him?" she asked, taking her coin sack in hand.

"Of course. I'm sure you've noticed I have a personal interest in your success." He closed the outer door to her wing and came to her.

"How much? I want to pay."

He shook his head. "I won't let you. It's done. Now, what can we do here in the city?"

She slumped to her cushion. She moved hair from in front of her eye with shaking fingers. "I'm not sure. If the prince comes to my room, I'm done."

"Even if you don't accept him in your bed? What if you tell him to leave?" He settled to a cushion beside her and took her hand.

She stared at his thumb rubbing wide circles from her knuckles to her wrist, round and round. Her thumping heart calmed and she caught her breath for the first time since Yoki had unwittingly delivered his bad news.

"Kirei?"

She sighed and closed her eyes. "It would only take one person seeing him come or go. If he comes a few nights in a row, my uncle can force my hand by sending third-night rice cakes to my chamber and presenting Prince Hansamu with a letter of committal."

"I see." He placed her hand on her knee. "I should go."

She searched his face, but he didn't meet her eyes. His countenance remained stoic. As he stood, she sensed that he was withdrawing. Did he begin to recognize the futility in hoping she could prevent Ojisan's scheming? The thought broke her heart, and she suppressed a need to cry. She'd known

Yūkan couldn't be hers. Not truly hers. So when had he engaged her heart? When had her hopes come to revolve around him?

"Will I see you again?" She winced. She shouldn't have asked. Where was her strength?

He took a second to straighten the lines of his clothes. "It'll depend on how fast Prince Hansamu and your uncle move. Under the circumstances, it might be best if we stop our lessons."

"Why?"

He merely shook his head, his lips forming a tight, thin line.

Gripping the edge of her cushion, she lowered her gaze. How would she get through her days without his visits? She'd go mad in the solitude of her wing, wondering when Prince Hansamu would attempt to steal into her room. Wondering what she would do. Wondering why her uncle had chosen that pompous ass instead of the bright, evocative, thrilling man who, this moment, walked out her door.

*   *   *   *

Fighting the urge to hit something, Yūkan strode to his carriage and climbed in. He'd never been more certain than now of how close he'd come to love. Lady Kirei far exceeded what he wanted in a wife. She had elegance, grace, and talents. More importantly, though, she was intelligent, kind, and thoughtful.

Her beauty had captured his attention. Her character had captured his affections. He'd never met a woman like her, and he never would. He loved her. Waiting for her father to prevent her uncle's misguided machinations was out of the question. Yūkan would have to intervene. Somehow, he'd become the wall between the prince and Kirei.

It wasn't like he had to concern himself with Lord Fujiwara's opinion. Her uncle already despised him. He had nothing to lose in that regard.

The minute he arrived in the Nine Fold Enclosure, Yūkan inquired after Ichijō's whereabouts. The emperor had just returned from a ceremony at the temples, which meant he likely changed robes for whatever came next on his agenda. If Yūkan hurried, he might catch him long enough to exchange a few meaningful words. Unlike before, he had an urgency to see his brother's rights reserved and the trade agreement secured.

He ran past his own quarters and to a long building at the center of the enclosure compound. To avoid delay, he adopted a proud bearing and marched right past two guards at the main entrance. Inside, he found Ichijō in a warehouse-like space that housed his hundreds of robes and accessories after the recent fire.

"Yūkan," the emperor greeted, offering a wave. He shooed a valet. "Enough fussing. This is good enough." When the servant disappeared behind a rack of fabric, Ichijō grinned. "I was hoping to see you today. What a tedious bore. And no end in sight until well into tonight."

"Sounds dreadful." Yūkan took a couple deep breaths then sank to a cushioned stool. "I need to speak with you about my brother, Fudōno, and our trading business."

"I'd like to talk with you, if only to take my mind off of this schedule of mine." He headed for a cluster of scroll-wielding ministers waiting at a far doorway. "Unfortunately, duty demands my time. I have to go."

"Would you have time if I wanted to talk about Lady Kirei?"

The emperor placed a hat on his head, waved farewell, and left. Yūkan punched the side of his stool's cushion.

"What about Lady Kirei?"

He spun and found Yoki sitting on a floor settee, a lap desk on his knees. "I thought you went home."

"I did. The emperor summoned me to handle some hasty correspondence. Now, what is it about Lady Kirei?"

"I think her uncle's made an arrangement with Prince

Hansamu."

He closed a bottle of ink and wrapped a brush in a stained bit of paper. "Really? Interesting but not surprising after I saw his carriage there. It's a good match for her, considering..."

"Considering what?" He stood, clasped his hands behind his back, and paced. "They're not well-suited. Hansamu's vain and shallow. She's beautiful, certainly, but not conceited. He doesn't understand her, much less can he truly appreciate her as a person."

"As a person?" His friend issued a brief but loud guffaw. "Are you saying *you* understand her and appreciate her as a person?"

He halted behind the stool and faced the aristocrat. "Of course I do. You and the emperor do, too. She wouldn't be a court favorite if not."

"We're not talking about me." Yoki's eyes twinkled as he took a rice cake from a platter. "So what does this business with Hansamu have to do with you or me?"

"I don't like it. Lady Kirei's upset. I want to help her."

His friend shrugged while he swallowed a bite. "This is a matter for her family. I can't get involved."

"I seek your advice, not action. As a friend." He dropped to the stool.

"Okay. As a friend, tell me this. Are you unhappy with the match because you want her for yourself?" He finished the cake and reached for another.

"Does it matter?"

"To me, a great deal. She's a dear, precious friend."

He scrubbed his hands over his tight face. "Damn it, yes. I want her for myself. Not as a casual lover or a concubine. I want her for my wife. She's amazing. She's my perfect match."

"She is."

"She deserves respect and honor."

"I agree."

Yūkan straightened. "Are you playing matchmaker? Is

that why you suggested the emperor make her my tutor? So we'd have to spend time together?"

Yoki smiled. "It wasn't my thinking at the time. I like you. You're honest and real. Ichijō and I wanted you close, which meant you needed to fit in among the *good people*. We chose her because she's from the provinces and would actually consider tutoring you. Any lady of Kyō would've sneered and dismissed you without even meeting you. Gentlemen were out of the question. I'd be lying if I didn't admit that I'm pleased, though. Does she return your regard?"

He put his head in his hands. "I don't know. She can be difficult to read. She doesn't discourage me. She kisses me back when I kiss her."

"Well, that's always a good sign." His friend chuckled. "We can't ignore the fact that she invited you into her bed."

Yūkan studied the nobleman who set aside the small wooden desk and stood. "So you'd support my marriage to Lady Kirei?"

Yoki took another rice cake and offered the tray to him.

"No, thanks."

He set the tray on its table. "Like I said, Kirei is dear to me. Ichijō's first wife adored her. Now Akiko loves her like a sister, and that means a lot to me."

"Why?"

"When the empress is happy, the emperor has less worries. That makes my job easier. Akiko may be young, but Ichijō loves her. I've watched Kirei turn down suitor after suitor. To be honest, none of them were worthy of her, anyway. You are. Other than me, you're the only one I can think of who is man enough for her."

Yūkan fought the urge to smirk. Yoki was anything but manly. In some ways, he was more womanly than some of the ladies in Kyō.

"She tells me I can't marry her if I want a career in the government." Unable to stay still, Yūkan stood and walked a circle around the stool.

"Do you want a ministry career?"

He stopped short. "No. I want Lady Kirei, but to win her, I have to be willing to stay in Kyō. And to maintain an acceptable social status, I have to obtain a position in one of the ministries."

"She's told you this is what she wants?"

He crossed his arms over his chest. "Isn't it?"

Yoki shrugged. "She doesn't confide in me. I think you should stay and use your family connection to Michinaga to get a government position that'll earn you a mansion in the fourth ward."

"What if I can convince her of my intent? Convince her to let me marry her? What do I do about Prince Hansamu?"

His friend shook his head. "Walk with me."

He joined him and headed for the door. "She sent a letter to her father today, but it would help if I could do something. In case the prince progresses faster than her father can respond."

The aristocrat glanced around then leaned his head close. "There's one thing you can do. It'll cause a scandal, so you'll need to decide if it's something you dare."

"What is it?" The muscles in Yūkan's neck bunched.

"Hansamu, with Fujiwara's consent, will attempt to force her hand. I know Lady Kirei better than anyone. She won't allow the prince in her bed. He'll have to make it appear as if he's spending night after night with her for the required three nights. The third night will involve *exposure of the event* followed by a formal letter of committal by her uncle where he'll express his official approval of the match. You can prevent this."

Hope mixed with dread in his gut. "How?"

"If Hansamu is sleeping in her wing of the mansion, there's only one way to prove he's not sleeping in her *bed*."

Yūkan's heart beat faster. "If her bed is occupied by another man."

## Chapter Sixteen

"Shinsetsu wrote to say he can come to our Day of the Monkey garden party tonight." Amai shuffled on sock-clad feet into the sitting room where Kirei plucked at her zither. She beamed. "He's coming!"

Kirei couldn't help but smile at her cousin's joy. It helped that this Day of the Monkey would earn her a worry-free night. Every sixty days, the Yin-Yang masters declared it essential that everyone spend the entire night awake to avoid being attacked and killed in their sleep by noxious powers circulating during the Day of the Monkey. Prince Hansamu couldn't share her bed if she wasn't in it. She chuckled.

"Will your brother be able to come?"

"No. He says the entire Yin-Yang staff will spend the night at the ministry, doing what they can to protect the city. At least Shinsetsu will be here."

Kirei offered the sweet young lady a smile of encouragement.

"And look." Amai came near and squatted. She unfolded a parcel of plain paper to reveal a coiled ribbon of embroidery sewn in brilliant shades of yellow, scarlet, and emerald. She rocked as she refolded the paper. "His aunt and uncle brought it from China. Isn't it gorgeous? Shinsetsu knows how to delight me."

"He really does." Kirei drank in her cousin's glee. "I've never seen a more up-to-date piece of embroidery. Have Zo attach it to the neckline of the mantle you'll wear tonight."

Amai giggled then gasped. "Exactly what I was thinking. Father tells me Prince Hansamu will attend. He wants you to wear your best silks, but I don't think you need to worry about gaining the prince's attention. I think you already have it."

"Me, too." Kirei played a thread of notes from her favorite Chinese tune, hoping she did a passable job hiding her displeasure. "What do you think of him?"

Amai fell backward onto a cushion and hugged her letter and parcel to her chest. "He's very handsome. More handsome than Lord Yoki, even. And he's from one of the best families. His mansion faces Red Bird Avenue, and only the finest families are allowed to have their homes facing the majestic avenues."

Kirei sighed. "I should be glad of his attention, shouldn't I?"

"You couldn't do much better." Her cousin sat up and gave her an earnest look. "You're not considering letting him take you as a concubine, are you?"

Careful to keep her countenance passive, she asked, "Why?"

"He's not suited to you at all."

If her self-absorbed, busy cousin could see what an ill match this would make, why couldn't her uncle? Or was there something else driving this? Had the prince promised Ojisan a price in exchange for his support?

"Perhaps. What do you think of Minamoto no Yūkan? He's improved, don't you think?"

"Thanks to you."

"I can't take the credit. He already knew Chinese poetry and music and the sutras. He seems naturally pleasing in his demeanor and interest in others."

Amai lay back and stared at the underside of the roof. "I admit I like him. I can't fault him for his handwriting or coarse looks. Shinsetsu's handwriting is worse and a number of ministers are uglier. You have to take some credit, though. His manners are much improved."

"True, though he spends time with Lord Yoki and Emperor Ichijō, so I'm sure they help him, too."

"He's very smart, isn't he?"

"It seems so to me."

"And he truly has an appreciation for beautiful things. He's got the finest carriage in Kyō, and his clothes are the very best fabrics. He knows a lot, too. I mean, he's studied, obviously. Yoki and Shinsetsu have both commented that they envy his education."

"Is that so?" Kirei asked.

"If he weren't so ugly, with his brown skin and square face, he might be the right man for you. Too bad he's not a true gentleman of Kyō."

"I'm not a true lady of Kyō," Kirei reminded.

"Yes, but Father would never approve such a match."

That was the problem. Would her own father have objected if he were here? "What of Shinsetsu and you? The two of you appear to be getting serious."

Her cousin rolled onto her side and propped her head on her hand. "I'm so in love it scares me. If he marries me, how will I be able to stand it when he adds consorts to our household?"

"I don't know." She let her fingers play a tune from muscle memory. "Jealousy is considered a reprehensible vice, but when we really love our men, how can we help it?"

Amai slowly sat up. Her mouth opened then closed. After a long second, she said, "Kirei."

"Yes?"

"You said 'when *we* really love our men.' You're in love?"

Her fingers ceased upon the zither. Love? She hadn't considered, but neither could she deny that she'd included herself in her opinion regarding jealousy. Love? Could she love Yūkan?

She wasn't sure.

"Cousin!" Amai grasped her by the arm. "Are you ill?"

She blinked and gave her head a shake. "No. Why?"

"You're gray. You look like you're about to fall over."

Kirei gripped the zither and realized she'd been wavering. She pressed fingers to her cheek which felt winter-cold. "I'm okay."

Her cousin let go. "Who is it? Who, after you've waited so long, finally won your heart?"

Amida Buddha save her from herself. "Minamoto no Yūkan."

\*    \*    \*    \*

"Thank you for the ride," said Yoki, stepping out of Yūkan's carriage.

"It wasn't any trouble. Your house was on the way." Yūkan followed the gentleman out and waved his driver to go park. He wanted to find Kirei and learn if she was still as worried as the last time he'd visited her.

The Fujiwara mansion blazed with internal lights, and laughter floated to the gate from the garden. Servants bustled and bowed as they assisted ladies with *kichō* and carried food and drink to guests.

"This ought to be fun. Kirei's uncle can be a bore when it comes to protocol, but he sure knows how to throw a party. I understand Lady Rippa plans to attend. You have to meet her. She's absolutely splendid."

"Splendid, huh? You must be having trouble getting into her bed."

Yoki laughed. "You spend too much time with me. You're getting to know me too well." He led the way through the east gate into the Fujiwara garden. "Lady Rippa is playing hard-to-get, but I'll win. She wants me. Besides, I like a challenge."

Ladies in bright, elaborate silks stood or sat in conversation around the beautifully landscaped garden. A group of young gentlemen stood in a circle on an island built into the garden's large pond where they kicked a ball in a game of *kemari*. A couple games of *Go* were in play in a wide pavilion that half sat over the pond's water.

Along the main wing's south veranda, gentlemen sat with their legs dangling. Behind them, ladies sat inside, the bottom wall section removed to show their gorgeous silk layers and blinds hanging low to hide their faces. Conversations there appeared lively, and bursts of spontaneous laughter rang over the party from that group in regular intervals.

Yoki grinned. "Lady Rikō must be in attendance. That clever lady has a way of keeping us laughing for hours."

Yūkan studied the voluminous arrangements of silk and wondered which she might be. With the ladies' faces always hidden, how did a gentleman know who he spoke to at any given time?

Women's laughter dominated the garden a moment before Prince Hansamu strutted from the west wing. The man grinned. Behind him, a row of ladies sat upon the veranda that edged Kirei's section of the mansion. Another round of their laughter lifted the mood, and Hansamu smiled bigger.

Yūkan swallowed. The prince would bring nothing but misery to Lady Kirei. She was right to worry. She was especially right to seek a way out of the forced union.

A plan began to form, and he touched Yoki's arm. "Will you have time to meet with me tomorrow?"

His friend scowled. "You sound serious. Stop it this instant. We're here to make light and flirt the night away."

He chuckled. "True, it's a serious matter I want to discuss with you. Tomorrow?"

Yoki sighed. "If I have to spend the entire night dreading this serious matter of yours, I won't have any fun. Can't we talk now? Surely we can find someplace quiet inside."

He shook his head. "We can't speak where there's a chance someone might overhear. And especially not here."

A servant hurried past and sent him a furtive frown. Yūkan sensed the need to move along, away from the gate opening before they stirred suspicion.

"This is about Lady Kirei, isn't it?" The gentleman checked the placement of his towering hat.

"Yes."

Yoki stamped his slipper-clad foot. "Damn it, Yūkan. My

whole night is ruined."

"Will you?"

"Of course. We'll take a trip to Mt. Hiei. A visit to a tendai temple will make the perfect excuse to get out of the city, and there are ample places to find privacy. We can invite Lady Kirei and her sweet cousin. I think the ladies could use an escape, too."

Especially Kirei. Yūkan searched the party. He located her across the garden. She stood beside her uncle, a beautiful silver fan hiding most of her face. Her dark eyes watched him, and he smiled. Her gaze cut away but found him again almost right away.

*I'm here for you, lovely lady. Count on me.*

"I see Lady Rippa," said Yoki. He gave Yūkan a slight bow of farewell and left.

He laughed then called, "She doesn't stand a chance against your charms."

The gentleman offered a tiny wave but kept to his path.

Kirei had moved from her uncle's side, and Yūkan searched the gathering for her. Someone played a cheerful tune, which set a happy background to buzzing conversation and an occasional giggle or chortle. The scent of pine and flower pollen perfumed the party far more effectively than any of the fragrances worn by partygoers.

He scanned faces, fans, and screens of state. Had she gone inside?

"Yūkan," she said close behind. "I'm glad you came."

"I'm always pleased to see you." He'd be pleased to see her every day for the rest of his life. He turned on his heel with a ready smile.

Her eyes above the edge of her fan sparkled in torchlight.

"Are you doing well?" he asked.

"Well enough considering everything. Better tonight since we have a crowd in attendance." Her smile reached her eyes. "Prince Hansamu can flirt with the ladies, and I have many excuses to avoid him."

He chuckled. The mouthwatering smell of grilling meat reached him, reminding him he'd missed his last chance to grab something to eat a few hours earlier. His stomach rumbled. Embarrassed, he pressed a hand to it.

"Come and eat," she said.

"You heard that, huh?"

Gathering the many layers of her green and yellow ensemble, she headed for the mansion's wing opposite the entrance gate. "Come with me. I'm hungry, too."

At an elaborate station arranged for serving food and manned by amply capable servants, Yūkan accepted a white dish of steamed rice heaped with seasoned vegetables and strips of grilled beef. Kirei had one with duck and eel.

"My screen is over here," she said, indicating a seating area where cushioned settees and silk-draped stools clearly set it apart for the party's elite. "Come sit by me."

"Of course." He marveled at his complete lack of discomfort. After a week of moving in the emperor's circles and acting as Lord Yoki's particular friend, he had grown accustomed to keeping company with Kyō's upper crust. Their acceptance astonished him since they didn't count him as a true gentleman.

The moon rose above the roofline of her uncle's east wing, and musicians began to play. A drummer, lute player, flutist, and a zither player approached by shallow boats along Lord Fujiwara's waterway. Their music preceded them. They floated under a bridge connecting the main building to the east annex, their red-painted boats a happy sight in yellow lantern light.

Yūkan held Kirei's dish while she settled behind her screen-of-state. As he sat on a mat beside her, he handed over her meal. He glanced at a group of men who played a game that involved throwing objects at a target. "Your uncle puts together a fun party."

"He does. I wish he worked as hard to see his home as

happy as his events." She used chopsticks to form a bite-sized ball of rice, placed a piece of grilled eel atop the rice then managed a dainty manner while moving the food to her mouth.

His heart thudded. "He won't relent concerning Prince Hansamu?"

She shook her head. "I won't talk to him about it. He'd only get angry. It could be the opportunity he seeks to force his decision, and I refuse to give him that. No, my silence buys me time."

He slowly chewed his food. In his attempt not to show his frustration, he released a heavy sigh. "You know how I feel about you."

"Yes," she said quietly.

The musicians moved past. Their joyful melody danced along a breeze that followed the winding narrow waterway. An owl hooted as if in time to the tune and caused applause and chuckles of enjoyment. Kirei's lovely features went soft and gentle in her amused smile.

"Dance! Lord Yūkan, dance!"

He set aside his dish and searched for the man who shouted the request. The melody grew louder, and he recognized it as Waves of the Blue Sea. He'd performed this dance for the emperor, and now Yoki waved him to stand. He shook his head.

"Dance!"

Lady Kirei cast him a curious, playful look, her eyebrows arched and a slight smile curving her lips. "Ever since Yoki told me you danced for the emperor, I've been interested to see you perform. Do you know this one?"

He sighed. "I do. My grandfather taught me."

Her dark eyes brightened. "It's one of my favorites."

Finding her hopeful anticipation irresistible, he leaned toward her without intending to.

"Will you dance?"

"For you?" He dropped his gaze to her alluring mouth.

"Yes. Dance for me, Lord Yūkan."

Before he could agree, Prince Hansamu hurried past. He
headed for a flat, grassy area at the pond's edge. Unfastening
his jacket, he announced, "I'll dance."

"Don't let him steal this chance," whispered Kirei.

"For what?"

Her hand, cool and gentle, found his. Her fingers curled
into his palm. "To show them. To prove you're worthy."

"Worthy of what?" The longer he stayed in Kyō, the less
interest he had in impressing this capricious aristocracy.

"Worthy of me."

He froze. His heart beat its heavy excitement against his
ribs. Was this some kind of declaration on her part? Some kind
of invitation? For certain, he wanted nothing more than to win
her devotion. Could something as simple as executing a series
of steps to music earn the approval he needed? It couldn't hurt.

He stood and offered Kirei a nod. "Only for you."

Untying his *kosode*, he headed toward Prince Hansamu.
At the pond, he pulled his arms from the sleeves and the silk
fell to his waist. He tied his sleeves around the band of his
*hakama*. His chest bare, he took a deep breath. Cool air sent a
shiver along his arms, but he didn't mind. The Waves of the
Blue Sea would have him beyond warm in a short time.

The musicians began the song anew. As the drummer
pounded an introduction, he took a place on the lush grass near
Hansamu. The prince cast him a brief scowl.

Guests quieted. For a moment, the night stilled until the
sound of water lapping at the musicians' boats created a music
of its own.

Then the lute player struck the first chord.

Yūkan pivoted on the balls of his feet to face opposite
the prince. The song began in earnest, and he danced with ease,
his movements a perfect foil to Hansamu's. He swung his arms
in large arcs, his fingers splayed. His muscles bunched and
clenched amidst his leaps and spins.

Sweat created a sheen on him and allowed the cool air to
prevent his overheating. Moving in time to the beat, he set his

features in the expression his grandfather had taught. Each motion came without thought, wrought of memory and delight in the players' excellent skill.

His heart beat faster and his breaths drew deeper as his exertion built a rush of blood and adrenaline throughout his body. It felt wonderful, especially after his weeks of near inactivity.

This dance brought fond memories to mind. A simpler time. A simpler place with people not afraid to show their love.

He glimpsed Kirei at her screen-of-state. As he executed a series of kicking spins, she stood. The glittering fan she held in front of her lovely face didn't hide genuine admiration in her gaze. He danced stronger than ever. Her good opinion meant everything.

As he assumed a deceptively serene pose in pause before a series of leaps, her fan began to slip.

Chapter Seventeen

Holding her breath, Kirei stared in fascination. No dance master could've taught Yūkan the impressive elegance he displayed in his interpretation. His partner, Prince Hansamu, was renowned for talent and striking good looks, but he paled beside Yūkan. All eyes were on the well-born trader.

Her heart beat rapidly at the sight of blazing torchlight upon his strong body as the music swelled. It made for a stunning climax in the dance. She had never witnessed such beauty in movement and expression as Yūkan achieved in that moment.

No guest moved. No one spoke. He held the entire assembly in thrall. Kirei more than any.

Sensations low in her belly brought her to life in a way she'd only experienced by his kiss. His masculinity created an awareness of her own femininity.

Behind her, a number of ministers wept at the gorgeous sight, and not a lady in attendance had a dry eye. The music waned, and Yūkan went still. He adjusted his stance. When music resumed, he swayed into the steps of the next movement. The fast melody had him dancing in nearly a blur.

Though his chest heaved and his color darkened, his motion appeared effortless. He didn't bear an ideal round, white face. His features had angles at cheeks and jaw, and he didn't wear cosmetics to cover his tan skin. He bore strength and grace in his bearing. Though his lips would never match the perfection of Prince Hansamu's flower bud shape, his mouth promised sensual kisses in its wide set.

His manly appeal and natural charm were hard to resist.

After this dance, Yūkan would attract attention and overtures from a number of ladies who watched with bright, interested eyes.

Her thighs trembling, Kirei sank to her seat. Drinking in his slowing resolution, she touched fingertips to her tingling bottom lip and hoped he would find a way to get her alone despite the crowd at her uncle's home.

He executed a striking turn, his entire body undulating like a wave while the music rippled to a close.

The night went utterly silent and still for a moment. With a single strike to his instrument, the drummer released them from Yūkan's spell. Everyone seemed to inhale on a collective breath. He bowed, and the partygoers exclaimed their approval.

Kirei wilted. For a rustic nobody, the man had won the hearts of Kyō's elite. He didn't represent the male ideal for beauty, but for her, he couldn't be handsomer. His strength, his appeal, his intelligence had combined to seduce her more effectively than any poem he could write.

The moment his eyes met hers, she knew. He'd won her, too.

When he picked up his jacket and headed her way, she lifted her fan higher and waited. His naked torso glistening in the moonlight had her practically panting as a wonderful sensation stirred in her loins.

"I should go," he said, his voice winded. He sent his jacket to the grass and untied his *kosode's* sleeves at his waist. "I need to bathe. I don't want to offend you or your uncle's guests with my odor."

Her heart thudded in disappointment. "You won't offend me."

A half-smile tugged the corner of his mouth while he tied the tape at the side of his *kosode*. "In an hour, I'll offend *myself*."

She pushed to her feet. "Then allow me to walk you to the gate."

"Of course." He plucked his jacket from the ground.

"You could stay and use our bath." She would gladly serve as his bath maid. Waving to a server to bring him a cup of water, she shivered in anticipation.

He accepted the cup and drained it. Handing the empty cup to the servant, he said, "I'm grateful, but perhaps your uncle prefers I go."

She glanced over her shoulder to where Ojisan spoke with Hansamu near the main building's veranda. Her uncle stared at Yūkan, animosity emanating from him. This uncouth country gentleman had outshone the good-looking prince, and she suspected he understood it had furthered her aversion to Hansamu.

Nodding, she met Yūkan's eye. "You're right. He wouldn't make a scene in front of his guests, but we don't want him angrier than he is."

She accompanied him to the gate then sent a man to notify his driver. Resisting an urge to trace the collar of his *kosode* as an excuse to feel his skin, she fingered her chemise's cuff edging. If only she could think of a way to go with him. Unfortunately, it would earn Ojisan's wrath. Their relationship had become tense enough as it was.

"Will you come tomorrow?" Kirei bit her lip. She'd never wanted to kiss a man so much as she did Yūkan in that moment.

"I thought we stopped our lessons."

"Yes, but ceasing may cause the kind of questions we want to avoid. You should come tomorrow."

"For a music lesson?" He gave his driver a nod as his carriage pulled to the gate.

"Perhaps your poetry could use some practice." Though she'd have difficulty keeping her hands off of him. After his dance, his strong body bared for her to admire, she once again considered taking him to her bed.

She smiled at the thought of the proper gentlemen who'd worked to win her invitation. They'd spit to learn she'd chosen this country trader over them. None could compare to his raw, masculine appeal. Many ladies found him intimidating and animal, but she thrilled at his brawn. Added with his intelligence and advanced learning, his physical appeal turned her on like nobody else's.

He went to his carriage door. "Don't expect me early."

"After being awake all night, nobody will rouse before midday tomorrow. Come when the sun is high. I'll be waiting." Excitement somersaulted in her abdomen.

He climbed in then gave her a wave out the window.

When he'd gone, she eyed the party. Noblemen laughed and drank. Ladies stood in groups behind their fans, their fine fabrics gleaming in torchlight. Her uncle fawned over his wife who sat behind curtains at the prime corner of his pavilion above the pond.

With Prince Hansamu nowhere in sight, she imagined he'd skulked away to bathe, apply fresh makeup, and soothe his wounded pride.

Uma came to her side. "You look lost, my lady."

Kirei sighed. "My reason for attending this event just left."

"May I get you anything?"

She took a step into brighter light. Nobody seemed to notice. Nobody waved or smiled her way. Nobody would miss her if *she* left. She couldn't remember a time in this city when so few eyes sought her at a public gathering like this. The unexpected anonymity made her smile.

She said low, "It's been a while since we went to The City of the Right."

Her maid nodded. "Two weeks. My source tells me there's a new family. They've taken a ruin that held together the most after the last earthquake, but it's on the other side of Suzaku Avenue."

Kirei's heart skipped a beat. "That's such a dangerous area. Thieves use that part of the city. I wish the emperor could rebuild, but what would be the point? The next earthquake or fire would demolish it again."

"Exactly. This is a family with a poor man and his wife. They have his old mother with them and two young boys. His wife is pregnant and due to deliver any time. They're on their way to Osaka but had to stop because she couldn't go further. They have no money."

"Then they'll be hungry. Come on. You gather rice cakes and I'll arrange a carriage. We need to move them into a protected part of the city until the baby's born and they can continue their journey."

"Yes, my lady." Uma bowed and headed for the kitchen.

In short order, they rode west toward The City of the Right. Their driver had given up warning her against these forays into the desolated, nearly deserted section of Kyō to rescue or aid the poor. No doubt he'd have told Ojisan of her adventures of charity if he weren't hoping to win Uma as his wife. Yūkan would likely be upset to learn she'd gone without him, too.

As they approached the southern gate to the Nine Fold Enclosure, she glanced at Uma then out the window at the palace compound's low wall. "Perhaps we should see if Lord Minamoto wants to come."

Her maid swayed with the rock of the carriage long seconds before she nodded. "He was very good to have along when we rescued Hen Na's girls. It would make me feel better to have such a strong and capable man with us when we enter the City of the Right."

Kirei waved their driver to the gate and instructed him to the palace guesthouse. She had Uma stay in the carriage while she hurried inside. A servant pointed the way, and she went to his door. With her hand poised to knock, she took a deep breath then rapped on the wood.

The door slid aside to reveal Yūkan with wet mussed hair and wearing only a pair of brown *hakama*. A slow smile curved his lips. "This is a pleasant surprise."

She blinked rapidly, at a loss for words. The sight of his

bared torso had an even more powerful effect on her here in the intimacy of his chamber than it had in her uncle's garden. Her fingers itching to touch him, she met his eyes, and the heat in his gaze perfectly mirrored the desire flaring within her.

She gave herself a small shake. "Would you be up for another rescue mission?"

His smile slipped a bit. "More charity?"

Not trusting her voice, she could only nod.

"I'm always up for an adventure. Come in." He stepped back and gestured for her to enter.

Tempted, she shook her head. She wanted him too much. One touch from him would have her ready and eager to forgo this jaunt into the City of the Right for a night in his arms. That family needed her.

"My maid and driver are waiting outside. I'll meet you out there." She retreated three steps along the hallway toward the exit.

He raked her with his gaze, his smile disappearing altogether. "Fine. I'll be a few minutes to get dressed."

She turned on her heel and fairly ran to the carriage. Climbing inside, she said, "He'll come."

She studied her trembling fingers as butterflies flitted in her stomach. What was it about this man that put her off her guard so easily?

When he joined them, he gave her a reassuring smile and took a seat beside her. He sat cross-legged, and his knee rested securely against hers. She liked the intimacy his casual touch implied.

They entered the area west of the imperial palace, a place in decay. A few head of cattle stood in statue-like sleep, left amidst overgrowth after a day of grazing among the ruins. Few houses still stood, and none occupied by aristocrats. The *good people* had abandoned the City of the Right, and when the crumbled structures were left as rubble, thieves had moved into the few intact homes remaining.

The carriage jostled over ruts and debris as they rolled

deeper into the desolated western section of Kyō. Kirei closed her eyes, concentrating on her task. The idea of children and a pregnant woman in this den of crime stripped her nerves raw. She hoped she could convince them to accept her help.

Her maid's informant proved reliable, as usual, and they immediately found the family. To Kirei's relief, it didn't take much to convince the man to move his family to higher ground. Yūkan's calm insistence went far to get the family moving quickly. She and Uma helped them gather their belongings while he lifted the two boys onto the roof of the carriage.

Shouts rang from shadows behind looming ruins along the street. The passing of their carriage hadn't gone unnoticed, and bandits closed in. Fighting panic, Kirei ushered the boys' elderly grandmother from the ruins in which they'd been huddled for who knew how many days.

The few coins the family had carried when they arrived were stolen the first night, and the grandmother's prized hair comb went missing the next day. They had no food among their belongings. Their situation had grown dire.

It took some difficulty to transfer the uncomfortable wife into the carriage. Yūkan and her driver had to practically carry the woman. The man loaded their few possessions onto the roof with the boys while Kirei helped his mother inside. Uma passed a couple rice cakes up to the children.

Shouts grew louder, and now she could discern broken bits of exchange in the darkness beyond the nearest crumbled buildings. Only small sections of the original property walls remained standing, and shadows moved along them.

"Thank you," the man said, bowing repeatedly. "A fine lady and gentleman like you shouldn't lower yourselves by helping people like us."

Kirei shook her head. While climbing in after the old woman, she said, "We're together in this journey of life and we have to help one another when and where we're able."

He bowed and joined the driver at the front with the oxen. Yūkan took a position behind the conveyance while Kirei climbed in. When the carriage rolled, the pregnant woman began to sob. The old woman patted her hand and made a comforting clicking noise. Uma stuffed a cushion behind the woman's back.

Kirei braced a hand on the carriage floor and leaned nearer the man's wife. "Why do you cry? You're going someplace safe where there's food for your children and comfort and assistance for you."

The woman wiped her tears. "I'm crying because I'm so grateful. Our entire village was destroyed by fire, and the lord who owns the land didn't replace the overseer who died. We had no way to rebuild and nowhere to stay. No one has helped us. No one until now. Until you."

Uma patted the woman's shoulder.

"I understand you go to Osaka. Do you have family there?" Kirei asked.

The old woman smacked her lips. "A traveler who passed through our village last year told us the fishermen in Osaka make good money selling what they catch. My son wants to provide for his family."

Kirei didn't see him doing well without a boat. "He's a good fisherman? He knows a lot about it?"

"No," she said. "How hard can it be? Throw a net and catch some fish."

She shared a worried glance with her maid. "Perhaps I have a better idea. If I give you my letter, my father will provide you a home and work in his province. The boys will receive an education, and you'll have the protection you need."

The old woman's craggy face sagged on a frown. "Why? You don't know us. Why are you doing this for us? What do you want from us?"

Kirei offered her a kind smile. "I'm doing this because none of us knows what tomorrow holds. You need help today, and I'm glad to be here to give it. Tomorrow, I may be the one who needs help. If Buddha smiles upon me, and if I've created enough good karmic ripples, those ripples may reach me on the other side of my good fortune and someone will be there to help me."

"So you're doing this as insurance against future calamity?"

She chuckled. "Partly. I'm also helping you because sometimes people simply need aid. Other than the emperor, I don't think anyone is better than anyone else in Buddha's eyes. Perhaps this life is a reality of suffering, but we are not meant to suffer alone."

The pregnant woman stopped crying. "If only we could be equal in each other's eyes."

"Precisely."

She and Uma settled the family into one of a seemingly endless line of humble cottages on a side street in the seventh ward where the eaves formed a solid line. Next door lived an excellent midwife whose reputation had earned her many requests for service among the birthing aristocracy. She would care for the family, especially after Yūkan gave her money to meet their expenses. Uma would get Kirei's letter of intro- duction to them in a few days.

The ride home was quiet despite busy streets. The entire city swarmed with activity this night of the monkey. It didn't distract her from her thoughts, however. If she abandoned her uncle to escape Prince Hansamu and return to her father, would she ever see Yūkan again? She sent him a questioning look, but he appeared lost in his own thoughts.

"Let's return to my uncle's party. If anyone asks, you left to bathe then returned."

His serious gaze caressed her face. "Not a lie, entirely. And what of your absence?"

"What absence?" She smiled. "I've been there this whole time. Lord Yoki will vouch it."

He barked a laugh.

\*     \*     \*     \*

His head pulsing in pain, Yūkan clamped a hand over his eyes and rolled with a groan. His empty stomach protested his unwillingness to rise, forcing him to curl around a hunger cramp. As a contradiction, however, the very idea of eating made him want to heave.

He had plans to visit Kirei today, so he tumbled from his mat and went to his hands and knees. He scrubbed a palm over his stiff face then stood.

Poetry. Ugh. He enjoyed reading it, but writing it made his brain ache. As if in agreement, his head pounded harder.

He got to his feet. He shouldn't have had those last two rounds of *sake* with Yoki right before the sun rose this morning. How would he impress his lovely lady if he couldn't think straight?

He donned a simple *hakama* and jacket to search out breakfast. The moment he stepped from his room, he froze. On the hall's opposite wall, a banner from the Masters of Yin-Yang announced that it was unlucky to travel south-east until tomorrow morning.

He slammed a fist into his hand. What nonsense. He would ignore it except they'd never grant him admittance into the Fujiwara mansion. Even if he ignored the ban, he'd be turned away at the door and accused of bringing evil spirits to the house. Damn it.

\*   \*   \*   \*

"Your uncle asks for you," said Zo, scurrying from the main building into the west wing.

Kirei glanced up, but her fingers continued to work music from her instrument. "Tell him I'm expecting company. Lord Yūkan couldn't come yesterday, so he'll be here today."

The maid's fleshy jowls jiggled. "I can't, my lady. Please don't ask me to go back and refuse him."

Amai stopped writing, her brush poised inches above her blue parchment. "Do you want me to go? I'm not afraid of

Father."

She removed her zither pick from her finger and set it aside. "You're sweet, but no. Your father will anger, and I don't want to cause tension between you."

Amai shrugged. "Okay. If Lord Yūkan comes while you're gone, I'll make sure he waits."

"Thank you." She stood and followed Zo into the main building.

Her red and silver fan caught late morning light shining from the garden view and caused darting reflections on the floor and upon round columns supporting the roof. The maid led her to a curtained area at the far side then retreated without a word.

"Ojisan?" she inquired.

"Come in." Inside his makeshift office, he tied a ribbon around a scroll then placed it on a stack balanced by a court courier. "Take those to the ministry. I'll bring these when I come."

The runner bowed slightly then exited where two curtain panels met.

"What can I do for you, Ojisan?" she asked.

"You'll be home today?" He dipped a brush into ink and signed an open scroll.

"Of course. Today is Buddha's birthday. I plan to entertain for the Washing of the Buddha."

"Good."

Her stomach tensed. He appeared too content. This couldn't bode well for her.

He set the scroll aside and chose another two. "Entertaining is what I want you to do. I've invited Prince Hansamu to come tonight."

A stone weight dropped into her center. What she dreaded most was upon her. "I can't promise, my lord. As handmaiden to the empress, I could be called to the Nine Fold Enclosure or the Ichijō mansion at any time."

He rolled the first scroll and slid it into a pre-tied ring of ribbon. "She won't summon you tonight."

"How—"

"Her Majesty has a sore throat. She's staying in bed."

Kirei straightened her spine. "I should go to her if she's not feeling well."

"You'll stay here. She doesn't require you, and you have no specific function to attend since His Majesty is performing the ceremony which accepts the offering of the gilt Buddha statue. They'll begin the washing of the statue in a little while, and I need to be there to participate." He gathered the other two scrolls. "I must go."

"But—"

"Do as you're told," he threw over his shoulder on his way outside. "Bring honor to our family."

By sleeping with that moron of a prince? She didn't think so. Shaking, she returned to the west wing. Yūkan still hadn't arrived. Had the emperor asked him to attend the ceremony?

## Chapter Eighteen

As guest after guest arrived at Kirei's Washing of the Buddha party, favorites she had met over the past year that included the resplendent Lady Rippa and the delightful Lady Rikō, it became clear that Yūkan would not attend. She played the dutiful hostess while fighting a cloying disappointment.

According to her previous arrangement, a priest presented a small guilt Buddha and a representation of his birth to the assembled guests. Laughter and vigorous vying energized the gathering as her male guests fought for position in the ceremony.

Soon, four priests paid their respects to the little statue, a miniature replica of the one presented at the imperial palace. While intoning words of praise, they poured colored water, each in turn, upon the statue's head.

"You didn't wait for me?" Lord Yoki asked near Kirei's ear, humor lacing his tone.

"Why should I wait for you? You're late." She glanced past him toward the east gate. "Did you bring Lord Yūkan?"

Yoki's handsome features darkened. "Your uncle convinced Emperor Ichijō that he needed Lord Yūkan's fine dancing skills to best honor Buddha's birthday in the palace's washing ceremony. I'm sure he doesn't believe it for a second, but the dance that took place here at his monkey party gives his words weight."

Trembling with anger, she tried for a calm demeanor as noblemen in attendance entered into her private ceremony. Their dance-like movements graceful and precise as each approached the statue, they poured colored water upon its head, made obeisance then withdrew in a leftward turn. Yoki joined them, his steps a tribute to the god.

When he returned to her side, Kirei said, "You're right, of course. My uncle worked to keep Lord Yūkan from my observance and he succeeded."

Prince Hansamu paid homage to the statue, his movements the finest of anyone's.

Yoki cleared his throat. "To be sure."

The priest approached the prince, waving madly and shouting, "No! No! Not like that."

The two men began a heated dispute over which steps were correct for this ceremony, and Kirei chuckled.

"I wish I could've attended the Washing of the Buddha ceremony at the palace," she said, giving her friend her full attention.

"This year's ceremony was remarkable. The Princess was escorted from her temple residence by all the ladies-in-waiting from the emperor's household. Each lady-in-waiting had eight pages attending her. The princess rode in a carriage that had projecting eaves." Yoki took on a faraway look as though he watched the retinue parading up Red Bird Avenue that very moment. "Behind her, the ladies-in-waiting followed in three silken carriages, six painted carriages, eighteen palm-leaf roofed carriages, and a couple of split bamboo. Lord Michinaga sent an escort to meet her and brought five gilded carriages filled with ladies from his own household. Their elegantly colored sleeves hung ostentatiously out the carriage windows as they passed through the south gate of the Nine Fold Enclosure."

Kirei smiled, able to envision the lavish display. The princess' serene smile and the ladies' playful giggles lightened her mood.

"Speaking of elegant ladies-in-waiting, why didn't you attend the palace ceremony?"

She shrugged. "I waited for a summons from Her Majesty, but it never came."

Yoki narrowed his eyes, making him appear as though

he slept standing. Then he turned and asked, "More of your uncle's scheming?"

She followed his gaze and found Prince Hansamu still in argument with the priest. Scheming indeed. To prevent a fit of her own, she said, "Tell me more."

He grinned. "High court nobles walked beside the carriages, and senior courtiers with palace officials met the retinue. Lord Yūkan stood in a position of honor near Lord Michinaga and was permitted to assist his aunt from her carriage when it arrived. Her jacket and robes were as resplendent as the princess'. I have only seen two festival parades that could compare in magnificence."

"How were you able to escape and not Lord Yūkan? I had hoped he could come today." Kirei flicked her fan in irritation.

"He hadn't yet danced. The meal hadn't begun when I found my moment to slip away. I did have a chance to speak with him. We think Prince Hansamu plans to attempt a first night with you tonight. Lord Yūkan wanted to formulate a plan with my help, and I had suggested we take a day trip to the tendai temple on Mount Hiei, but there hasn't been time."

It reassured her that Yūkan hadn't given up. She studied Hansamu whose argument with the priest had progressed from edgy polite to open irritation. Guests chortled, and the prince seemed to enjoy the attention. He hadn't spared her a single glance.

The weight of sadness settled into her chest. "If only Ojisan wasn't moving so fast and we had more time. I regret staying. I should've returned to Shinano Province two weeks ago."

Yoki tugged on her sleeve, kindness shining in his tapered gaze. "How could you bear it, dear lady? How could you face that place of pain and loss?"

"I don't know." She fought a weariness that threatened her usual resolve. "I only know that letting my uncle make these decisions was a mistake. Meeting Lord Yūkan made me want things I shouldn't. Where else do I have to go?"

Her friend slowly shook his head.

"It doesn't matter." She returned her attention to the prince who completed the steps to his dance under fierce frowns from the four priests. "I cannot leave quietly now. There would be damning questions and damaging gossip. I won't be the cause of dishonor to my family, and I refuse to take the chance that Amai might suffer the social ramifications. No, it's too late now. It's too late."

\*   \*   \*   \*

Inhaling a deep, steadying breath, Yūkan stepped from his carriage. A rejection from Lady Kirei would devastate him. He had to tread carefully. He dismissed his driver with a wave and stared at Lord Fujiwara's imposing residence.

Yellow light from the mansion's main building gleamed on dew-moistened pebbles landscaping the ground fronting the steps. Beyond the bridge leading to the west wing, the estate appeared dark. Since nobody moved about, he climbed to the veranda, skirted the larger structures, and went straight to her and Amai's private wing. Her uncle had power, but Yūkan refused to fear him. This was too important.

He bypassed her door and went to the bamboo shades that formed the upper walls near the northernmost section that housed their bedchambers.

"Lady Kirei," he whispered, praying he had the right room. When no answer came, he gently rapped upon a wooden partition between two blinds and whispered louder, "Lady Kirei."

A bird chirped inside, and bedding rustled. She didn't say anything, however.

"It's Yūkan," he said, beginning to suspect he had Lady Amai's chamber. "May I come in?"

The rustling grew louder, then a blind shifted. Kirei's face appeared, pale and lovely in the moonlight.

"I thought you might be Prince Hansamu." She untied

the shade's mooring and lifted it aside so he could climb over the bottom wall section.

He removed his shoes and vaulted over the sturdy partition and into her room. As she secured the blind, he took in the unusually large sleeping area. A covered birdcage hung from a rafter above a brazier that provided a faint glow and sufficient heat for this space. The entire wall behind her futon consisted of floor-to-ceiling drawers - her impressive wardrobe.

Framed silk needlework portraying white and red cranes on pine branches hung on either side of her door, and her wooden writing box sat in the far corner. Other than her bed, a stool, and two square silk cushions, her dark wood floor was clean and bare. He moved one of the cushions close to the bed and sat.

"I wished you could have come to my Washing of the Buddha ceremony," she said, settling gracefully atop her bedding.

He took in her hair pooled on the floor beside her and the faint pastel of her few silk layers. Taking her arm, he slid back her soft sleeve and encircled her delicate wrist. "I wanted to, but Ichijō asked me to attend his feast following the Washing of the Buddha at the palace. I danced for them. Afterward, I spent a few hours bribing servants for Hansamu's and your uncle's schedules. Lord Yoki told me he had learned the prince planned to come to you tonight, and I had to get here before him."

"I see." She lowered her gaze.

Releasing her wrist, he gave her bed a nod. "You sleep like I do when I'm home, with a futon and proper covers. These Kyō aristocrats sleep on straw mats and cover themselves with their clothes. Very unsophisticated, in my humble opinion."

Kirei nodded. "The more I learn of you, the more I respect your opinion. You have no reason to call it humble."

"Have you heard from your father?" he asked.

Shifting her hips to her heels, she adjusted the plain neckline of her simple white robe. "Not yet. When I sent my letter, I suspected his reply wouldn't come in time. Each day that passes convinces me more that I was right."

"I might have a solution, if you're amenable." His stomach clenched. He straightened his shoulders, preparing to address her rejection with a brave face.

Her dark eyes studied him a long minute. "One moment. I'd like to see you properly."

She rose, went to the brazier, and used a long, thin stick to gather a flame to light a lantern. She hung it on a hook near her wardrobe and returned to her knees in front of him.

Some of her hair fell over one shoulder down her front, and she stroked it with both hands. "I think I might already know what you have in mind, but tell me. Maybe I'm wrong."

She glanced fleetingly into his eyes before returning her gaze to her lap. Her beauty paralyzed him. Would she let him touch her? Would she honor him with the most precious gift she had to give?

He released an arrested breath, crossed his legs and clutched both of his knees. "Let me stay the night, and again tomorrow, and again the next."

She sat unmoving. Did she even breathe? Stiffening his spine, he braced for her rejection.

\*　\*　\*　\*

Heart pounding, Kirei fought tears – tears of joy and tears of terror. She'd wanted nothing else for days now, but with the moment upon her, she froze.

If she said yes, she'd get what she wanted. A husband she truly loved, desired, and respected. Life in the country, if she convinced him to leave Kyō. A future focused on learning. Focused on true beauty rather than the superficial shimmer created by this city's nobility. Focused on meaningful, purposeful charity and change.

Yet if she said yes, he'd learn she was untouched. A virgin of her age was significantly unnatural. Some might go so far as to claim an evil spirit had possessed her. Did Yūkan fall in with that group?

Also, her uncle would never consent to provide his letter after their third night. Would her father approve? She wanted to believe he would want her happiness.

He cleared his throat. "Were you wrong?"

She forced her disinclined lungs to work. "No. Your proposal is what I thought."

He didn't say anything. Didn't move.

Trying to ignore the icy fingers of fear gripping her racing heart, she slid closer to him. She whispered, "I want so much to say yes, but I have a secret. If you learn my secret, you may not want me."

"Your voice is shaking."

She nodded. "I have too much to lose."

He took one of her hands and tilted her chin until she looked him in the eye. "You have nothing to lose. I know your secret."

Her stomach plummeted. He couldn't. "What do you think you know?"

His angular features grew harder. "That you've never taken a man to your bed."

She gasped. How? She'd clung to this secret for dear life every single day since her arrival in the imperial city. She hadn't even told Uma or Zo.

"I'd be honored to be your first...and only."

A sob escaped her lips as emotion overwhelmed her. Despite her tutoring and his adept ability at fine arts, he couldn't be more different from the noblemen of Kyō. Different in the best ways.

"When did you know?" she whispered.

"I began to suspect our very first morning on the foothills of Mount Hiei when your cousin talked about the virgin lady who was possessed. You stiffened. I saw."

She trembled but couldn't stop.

"In the weeks I've been here, not one gentleman has

spoken of an intimacy with you. You're so greatly admired that such an honor would be a bragging right. I suspect many think you sleep with Lord Yoki, and that's why you've never been questioned."

Of course it appeared so. Yet she had let Yūkan into her closest circle, and he was observant. He'd seen what she'd refused to say.

He released her hand and opened his arms. She leapt into his hug, wrapping her arms around his shoulders. Relieved to not be alone in her secret any longer, she touched her cheek to his. A tear escaped her lashes, and she brushed it away.

"Say yes," he whispered, squeezing her lightly.

She continued to tremble but no longer in fear. "Yes. I love you, Yūkan. Yes."

His sigh sounded heavenly in her ear. "I'm so glad you said that. I love you, too."

"What now?" She held her breath, despising her lack of experience.

He chuckled and gently put her from him. Cocking his head slightly, he smiled. "For once, I'm the expert."

She released a breathy laugh.

"Follow my lead." His gaze raked her from head to knees and back.

Flutters began in her belly. Her heart slowed, but not by much.

His eyes met hers while his fingers unfastened a tape tying his *uenoginu* closed. He untied another inside then shrugged out of the bulky garment. The V of his thin white under robe delved deep, showing a fan of straight black chest hairs.

She stared. She itched to brush her fingertips across them.

"Now you," he said.

"But—"

"No argument."

"A lady is expected to open amidst many layers of silk,

like a flower."

He shook his head. "A woman is expected to please her man. My pleasure starts with seeing you."

Her nipples hardened at the very idea of his eyes on her naked breasts. The man was too handsome, too sexy for words. Pleasing him was her greatest desire, so she stood then shrugged out of three *uchigi* in varying shades of peach and her dark green chemise. She loosened the tie at her waist and let her dark purplish red *hakama* sag to her feet so she wore only her *kosode*.

He stood, went to the brazier, and stirred its coals. Immediate heat raised the room's temperature. Facing her, he stepped out of his pants, leaving him in only his knee-length *kosode*. As he stepped from the fabric, his long legs bore the same dusting of dark hair as his chest, and his muscles attested to his enjoyment of climbing and dancing.

He came to her and helped her to her feet. Deftly, he untied the fastening of her robe then smoothly slid the silk aside to bare her shoulder.

"You're beautiful," he said. He placed a lingering kiss to the curve of her neck.

She boldly touched his chest. Finally, she got to touch him this way. The hairs there felt thick but soft.

"With me," he said low, working his firm, pliant lips up the side of her throat, "there are no rules. Learn my body. Explore."

He removed her *kosode* from the other shoulder. It fell to the floor, baring her completely. She'd expected a sense of vulnerability, but instead, she experienced a remarkable liberation. More than telling her he considered her beautiful, here like this, he showed her how he saw her.

His appreciation translated in the graze of his fingertips up her spine and the path of his lips from her throat to her breast. He went to his knees. When his hot mouth closed over her aching nipple, he awakened a new need in her.

She sent her fingers into his hair and sucked a breath of

delight through her teeth as he pulled upon her taut bud. Between her thighs, the throbbing she'd felt when he danced at her uncle's party began, but more intense. More insistent.

He stood and removed his short robe. Yūkan was glorious in his nudity. People talked of repulsion and disgust at the sight of undressed bodies, but his form intrigued her on a deeply sensual level. He had muscled arms and shoulders that flexed and bulged as he moved.

His broad chest, though infinitely more masculine next to Prince Hansamu's scrawny thinness during their dance, now appeared almost imposing above the fit taper of his rippled abdomen and the slimness of his hips.

His penis jutted, intimidating yet inspiring in its silent promise of pleasures to come. She'd heard accounts of the sexual act, but she already deduced that hers would be unique. She was a woman. Everyone she knew had lost their virginity as girls.

Here was no Kyō aristocrat intending to seek gratification at the expense of hers. Yūkan had taught her in a few minutes that his pursuit of beauty in the act went beyond artistic visuals. He appreciated her form as nature created perhaps more than he appreciated a flower's or tree's form. He would derive a thrill in her pleasure, not only his own. He wouldn't put effort into it otherwise. She smiled. Subtlety had never been his strength.

She backed to her futon, but before she could sink to her bedding, he reached her in two strides and held her close. Her breasts pressed to his chest. His rod pierced the fissure of her thighs and rested its rigid length against her pulsing, swollen crease.

Moisture eased into her folds. Everywhere he touched, his skin felt warm. He made her tingle. The *good people* didn't know what they missed by depriving themselves of the amazing arousal generated by the coming together of skin like this.

Savoring the contact, Kirei closed her eyes. This man loved her. He showed her he meant it through his touch. He made it clear through the adoration in his gaze. She'd never felt more cherished.

She parted her lips as he lowered his face to hers. Their mouths joined in a kiss so passionate her mind reeled. Deepening his pressure, he urged her to open wider. When their tongues engaged, her knees weakened. He went with her to the bed.

With her heart thudding, her breathing shortened to panting as her excitement increased. His lovemaking was an assault on her senses. His mouth devoured. His hands tested, measured, and teased. His body moved against her. He even smelled deliciously of cinnamon, sandalwood, and cloves. Her nerves escalated in their receptiveness until she wanted to scream.

Her entire body fairly hummed under him.

He spread her legs and planted his knees between hers. Using his new position, she explored him. He didn't possess a single soft spot. Every inch of him was hard. Masculine. Strong.

The throbbing grew unbearable, and she whispered into his kiss. His large hand splayed between her breasts then skimmed her abdomen to the place of her momentary torment. When he slid fingers between her swollen, slick folds, she gasped in relief.

His mouth working back and forth across hers, he stroked her flesh. Relief soon shifted to a more powerful need – the need to have him inside.

"Please," she said against his lips.

His fingers went to her ready opening. She felt the tug of her flesh where he tested her hymen.

He broke the kiss and gazed at her. Intensity radiated from his countenance and from every point where his body touched hers. "You're completely intact. This is going to hurt."

"I'm prepared. Please. I can't wait." She tilted her pelvis, begging for his entry.

He made an adjustment then his erection pushed at her opening. "Wrap your arms and legs around me and hold tightly."

Shaking in anticipation, she did as he instructed.

He descended, taking her lips in an open-mouthed kiss as he thrust his hips. She tore, engulfing his penetration in an inferno of pain. She screamed into his mouth.

Tears welled and spilled into her hair. She clung to him where he braced above her, fully seated inside and unmoving.

He lifted his lips from hers. Concern puckered his brow. "Are you okay?"

"No," she whispered. "I'm on fire."

"We can wait."

She shoved at his solid chest. "I want you out."

He didn't budge. "It will hurt worse if I pull out now. Let it subside. I promise it stops burning."

She didn't believe him. Flames of agony licked at her tender flesh, bringing another set of smarting tears.

"Relax," he said, his tone gentle. "Trust me."

She inhaled on a shuddering breath then forced her body to ease on a slow exhale. The pain lessened. Sending him a hopeful glance, she did it again and again until the burning ceased altogether.

"Feel better?"

She nodded.

"Okay. This is going to hurt, but not like before. Bear with it, and I promise pleasure will override the pain. Can you do this?"

She released a shaky breath. She had committed to this. A minute ago, she'd begged for it. She would wrong him, and maybe herself, to abandon their union.

"I can do this," she whispered.

He lowered until his cheek brushed hers and he slowly withdrew. It burned. She drew a sharp breath through her teeth. Right away, he entered at the same speed. Each pass hurt less until a tightening need began to coil at her core.

She relaxed into his movement. As he set a rhythm, she raised her knees to hug his hips. She met him thrust for thrust, pure pleasure forcing tiny gasping mewls from her throat.

Her blood raced. Her heart pounded. Her lungs labored. Every pump of his hips tightened the coil further. Increased her pleasure. Brought her closer to some elusive goal for which she strained.

"Please," she begged, not sure what she asked but needing it nonetheless.

His body went harder under her fingers. Without breaking his rhythm, he raised until he looked down upon her. His countenance bore tremendous tension as his lips thinned and his skin stretched over his cheekbones.

"I can't..." His voice rasped, deep and guttural. "Kirei. Aah!"

He reared, bucking against her. The coil snapped and a brief flash of intense pleasure stiffened every muscle in her. She felt her body squeeze his length once then relax.

It disappointed her. Somehow the building pressure had held a promise of more.

Yūkan groaned. He withdrew then flopped to the bedding next to her. "I'm sorry."

"Why?"

"I wanted you to get there."

She rolled to her side and winced at a painful pull. She dug her elbow into her pillow and propped her head on her hand. "Get where? Because I sensed it, but I didn't reach it."

"Exactly." He gathered her close and covered them with her soft cotton counterpane. "Ecstasy. It's difficult for a woman to achieve the first time. Maybe since you had so much pain, it was even harder for you. I thought there might be a chance. I tried to get you there, but you felt so amazing around me. I couldn't stop my own. That's why I'm sorry. I think you were close."

"Maybe." She rested her cheek to his chest and listened as his heartbeat nearly matched hers in tempo. "It was good, though."

"It was?"

She closed her eyes. "Women talk about it. I thought I knew what to expect. It was so much more than I anticipated. What we did tonight is different than how anyone else I know does it. They don't see each other undressed. In fact, they only remove their outer robes. They never touch skin to skin."

"Do you find my naked body disgusting?"

She smiled. "Your naked body is one of the most magnificent things I've seen."

His fingers drew lazy circles at her nape and across her upper back. She melted into him and hummed her approval.

"I liked it very much," she whispered. "Despite the pain at the beginning."

"Then you'll like it better when I come to you tomorrow night. I would take you again tonight, but you're already going to be sore."

Her walls tightened pleasurably when she imagined him entering her, but a twinge of pain at her opening had her agreeing. No more tonight.

"Wake up, lovely Kirei." She blinked. When she shifted, a stinging between her legs made her gasp.

Yūkan wore his *kosode* and pants. His disheveled hair came forward over both his shoulders. He squatted at her bedside with a reluctant expression. "It's morning and time for me to go. I don't want to."

Footsteps sounded in the hallway outside her door.

A sadness tugged in her chest, and she realized she didn't want him to go, either. She'd miss him. "You'll be back tonight?"

He grinned, and his masculine beauty made it impossible to breathe for a second. "I'll be here. Rest today. I'm going to have you awake for long hours tonight."

Her body stirred to acute awareness. Not trusting her voice, she nodded.

He glanced at her door and said, "Kiss me."

Wincing, she sat and wrapped her arms around his middle. She adored the feel of his firm, male body against her.

He lowered his mouth to hers, sending her head backward.

The door made a slight knocking sound on its track as someone touched it. It shished open then a muffled squeal filled the room.

Yūkan slowly released her mouth then added a sweet peck as if nothing happened. He stood.

In the doorway, Uma clutched the doorframe. A white linen towel pooled on the floor at her feet. Zo arrived and gazed over Uma's shoulder. Her plump lips formed an O as her thin eyebrows arched.

He collected his *uenoginu* from where he'd dropped it near the now-cold brazier. Smiling, he untied her blind and slipped outside.

## Chapter Nineteen

Kirei fell to her pillow and sighed. The man was entirely too sexy.

"My lady!" Uma shuffled to the bed with Zo at her heels. "You're naked."

"Very." She fought an urge to giggle.

"I'm confused. Why that gentleman?" Uma asked.

She met her maid's eyes. "Did you see him?"

Uma huffed but Zo blushed pink.

Kirei folded her hands behind her head. "You're forever commenting on how I'm different from the ladies of Kyō."

As Zo waddled out, Uma smoothed her fingers over her swept up hair. "You're *better* than most, my lady. You deserve a prince. A proper gentleman raised and educated here, at the least."

She groaned her frustration. "You know I don't want to be a consort. I want a husband. Legitimate children. A life lived in the open. The idea of a man hiding me behind closed doors for the rest of my existence makes me want to scream. I won't do it."

"This gentleman can give you what you want?"

She sat up, sinking teeth into her bottom lip at the telltale sting between her thighs. "He's like me. He hails from the very best family. He just wasn't lucky enough to live in this city. Have you considered I may not want to live here, either?"

Her maid moved about, gathering yesterday's *uchigi* layers and her discarded *kosode*. "Don't say you want to leave. It breaks my heart."

"There's so much I want to do. I love reading Chinese

works, and nothing gives me more satisfaction than to help someone in need. Do you think there's a single nobleman in this city who will allow me to do those things? Yūkan not only supports my good works, he accompanies and helps. Ladies are discouraged from reading Chinese, and the idea of my dealing with poor people, much less giving them aid, would send more than a few into hysterics. Not Lord Minamoto. He's different. He's like me."

Uma stopped working and drooped where she stood. "I know you speak the truth, but how will we do without you? Your cousin is sweet-natured, but you breathed life and excitement into this house when you came."

"Uma."

Her maid pouted.

"I can become a city gentleman's consort and move to his house, or I can take Yūkan as my husband and hopefully move to the country. Either way, I'll leave my uncle's home. Wouldn't you rather I found happiness and freedom in my move?"

"Moving to the country will be a form of exile, won't it?"

"It's not exile if I want to be there." She flung aside her covers.

A reddish brown bloodstain marred the bedding beside her. Uma stared at it a moment.

Kirei's heart thudded against her ribcage. "You'll keep my secret?"

Her maid headed for the door. "Of course. I always have."

*   *   *   *

A knock on his door woke Yūkan from a dead sleep. He tried his voice but could only manage a ragged croak.

The knock sounded again. "Yūkan. What are you doing in there?"

Yoki.

He cleared his throat and rubbed his eyes then sat. His back ached. He'd burn that straw mat if he could. "Come in."

His friend entered on a flourish, his stiff orange silk *karaginu* rustling as it rubbed against his maroon *hakama*. He lifted one eyebrow. "You're sleeping?"

"As a man will do when he spends the night elsewhere." He heaved to his feet and kicked the offending mat.

"Oh-ho! Is this *elsewhere* a certain Fujiwara estate in the Fourth Ward?"

"It is." He scrubbed his palms over his stiff face and combed fingers through his hair. "Send a servant to tell my driver to ready the carriage, would you please?"

Yoki poked his head into the hallway and made the arrangement then slid closed the door and sank to a cushion. "I hope you're prepared for war. Lord Fujiwara has plans for his niece."

"She's worth the fight."

"I should say so. Who saw you?"

"Her two maids and three gentlemen on the street. I made a show of it by leaving through her window, leaving my hair loose and waiting until I walked her block before donning my jacket."

"Good thinking. I've trained you well."

He chuckled. "So has Lady Kirei. I sent her a poem with a sprig of plum blossom attached."

"Did you?" Yoki beamed. "I feel like a proud papa...well, what I imagine a papa might feel. Speaking of children, I've decided to marry."

Yūkan froze where he bent over his clothing chest. "To whom?"

His friend shrugged. "I haven't decided."

He laughed. "Any prospects?"

"There's a pretty girl from the Tōru family living one street up in the Third Ward. She seems sweet but has seductive eyes. I like that. She might actually hold my attention an entire month before I get bored and start wandering again."

Yūkan chose a fresh under robe and a smart new *karaginu* in patterned brown watered silk. Over a pair of off-white raw silk *hakama*, it would lend him a natural, finished appearance Kirei admired. "You were raised wrong."

"No, you were raised wrong. We've already had this discussion."

"I've met two imperial ministers who are solely devoted to their wives."

Yoki tapped his knee with a tapered, almost womanly finger. "I'm not saying there's anything wrong with husbandly devotion. And for a time, it'll be tolerated. If they're interested in promotion and success in their careers, though, they'll take concubines and possibly an additional wife into their households."

He fastened the ties of his pants and shook his head. "You make me want to reconsider my decision to establish a household here."

"This city is brimming with patrician beauties. Are you telling me none of them tempt you? You plan to devote your entire love life to one woman?"

Yūkan smiled. "This one woman is Kirei. No one compares."

His friend cocked his head. "You've got a point there. She'll age, you know. Who knows what childbearing will do to her. She may not be a great beauty forever."

"She will be to me." Though he suspected she would retain her stunning good looks well into her senior years. She showed the same markers his grandmother had possessed, and his grandmother had been a renowned beauty until she died at the age of sixty-seven.

"Oh, Great Buddha. You love her, don't you?" Yoki rolled his eyes.

"Of course. And in two nights, she'll be mine." He shrugged into the *karaginu* and adjusted its collar smooth around his neck.

"It won't last. Love is fleeting. Don't use it as a compass

to make plans that change your life."

He tied the internal stay at his hip then wrapped the robe's front across his chest and secured the closure. "You're *good people*, Yoki, but you're a fool. There's nothing more important or life-changing than love. I look forward to the day you find it. Then we'll see who's offering and who's seeking the advice."

His friend barked a laugh and stood. "I guarantee that day will never come."

Yūkan's stomach rumbled so loudly Yoki stopped in his path to the door. "Sorry. I need to get something to eat."

"Let me take you out. We have a big night ahead. I've arranged to procure you an invitation to the Minister of Agenda's drinking party. It's practically a promise to grant you an interview. I've asked him to mentor you. The emperor won't ignore you much longer." Yoki opened the door and waited.

"Not tonight." He swept his hair high, twisted it into a tight topknot, and secured it with a thick steel clip. "I have an appointment."

"This is your career, Yūkan. What appointment is more important than an interview with a potential sponsor?"

"One with a certain Fujiwara lady of great reputation." He chose a stick of incense, one he'd mixed by his own design for a change, and inserted the tip into his brazier. It immerged smoking, and he infused his clothing with the smoke before extinguishing it in a shallow dish of water.

"Lady Kirei?" His friend's eyebrows came together over the nearly nonexistent bridge of his nose. "Two nights in a row? It's just not done. Especially considering..."

"That she's a virgin?"

Yoki cast a horrified glance over his shoulder to the wide palace hallway. He hissed, "Nobody knows."

"You did. I'd guess her maid did. I knew, too."

"Thanks to me."

He brushed past his friend and strode for the exit. "I suspected all along. It no longer matters. She's not, anymore.

And yes, I'm going back tonight."

Yoki half-jogged to keep up, his gait bouncy and comical. "It simply isn't done."

"It is."

"Only when—" His friend gaped. He halted and slapped a hand over his mouth.

Yūkan sighed and turned on his heel five steps shy of the courtyard door. "Don't act surprised. You know I love her."

His friend took a stomping step. "Then love her, but don't take her as your first. Take a *wife* first. Then add her as a consort."

"I *am* taking a wife first. My first. My last. My only."

Yoki's countenance darkened and the corners of his mouth turned downward. "That's career suicide. Have I taught you nothing?"

Yūkan despised this social tug-of-war. He took his friend's wrist and led him outside to his waiting carriage. "I don't have a choice. If I don't do this, Prince Hansamu will take her with her uncle's blessing. I won't lose her."

"I can't argue with that, but the cost is too high."

He let him go and opened the carriage door. "I might agree with you if I cared about a ministry position. I've already worked and retired from a career I enjoyed. I have my fortune. I'm only agreeing to this nonsense for Kirei's sake. I need to be respectable so I'm seen as worthy of her and so she can keep her social standing."

"It's not nonsense."

He closed the door and leaned to the window. "Really? You hold an illustrious position. Tell me one accomplishment you made today that benefited or provided an improvement to the people of this city. Better yet, tell me one such accomplishment you made this year."

Yoki's forehead wrinkled. He opened his mouth, cutting his eyes sideways in contemplation. Then he snapped his lips closed.

"That's what I thought." Yūkan rapped on the carriage

ceiling, and the conveyance jerked forward. "This is more than me and what I want. It's about Kirei. It's about my brother."

*　*　*　*

Kirei enjoyed a rare soak in her uncle's hot water tub. The tub was so large that it practically filled the small *furoba*, and Kirei could reach out and run fingertips along the room's cool, smooth wall. Her maid brought a fresh bucket of water and poured it in. Steam skated along the bath's surface, swirled in an elegant circle, and lifted into an elaborate curling line like smoke from incense.

"Feeling better?" Uma asked on a bow as she set the bucket in a corner.

Kirei rested her head back on the edge of the tub's tall wooden side. She took a deep breath, enjoying the rich loamy scent created by the light rain outside. "I didn't think you knew."

Her maid released a breath that sounded like *pah*. "Amai has had nighttime visitors since she was sixteen. Zo and I always have to take care when talking near her chamber in the morning. You, however, never do. We can come and go as we need. It didn't take me long after your arrival to figure out you weren't breached. Especially since you don't keep *kuma tsuzura* in your chamber. Amai always has *kuma tsuzura* tea after her nighttime visits to prevent an unexpected pregnancy."

Kirei put her hand on the flat stretch of skin below her bellybutton. She hadn't considered a baby might result from Yūkan's visit last night, but she had to. "Maybe I should drink some. Have I waited too long?"

Her maid slid a stool with a grating screech to the tub behind her, removed the cord binding her hair, and began brushing. "It's not too late. I'd be happy to prepare this tea for you...if it's what you truly want."

She opened her eyes and stared at a narrow wooden beam that ran from one wall top to the opposite. Daylight filtered in from steam vents where the walls didn't quite meet thick roof supports. Though the room was attached to the east colonnade and kitchen, it smelled of pine and clean air, as if she bathed outdoors.

Uma's soothing fingers massaged her scalp following each scrape of the brush. "Yūkan is a fine gentleman. As much time as Lord Yoki spends with you, I thought he might be the one to win you, but I understand your choice. I'm sorry for questioning it this morning."

"Yoki?" Kirei laughed softly, trying to imagine her friend attempting a romantic overture. He was a philanderer in the extreme and had no difficulty charming his way into nearly any lady's bed of his choice, but he held no appeal to her whatsoever. "Why didn't you mention you knew about my virginity?"

"I didn't want to embarrass you, my lady. Besides, the less said on that subject, the better. What's the saying? Walls have ears?"

"Yes. Thank goodness for singing floorboards, though this house has far fewer than I'd like."

"Exactly. That wasn't a rumor we wanted circulating. You'd have been shunned, and you definitely wouldn't have become a favorite of the empress. Lord Fujiwara has benefited greatly by your social success."

"My uncle knew?" Her heart skipped a beat.

"No, and be thankful. He wouldn't have hesitated to declare you unfit and banish you back to the country in disgrace. I guarded your secret most diligently from him."

Banished to the country. It sounded so good, even if home held such haunting memories. It was the disgrace part she had to avoid. Though she'd been unhappy in Kyō, she wouldn't regret it. She'd met Yūkan here. She'd fallen in love here.

A young maid from the staff of her uncle's first wife looked in, her eyes wide. "Pardon me, but Prince Hansamu is here."

Kirei shrugged. "What has that to do with me?"

The maid bowed. "I'm sorry, my lady. Lord Fujiwara is entertaining him right now but requests your presence. He asks you to bring your poetry and a story or two. The prince is expected to stay late."

Uma's hands stilled.

Kirei stiffened. Her uncle and Hansamu were making their move. Yūkan had waited too late to begin his bid of seduction. Time had run out.

## Chapter Twenty

A light drizzle cast a sheen on the imperial city's well-tended avenues as Yūkan rode through the upper wards. Night wouldn't descend for hours, but cloud cover lent an air of premature evening. He hoped Kirei wouldn't mind his coming so early, but he couldn't wait to see her.

As though well-practiced, his driver guided the ox they had borrowed from Lord Yoki to the north gate of the Fujiwara mansion. Kirei stood outside the door to her wing, her hair twisted into an elegant arrangement atop her head. She wore an array of pinks and frosted purples that somehow brightened the gloom of the late afternoon. Despite a fan hiding her face, she had her head bent low.

Her uncle yelled and waved his arms, which caused the long sleeves of his *karaginu* to wave wildly. Beside him, Prince Hansamu stared expectantly at her.

Not wishing to make her already difficult situation worse, Yūkan fought the urge to rush to her rescue. His appearance would surely push Lord Fujiwara into a rage, so he sank deeper into the shadows of the carriage's interior and waited.

Her lovely profile turned a bit, and she caught sight of his conveyance. She said something, bowed to her uncle, and headed for the north entrance.

"This is unacceptable!" her uncle shouted. He didn't follow, however.

Yūkan didn't dare let the men see him, so he waved to his driver through the opposite window. The driver opened the door on the mansion side, and Lady Kirei entered without delay.

"Are you okay?" he asked while she arranged her robes and his driver took position at the oxen's head.

"Mm-hmm," she said, her lips not moving. She offered a curt wave to the men when the carriage began rolling. She held a straight posture until they reached the next block. Then she lowered her window's blind and sagged against the wall. "That was a scene."

"I saw it, so I have to agree." He moved aside layers of silk to find her soft hand. "I take it we won't be spending the evening at your uncle's house."

She released a half sob and dropped her fan to her lap.

He slid his cushion to hers and gathered her close.

"Can we please get out of the city? I know it's late to begin a trip, but—"

"Of course." Though he was glad for any excuse to leave Kyō, her obvious distress churned his stomach. He opened his door and stepped out. Walking beside the slow-moving conveyance, he instructed his driver to switch out the ox for his horse and take them into the mountains.

"Thank you," she said when he climbed inside.

"Do you mind if we stop at the palace for a time?"

She gently smiled. "Actually, it's ideal. I escaped by saying I had been summoned by the empress. It was a lie, but your fancy carriage arrived at just the right moment."

"I'm glad I could help." He held her close.

Resting her head on his shoulder, she said, "I thought I was doomed."

The carriage lumbered over a steel bar forming the frame base of the Nine Fold Enclosure's ornate eastern entrance. It bumped and tipped so hard, Yūkan lost his cushion.

Kirei laughed and lifted a hand to check her hair.

Positioning his cushion under him, he said, "I want to hear about it, but let me go inside and get us a few provisions while my driver switches the ox for my horse."

She gave him an elegant nod.

He strode to Yoki's lushly appointed and rarely used apartment and collected a floor settee with a connected back and armrests that accommodated two people. He also borrowed a padded lap throw that he gathered into a makeshift sack and filled with a sealed bottle of *sake*, two cups, a wooden box containing dried fruit, and a flute.

He carried his load through the wide hall, past his own small room, not caring who noticed him. Footsteps slapped the floor behind him, but he didn't turn. He wouldn't keep his gorgeous lady waiting a minute longer than necessary.

"Yūkan," came Yoki's winded voice.

"I'm busy," he said over his shoulder.

"Wait."

"No." He moved outside, and his heart beat faster at the thought of spending the night to come with her in his arms.

His friend reached his side, their feet crunching on gravel coating the courtyard. "I think I can get you time with the emperor tonight. Empress Akiko is indisposed, and I know for a fact that he has no official plans."

Yūkan halted. This was his very purpose in coming to Kyō in the first place. Had the afternoon gone smoothly, he'd be in Kirei's wing of the Fujiwara house and missing this opportunity entirely. He had to believe that events had unfolded in such a way as to make this possible, and he couldn't ignore it. This could be his only chance.

"Okay. Give me a second." He headed for the carriage, which stood unattached to any animal. His driver wasn't in sight. He assumed he'd left to put away the ox and fetch his horse.

"Aren't these mine?" asked Yoki, taking the bag. "You're getting them wet in this rain."

"Yes. Careful, that's just a lap throw."

"Where were you going with my things?"

"On a midnight tryst."

His friend's countenance lit. "I love a tryst."

"I'm sure you do, but this isn't your tryst. It's mine." He shifted the settee and opened the carriage.

Kirei had gone.

\* \* \* \*

"I'm glad you came. The empress wouldn't let us send for you, so how did you know she wasn't feeling well?" Sei waved as Kirei left the empress' curtained sleeping space in the First Ward mansion.

"I didn't know," she whispered. "I had stopped at the palace on my way to Mount Hiei, and Uki saw me."

"It's good. Now Akiko will sleep. You have a way of putting her at ease that the rest of us don't have." Sei led the way to the empress' small garden but stayed on the covered walkway. "Why are you going to Mount Hiei at this hour? The night will be half over before you reach the first temple."

Kirei smiled. "For once, I'm not going to pray."

"I really wish you'd blacken your teeth. Your smile gleams horribly in the torchlight." The lady-in-waiting went still. "Wait. Not to pray? You're going to meet a man!"

"Ssh." Kirei chuckled at the woman's enthusiasm. "I'm doing better than that. I'm going *with* a man in the same carriage, and we're spending the night."

"Scandalous." Sei giggled. "I feel special. You're so discreet none of us ever know who you're sleeping with or when or where. Will you tell me who?"

She hesitated but figured everyone would know in a few days. She was only sorry they couldn't sleep in her chamber as tradition prescribed, but Prince Hansamu made it impossible. "I go with Lord Minamoto no Yūkan."

Sei's features lost their lift. "He's from the country, isn't he?"

"So am I." She stood straighter and raised her chin a notch.

"You're not countrified, though. You're beautiful and

smart and the most refined lady I know. Maybe more bookish than I like, but I can overlook it in light of the wonderful poetry it helps you write."

"Like the way you overlook how I don't blacken my teeth or pluck my eyebrows?" Kirei took a deep breath to stifle a surge of anger. "Lord Yūkan is immediate nephew to Minamoto no Rinshi. He's richer than most of the noblemen here. If you had seen him dance at my uncle's party, you wouldn't question his refinement."

"Well, he's not handsome in the way our Lord Yoki and Prince Hansamu are, but there's something about him, isn't there? Something so manly and strong that it almost beckons the woman in us, don't you find? I can't fault you for this attraction. It may not be artistically alluring, but I can't deny the natural appeal. It's classic."

Classic? Kirei averted her face and fought a smirk. "He's probably wondering where I am. I need to go."

"Do you mind if I come?"

Uki came around the building's corner. "Come where?"

"Lady Kirei's going with Lord Yūkan to Mount Hiei tonight."

"That sounds romantic."

Kirei laughed outright. "Bumping along mountain roads in the darkness is hardly romantic."

"My brother will let us use his carriage," said Sei, grinning.

"I'm not going to stop you if you follow us." Kirei caught Sei's contagious smile. Maybe this wasn't such a bad idea. Wouldn't they need witnesses to their second night together in order to make their scheme work?

Uki squealed in delight.

They both hushed her.

"Don't wake Her Highness," warned Kirei. "I'm going. Do what-ever you like."

"There's no rush." Uki offered a courteous bow and headed for her room in the outer ring of chambers surrounding the empress' quarters. "I saw Lord Yoki taking Lord Yūkan to the emperor's offices right before I fetched the empress' water pitcher at the palace."

*   *   *   *

"This is about my family." Yūkan bowed low.

"Please stop bowing. It's distracting." Emperor Ichijō indicated a neat stack of colorful silk cushions in a corner. "Sit. Visit with me a while."

Finally he received an official invitation to sit with Ichijō. Why did it have to be tonight?

Yoki tossed a green cushion on the bare wood floor and sat. "We can't stay long. We have a secret rendezvous."

The emperor's eyebrows lowered. He gave Yūkan a hard look. "It wouldn't be with a certain royal favorite, would it?"

Yoki laughed. "Of course it would."

"Then the rumors are true." Ichijō rubbed his chin. "Do you think Fujiwara suspects? He won't be pleased."

Yūkan dropped a red cushion next to his friend's and joined them. "Does it matter?"

A lightness entered the emperor's eyes. "I think the best of Lady Kirei. She deserves the finest of everything."

"The finest meaning material possessions? Because you can't mean the finest in circumstances. Kyō society dictates that no man worth anything can take her as his wife; so she either remains single or she accepts a nobleman's protection by becoming his concubine. How is that the finest?"

The emperor cleared his throat and folded his hands in his lap. "Indeed. My father spoke highly of both your grandfather and your father. He considered them friends. He valued their honesty."

He didn't dare speak until he understood where the emperor headed with his words. Had Yūkan overstepped?

"I can tell you don't withhold your honest opinion any more than they did."

"No, I don't, Your Majesty. I've learned in my travels that most men value wisdom and truth as highly as they do currency. Sometimes more. I was taught to seek these virtues and demonstrate them at every opportunity."

A slow smile lifted Ichijō's features. "These are virtues I value, as well. I believe we would be wise to continue the friendship of our fathers."

Yūkan relaxed. "I agree. Fudōno has taken over the running of our trade business. I hope he'll be welcome to bring our goods to this city for sale."

"He's welcome here. We're glad for a steady influx of fine Chinese wares. Be sure to tell him to bring his imports to the Nine Fold Enclosure first. I'll want my pick of his best. If he'll do this for me, I believe I can influence the transportation ministry to continue to waive fees and taxation of the Minamoto Trading Company. Keep paying your rice shares and we'll have no reason to complain."

Yūkan bowed where he sat. "Thank you, Your Majesty. Your terms are generous, and I will write to Fudōno as soon as possible. There is another matter of great importance I wish to discuss with you."

"I'm listening."

"There's a silk dyer in the Eighth Ward – a man by the name of Hen Na. He's been enslaving young women from the country to work in his warehouse. Is this a common practice in Kyō?"

"Certainly not." Ichijō gave a pointed nod toward Yoki.

"Yes, Your Majesty," said the gentleman. "Hen Na. I'll make a note of it and have a ministry investigation begun."

"Good." The emperor gestured to a clerk who presented a scroll. Ichijō unrolled it and accepted an inked brush. Offering a small smile to Yūkan, he said, "I don't want to keep you too long from your lovely lady, but I need to make two things clear."

"Yes, Your Majesty."

"First, I cannot interfere. Lady Kirei is Minister

Fujiwara's niece and ward and, therefore, subject to his machinations and decisions." He signed the scroll then turned it and offered the brush to Yūkan.

He recognized the original agreement of their fathers. He signed directly beneath his father's signature then handed the brush to the clerk. "Are you aware that his decision involves giving her over to Prince Hansamu?"

Ichijō gave a brief nod. His eyes twinkled when he said, "Second, I privately support anything you can do to thwart him. Lady Kirei is dear to my wife and me. I want to see her happy."

Yūkan shared a smile with Yoki. "Of course, Your Highness. I'll do my best."

"I hope your best is good enough. Now go to her. Lord Yoki, you go with them. I can't think of a more reliable source of gossip when you return tomorrow, and write a poem about how the famous Lady Kirei spent her night."

## Chapter Twenty-One

"There you are." Kirei came through the palace's East Gate entrance with Sei and Uki, going to Yūkan. "You spoke with the emperor?"

"I did." He held out a welcoming hand, his expression kind.

"It went well?"

"Very."

Lord Yoki came from around the back of the carriage. "Let's get out of this rain."

"He's coming?" she whispered.

"By the emperor's order. He's to write a poem about us and our night."

"How charming." She smiled, recognizing Ichijō's support.

"Yeah, real charming. Who are they?" Opening the carriage door for her, he indicated Sei and Uki with a tilt of his head.

"Ladies-in-waiting like me." She let him help her inside. "They're coming, too. As witnesses."

He scowled at Yoki. "Find your own way. This carriage is full."

The aristocrat opened his mouth to speak, but noisy crunching from an approaching carriage interrupted. He studied the two ladies for a second, his lips pursed, then he smiled a wolfish grin. "That's Lady Sei. I'll ride with her. I may have to write a poem about *my* night."

Yūkan closed the door. While he went around to the other side, Kirei took in the interior's transformation. The entire floor was hidden by cushions. She sat upon a settee she could tell was particularly plush, even through her twelve layers of silk. In a corner near where he climbed in, a swath of material formed a sort of nest for a *sake* set and wooden box. She'd never enjoyed such comfortable accommodations in a conveyance.

When the carriage began to roll, he got to his knees and held out his hands. "Let me help you out of your wet layers."

Her heart stuttered at the idea of him undressing her. Tucking her fan in her sleeve, she met his gaze. She untied the belt of her *karaginu* and shrugged out of it. She lifted her hips while he pulled it out from under her. As her stomach quivered amidst a flutter of anticipation, he laid her robe across the cushions. She unfastened her *mo* from around her waist, pulled it free, and handed it to him.

She got to her knees right when the driver took them over the gateway's metal bar. She laughed as she lost her balance and toppled. He helped her remove her intricately woven *uwagi*.

She'd forgone donning an *uchiginu* of stiff beaten silk when Uma had assisted her in dressing for her escape. She didn't want that heavy layer slowing her. Now, in a patterned purple gown of smoothest Chinese silk, six layers of barely-there gossamer *uchigi* in graduating shades of lavender and pink, and her soft white *hitoe*, she relaxed against the settee's back on a sigh.

He removed his own *karaginu*, and she noticed for the first time how well-appointed he appeared. His color and fabric combinations spoke of a fine, artistic mind. His topknot looked neat and clearly stated his position in the hierarchy by its superb placement and hint of a twist.

He hadn't done anything to hide the natural brown of his skin, and thank goodness. The rain would've made any face powder into a hideous mess. Besides, she'd grown accustomed to his dark coloring. In fact, she liked it.

"You're happy this evening." He settled beside her and

pulled her close.

She put her cheek to his firm chest. "I am. I'm with you. We're leaving the city. I've escaped my uncle's excellent attempt to put Hansamu in my bed tonight. All very good reasons to be pleased."

His chuckle rumbled under her ear, and his pale *kosode* felt warm and soft against her skin. He smelled wonderful, and she inhaled deeply.

Where her robes gaped, she pressed a palm to the waistband of her *hakama*. "My maid offered to prepare *kuma tsuzura* tea for me today."

He was quiet for a time. Then he asked, "And?"

"I didn't accept. Should I have?" Her stomach knotted.

"No." He kissed her forehead. "No. The idea of having a child by you pleases me more than I can say."

Joy warmed her from the inside out. "I'm sorry for judging you harshly and treating you badly when we first met. You have a better character and more generous spirit than most of the so-called *good people* of Kyō."

"You don't need to apologize. What matters is that you gave me a chance when many others wouldn't. Thanks to you and Yoki, and hopefully with Emperor Ichijō's friendship, I'll be able to give you the life you want."

Pushing to a sitting position, she asked, "What life do I want, Yūkan?"

He straightened from the arm of the settee. "The life you have here in the imperial city, as a royal favorite. Wearing the finest silks, surrounded by *good people* who admire you, and enjoying the artistry that can only be found here."

Her heart sank. "You think I want to live here?"

"Don't you?"

The carriage bounced over a pitted section of road, letting her know they had left the city, and the distinct odor of a pig farm permeated the air.

"Do you smell that?" she asked.

"Of course."

"That's a country smell. So is the scent of fresh rain on overturned soil. How about the fragrance of rice stalks when the wind blows through them? I miss these. I miss the sound of women singing during the rice harvest, the laughter of children chasing puppies, and the hum of wind when it brushes through rocky mountain crevices."

He caressed the curve of her cheek. "You seem to thrive in this society. Your talent and beauty put many of these aristocrats to shame, yet they love and appreciate you."

"They appreciate my aesthetic, not me as a person. I know you value them. You came to take lessons from me because you want to emulate them and be accepted by them. I think it's *you* who wants to live in Kyō." Her heart sank lower.

He simply shook his head.

She began to hope. "If they knew me, truly knew me, they'd shun me."

"Why?" He arched his eyebrows.

"Before last night, I was a virgin. That alone would've had people screaming for my banishment and accusing me of being susceptible to evil spirits. My uncle is no exception. I despise their selfish, self-righteous ways. Lord Yūkan, our births are no lower than theirs, yet they condescend to us because of where we lived. They treat lower classes little better than animals and address charity like a religious requirement rather than a social necessity."

"I see."

"Do you?" Frustration throbbed like a pulse in her neck.

"I believe the same."

The fight left her in a whoosh, and she slumped against the settee's back. "You do?"

"Every bit of it. Well, except the susceptible to evil spirits part. I love that I was your first."

A smile struggled its way to her lips. "I wish I had known you before my father decided to send me here. Well, before I had asked to, actually. Then we could've saved this trouble and nonsense."

He shook his head. "I was traveling the world in trade until three months ago. If you'd known me before now, it would've been fleeting at best. No, this is how it was meant to be between us. I had to be free of work to properly win you."

Kirei laughed. "Win me? Was I really so difficult?"

He smiled. "Yes. You were stubborn, but in a good way. You won't settle for just any gentleman, and you showed me that if I wanted you, I had to earn the privilege of your consideration."

Guilt heated her cheeks, and she swallowed. "I was strict. I admit it."

He chuckled. "Good. Now come here and kiss me. Show me you've set aside your hardness. Be soft for me."

Her heart swelled with love as she leaned against him. She touched her lips to his, and he didn't let her kiss him long before he claimed control.

He parted her many robes and hugged her, chest to chest. Only their thin *kosode* stood between them. His heat came through, as well as the firm feel of muscle, and her nipples hardened.

Growling low, he urged her to open. His tongue met hers in a smooth, sweet stroke that tasted of refreshing cucumber and tangy ginger. His hands slid under her innermost *uchigi* to skim her thin *kosode* up and down her spine.

If only this could be their third night. Then she could surrender, knowing nothing threatened their togetherness.

\*   \*   \*   \*

Leaving Kirei snacking on fruit in the carriage, Yūkan negotiated accommodations for them, for the three hangers-on still traversing the dark mountain pass, and for their drivers. He carefully adhered to the rules of temple protocol, getting the housing monk up from bed and providing a sizeable donation to the temple, which had the man bowing and leading the way in no time.

After checking the rooms and finding them more than satisfactory, he sent the monk to meet the other carriage. Yūkan returned to Kirei who looked cozy and content in the padded luxury of his conveyance.

Offering a hand, he said, "Come while away this rainy night with me."

Her smile widened, but he glimpsed it only a moment before she hid it behind her fan. She accepted his hand and let him help her out.

When she hesitated, he asked, "Are you alright?"

"Listen." She closed her eyes and tightened her grip on his hand. "The rain gently patters the leaves high up, but by the time it trickles down here, it has gathered into large drops that splatter on the wet earth."

A steady popping sound filled the night as water bombs fell from the trees near and far. He smiled. The doleful cry of a deer came through the darkness.

"She calls for her lover," he whispered.

Kirei opened her eyes and locked gazes with him. His heart pounding, he licked his lips, fighting the urge to lower her fan and claim her lips. A shout interrupted, however, as the second carriage approached.

"We're getting wet," she said quietly.

"Right. Let's go inside." He led her along a wooden walkway protected by a temple eave.

At an open courtyard formed by a ring of varied buildings, he escorted her past a blazing torch that hissed in the rain. A long, fine residence appeared as if it had been plucked from a *shinden* in the city. It ran the entire length of the courtyard, its sloping bark-shingled roof and lit outdoor lanterns inviting in the night.

Rather than bamboo shades and bottom screens, the outer walls of this structure actually had solid wood walls carved to look as though made of indented block squares. He gave her soft, cool fingers a squeeze and climbed to the dry veranda. His manhood stirred, eager with the need to get her into true privacy.

At the rear, he stopped at their room and slid open the door. She slowly lowered her fan and grinned.

"Do you like it?" he asked.

"It's very nice." She stepped from her shoes and went in.

He breathed deeply of her perfume as she passed but didn't linger to savor it as a true gentleman of the imperial city should. He removed his shoes and followed, closing the door behind him.

She stood at a large round pillar and fingered its elaborate carvings. "This craftsmanship is excellent. Now I see why my friends enjoy coming to the temples when they want a tryst. These rooms are as comfortable as our homes."

He removed his jacket and went to a corner brazier. It had hot coals, so he added fuel. Immediately, the room began to grow warmer.

He knocked on an inner wall. "Look. Solid wooden walls. Not curtains or removable screens. We have complete privacy."

She tucked her fan in her sleeve, her gorgeous eyes widening a fraction. "I don't think I've ever been in a building where I had privacy like this."

He chuckled. "Me, neither. It's something to think about. Maybe we should add solid walls to my home when we get to Echigo?"

Her slight smile disappeared. "I'm scared."

In three strides, Yūkan reached her. He searched for her fingers among her layered sleeves then took her hands in his. "I promise it won't hurt tonight."

She shook her head in a faint movement. "I'm talking about my uncle and Prince Hansamu. They have wealth and power. We're fortunate Ojisan didn't go to the palace today. He didn't hear the gossip about us."

He nodded. "I don't think he'd have let you leave his house without an official imperial escort this evening."

"Or he would've come to the palace with me and stayed close. By the time we go back tomorrow, he'll know what we've done. A third night could be impossible."

"Not impossible. I have wealth, too. Maybe he shouldn't underestimate my connections and determination."

Her gaze softened. "I love you so much. Our third night is everything, but my uncle has the ability to prevent it."

## Chapter Twenty-Two

"Let's have our second night before we worry about the third." Yūkan released Kirei's hand and shifted her hair from her shoulder. He buried his face in the curve of her neck.

She wanted to be naked and in his arms, but she also didn't want to rush. If her uncle thwarted their efforts, this could be her last night with the man she loved. She would savor every second.

He slipped off her many layers as though they formed one thick coat. The weighty material settled to the wooden floor with a heavy sigh, leaving her light and freer to move. He kissed a line along her taut tendon, and she quietly moaned as he followed her collarbone to the round of her shoulder.

She raised her arms, causing her breasts to ride a bit under her plain, thin *kosode*. Her nipples hardened in acute awareness. Everywhere he kissed, her skin tingled.

While she untied his topknot, he moved lower and captured one of her nipples through the silk. A shock of pleasure shot from her breast to her crease. As a delightful throbbing began along the folds between her thighs, she gasped.

His hair fell past his shoulders, and she combed her fingers into its thick, straight ebony strands. The intimacy in this small liberty made her heart race. He shrugged out of his jacket. When it landed, something hard hit the floor with a brief clatter.

She didn't waste breath to ask since he worked to unfasten the tie of her *hakama*. She needed all the air her lungs could get as he dipped a hand inside and cupped her now aching folds. Her entire body thrumming with need, she arched in a silent plea for more. As if in answer, he slipped his finger into her wetness.

"Yes." She grasped his broad shoulders and tipped back her head.

His mouth touched hers while he intimately caressed her. Her loosened trousers dropped, the stiff raw silk maintaining its structure enough to allow the waistline to rest at her knees. He added pressure to his kiss, and she opened.

A deep, raw sound of need rumbled in his throat. His tongue met hers in a sensual dance, a continuation of the promising kisses in his carriage. The kisses that had made time speed by. The kisses that led to this moment.

"My beauty," he said, taking a step back and releasing her.

She swayed. Her head swam in an ocean of expectation, and her body pulsed with growing desire.

He removed his *hakama* and tossed it onto a straw sleeping mat that occupied the center of the room. He took her sea of silk and folded it into a makeshift mattress. Squatting, he arranged the layers smooth.

"Come," he said low, holding out his hand.

Her heart skipped a beat. The man looked so sexy, with his broad shoulders, long hair, and muscular legs. For tonight, he was hers. If she had enough good karma from her charity and genuine wish for the wellbeing of others, perhaps their plan would find success and he'd be hers for the rest of their days.

She took his hand. "You feel like my destiny. Ours wasn't a chance meeting, was it?"

He stood and gazed at her. "No. I feel it, too. I felt it the first time I saw you. Our love transcends this earth. I've loved you before and I'll love you again. I'll love you for all time."

The truth of his words suffused her soul with rightness. "Yes. For all time."

He opened her *kosode* then his own. His jutting member offered proof that his arousal matched hers. Without releasing her hand, he went to the bed of pink and purple silk. He drew her down on top of him.

Their mouths met in a passionate kiss as their bare torsos came together. A hum of satisfaction vibrated her throat. She'd wanted this every minute of this day.

As he drew a swath of white silk atop her, his scent enveloped her. The fragrance she'd chosen carefully hours earlier rose from her *uchigi* and mingled with his. The two scents suited, creating a new perfume so delicate and delicious that it invited her to inhale deeper.

He swept her hair to one side. Through the wall, muffled laughter announced the arrival of Yoki and Sei. Then the door to their room slid open and spilled cold air across the floor. Kirei shivered, and Yūkan pulled his *karaginu* close over her.

Uki grinned in the doorway then looked to where their legs protruded. Her expression soured. "You're undressed? That's disgusting."

Irritation tightened Kirei's gut. "Get out."

"Just had to make sure. You wanted an eyewitness." Uki closed the door and laughed. Her giggles faded as she moved away along the veranda.

Yūkan's gaze caressed Kirei's face, which stirred her to renewed desire. He said, "We should've brought a man for her...to give her something to do."

She shook her head. "I don't want to think of her. I only want your hands and mouth on me so I can't think."

His countenance relaxing into seriousness, he released a raspy groan. He cupped her nape and pulled her into a passionate kiss that granted her wish. Closing her eyes, she blindly explored the hard planes and dips of his body. His hands skimmed over her curves, leaving a trail of goose bumps in their wake.

His fingers brought her breasts to life, hardening her nipples and increasing the moisture at the juncture of her thighs. He took her by the hips and adjusted her position so his erection pressed into her slit. Her heart pounded. Her folds throbbed. Deep inside, her woman's core pulled, begging for him to enter.

Breaking from the kiss, she pressed her face into the warmth of his neck, her breaths panting in short bursts. "Please."

On a sexy moan, he sent his arm across her back and flipped them in a single move. She gasped then chuckled.

When he locked eyes with her, her humor fled. He hiked her knees to his hips, and his mouth claimed hers at the same time he entered her.

She stiffened, but rather than pain, sheer pleasure shot though her. He slowly stroked in and out. With each thrust of his hips, her pleasure climbed. Her pulse raced. Her temperature rose.

"Yes," she said on a labored exhale.

He increased his pace. Rocking her pelvis, she matched his rhythm. Each thrust took her into deeper pleasure. He lifted his upper body, ending the kiss, his hands braced on the bedding at either side of her shoulders as he pumped into her. His handsome face hardened in concentration, and he closed his eyes.

Then her walls closed around him. Ecstasy took hold of her. It clenched every muscle and squeezed a band around her chest, making it impossible to breathe. As pleasure shook her to her soul, she clung to him.

*   *   *   *

The earth seemed to tremble as Yūkan's release surged and he came. Kirei went limp, and he collapsed beside her. Working to catch his breath, he lay still, trying to gauge the earthquake. Nothing moved. Had he imagined it?

He gathered her against him, soaking in her soft warmth. When had she become a part of him? The idea of leaving her at her uncle's house the next morning sent a sharp jab into his chest. She somehow completed him, and it made him nervous to think they hadn't yet finished the binding ceremony.

One more day. One more night. Uma would ensure they received the necessary third-night rice cakes, which would lend their connection the religious sanction required. The only piece missing would be the formal letter of committal. He was following every rule, but he couldn't make others do the same.

Certainly not her uncle.

They would also have to forego the feast with her family and friends. He raked fingers across his scalp. Assistance from her attendants wasn't enough. He needed approval from her family. As of tonight, he didn't have it.

His gut twisted painfully. He'd given her his heart. He was prepared to spend the rest of his life with her. In fact, he couldn't imagine a future without her.

He needed help from someone who understood the rules of these strange aristocrats. Someone who knew the ins and outs and might identify a loophole for this situation. He needed Yoki.

The sound of birdsong and laughter woke him the next morning. When Kirei sighed, curling against him and laying her head on his chest, he kept his eyes closed. He wrapped his arm around her slight frame and inhaled the sweet, sleepy smell of her. The room had a chill, but in their cocoon of silk, he enjoyed a cozy warmth he hadn't experienced in a long time.

The door slid open and Uki bowed. "Good morning."

"Go away," Kirei mumbled, not moving.

The woman chortled. "Aren't you hungry? I brought breakfast."

"I'm not ready to move," admitted Yūkan.

"You have to." Uki carried in a tray bearing bowls of rice, cups of water, and a variety of sliced fruit. "We need to leave soon. The sun is already well past the horizon."

"Go away," Kirei repeated.

"Fine, but don't take your time. Lady Sei is up and dressed. She's waking Lord Yoki right now."

The door closed, and Yūkan kissed Kirei's forehead. "If only we could run away. I would take you to my home in Echigo."

"I can't disgrace my family that way, though it's tempting. So tempting."

He located the sleeve of his *karaginu*-turned-blanket and withdrew his flute. "Nobody understands that better than I. Both your father and your uncle are imperial officials. You wouldn't want to compromise their careers. I have my brother to think about. We have to carefully plan our moves to protect our families while trying to win a life together."

"Exactly."

He raised the flute to his lips. Why couldn't he think of any ideas to gain family approval? Even just the appearance of it would suffice. Closing his eyes, he poured his affection for Lady Kirei into an impromptu melody. It came out as lilting and exquisite as her. The cheerful tune, however, didn't override his pensive mood.

Kirei rolled from their bed and hunched against the chill. She padded to the brazier, stirred its dying coals, and added fuel. After bringing the tray close, she slipped in beside him.

"Are you playing a tribute to the beauty of the new day?" she asked.

He shrugged. His song was more a tribute to her than anything else, but he didn't want to stop playing. Not yet.

She reached over him, chose a slice of yellow fruit and took one of the cups. "You're truly becoming a gentleman of Kyō."

A few days ago, he'd have preened from her compliment. Now, it provided inducement enough to stop his playing.

He set aside the flute. "Do you want to live in the imperial city?"

"Do I have a choice?" She drank, gazing at him over the cup's rim.

"Yes." His stomach gurgled, partly from hunger and

partly from anxiety. "Your uncle would prefer you stay. You're doing wonders for his career."

She rolled her eyes. "I barely respect the man. I wish you could meet my father. You'd see how very different they are. I'm glad Ojisan has benefited from my coming to the city, but I couldn't care less what he wants."

He took in her sleep-puffed eyes, pale countenance, and mussed hair. He'd never seen her so unkempt or beautiful. Unable to resist, he caressed her smooth cheek. He needed a clear yes or no. "You haven't answered me. Do you want to live in Kyō?"

She slowly chewed and swallowed the fruit. When she faced him, worry etched lines around her eyes and mouth. "You came to this city to meet Emperor Ichijō and ensure that Fudōno can sell his imports here. Ichijō sent you to me so you could learn the manners and refinements necessary to be accepted by the *good people*. You have, so I assume you want to live here."

Frustration clenched a fist in his gut. Why couldn't she simply give him a straight answer? "Are you happy here?"

"Happy enough." A small smile stretched her lips. "I'm happy with you, which says a lot. I didn't think happiness was possible."

"Why not?"

"Though my father made the decision to send me here, it was at my request." She went still, her eyes staring at her cup of water. "You see, I thought myself in love at one point. Warui was a military man. The son of Shinano's *shugo*, the province's military agent. He was handsome and charming. When I refused to lay with him, however, he turned ugly. Abusive. He hurt me."

Anger flashed through Yūkan, making him shake. "He hurt you badly?"

"He broke my arm. My face was so bruised and swollen that my mother didn't recognize me when my father's men carried me home."

To look at her loveliness, nobody would know she had taken such a beating. He raked his hands through his mussed hair. "I want to kill him."

When she trembled, his heart softened. He took her cup and set it aside then brought her under the covers with him.

"Warui is already dead," Kirei said quietly, her arm coming across his abdomen as she settled her head on his chest.

She was such a gentle woman. He couldn't imagine any man wanting to hurt her. He wanted nothing more than to protect her.

"I didn't know until much later, after I had recovered and could leave my bed. Nobody told me." She snuggled closer, and he tightened his arm around her. "My brother, Mezurashii, had sought him out and attacked him for what he'd done to me. If I had known, I'd have tried to stop him."

"Mezurashii was punished?" he asked, hating the pain she had suffered but glad she shared this with him.

She released a sob that tore at his heart. "My brother lost his life. They had fought with swords. Neither survived the battle. Mezurashii died because of me. After that, I couldn't stay. Everywhere I went reminded me of them. Just sitting at home made me miss Mezurashii so painfully that I did little more than cry most of the time. I had to get away. Kyō was the only place I had family. The only place I'd have a future that didn't haunt me."

He gave her a squeeze then sat up. His *kosode* slipped off his shoulder, and he righted it then stood. He didn't bother closing it as he paced. She'd seen every inch of him. Touched him everywhere.

He hesitated. "Kirei, what if I'm not happy in the city? You said you were tempted to leave with me and go to my province, even if you can't."

She watched him, her features revealing nothing.

He resumed pacing. "Could you be happy living someplace other than the imperial city? Because what you said in the carriage about the shallow nature of the *good people*...well, it made me hope."

"Hope for what? You want to leave? I thought you were being romantic when you suggested we leave instead of returning to Ojisan's house."

He flexed stiff fingers then balled them. Living in the imperial city would make life more difficult. More complicated. Yet he couldn't escape how she'd treated him at the beginning when he'd first arrived from the country. She'd apologized for it and had talked of missing life in the provinces, but how far would she go? Would she resent him for asking her to live anywhere but the city? Would living in the country be too difficult after what she'd suffered in Shinano?

She stood and came to him. Halting, he adored how she didn't attempt to hide her nudity. The way her gaping *kosode* barely graced her slender shoulders and flowed past her curves. It gave her an ethereal, fragile quality. She was no wilting, mindless beauty, however. She had a mind stronger than many men, and her sense of right and proper rivaled any of the imperial ministers. Was he wrong to ask her to leave the center of Japan's high society?

"Do you, Yūkan?" She tilted her head slightly. "Do you want to leave?"

He took her hand and went to stand next to the brazier. Heat warmed the back of his legs and penetrated his thin under robe.

Meeting her gaze, he quietly said, "It was never my intention to live here. I only began taking etiquette lessons from you because Emperor Ichijō wants me to stay. I continued because you fascinate me."

Her small, pert breasts rose and fell on a long breath.

"But I'll stay if it's what you want. There are things I want to do, but I have no set plans. I've earned my wealth and retirement. I can live anywhere."

"You know I was raised in the country?"

He nodded.

"My parents still live a provincial life. My father loves his position as an imperial official in Shinano." She lowered her eyes to his chest. "I miss it. I don't miss what happened there, but I miss that life."

"You told me." He held his breath.

She eliminated the small distance between them. Wrapping her arms around his middle, she put her cheek to his chest. Her curves pressed to him, and she inserted a knee between his.

Closing his eyes, he hugged her, soaking in the satiny feel of her.

"I'm not happy in Kyō," she whispered. "I didn't want to come. I had to. My father thought it was best, too. I want to leave with you, but we have to do it properly."

He inhaled with overwhelming relief. Thank the gods, he would take her from the city. "I agree. Too many people stand to get hurt if we fail in this."

She lifted her cheek off of his chest and gazed up at him. "We may not succeed. If my uncle decides to publicly deny you, we don't have anyone to intercede. Only my father has the power to openly deny Ojisan's plan."

He placed a kiss on her forehead to hide his dread. He had to find a way. He wouldn't leave without her.

## Chapter Twenty-Three

Kirei stared out the carriage window at passing trees and blue sky while her stomach fought knots. She had no idea what awaited her at Ojisan's mansion, but she suspected it would involve yelling and arm flailing.

Yūkan held her in silence, and she took strength from him. She finished the last dried cherry from the wooden box and wished they'd stayed at the temple compound. Of course, remaining had been impossible. The third-night event had to take place in town for family to witness.

As the sun passed its zenith, his carriage pulled under the covered entrance to her uncle's east gate. She rolled in his arms. Her heart pounding and tears smarting, she kissed him passionately. She didn't want to leave him for even a minute.

The conveyance jiggled as his driver climbed from his seat.

Pulling away, she smoothed her hair. "I should go inside."

"Do you want me to come with you?" He pushed off the settee to his knees, a furrow forming between his eyebrows.

"It's not done," she said with a shake of her head. She loved that he offered, however.

"I'll send you my next morning letter as soon as I get to my room at the palace...though it's afternoon."

She chuckled, despite concern for what waited for her inside. "This time, I promise to write back."

He kissed her, a sweet peck that spoke of companionship and commitment more than passion. "I'll see you tonight."

The driver opened her door.

She kissed Yūkan's cheek. Not trusting her voice past a thickening in her throat, she exited and hurried through the gate without a backward glance.

Bracing for a scene by her uncle, she followed the covered walkway that led from the kitchens and bath to the east wing. Her mouth went dry as she climbed the steps and followed the veranda around front along the main building and past the west to the wing she shared with Amai.

An eerie silence set her nerves on edge. No gardeners worked outside. No servants moved between buildings. Was this a pre-storm calm? Did they wait with held breaths for the anticipated explosion?

When she reached her wing's door, she stopped. She took a deep breath, slowly let it out, and went in.

Nobody met her.

"Uma?" she called.

Nothing stirred.

Her zither and her lute were missing from the music wall.

"Uma? Zo?" She headed for her room.

Zo came around a corner at the far end of the hall. Her round face looked redder than ever, and she wrung her hands.

"Where is everyone? And who moved my instruments?" She reached for her chamber door.

"My lady—"

Kirei stepped inside and froze. Her room was emptied. The brazier stood cold in one corner. Two drawers on her wall wardrobe were pulled open, proof that her clothes no longer occupied that space. She faced the maid.

Zo shook her head, a tear coursing a fast track from her left eye to her jaw. "It's too terrible."

Kirei's knees threatened to buckle, and she grasped the doorframe. "Is it my father? My mother?"

The maid continued to shake her head. "Lord Fujiwara ordered your things moved last night. He woke everyone. Uma's not here. She took the last of your belongings over and hasn't returned yet."

"Where?" Kirei put a hand on the woman's shoulder, praying her maid would say her things had gone to the empress' residence in the First Ward. "My possessions were taken where?"

Zo's eyes widened and she opened her mouth. She snapped her lips closed then opened them again. She whispered, "To Prince Hansamu's mansion."

A bolt of electric shock zapped through Kirei's brain. Her vision blanked to white, and her knees gave out completely. She grasped her maid by the shoulders. "Where is my uncle now? This will not happen."

Shaking her head, Zo sobbed then said, "He has gone, my lady. Your uncle has taken his primary wife to attend a house party hosted by the princess. They won't return until late tonight."

"Then I'll stay and await his return." Kirei found the strength in her legs but realized he had won. She couldn't remain. Even now, the sounds of his ladies and staff gathering along the veranda carried to her chamber. This was the formal farewell. If she remained, her uncle's second wife would come and try to make her leave. It would become a screeching scene. An undignified sight. Fodder for distasteful gossip. She refused to lower her standards of conduct to that level.

Lifting her chin, she squared her shoulders and strode from her chamber at a stately pace. She would manage a regal leave-taking, and when she found time alone at the prince's mansion, she could formulate a plan of escape. She had to. The idea of life without Yūkan was unconscionable.

\*    \*    \*    \*

"That's not possible." Yūkan glared at the messenger boy. "I left her not two hours ago. Are you sure you went to the Fujiwara house in the Fourth Ward?"

"Yes, my lord." The boy handed him his undelivered

letter. "The Minister of the Center's mansion. I've been there many times."

Yūkan reluctantly accepted the parchment. "What did she say?"

"I didn't get to see her, my lord. Minister Fujiwara's majordomo said Lady Kirei would no longer be accepting correspondence at her uncle's house. He said to return the letter to sender, so I did." The messenger bowed then ran as if Yūkan would chase him.

He stared at his deep purple folded letter. This made no sense.

A knock sounded at his open doorway, and Yoki stepped in. "Have you heard?"

"Well, I heard something, but I don't know what it means."

His friend's pale features appeared washed out from underneath rather than from powder. "Tell me."

"The messenger I used returned my letter." He brandished his paper. "He says she's not accepting mail."

The aristocrat offered a solemn nod. "It's true."

"Why?" His chest tightened at the possibility that she'd changed her mind. He couldn't believe it, though. Her uncle had something to do with this.

"She's not there anymore."

Yūkan's head spun. "Where is she?"

"Prince Hansamu's house."

A frightful pressure began to build behind his eyes and in his chest. A buzzing overwhelmed his hearing, and his skin suddenly felt too tight for his body. He slammed closed his eyelids, resisting the urge to imagine that weak-armed philanderer's hands on Kirei. It didn't work.

"I'll kill him," he said low.

Yoki put a staying hand on his chest. "Listen to me first."

Opening his burning eyes, he crumpled the letter then threw it across the room. "That conniving, sneaking—"

"In fairness, her uncle could say the same of you."

A red haze of rage dissipated from his vision. His friend was right. "I love her. Hansamu's incapable of love. Not this kind, anyway."

"Will you please listen to me a minute? It's not as bad as you think."

Yūkan's hands itched to strangle somebody. "She's been placed in another man's house. Set up to be another man's lover. How does it get any worse?"

His friend retreated a step and stroked the miniscule beard gracing his effeminate chin. "You know Lady Kirei better than I, and that's hard to do. Nobody else comes close to understanding her like us."

"So?"

"Will you stop checking the doorway? Neither Prince Hansamu nor Lord Fujiwara are going to come here. They're probably scared of you."

"They should be." He fisted his hands at his sides. Everything in him screamed to find her and take her from this ridiculous city.

"Breathe." Yoki chucked him on the shoulder then stumbled a step backward and tottered as he nearly tripped over a cushion.

"I'm breathing." Yūkan clenched his jaw to keep from shouting.

"Won't you sit?"

"No."

Yoki sighed heavily. "Fine. Like I said, nobody knows Kirei like we do. I know Prince Hansamu well, too. I've known him since we were boys. We went to the university together."

Irritation stiffened the muscles in his neck. "And like *I* said before...so?"

"So you know she's not going to simply admit him into her bed."

"True." He relaxed a fraction.

"I promise you that Hansamu won't force her. He might want to, but she's a royal favorite. He won't risk the gossip."

Yūkan gave his head a shake. This level of anger wasn't conducive to straight thinking. "Won't he try to seduce her?"

His friend barked a laugh. "Hansamu? Seduce Lady Kirei? He's not smart enough. She'd see right through his attempt."

"Then what's the point of moving her into his house...unless it's a way to keep her from me?"

Yoki arched his eyebrows, and his tiny mouth formed a slight, expectant smirk.

"I see," said Yūkan, sinking to a cushion.

His friend sat facing him. "I don't think you do. Not entirely, anyway. The prince isn't really interested in Lady Kirei. She's not even a conquest."

"Then why has he been pursuing her?" He rubbed his aching forehead.

"Hansamu is a collector of rare and beautiful things. He likes owning things other people covet and value. Is there another person in this city more beautiful, rare, or valued than our Lady Kirei? She's invited to every party. Every event. The ones she chooses to attend is a social nod to the host or hostess, even if she doesn't intend it. Both the emperor and empress adore her, and she was handpicked for royal service by Michinaga himself."

"He views her as a possession in his collection?" The idea stunned and horrified him.

"Yes."

"Her uncle not only allowed it, he encouraged it. Pushed for it."

"Of course. It creates a connection directly to the emperor's line for his branch of the family. Both her uncle and her father will benefit politically from this match."

Yūkan's head began to hurt. "Neither her uncle nor Hansamu have taken into consideration what she wants or needs."

"Why should they?"

"She's important."

"She's a woman. A pawn."

"This is idiotic. Is this why her father sent her here? So she could be used and made miserable for the furtherance of his career?"

Yoki shook his head. "Do you know her father is a great poet? Seven of his poems have been chosen to be included in the collection of poems commissioned by Ichijō's father. He personally taught Kirei and her brother. I consider her education far superior to any of the gentlemen of my acquaintance, including mine. Her father loves her. Why else would he pour so much of himself into her? No, I don't believe for a second that he wanted this for her."

"I don't understand. He sent her to his brother. Doesn't he know Lord Rikō's motives?"

"I doubt it. As far as I know, her father hasn't been to Kyō in eight years. I can promise you her uncle hasn't left the imperial city. Ever. They may be brothers, but at this point, they're as good as strangers. How could her father know Minister Fujiwara has become consumed with ambition?"

"Then you don't think her father would support this?"

"I don't think he would."

Yūkan began to hope. "She's expecting a letter from him. Under the circumstances, I doubt she'd get it now. Her uncle would keep it from her."

"Probably." Yoki narrowed his eyes, which made them appear closed.

"Prince Hansamu may not plan to bed her tonight, but I still do. Tonight is our third-night event. I'm not losing her over her uncle's unsupported scheming."

"That's bold, even for you. Will you march into the prince's house and demand to claim his new concubine under his own roof? You realize, don't you, that he's as aware as her uncle of what you're trying to do. Hansamu has reason to prevent you."

"I'm not surrendering. They've made a strategic maneuver. Now I have to think of an equally effective counter maneuver."

Yoki stood. "You'll commit social suicide. Emperor Ichijō will be forced to banish you. For bringing dishonor to the Minamoto family, Michinaga will have your trade agreement destroyed and blacklist Fudōno. Who knows how badly Kirei's family will suffer. Don't do this."

The icy fingers of dread crept up his spine and sent hairs on end at his nape. "I can't let her go."

"Well, don't do anything impulsive. Give me some time to contemplate a few ideas."

His friend left, and Yūkan went to his small window. He was beginning to despise this city of walls. He'd give Yoki time, but not much. One way or another, he'd get to the woman he loved. He'd get to her tonight.

## Chapter Twenty-Four

Rubbing tired, gritty eyes, Kirei shifted her stiff legs. With so little sleep the night before, during her jaunt with Yūkan to Mt. Hiei, she needed a nap. She refused to sleep, however. She couldn't afford to let down her guard in this new household. She hated Ojisan for doing this.

Prince Hansamu had actually posted a guard at her room divider, as if she could simply walk out. Where would she go? Her uncle's house was fifteen miles away two wards up. Hardly walking distance. Not that he'd welcome her there. Yoki would, but he didn't live any closer.

She couldn't simply sit there in the cold dark, however. She had to try. To keep her silks from rustling, she slid across the hardwood floor to the single blind-covered outer section of her small partitioned room.

She rolled the bamboo and blinked against bright daylight. Hammering sounds popped and echoed from a distance. For a fleeting moment, she considered Hansamu might have hired workers to build a new wing for her. She didn't plan on staying to find out.

Gazing at the cage with her birds, which hung on a cord tied to a low ceiling beam, she wondered at their silence. They simply stared at her as though sensing her unhappiness. She didn't want to leave them but, under the circumstances, she couldn't attempt an escape with a cage in hand.

She slowly got to her feet and glanced toward the guard. His shadow made no move on the other side of the rice paper wall screens. Biting her bottom lip, she parted her many clothing layers and stepped over the window's base and out onto the veranda.

A number of servants and rough-looking laborers moved about the north and east grounds. Kirei straightened and scurried past her open window. Straightening her robes as she went, she headed to the enormous south garden.

Gardeners worked around the prince's pond and at patches of artfully arranged vegetation below the main building's southern veranda. Also, a number of elegantly clad women sat on the lawn and played a game of Go. Nobody glanced her way.

Her bare feet arched when she reached the chilled, wet walkway leading past the east wall exit. She stopped to assess the mansion's rear layout. Hansamu's estate had a different design layout than Ojisan's, and she wasn't sure where he kept his carriages.

At the end of the colonnade, she stopped. A great, open hall provided another set of steps and veranda. Beyond it, a huge pavilion formed the end. She had gone the wrong way.

Across the garden, a series of smaller buildings attached to the western colonnade and another large pavilion. She was completely turned around.

Had Yūkan learned of her uncle's double-cross? Did he rage or plot? Or did he surrender? If he loved her as much as she believed, he wouldn't abandon her.

She couldn't wait for him to rescue her, however. If he failed, how long until a sedentary life with no intellectual stimulation numbed her brain enough to make Prince Hansamu appealing? Poetry and games didn't provide the kind of diversions she needed. She thrived on conversation and debate. Reading. Writing. Meeting new people and helping those less fortunate.

She'd get none of that here. Hansamu was famous for his possessive nature. Once he considered something or someone his, he didn't share. Eventually, Empress Akiko would weary of his complaints and stop summoning her. Then Kirei would become a human mushroom, kept in the dark, rarely moving, her brain turning to porridge.

She trembled in panic. She had to get out of this place.

"Lady Kirei," came a man's voice immediately behind her.

Closing her eyes on a defeated huff, she turned on her heel.

Her guard bowed. "I'm available to escort you when you want to take a walk, my lady."

She bit her tongue. He was just doing his job.

Dangling her shoes from two fingers, he said, "I thought you might want these."

"Thank you," she said dryly, liberating her footwear from his callused hand. "I need a carriage. The empress wasn't feeling well last night, and I haven't had a chance to check on her."

"Not without Prince Hansamu's approval." He bowed. "I'll take you to your room."

She edged past him, asking, "So, where does the prince store his carriages and oxen?"

Pressing hard-looking lips together, the man didn't answer.

*    *    *    *

"We can't go through the streets with a horse harnessed to your carriage, my lord."

Yūkan gave his driver a stern look. "I'm serious. The rules be damned. Go get my horse because we're not coming back to the palace. We're leaving the city the moment we have the lady."

"A kidnapping? That's not like you," said Yoki as he approached.

The white ox his driver had attached to his carriage stamped and blew blasts from flared nostrils. Tack jingled in the quiet night.

He faced his friend. "Do you have a better idea?"

"I do. Leave this ox harnessed. You'll be back."

Yūkan resisted an urge to shove the aristocrat. "Care to tell me your plan?"

"Get in." Yoki stepped toward the carriage.

"You're coming with me?" That put a halt to his hopes of escaping with Kirei. "Tell me your idea."

His friend gently pushed him at the doorway. "Don't you want to be surprised? If you know everything, nobody will believe you didn't arrange this."

He climbed in and scooted to make room. "If everything's arranged, won't it appear so?"

Yoki got in. "We're headed to Prince Hansamu's mansion, aren't we?"

"Yes." Frustration gave the word a bark-like quality.

"Good. I can tell you this much." Yoki grabbed a handhold when the carriage rolled forward. "You're going to get Lady Kirei out of Prince Hansamu's house. I learned that he's at Lady Kowaii's poetry party tonight. I don't know why. He may appreciate good poetry, but he couldn't write a passable verse if his life depended on it."

"We're talking about Kirei, remember?"

"Right. Sorry. I'll tell you what's next after you get her out of the prince's mansion." Yoki's voice warbled as they jostled across the palace's south gate brace and onto Red Bird Avenue.

"You mean after *we* get her out." Yūkan despised the ox pace. A horse would take a fraction of the travel time, though they'd attract attention.

"No. You. I'm already too involved. The emperor may support your methods, but his ministers won't. I have to work with those gentlemen."

"Then why are you here?" Willing the ox to go faster, he gripped the window frame.

"Because Ichijō told me to."

He studied a telltale quirk of his friend's lips. "What else?"

"Who says I need any other reason?"

"What else?"

"Fine. If we succeed, the ladies will consider me heroic. They won't understand why Lady Kirei chooses you over the prince, but they'll think I'm romantic for helping her get the man of her choice." Adjusting his hat, Yoki sat a bit straighter.

"Do the *good people* think of nothing but beauty and appearances?" Yūkan released a disgusted sigh.

"Mostly."

"I don't understand it. There's good to be done, but nobody here seems to think about anything other than a moment's pleasure or outdoing a rival."

"You sound like Lady Kirei."

"That's the kindest compliment you could pay me."

His friend hesitated. "We do charity. We feed the poor."

"Because you want to, or because it's required by doctrine?"

Yoki looked away and straightened his already straight hat.

"That's what I thought. Now tell me what you have planned for me after I rescue Lady Kirei."

"You take her to Lord Fujiwara's house."

A lightning bolt zapped Yūkan in the spine. "Absolutely not."

Facing him, his friend tilted his head. "Where would you take her? To the palace?"

"To the country."

"That's the worst thing you can do."

Yūkan crossed his arms over his chest. "Why?"

"You don't have her family's formal letter of committal. Without her father's or her uncle's official approval of your marriage, taking her away will be construed as abduction. Emperor Ichijō won't be able to advocate your match, secretly or otherwise. Do you really need me to list the ill that will befall your two families?"

"Taking her to the Fujiwara mansion isn't going to win me her uncle's letter. What would be the purpose?" He truly despised the politics of high society.

"You have to trust me."

"You ask a lot." Especially since he had so much to lose.

Yoki glanced out the window. Despite his turmoil, Yūkan had to admit that golden lamplight reflecting off glittering willow trees lining the massive avenue appeared warm and inviting. Too bad the city's people weren't equally so.

"We're almost there." His friend waved toward a tall white wall that looked no different from the hundreds of others throughout the grid-bound city. "Do you know where she's located?"

"Of course not."

"Then how were you planning to find her?"

Yūkan clenched his jaw a few times in frustration. "I was going to ask whatever servant I encounter."

"That won't work. Listen, Prince Hansamu has a west wing similar to Lord Fujiwara's. He had a building added to its north as housing for his concubines. He's having an extension built, and he's got her quartered in a partition of the concubine's building *opposite* of the expansion side."

Yūkan shook his head. "How do you know this?"

"The servants talk. My majordomo knows everything that's going on. There are few secrets in Kyō."

"I suppose not." No wonder couples used the temples on Mount Hiei for their trysts.

His driver pulled to a halt at the wall, well away from Hansamu's north gate. As Yūkan exited, Yoki wished him success. He bit his tongue. He didn't need well wishes. What he needed was a helper.

He found the north gate closed and unmanned. He had to go in this way, however. Entering at the east or west gate would draw too much attention.

His grandfather's voice floated to him from the past. "Don't do this, boy. Breaking the rules only gets you trouble. Think of what happened to your father. Think of your family's honor."

He shook his head. "Lady Kirei is worth breaking the rules. She's worth risking honor."

He relaxed his fisted hands and pressed fingers to the gate's cold wood. He inhaled deeply while the weight of his father's death suddenly lifted. He had made a poor decision from lack of experience, and it had cost his father's life. Because of it, he'd striven to conform and comply. It had served him well as a traveling merchant, but he'd had to deny his very character. He was no longer a child, however. He had to trust his own mind.

As a boy, he'd questioned. He'd pushed boundaries. He'd challenged the status quo. Squaring his shoulders, he smiled. He would no longer deny his instincts. He would no longer doubt his motives. From now forward, he would make his choices not because of social dictates but based on logic and rightness. He was a man. Kirei was his decision.

Everything about her presence at Prince Hansamu's mansion was wrong. He would right it. Now.

He stepped back and assessed the wall. At six feet high, the wall would allow him to scale it with difficulty and likely some notice. The shorter gate, however, had deep carvings and iron handles. He grasped the top edge and used the carvings as footholds, climbing over in seconds.

The three largest wings of the mansion faced north but had quite a bit of lawn between them and the wall. Nobody moved about on the north side, but that didn't surprise him. Servants had completed their outdoor duties by this time of night, and Hansamu's wife and concubines had no reason to be out front.

He unlatched the gate and waved his driver in then raced across the lawn to the west wing. The new construction Yoki had mentioned sat in darkness while slivers of light spilled from shutters on the occupied building. He climbed steps to the veranda and made his way to the side his friend had said she stayed.

"Lady Kirei," he whispered as he stole along the walkway.

He counted six partitioned sections on this side. Which was hers? "Kirei. It's Yūkan."

A bamboo blind rolled upward, spilling an anemic light across the veranda's dark brown boards.

"Lord Yūkan?" came a man's whisper.

He froze. Had Yoki been wrong about Hansamu's absence? Turning slowly on his heel, he braced for a call to guards.

"It is you." Lord Shizuka peered out. A sleepy-eyed lady sprawled behind him, wearing a mere three layers of *uchigi* in disarray, and blinked at him from the dim interior.

"What are you doing here?" Yūkan gripped the bottom wall portion. "Never mind that. I see what you're doing. Where's Lady Kirei?"

His friend glanced over his shoulder at Hansamu's concubine.

She smiled. "Two sections down, closer to the corridor leading to the main wing." She grabbed his friend's foot and tugged.

"Good luck." Shizuka chuckled and let the blind drop. A loud giggle followed.

Blinds cracked further back, but he hadn't come to socialize. He had a mission. He whispered, "Kirei."

Ahead, a blind rolled up. He hurried, sure the light came from his lady's room. He reached the window where she sat swathed in layers, her eyes pleading and wide above the edge of a fan.

Blocking his way to her, however, stood a palace guard.

## Chapter Twenty-Five

"I can't go with you." Kirei's heart broke. He'd come for her. It meant everything.

"You can and you will." Yūkan came a step closer.

The guard made to draw his sword, but Yūkan took another step then spun in reverse and planted a back-fist into the guard's face. The man collapsed in a heap.

Kirei cried out and pushed to her feet. "You shouldn't have done that."

"Come with me." Yūkan held out a hand.

"The scandal will destroy both my uncle and my father. I have to stay or escape on my own."

He shook his head. "You have to trust me."

Her brain demanded she stay, but her heart screamed for her to go with him. She'd never wanted anything more. Covering her face, she hunched her shoulders and said, "I can't."

"Kirei."

She peeked between her fingers. He appeared so calm. In control. "But this breaks the rules."

"I'm done with rules that make no sense." His jaw muscles flexed.

Had he figured out a solution? Trembling set in with her effort to keep from rushing away with him. She'd only trip on her robes, anyway. "Hansamu will come for me, and you'll have to let me go. I don't want to go through that."

He climbed inside and took hold of her sleeves. He looked impossibly handsome and confident. "Come with me tonight. If everything goes according to plan—"

"There's a plan?" Her heart skipped a beat then began to pound with hope.

"Yes." He gently pulled her to the window. "It begins by leaving this room before another guard comes to try and stop me."

He skirted the downed man then bent and lifted her silks. For the second time that day, she escaped through the window.

"Where are we going?" she asked, heading for his carriage at the end of the veranda.

"To your uncle's house."

She stopped short, and a stone weighed heavily in her stomach. Behind her, his steps landed hard. When she faced him, he fought for balance. "That's not a good plan."

"This is our third-night event." He turned her by her shoulders and urged her forward. "Where else do you propose we do that? Here?"

Her jaw gaped at the very suggestion, and she snapped her mouth closed. She reached his carriage where he unfastened a couple of clips and lowered the entire rear panel so she could climb in through the back. Someone sat inside but her gaze couldn't penetrate the darkness to discern features.

"Welcome to our little adventure," said the figure.

"Lord Yoki?"

Her friend offered a sheepish grin and scooted, giving her room to settle. "At your service."

"This is *your* plan, isn't it?" she accused in a loud whisper while Yūkan closed the carriage.

"Mostly." Yoki's stiff silks rustled, reminding her of the sound balls of crumpled paper made when a breeze caused them to rub together.

Yūkan's deep voice penetrated the gloom as he spoke to his driver.

She wished she could see him better, but the lanterns inside the box hadn't been lit. "What is this about us going to Ojisan's house?"

"I don't like it either," said Yūkan, coming in through the carriage's side door.

"There must be someplace else we can go." Kirei's stomach churned. Facing her uncle after his deception was a confrontation she couldn't handle tonight.

The carriage began its roll across the north lawn's uneven surface. She planted her hands on the floor to keep from falling over.

"You need at least an illusion of family support for your third-night." Yoki crawled to the far wall and sat opposite her.

"But he doesn't and I'm no longer welcome to live with him. He's not going to accept me, especially with Yūkan at my side." She swallowed against a forming lump.

"I said an illusion. We know he doesn't support your match."

"Then what makes you think he's going to allow us into his house?"

"He's not." In light from the street seeping through the window, her friend rubbed his palms across his knees.

Yūkan removed his hair tie and vigorously shook his head. He climbed out and closed the north gate then returned.

Leaning toward her friend, Kirei said, "This is entirely your plan. I should've known. This isn't going to work."

Yoki offered her a sour scowl. "Have some faith."

Taking her hand, Yūkan gave her a reassuring squeeze. "We have to give it a try."

She searched his gaze in the gloom, unable to read his shadowed features as they passed between street torches. He was right. She had only two alternatives. The first, remaining with Prince Hansamu and possibly never seeing Yūkan after he returned to his country estate, was out of the question. That way led to madness.

The second, leaving Kyō with him and never looking back would ruin both of their families. They relied on political privilege and hierarchical connections to maintain their honor and livelihoods. A foolish act on her part could undermine that.

The carriage turned onto Red Bird Avenue, causing them to lean. Yūkan closed the blind on his window then took her hand and gave it another squeeze. Finding it difficult to take courage, however, she swallowed against a lump of dread.

She couldn't simply arrive on her uncle's veranda and expect acceptance. Had she escaped from a hole just to leap into a pit? "Do you know if Ojisan's home tonight?"

"He will be later." Yoki shuffled forward until the robe covering his knees nearly touched her *uchigi*. "I've been working this afternoon to call in favors and make arrangements."

"It might help if you shared these arrangements with us," said Yūkan.

She leaned against him, comforted by his strength.

Her friend swayed side to side then straightened his black hat nearly scraping the ceiling. His pale face appeared ghost-like in the dim interior. "I'll tell you that we're going to the west gate. I already told the driver."

"When?" asked Yūkan.

"When you were getting Lady Kirei from her room at Hansamu's house."

"You're a wily badger." Kirei poked her friend's hand and forced a smile.

"Put those ghastly white teeth away." Yoki shook his head. "You never take my advice. You'd be so much more up-to-date if you'd only stain them like a lady should."

Her heart warmed at how her friend tried to use their old argument to diffuse the tension. "You can't say never. I'm taking your advice tonight, aren't I?"

"Only because you have no choice."

Yūkan gently tightened his hug. "Believe me when I say that's true. If I had any better idea, the Fujiwara mansion would be the last place we'd go."

Yoki sniffed. "You two are the most ungrateful friends a gentleman could have."

"Would you be grateful if I led you to a sure fight with

the one man who stood between you and your heart's greatest desire?"

She closed her eyes. Yūkan called her his heart's greatest desire. She loved him more than life.

Yoki cleared his throat. "Worry and pessimism weaken your spiritual resistance. They make you liable to fall prey to evil influences. Don't you know that negativity opens you to evil spirits? Do you want to be possessed or fall ill?"

Yūkan chuckled. "I should blindly trust you and be glad to do it?"

"Absolutely."

"What's the worst that can happen?" It couldn't be worse than her bleak prospects only an hour earlier. Her friend's resolute posture made her smile in earnest.

Yūkan kissed the top of her head. "Let's not contemplate that."

"There's the attitude you should have," Yoki praised. "Have faith. Honestly, what can you expect, anyway? There's an elegant ritual in which we conduct our love affairs, and you both have barely complied with this tradition. You have to trust me to know how things should be done. Nobody knows better than I."

Kirei snuggled against Yūkan. "Nobody has more experiences with secret nightly trysts or a stronger aesthetic sense than you, dear friend."

"That's right." He sat straighter. "Besides, the emperor understands how it is and he conspires with me. Your uncle doesn't stand a chance against such a team."

Drawing a deep, steadying breath, she hoped her friend was right. As they arrived at her uncle's west gate, she gripped the silk of her soft chemise within her many sleeves. The muscles of her neck and upper back clenched.

"Stay behind me," Yūkan said. He opened his door.

Before he could climb out, however, Yoki cleared his throat. "Wait."

Yūkan slowly pulled closed the door but said nothing.

"Lady Kirei," came a woman's whisper.

Yoki lifted the blind of his window, and Uma's concerned features appeared in the opening. She gave a small wave for them to follow her.

Yūkan took Kirei's hand and scooted out. He helped her exit, and she hurried to the gate as fast as her voluminous robes allowed. Having Uma involved provided her a fair measure of reassurance. Other than Ojisan's majordomo, nobody knew this estate better than her maid.

Uma led them inside the wall and to the northern corner of the west wing where torchlight didn't reach. In shadow, she stopped. She touched a finger to her closed lips.

Cutting her gaze to where the veranda met with the west corridor, Kirei listened. A man's voice rose above a rippling of garden water and chirping of crickets. A distinctly female giggle silenced the insects for a moment.

"Amai and Shinsetsu," whispered Yūkan.

Uma nodded then headed around front. At the main door to her cousin's wing, her maid soundlessly ushered them inside. Men's boisterous laughter burst from the main building's veranda, proof that Ojisan's concubines entertained their lovers in his absence. The noise covered their steps as they rushed to Kirei's old room.

Uma closed the chamber door behind them, leaving Kirei alone with the man who owned her heart. Her pulse raced. Her temperature rose. She wanted nothing more than to shed her silks and press against his hard body.

The brazier glowed with heat. Above it, a lantern cast an orange glow on the room. The unmistakable scent of Uma's personal cherry and pine extract cleaning oil emanated from the floor.

A luxurious futon with white cotton linens waited at the room's center. Uma had indulged her.

Smiling, Kirei shrugged from her jacket then dress. They pooled on the train of her chemise, which protruded from the layers of her six *uchigi*.

Yūkan's dark eyes grew sultry. He unfastened his coat and added it to her discarded garments. "Yoki and Uma had this figured out."

She nodded in thick anticipation and worked at untying his *hakama*. Her fingers trembled, but she didn't let them slow her.

"Do you think we'll have interruption?" he asked.

She shook her head, not trusting her voice. As he swept her long hair over her shoulder, his hot hand cupped the side of her neck then caressed to her collarbone. He slipped his fingers into the V of her *kosode* and traced the inner curve of her breast.

Closing her eyes, she held her breath. This was it. Night three. Even if Ojisan didn't present a letter of committal, Yūkan would forever be the man of her heart. The love of her life. Her soul mate.

She dropped out of her six *uchigi* at once, immediately lighter without their weight. While he stroked her breast, he used his other hand to unfasten his pants. She untied the string fastening her own *hakama* then kicked them off.

Tremors of desire cascaded from his touch. She untied the stay holding closed his *kosode*. When it gaped, she splayed her fingers across his firm muscled chest.

She adored his hard man's body, so unlike hers. She enjoyed his strength. Sensed a certain security offered by his size and ease of movement. No other man of her acquaintance could compare.

"You are everything I want in a husband," she said, meeting his gaze. "I love you."

He skimmed his hand from her breast up her throat and cupped her jaw. His gaze held an intense affection as he studied her. Then his eyes moved to her mouth. His lips followed.

Firm yet pliant, his mouth worked across hers. She melted against him and sent her fingers into his long, loose hair. It felt smooth and thick and retained warmth from his body.

He pressed harder, demanding entrance, and she relented in delight. She opened. His tongue, sweet like vinegared rice, swept inside. She welcomed it with a sensual dance of her own. Her nipples hardened in response to his heat coming through the thin white silk of their *kosode*.

He consumed her. She ran her hands over his unyielding planes and solid ridges. As she had no way to know what tomorrow held, she had to lose herself in this night. She had to savor each moment.

When her *kosode* slid from her body, she broke the kiss and chuckled. She'd been so engrossed in his kiss that she hadn't felt him untie her undergarment's fastener. She divested him of his and led him to the futon.

Sinking onto the rich bedding, she marveled at how just the sight of him sent butterflies aflutter in her belly and moisture seeping into her crease. This man had been nothing but a country buffoon who actually had horses drawing his carriage through the city when she'd met him. Now, he'd become everything. Her strength. Her moral compass. Her light in society's darkness.

Extending her arms in invitation, she smiled at her handsome Lord Yūkan. She wanted this night to be the beginning of their forever. If there really was life after death, as doctrine taught, she could face eternity in paradise with him. The deeper she fell in love with him, the more she believed.

Yoki would cry if she told him that tonight was less about ritual and tradition, and more about beauty within pleasure and spiritual connection. Tonight, she would ensure Yūkan understood how much she admired and loved him.

When he settled to the mattress on his knees, she put a hand to his chest and eased him to his back. His jutting member, thick and richly veined, told her he shared her desire. It fascinated her.

Folding her fingers around it at its base, she kept her gaze fixed to his features. His lips parted. His eyelids lowered nearly to his pupils. At his neck, his pulse throbbed in time to the throbbing in the folds between her thighs.

She put her lips to his tip. His chest expanded on an audible breath. Smiling at an unexpected rush of power, she licked his length. He moaned, rising to his elbows. Kirei controlled his pleasure, and it increased her own.

A pearl of moisture formed at his tip, and she licked it. Salty sweet spread along her tongue. He was delectable. Arousal burned like fire in her blood. She took him into her mouth and explored his textures. To her fingers, he was silk wrapped around a wooden rod. In her mouth, however, he was smooth as a maple leaf and as sweet and varied in contour as an imprinted rice cake.

She flicked her fingernail over his dark nipple and reveled in its puckering response. His member was broad and heavy in her hand. His glistening crest beckoned her, and she grazed her lips across its velvety texture.

His groan drove her to take him into her mouth. His rigid manhood flexed as she swallowed. Gently, she cupped his writhing testicles and tenderly squeezed.

## Chapter Twenty-Six

Yūkan fought for breath through his pleasure. Her beauty threaded between his thighs as she appeared to savor every inch of his engorged length. He wanted to bury himself deep inside her.

"You are more woman than any woman I've met," he said, his voice strange and tight to his ears.

He gazed at her stunning, naturally pale features and swept his fingers into her endless silken hair. He strained against a need for release as her shapely, lips worked his shaft. While she gained in pace, her dark eyes never strayed from his.

Her surprisingly talented tongue worked him, and her gaze held a victorious glint that threatened to topple his carefully restrained need. Her inexperience didn't matter. What mattered was her eagerness to please. Her gentle handling of him and her open curiosity. Nobody had aroused him more than she did in this moment.

Her fingertips found pleasure points buried under the base of his sac. His entire body shuddered in excitement. Sparks of need shot through him. Her sensual sloe eyes searched his soul and mirrored his desire.

He dropped to the sheets in surrender. He belonged to her.

Always had.

Always would.

He moaned on a tremor as an electric charge zipped along his spine. A lifetime of this wouldn't be enough.

At the brink of his control, he took her by the shoulders and drew her upward across his body. Her soft skin was heaven against him. Her hard nipples pebbled next to his chest. Enjoying the sensation, he braced his arm across her back to keep her there.

He urged her knee to the outside of his hip and entered her hot, wet passage on a slow thrust. She tucked her lovely face into the crook of his neck as he filled her. Seated to the hilt, he held still.

Her scent met his nostrils in a sensual waft of femininity, a mixture of earthy desire and her unique perfume creation. He buried his nose in her hair and inhaled her fragrance.

Her sweet breaths quickened. Her honeyed walls cradled his aching length, offering some relief. She had him so primed for orgasm that he feared finishing before she found her pleasure.

Reaching between their bodies, he found her weeping slit and inserted his fingertip between her folds. She released a womanly sigh. Her hips tilted into his touch, and she began to kiss his throat.

When he located her clit and gave it a circling caress, she tightened around his shaft. Pleasure wrenched a moan from his throat, and he realized she moaned with him. Her tongue darted and alternated with sucking kisses along his jugular in time to his stroking finger.

She gasped and arched. Her passage gripped him, pulling him deeper and multiplying his excitement.

Heart pounding, Yūkan rolled, taking her beneath him. Her eyes locked with his as he thrust in an age-old rhythm that promised ecstasy. He climbed swiftly to the point of explosion. Still, she beat him there.

Her mouth open on a silent scream, Kirei arched. Her walls squeezed, surging him to his own release. He shook under the force of his expulsion. He had never come so hard in his life.

He dropped to his back beside her. Bringing the covers with her, she curled against his side and draped her arm over his chest. She rested her smooth cheek on his shoulder.

"I'm yours," he said. "You have my heart. My loyalty. My protection."

"I love you." She sighed and cuddled closer.

Before this moment, he hadn't imagined he could love a person as much as he loved her. He pulled the cover around her and up his legs, drawing it to his naval. He had to concoct a way to legitimately get her out of Kyō and away from these people with their twisted sense of right and wrong, good and bad.

Kirei had talked of living in the country and how she missed it. Could she be happy on his northern estate? Could she learn to love living near the sea?

\*    \*    \*    \*

Voices. A man shouted. A woman screeched. No, two women. Kirei cracked open the lid of one eye and groaned. How had morning come so soon? She snuggled closer to Yūkan. If she could wake in his arms every day for the rest of her life, she'd consider herself the most content woman in Japan.

The voices grew nearer along the west wing. She picked out Ojisan's shout.

Her maid cried in a high-pitched tone, "My lord, don't go in there. It's unseemly."

Recognizing Zo's wail, she gave Yūkan's shoulder a shake. "Wake up, my love. We're about to be invaded."

He wiped a hand down his face and sat. "This is going to be ugly."

That was no joke. She clutched the sheet to her chest.

"Get out of my way," bellowed Ojisan a moment before her bedroom door slid open. Red-faced and disheveled, his *kosode* sagging at his thin chest and his house robe half off of one shoulder, her uncle glared at her.

Her stomach lurched. She sat and put a hand on Yūkan's thick arm. "I won't go back to Prince Hansamu's house. We just spent our third night."

Hansamu's face appeared past Ojisan in the doorway. He wore a disapproving scowl. She didn't care.

"I mean it," she said to the prince. "I'm not going to live at your mansion."

Ojisan's face darkened to an alarming reddish purple. He opened his mouth to speak. His gaze dropped to the floor next to the bedding, and his mouth snapped shut.

Kirei leaned forward. On the finest porcelain saucer sat a perfect presentation of third-night cakes. Wearing a too-satisfied smirk, Uma sidled into the room and hung Kirei's birds above the brazier.

Yūkan chuckled. "Good. I'm hungry."

Ojisan sputtered and gave her maid a shove. "Remove those this instant!"

Yūkan took two in one hand and gave one to Kirei. "Too late."

A familiar voice called from the entrance to her wing. "Hello?"

"Yoki," she whispered on a smile. She took a bite of her delicious *mikayomochi*.

The gentleman came into the hallway and declared, "There you are, Prince Hansamu. I went to your estate to see if you and Lady Kirei wanted to join me for a jaunt to the High Priestess' residence. Lady Rippa wants to bring society into that lonely princess' life by hosting a day party."

The prince rolled bored eyes.

Kirei hid her widening smile behind her hand. Yoki was lying. He knew how much she disdained the High Priestess' fake nature and condescending way.

Her friend elbowed into the chamber. "What do we have here?"

Zo came in with wine.

"Stop," shouted Ojisan. He glanced at the emperor's Supreme Minister of Personal Affairs and clamped a hand over his mouth. He squeezed closed his eyes.

"What?" Yoki acted confused. No wonder he did so well

at court. He was a consummate player. "You give your niece leave to partake her third-night in your home and go to the trouble of providing third-night cakes and wine yet stand there and pretend affront? What would Emperor Ichijō think of such a two-faced attitude?"

Kirei was going to owe her friend big after such a performance.

Yūkan stretched and grabbed his *kosode* from where he'd left it on the floor last night. He shrugged into the wrinkled silk then stood. "The commitment is made. It's done."

Hansamu thrust an arm into the room and wildly waved his hand. "This is not done. Lady Kirei is my concubine. She's mine."

Both he and Yoki sent withering stares at the prince. The proud man withdrew his arm and retreated a step.

"Where is the letter of committal?" her friend asked her uncle.

"The one I gave Hansamu?" Ojisan jutted his weak but stubborn chin.

Yūkan barked a laugh. "Even I know no such letter can be presented without a third-night. The prince has never been intimate with your niece much less shared a third night with her. I have."

She admired Yūkan's calm, matter-of-fact tone and posture. These men might consider him a boorish trouble-maker lacking good taste and manners, but at the moment, he outshined his so-called betters with his refined handling of her uncle's bad behavior.

"You can't know that for certain," said the prince.

"I can and I do." Yūkan absently tied the closure of his under-robe as if they spoke casually of nothing more important than whether or not they thought it might rain.

Kirei's heart skipped a beat. She met her uncle's darting glance. She stood, taking the cover and wrapping it about her body.

Ojisan sized up Yūkan who met his gaze squarely and

confidently. A glint of fear touched her uncle's eyes. They widened a fraction as they slid to Kirei.

She nodded. "Believe it. It's true."

"What's true?" asked the prince.

Uma folded her arms. "I can attest to it. I washed her bedding after their first night."

"By the gods," whispered her uncle.

"What's going on?" demanded Hansamu.

Yūkan took a step nearer her uncle and said low, "This isn't something you want known. Imagine how the *good people* will react to learn she'd been among them for a year in such a vulnerable state. They'd see it as your fault. You're her guardian. It was your responsibility to ensure she was acceptable to move among your peers."

Ojisan paled a shade. "How did I not know this?"

"Know what?" Prince Hansamu stomped.

Kirei ignored him and went to Yūkan's side. "You weren't paying attention. Since coming to Kyō, I've brought nobody here."

Ojisan shook his head. "My brother said there had been a man in Shinano Province. A warrior's son. Besides, you had plenty of opportunity. Entire nights spent out. Trips to Mount Hiei. You returned from parties the morning after so many times, I assumed..."

She slowly shook her head.

"You've ruined me," he whispered, disbelief causing his mouth to sag.

"Not if you provide a letter of committal," said Yūkan.

Hansamu shrieked. "Now wait a minute—"

Zo planted her hands on the prince's shoulder and began pushing. He protested, trying to fight the maid, but he couldn't get past her sheer size and weight.

When Hansamu was out of earshot, Yoki studied his fingernails and said, "If you have any wish to protect your reputation, your family's honor, and your government position, you'd be wise to write that letter."

Ojisan fixed his robe with a jerk. "You knew? How many people knew she was a virgin?"

"Everyone in this room."

Her uncle glared at her maid.

Uma merely shrugged. "I served her every day since she moved here. It's something a servant notices. I promise you, my lord, that her secret has stayed close. Nobody else knows."

"Though," said Yoki on a bored note, "now that it no longer matters to Kirei's continued social acceptance, it would make for fun gossip. I imagine the *good people* of Kyō would keep it as party conversation for weeks. It's such a juicy and horrifying morsel, it may even circulate for months. Somehow I don't believe your social or political standing would survive."

Ojisan trembled. From fear or anger, Kirei couldn't tell. She suspected it might be both. She gave him a pleading look. "My lord, I don't want to see you ruined. I only want to be happy. Please give us your letter."

"What will you do if I refuse?" he asked.

She glanced at Yūkan's handsome face. "I'll leave this city with my husband, Ojisan."

He staggered backward a step. "Without family approval? That would destroy us all. Have you no sense of honor?"

"My sense of self-preservation is stronger at the moment than my sense of honor. Maybe I'm being selfish, but I adamantly refuse to return to Prince Hansamu's house. One way or another, I'll live with Lord Yūkan."

## Chapter Twenty-Seven

"He's provincial," Kirei's uncle spat, slicing his hand through the air.

Yūkan curled his fingers into a fist. Why was it always about where he'd lived?

Yoki's features hardened. "You're a fool, Lord Rikō. He has the court's support. This match has Emperor Ichijō's blessing."

Yūkan wanted her family's approval, but he secretly rejoiced that she'd said she'd be with him no matter what. Unfortunately, he didn't have that luxury. Fudōno's success depended on his doing this right. Scandal and dishonor weren't an option. He had to fight for a letter from this Minister of the Center.

He went to his discarded clothes and stepped into his patterned silk *hakama*. As he tied its string, he said in as serene a voice as he could manage, "Maybe you should think of it this way. If you give me your letter of committal, you'll be pleasing the favorite nephew of my aunt. I am a Minamoto. My aunt is Lady Rinshi."

The bald minister puffed out his unimpressive chest. "I have met Michinaga's principle wife. I know her."

"Then you know she is mother of our empress. She is wife of Japan's ruler-in-practice, and that should she decide to dislike you, she could personally make your life impossible."

"Is that a threat?"

He scooped his *karaginu* off the floor and shrugged into it. Even with it open and casual, he now stood in greater splendor than Kirei's *ojisan*. Yoki also wore his usual finery, which put the older man at a distinct disadvantage in his own house.

Yūkan joined Kirei and put his arm around her shoulders. Their third-night event had finally placed him in the position as her protector, and he wouldn't relinquish it.

"Answer me," shouted Lord Fujiwara. "Are you threatening me?"

"No threat. I make you a promise," he said in a calm, quiet tone.

"How dare you? I am related to Michinaga himself. I don't need his wife to side with me."

"Really? So you have His Excellency's ear? You can go to his home anytime and court influence with him?"

Fujiwara cleared his throat. His gaze went to his feet.

"Exactly. You can't, but my aunt can."

Yoki went to the doorway. "We're finished here. Lady Kirei and Lord Minamoto have had their third-night event. Rice cakes have been served and consumed by the couple, signifying they have religious sanction of their marriage rite. Most importantly, we've established exposure of the event. If Hansamu won't get word out, you can rely on my doing it, that's for certain. Now give this delightful couple your official approval of this marriage. Give them your letter."

Her uncle's face lapsed in resignation.

"Good." The aristocrat offered Yūkan an eager grin then turned to Fujiwara. "Lord Rikō, you make plans for the marriage feast. I'll arrange for a priest to come tonight and recite *norito* rituals and wave a branch from the *sakaki* tree to purify their union."

"I'll have a letter ready," said her uncle, his face going from red to pink. "All I ask is that you keep this morning's upset to yourself."

"Of course." Yoki sighed dramatically. "I guess an excursion to the High Priestess' house is out of the question. There's simply too much to accomplish today."

The heavy maid came and stood behind Uma. Quietly,

she said, "Prince Hansamu remembered an appointment he had. It was necessary that he leave."

Convenient. Yūkan gave Kirei a gentle squeeze. The prince was one less issue they needed to address that morning. The man wasn't particularly bright, but at least he had the sense to recognize when he'd lost a battle. Thankfully, social pressure would ensure he'd not speak of this. It would only make him appear weak and inept.

The defeated minister strode toward the main building, and Yūkan left Kirei with her maids. He accompanied Yoki to the west gate.

"That was fun," said his friend, rubbing his hands together.

"You have a distorted idea of what's fun."

Yoki chuckled. "I'm bored. What do you expect?"

"Thank you for helping us. Kirei and I couldn't have accomplished any of this if it hadn't been for your planning."

"It was my pleasure. You can't believe how much it was my pleasure." He laughed and signaled a servant near the gate to summon his carriage. "Though if I had known you'd stripped naked, I'd have hesitated. That was disgusting."

"I know your opinion on nudity. No need to go into it."

His friend pressed his lips together. "Hmm. I'll see you tonight."

Yūkan returned to Kirei's chamber where her maids had already dressed her in a multitude of blue-green and coral shades of *uchigi*. They had smoothed her floor-length hair and now assisted her into a tan *uchiginu* edged with embroidered butterflies of every color. When she glanced his way, her dark eyes softened in affection and a tinge of pink blossomed in her pale cheeks. She stole his breath.

In a corner, her cousin quickly lifted a painted fan to hide her face and ceased a rambling telling of what she and Shinsetsu had overheard of her father's tirade. "Lord Yūkan. What a pleasure to see you."

He bowed slightly. "Lady Amai."

She stood and bowed a respectful depth that took him aback. She said, "I was wrong in my prejudice against you when we first met. My father is wrong to continue in his low opinion of you. I think you're a perfect match for my cousin. In your manner, your education, and your thinking, you're truly a gentleman."

"Thank you." He glanced at Kirei who smiled and gave him a nod.

Amai took a step forward. "Please tell me you won't take her from Kyō."

He sighed. "I can't make any promises. I don't know what tomorrow holds."

Her delicate eyebrows lowered. "Why not?"

"Amai," said Kirei, accepting a folded fan from her maid and moving to his side. "We've had a very difficult couple of days. Give us a chance to talk and decide what to do."

Her cousin sent her a worried look but bowed in acquiescence.

"Let's go to the veranda overlooking the garden," he suggested. "It's nice weather."

He led the way. After collecting two large cushions from her main sitting area, he lifted a bamboo blind and removed a wall section so she could step outside. He placed the pillows side-by-side and waited until she settled before he sat.

Zo brought cold grilled pheasant, fruit, and cups of fresh pressed juice. While they ate, the sun burned dew from blades of grass, and a fine mist rose from the garden waterway. An overhanging eave kept them in shadow, which he preferred. It offered a measure of privacy and remained cool.

"I didn't think my uncle would relent." She drained her cup and set it next to the plate of fruit.

"Me neither. Lord Yoki backed him into a corner, though."

"Yes, but it was your words that forced his hand. He wouldn't have agreed to write his consent if you hadn't made him truly see how his lack of approval threatened his entire way of life."

He smiled. "I did my best. There's too much at risk for me to give up."

"You mean your brother and the business?"

He stared across the garden, but his mind went to his home estate and their three ships at anchor near the village. "Yes."

"With so much to lose, I wouldn't have faulted you for leaving me."

Her words yanked him back. He took her hand. "Kirei, I knew the moment I first saw you at that perfume party that you were different. Special. And after our conversation during sunrise on the side of that mountain, I knew you were meant to be my wife. I love you. Last night when I came for you at Prince Hansamu's mansion, I intended to leave with you. To take you to my home in the country."

"But your brother's success rests on the contacts you establish here in Kyō. I imagine our children and his, should they choose to continue in trade, will rely on these contacts, too. We were wise not to go." She sank straight white teeth into her bottom lip.

He chuckled. "Fudōno and our business will never come before you. No, I stayed because Yoki had a plan. Because he convinced me that my way would hurt too many people, including you."

She nodded. "My father would've suffered for my scandal. He'd probably lose his post. I'd have been unable to forgive myself for that."

He breathed a heavy sigh, grateful to his friend for saving him from himself. "This way was much better. The confrontation with your uncle this morning was as difficult as I expected, but it helped to have Yoki doling threats in the argument and to have you by my side."

She skimmed her smooth, warm fingers over the back of his hand. "I know we want to leave the imperial city, but the emperor wants you to stay and take a position in the government. What will you do?"

His stomach clenched. The time for questioning and probing had past. He'd made her his wife, and now he had to choose a path for their future.

"If we stay, I will have to start a new career. Learn a new set of responsibilities. I'll never take another wife or any consorts, so my advancement will be limited. All the power and prestige held by my aunt and Michinaga can't change the fact that I was raised in the country and married a woman from a similar background. Our children will never grow to greatness under our stigma, but our grandchildren might stand a chance."

She nodded and looked to their connected hands.

Studying her lovely face, he said, "Yoki's a dear friend, and the emperor seems to be a good man who would enjoy spending time with me. You'd be able to continue as a court favorite and enjoy the refinements available here in the city. Nobody wants you to leave."

She gazed into the garden.

He ran fingers through his loose hair and wished he could read her expression. "On the other hand, you told me you miss the country and its freedom. You said you want to leave this city."

Her gaze met his. "I do. I truly do."

He studied her a long moment, trying to discern her mood. "Then I'm just going to say it. I have an extensive Chinese library and every instrument available. My home is large. Larger than your uncle's. It's beautiful. I designed it, and it offers every comfort you'd find here. I miss it."

"Then let's go."

His heart drummed loudly. "Really? What about what the emperor wants?"

She smiled, and her smile reached her eyes. It made her glow from within. "Really. Ichijō won't hold our leaving against us. He's not selfish like that. And I've never enjoyed living in the city. There have been moments of fun and rewarding interaction, but it's not home. Does that make sense?"

"It does." He ran his fingers along the silky length of her hair past her shoulder. "Do you think you could like living near the sea? Do you think you might want to do some traveling?"

Her smile grew. "There's only one way to find out."

His breath hitched at her incredible beauty. At her depth of character and spirit. He whispered, "I want to show you the world."

"I want to see it. I'm excited. Can we go to China and share poetry with their renowned poets? I'd love to purchase books on Buddhist philosophy. Do you think we could visit Korea? The traders who come from there are some of the nicest and most well-read people I've met."

He laughed, overjoyed by her enthusiasm. "Yes. We can do those things and more."

Uma came to the opening and bowed. "My lady, your father has come. He's here. Now. Your uncle is receiving him this instant."

Kirei shared a happy glance with Yūkan then let him help her to her feet. Her father. Here. Yūkan hadn't expected such a complication. Only one man could destroy what they'd worked so hard to win that morning, and he had just walked through the door.

## Chapter Twenty-Eight

No wonder a letter hadn't come. Kirei's father hadn't sent one. She retrieved her fan from her sleeve and concealed her face as he and Ojisan entered the west wing. Her father smiled as she bowed a greeting.

Yūkan stood at her side and waited. He seemed to lend her his unyielding strength. How had he come to understand her so well? Holding her breath, she resisted an urge to lean on him.

"My dearest daughter." Still smiling, her father spared Yūkan a glance then came to her. "I hope you're well. I was upset to learn in your correspondence that Rikō sought to make your match solely for his own gain and without a thought to your happiness."

Ojisan remained in the doorway, his scowl more petulant than fierce.

"I sent you to Kyō to give you the chance to meet a nobleman who shares your curiosity, sensitivity, and thirst for knowledge. You could never find that among the hardened, rough-edged military men of our province. And I know you needed to get away. Too many bad memories made your life miserable in Shinano."

"Thank you, Otōsan."

"Let my brother earn advancement on his own merit. I don't seek any more than I already have. You are a pawn for neither of us."

Yūkan put a hand to Kirei's back, and she could feel his reassurance pressing through the layers.

"You wrote of a country gentleman in the imperial city.

Minamoto no Yūkan." He turned his gaze to Yūkan. "You are the son of Rinshi's brother, Tokinaka?"

"Yes, Lord Fujiwara. Minamoto no Tokinaka was my honored father. The best of men."

"I knew Tokinaka when we lived in Kyō twenty years ago. Yes, he was one of the best men I ever met. If you are anything like him, I approve. Please promise me you'll both come to Shinano so Kirei's mother can meet you."

"Of course, Lord Fujiwara. I am only sorry she couldn't be here for the third night feast."

Her father returned his attention to Kirei. "She wanted to come, but I had to travel quickly with no time to plan. I had to get here and try to undo the damage my brother sought to wreak. It seems you've done well on your own, however."

Kirei smiled. "With the help of friends, Otōsan."

He kissed her forehead then gave her uncle a shooing wave before heading to the mansion proper.

Lowering her fan, Kirei beamed at Yūkan. "My father knew and respected your father. If only he had come three days ago. We could've avoided so much heartache."

"If I hadn't been so determined, and Yoki hadn't been such a caring friend to us both, he might've come too late. You could still be at Prince Hansamu's mansion, and by now, you'd be too ensconced to pull out of his household without scandal."

She leaned and rested her head against his shoulder. "As it is, I didn't spend even one night under his roof. I could've been visiting for all anybody knows."

"Thank the gods."

"We still need a letter of committal."

"Your father will write it, which is good. Your uncle would've made us wait, I suspect. I won't take you out of the city without one."

"I agree. So how soon can we leave?"

He chuckled, and it lightened her soul. They returned to the veranda and their waiting cushions.

Amai's damask rustled as she shuffled along the veranda

toward them from the main building. "You'll never guess."

"Then tell us." Kirei gave Yūkan her back. He wrapped his arms around her and drew her against him. Safe and content, she rested her head on his chest. He set his chin atop her hair.

Her cousin squealed than sank to the wooden walkway in front of her. Her fan trembled before her face. "Father spoke to me. He said since he doesn't have to write a letter of committal for you, he may as well write one for me."

"You and Shinsetsu?"

Amai nodded vigorously. "He said if we want to consider last night our first night, we can celebrate our third-night event the day after tomorrow."

"Do you think Shinsetsu wants you for his primary wife?" asked Yūkan.

"He does. He's already asked me for my devotion. We were waiting because he didn't think Father would approve until he got a promotion. Shinsetsu's rank only qualifies him for a residence in the sixth ward."

"Then you'll live here until his promotion," he said.

"Of course." Her cousin fluttered her fan. "I'm so happy. I'm going to write to him immediately."

Kirei's heart sang for her sweet cousin. "His marriage to you will practically guarantee him a promotion. I'm thrilled for you."

Amai hesitated, and moisture pooled at her lower lids. "To think, dear cousin, that I met Shinsetsu the same night you met Lord Minamoto. Now here we are, both married to our loves only days apart. It's a blessing. The gods are smiling on us. I couldn't have imagined being so happy."

"I feel the same." Her heart swelled with love for the man who held her so sweetly in the dawn of their new life.

When her cousin stood and went inside, Kirei wondered if Amai would be able to hold onto her happiness. Especially when Shinsetsu brought a concubine into their home, or worse, a second wife. And he would. Ministers who wanted to remain in the city had to.

She snuggled closer to Yūkan. She'd fallen in love with a man she could trust. A man who gave her equal love and devotion. A man who would encourage her study and interests rather than discourage.

It made sense that she found her true love in a man raised in the country. That they'd had to come to Kyō, a place where society disdained people of their provincial background, in order to meet, however, amazed her.

"We should wait to leave," she said, though it was difficult. If she had her way, they wouldn't wait for tonight's feast. She'd be content to let a country priest sanctify their marriage. Her father had traveled so far, though. She couldn't simply go.

"For Amai?" He kissed the top of her head.

She closed her eyes, soaking in his closeness. "Yes. She'll want us here to help her celebrate in a few days."

"I'll send my driver to the Nine Fold Enclosure for my things. I'll send Uma to fetch your belongings from Hansamu's house, too. Now that we're officially joined, I see no reason why I should be anywhere but with you."

"I can't tell you how glad I am you came to town. I can't imagine spending another day without you."

He put a finger under her chin and tipped her face. His mouth descended to hers. Her body came instantly alert. Alive.

As she allowed his tongue entrance, he slipped his hand inside her *kosode*. He played her like a rare and prized instrument, bringing her nipple to harness with an expert touch and making her dizzy with need. Desire rippled through her.

Reluctantly, she broke the kiss. They had tonight, tomorrow night, and the rest of their lives to satisfy her passion.

Warmth caused by his kiss chased the refreshing chill of their shadowed veranda, and she used her fan to cool her cheeks. "I'd like to visit with my parents before we go to your home."

"There's no question. We can go with your father when he returns. I look forward to meeting your mother. We're not on a schedule, so we can visit Shinano as long as you like."

She took his hand from her arm and pressed her lips to the backs of his fingers. "I adore your generosity, but I wouldn't want to stay longer than two weeks. I'm actually anxious to see my new home. I'm sure Fudōno is looking forward to seeing you, too."

"I already wrote him of my success with the emperor. By the time we reach Echigo Province, he'll be back from China."

She sat up and faced him. His good looks gave her pause, and she smiled to think she'd never tire of gazing at him. Never tire of being with him. Other than her father, Yūkan was the only person who didn't bore or weary her after a while.

"What is it?" he asked. A slight smirk played about the perfect bow shape of his lips.

"The heat of summer is approaching. We won't have these cool mornings and evenings much longer. I'd rather be traveling now than when the heat will make us miserable."

"Me, too. How about we plan to leave the morning after Amai's wedding feast? It's only a few more days."

She glanced at the cherry blossom tree that caressed the eave above. Nearly all its blossoms had given way to green leaves.

"A few more days. Yes."

She'd gladly leave behind her conniving uncle. Gladly leave behind the fickle *good people* of this imperial city. Gladly leave behind endless walls for open countryside and majestic mountains.

Yes, loving Yūkan opened the door to true, limitless happiness. The kind of happiness her parents had. The kind of happiness she'd always wanted.

Beaming her joy, she wrapped her arms around Yūkan's neck. She kissed him with every ounce of love in her. For him, she wouldn't hold back her passions or herself. He would have all of her. Without restraint. Forever.

**COMING SOON**

Chapter One

Sumpu, Japan
March 30, 1616

When had she lost all choice in her life? Only days ago, Saiko lived free and independently in Mito, managing her youngest brother's castle and learning the art of swords. Now, she sat in her father's castle with life flipped. If she had come home to stay, perhaps she could enjoy some peace. Her return, however, was temporary. Frighteningly temporary.

Her father loved her. He never let her doubt it. But when he issued an order, he expected it followed. It didn't matter that her oldest brother carried the title of shogun. Her father, Tokugawa Ieyasu, still ruled Japan.

Saiko fisted a hand, wishing she had a bow and arrows. What she wouldn't give for a bit of target practice right now. She missed her younger brother in Mito. He'd taught her how to shoot.

Five years in a country setting had given her a chance to grow close to Yorifusa in a way she'd never had here in Sumpu as a child. She smiled, remembering when she'd first arrived in his province and how he'd taught her to ride horseback. He used to race her across a field next to his castle. She'd gone to Mito as an untried, curious girl. While there, she'd become a woman with skills – skills that would go to waste once her father consigned her to live far away at the imperial court.

Duty. The word had never left a bad taste in her mouth before. Never been a burden. Now, she cursed it with every ounce of her being. What had she, the youngest child of Japan's most powerful man, done to deserve such a sour fate? Why had he chosen her to serve as a mere consort to the emperor?

"It's not right," she whispered into the cool air of her chamber.

She wished she could slide open the shutters on her window, but the cold temperature outside would plunge her room into an unbearable chill in minutes. Only a brazier warmed her chamber, and its meager heat couldn't stand against the last of winter's icy grip. Besides, she had too many people in her room at the moment. It made no sense to subject them to misery so she could catch a breath. Coming home reminded her how she, as a princess, should expect no privacy. At the emperor's palace in Kyōto, she would have even less.

Living in Mito had spoiled her. Saiko had worn trousers and ridden. She had learned archery, sword, and how to fight with hands and feet. She'd come and gone on her own schedule.

She cast a longing glance at the window. Did it snow? Did the sun shine? She hadn't seen the sky in two days, and the confinement had her ready to come out of her skin.

Facing her, her tutor bore the sober expression of a man who had participated in one too many meaningless conversations. His dull eyes drooped a bit at the outer corners and seemed to fight the weight of his slumping eyelids. The whites had turned the color of bile, from age she suspected. Saiko lowered her gaze to keep from glaring at him. He had droned on about the proper handling of servants for too long already, and apparently had much more to say on the subject.

The left side of her rear end had gone numb, and she fidgeted on her silk cushion. The seam of her sock scraped across tightly woven *tatami* straw matting covering the floor, creating an unpleasant screech. On cushions near the brazier at the far end of her room, her ladies-in-waiting sat with heads together in soft conversation, the whispers barely registering. Their bright kimonos brought to mind spring flowers and made her long for warmer days.

Raising her hand, Saiko put a stop to her tutor's monotone lecture. "I'm humbly grateful for your wisdom, Hayashi-sensei. You'll surely have me ready for life in the imperial palace. As I've spent the last five years managing servants and the running of Yorifusa-san's castle in Mito, however, I believe this area of my education has been thoroughly addressed." With a serene smile, and feeling anything but, she stood. "Now might be a good time for me to get some air. I believe I'll take a walk in the garden." When he opened his mouth to protest, she shook her head. "Master Hayashi, your patience with me is admirable. Please take a rest and have some tea. Or perhaps, as my father's advisor, you have responsibilities that require your attention elsewhere?"

The sagging skin of his thin face and his protruding ears jiggled with indignation as he stood, but he simply nodded and bowed. His height had the narrow, twelve-inch-high black lacquered hat towering atop his head nearly brushing the ceiling when he straightened. He went to the brazier and gave his palms a warming then a rub. "I'll be gone a few days. I travel to Kotu."

Her three ladies ceased their whispered conversation and cast him uneasy glances.

She frowned. "But Kotu is less than a day's ride on horseback."

"I travel only in my personal carriage. It's slow but more dignified than riding on a horse." He bowed then headed for the door. He sniffed. After another bow and a stiff rustle of his black minister's robe, he left.

She shook her head. How was riding a horse undignified? And how had he, an aristocratic sycophant, obtained a position of honor within the shogunate? Shuffling to the door, she stayed her ladies with a gesture. She slipped on her platform *geta* sandals. She didn't bother searching for boots or a down-filled coat. A walk alone in the garden for a few minutes meant her sanity, and the temperature outside couldn't deter her.

"But Princess..." her first lady protested, leaving the brazier's warmth to join her at the door. She had thin but not unpleasant features, and her warm, dark eyes almost always shined with some secret pleasure or joke she never revealed.

"I need this, Okiko-san." Waving sweet smoke from an incense burner over her hair and clothing to freshen her scent, Saiko shook her head. "I won't be gone long."

Fisting her hands, she let the bite of her fingernails into her palms remind her not to complain. Wars had left samurai lordless, homeless, and starving. Despite a growing peace, minor uprisings around the country still caused unrest and displacement, and the roads contained a steady stream of villagers who had lost their homes and livelihoods. Saiko wore the finest silks, never went without a meal, and faced a world of opulent luxury in the palace of the figurehead emperor. True, she would serve as nothing more than a sexual servant to a man who no longer held any power or authority, but she would appear ungrateful and undutiful if she lamented. She had to bite her tongue as she practically ran from the chamber.

With the need for escape quickening her step, she hurried from the castle, ignoring every stare on the way. She should consider this move an honor. Her father trusted her to represent the Tokugawa line. If she bore a son to the emperor, such a child could end the uprisings and secure Japan's peace by binding the shogunate to the royal seat. So why did she struggle with the idea? Why did she alternate between anger and despair?

She glanced over her shoulder to make sure Okiko didn't follow. Her two-story quarters formed a structure among a grouping that formed the 'second circle,' a ring of buildings that surrounded the inner citadel where the main tower loomed along with the areas where her father conducted his business of running Japan.

She sighed with relief as she stepped into the winter chill of the garden. The cold air had a clean, odorless scent so refreshing after the stale, stagnant air that permeated the fortress. It cooled her cheeks but didn't penetrate the three layers of thick silk she wore. Despite the season, the landscaping held tremendous loveliness. Pale winter flowers bloomed, evergreens swayed in a slow breeze, and even dormant trees reached bare branches to the sky as if in celebration of the day.

Spring showed signs of life, though. Miniscule buds began to form on overhead branches, and a hint of green peeked through the straw-colored remnants of last year's grass. Drawing her fingers into the warmth of her sleeve, Saiko smiled. Spring was her favorite season. She adored the renewal and the colors.

She didn't share most everyone else's fatalistic view of life. Waiting for the next disaster. Ruminating on death. What did it accomplish? No, she wanted to savor every second and breathe in the joy of her existence like her mother had.

Then again, Saiko would have more joy if she had *some* choice in her future. Was she so wrong to want romantic love? Why did *duty* have to preclude it? And why did her father not want for her what he'd had for himself with her mother? Her parents had been the perfect example of what love could be. Kind. Consuming. Forever. She wanted nothing less.

She moved along a stone-laid path next to the happy gurgle of a winding brook that snaked through Sumpu Castle's south garden. Layers of silk and linen under her elaborate, flowing blue kimono continued to keep the chill at bay but wouldn't keep her warm for long. It didn't matter. Gardeners had placed a tall, lacquered wood cover over her bridge. It blocked the breeze, and three lanterns inside provided light and some meager warmth at the highest point on the arch.

Before she turned a corner where the path continued behind a hedge of evergreen bushes, she glanced once more over her shoulder. Nobody followed. She hiked her hem to her ankles and went as fast as her *geta* sandals allowed. The exercise warmed her and made her smile. When her stone bridge came into sight past a row of dormant cherry blossom trees, she slowed.

Her bridge. So beautiful. So peaceful. Rich wood planks carved with flowers and trees then coated with a hard clear lacquer formed the walls of the bridge cover and glowed brightly in the muted winter sun. A cheerful red wood framed the long curved box at top and bottom edges and formed a crested roof decorated at each end with red dragons roaring silently to the sky.

Supporting it, her pale stone bridge sported enormous magnolia blossom branches chiseled into the side. It gently arched over the brook, and golden light shone from the opening nearest her.

She might never see it again after she left. Tears smarted. Other than the last five years spent in Mito helping her brother with the administration of his domain, she had lived here in Sumpu. This was her home. But not for much longer. A tightness formed in her chest, and she pressed a fist to the trapped sensation behind her ribcage.

Life had never seemed this unfair. Since returning less than a week ago, she'd had a chance to visit the garden only once. Sumpu Castle teemed with strange faces. Her father had explained that his veteran servants and retainers had gone to Edo to serve her brother, the shogun, and she recognized only a few who stayed at Sumpu.

Her gaze trained on the warm glow at the bridge's entrance, she slowly headed for what time inside the shelter meant. Freedom. Peace. If only for a few minutes. Saiko grasped the end of the handrail and swung into the bridge with a hop.

A man stood inside, and she yelped with alarm.

Dressed in shades of gray, he wore his long hair in a knot at the crown of his head. A slung *katana* long sword rested across the small of his back, and a smaller blade hugged the front of his neat *kosode* at an angle, proclaiming him elite samurai. Barely moving, he cut a hard gaze sideways and gave her a once over. He drawled, "My lady."

He'd called her *my lady*? Did he not know who she was? "Pardon me. I didn't realize anyone..."

But this was her bridge. Her father had ordered its building from Edo artisans the day of her birth. This man should apologize and leave. Not her. She released her kimono, and its heavy silk hem slid past her feet to rest on the stone.

He traced artistic detailing of a tree carved into the wood and said in a deep, smooth voice, "I'm told this garden has seventeen bridges."

He had a nice voice. So what? "It does."

"Yet I'm drawn to this one. I haven't seen many stone bridges. I like its sturdiness. It promises peace and time alone in quiet solitude."

He spoke her very thoughts. She offered a mild nod. "Yes. It's the place I come the most. Though time alone is hardly possible with two of us here."

Keeping her gaze slightly averted in courtesy, she fought the urge to look him in the face. Study his visage. Search his eyes and any secrets he kept. When his gaze sought the carving his finger traced, she took her chance.

He showed no hint of reaction to her sarcasm. Strength, unforgiving and unrelenting, lined each angle and plane of his handsome face. A scar, old if the brown shade of it indicated properly, tightened his skin from the corner of his left eye to the lobe of his ear. No doubt it marked a moment in battle. His dark skin attested to long hours outdoors. And though not considered an attractive attribute, on him his coloring added to his rugged, manly beauty.

Who was this man who made her breathe faster? Made her heart beat harder? Who was this warrior whose strength affected her physically without his touching a hand to her? The very thought had her stomach clenching with delighted anticipation.

He gave her his full attention, his black stare assessing and hard. She dropped her gaze. Would he try to demand she leave? If he did, she *would* meet his eyes in a confrontational glare, and firmly put him in his place and off of her bridge.

He didn't wear weathered crags and creases upon his skin or the longer facial hair of the samurai she had seen in her father's service. This man had smooth, clean planes of youth. In his stare, however, glinted an edge of experience. He had seen battle. Horrors. Pain. He was special. Different. In a near whisper, he said, "Tell me about your tears."

Her tears? Wiping the tip of a finger across her lashes, she encountered moisture. She took a step closer and found the warmth trapped inside the bridge cover from the overhead lanterns. Something tentative in his demeanor had her less eager to see him retreat. "It's nothing. Just a moment of weakness. Are you newly arrived?"

"Yes, my lady. I fought with Tokugawa Ieyasu-shogun during the Osaka Summer Siege then stayed to maintain the castle's military defenses until his son assigned a *jodai*. When I returned, I came to Sumpu to serve him."

"I'm told the Toyotomi clan is destroyed and their samurai with them. You must've fought well." She took another step closer and felt warmth on her cheeks.

"I was fearless." His statement held no boasting. "It's easy to be fearless with two hundred thousand samurai at my back."

"Tokugawa Ieyasu-shogun led the fight in the Osaka Summer Siege. Only the best serve him." Saiko ran a hand along the planks, enjoying the texture of the carvings on her palm and fingertips. She tingled at his nearness. Fine hairs stood on end along her arms and nape. When he spoke, his voice warmed her as if she eased into a hot spring. No man had ever affected her like this.

"Yes. I served the retired shogun at Osaka." He chuckled. "*Retired* is used loosely, of course. His son holds the title, but Tokugawa Ieyasu-shogun still rules from this castle. And you, my lady? What's your role here?"

She tried to read him, but his expression offered nothing in the way of his thoughts. Opening her mouth to tell him her name, she paused. She liked that he didn't know her identity. He talked to her as an equal rather than a princess – something she only experienced with her father and brothers.

In the distance, Okiko's call carried on the breeze. "I must go. I have duties and responsibilities. But I'll try to come tomorrow."

He gave a solemn nod. "I have duties, as well. I'll try to come tomorrow. I'd like to talk more."

She backed from the bridge, reluctant to look away from his rugged yet eloquent strength. "Tomorrow."

Holding her breath to fight a grin of anticipation, Saiko turned and gathered her kimono in fists before running for the castle. Cold finally seeped through her clothing now.

Her first lady met her and held the door. "You're flushed. Do you feel unwell?"

"I am too well, Okiko-san. Too well." Settling her dignity around her like a cloak, Saiko entered the castle with her head held high.

*   *   *   *

Standing on the bridge long minutes after she left, Takamori dared not hope. After all he had seen and done, could he find happiness? Love? Battle and bloodshed had made him into a hardened, heartless warrior. Hadn't it? Yet when the gorgeous lady had drawn closer by inches, his heart had pounded. Maybe he wasn't as heartless as he'd thought.

With his thumbnail, Takamori traced the Hosokawa family crest inlaid in gold onto the end of his *katana's* hilt. He hailed from an illustrious warrior family, one that had enjoyed favor by the Ashikaga shoguns because of loyalty, and who had served in influential positions within the government as a result.

He wanted most to honor his family. To do justice by his ancestors and to have future Hosokawa generations remember him proudly. His acclaim in battle, and now his service as military leader to the powerful Tokugawa shogunate, accomplished this, he believed. Yet he couldn't claim ambition in any sense. He had only ever wanted to serve and serve well. Now, he wanted...what?

He exited the refuge of the bridge from the opposite end and strode for samurai quarters. His thoughts warred with his desires. The lady had stirred something in him. He wanted to see her again.

He tired of fighting. It no longer defined him. Every minute he could spare these days, he read or wrote. He sought learning. Betterment. A feeding of his mind and an appreciation of nature he had ignored until this blossoming peace brought by Tokugawa Ieyasu afforded him the gift of time.

As he approached samurai quarters, he admired the unusual architecture. The main entrance fronted a center section, which rose high like a temple. Square windows ran in a line above the entrance's lower roofline which wore a sharp A-shape with a fancy crest and dragons arching in flight from each of the four corners. Two one-story dormitories flanked either side of the center section, sporting battlements along the tops and leading to the castle's outer protective wall.

Inside, the clang of swordfight echoed through the large entryway. Crossing to double doors, he went into an enormous exercise room where samurai practiced bare-chested with their metal swords. No practice swords for these seasoned veterans. They blocked as well as they attacked, and occasional nicks served as reminders to improve speed and reflexes. Flashes glinted off of shiny blades from daylight streaming through high windows in the upper surround.

"Marshal," someone shouted, and practice stopped. Warriors, sweaty and breathing hard, faced him and bowed.

Returning the bow, he gruffly ordered, "Resume."

His brown-skinned second-in-command approached across hardwood flooring and sent his *katana* into its scabbard with a crisp movement that spoke of superb technique. What he lacked in height he made up for in sheer strength. His muscles bulged and gleamed with sweat. No man had ever taken Shosan down in hand-to-hand combat.

Despite the violence they'd seen and committed these past years in battle, his friend had clung to his humanity and humor. A gentle, teasing light shone from the wide gaze in his square face as he asked, "Did you find the perspective you sought?"

"I found a different perspective altogether, Shosan-san." Takamori took his two swords in one hand, untied his waistband with the other and removed his outer robe. Maybe some practice would take his mind off of intelligent shining eyes, trembling lips, and skin so delicate and flawless as to make a woman from Edo's pleasure district jealous. Peeling off the upper layer of his innermost robe so it hung at his waist, he rubbed a hand across the skin of his chest. He winked. "Spar with me? I promise not to cut off your head."

Arching his eyebrows, Shosan laughed and put a hand on the hilt of his *katana*. "I don't know what you found in that garden, but this is a vast improvement over the growling bear you were when you left. Did you drink a magic elixir? Tell me where to find it."

Takamori dropped into horse stance and drew his sword. "Magic, maybe. But no elixir. And I'm going for more tomorrow."

\*    \*    \*    \*

Fighting the urge to scream, Saiko pressed her lips together to keep from spewing the words that wanted to spill from her. Words outlining the injustice of this fate her father had assigned her. Words telling him what she had wanted from life. Words that would only cause them both pain.

Avoiding her father's glances, Saiko sat in the first seat of the table closest to the retired shogun's high table. Her father, though a warrior, understood finery, and his great hall reflected his sumptuous taste. Purple damask covered every wall but the one behind him. That one gleamed, its shiny black paint reflecting every light in the room. Huge pillars, glowing in gold, supported a ceiling two stories high. Each person in attendance sat upon a black silk cushion and shared a low, black lacquered table with one other diner.

Large ink drawings framed in black hung at equal intervals against the damask. High on the black wall, seven sheathed samurai swords from various periods throughout Japan's history hung on display, one above the next and twelve inches apart. Everything implied elegance and cleanliness, even the pristine hardwood floor beneath her cushion.

Along the far wall, a bank of wooden folding screens painted in elaborate battle scenes blocked a multitude of doors. From behind them came a parade of servants bearing trays. Her father received his meal first, and then her middle brother and she were served.

The food provided a further tribute to perfect beauty. Not a single grain of rice strayed from round molded mounds presented in rice bowls the exact shade of purple as the walls. Vegetables formed lovely flower petals upon gold saucers. Even noodles in a rich broth seemed to perform a complex dance as servers gently placed the dishes before each diner.

Across the aisle, her brothers sent her a questioning look, but she ignored it. She ate in silence, her chopsticks not making a sound. At her side, Okiko breathed worried sighs between bites of her own meal.

"He won't chastise you," Saiko whispered.

"But I'm your first lady-in-waiting. I'm supposed to care for you." Okiko's chopstick clinked a nervous chatter against the edge of her soup bowl.

Saiko released a heavy breath. "My father knows me. He understands that if I decide to do something, there's nothing you could do to stop me short of pinning me to the floor." She bit back a smile, imagining her friend attempting to hold her down.

As dinner drew to a close, she released an uptight

breath. Her father studied her, so the time had come. Forcing her shoulders to relax, she calmly set her chopsticks aside.

"Daughter, I'm informed you had some time alone this morning." His eyebrows came together to form a fierce scowl. His hair, though completely white, hadn't grown thin, and his topknot could compete against any young samurai on his estate. His age of seventy-two didn't detract from his power or his ability to wield it, either. The glistening richness of his black *kosode* decorated with white hash marks added to his aura of power, especially in contrast to his pale gray *hakama* trousers and the black wall behind him.

Still, she loved the old man and refused to let him intimidate her. She stifled a chuckle, stood and bowed low. "Yes, Father. Master Hayashi has been merciless in preparing me for my new life. I thought it wise to take a short break to give us both a rest so his great knowledge could sink into my tiring mind."

"I see." He cleared his throat then roared, "And you could not take a companion with you?"

The huge room went utterly silent. Behind her, two aristocratic diplomats from Kyōto gasped.

Saiko glanced at her father through her lashes, batted them briefly then bowed her head lower. "I find it easier to clear my mind when I'm alone, Father. But if you deem it necessary that I take a companion, I'll do as you say. As your obedient daughter who loves you so dearly, I'll do as you say." She snuck a peek through her lashes, sinking her teeth into the soft flesh inside her bottom lip.

One side of his mouth quirked, and he rubbed both hands over his face. "We're well protected here. As long as you stay inside the castle's walls, I see no harm in your having time alone. I imagine you have much to contemplate in these last days here. You may have time each morning to walk in the garden."

Fighting a smile, she stepped from behind her table, went to her knees and touched her forehead to the floor.

"Thank you, Father."

"Come show me your love."

She stood and moved forward. Before him at the high table, she whispered, "I don't want to leave. But I love you. You say this is best for our country, and so I'll go and do my best to make you proud." Her bottom lip trembled and she tucked it in to hide her weakness.

"You do make me proud but you're a woman, not a child. Now that Yorifusa has taken a wife and no longer needs your assistance in Mito, you have a greater duty to see your family and your country succeed."

She nodded. "I just wish it were about love rather than politics. But I'll do what I must."

"I know you will." He turned his cheek, and she leaned across the table and kissed it. "Now be good to Master Hayashi. He wants to see you shine in Kyōto."

"He does. I know." She returned to her seat and tried to finish her meal, but fluttering in her stomach made her appetite wane. Time in the garden every day. To see the samurai every day. If her father knew about the elite samurai on her bridge, she doubted he would show such generosity.

Despite it, she looked forward to tomorrow in a way she hadn't in a long time.

## ABOUT THE AUTHOR

Laura Kitchell lives in Virginia. She is a member of Romance Writers of America and Chesapeake Romance Writers. She lived in Japan as a child and has a love and respect for Japanese history and culture. Contact her at laurakitchell@cox.net, visit her website for events, excerpts, and upcoming projects at www.laurakitchell.vpweb.com, and follow her at laura.kitchell.1@facebook.com.

# BIBLIOGRAPHY

----, *The Diary of Lady Murasaki*, Translated and introduced by Richard Bowring, London, 2005.

Dalby, Liza, *Kimono – Fashioning Culture*, London, 2001.

Deal, William E., *Handbook to Life in Medieval and Early Modern Japan*, New York, 2007.

Morris, Ivan, *The World of the Shining Prince,* New York, 1994.

Made in United States
North Haven, CT
08 April 2022

18056524R00173